Also by Antoine Vanner

Britannia's Wolf
The Dawlish Chronicles, Volume 1
September 1877 - February 1878

Britannia's Reach
The Dawlish Chronicles, Volume 2
November 1879 - April 1880

Britannia's Shark
The Dawlish Chronicles, Volume 3
April – September 1881

Britannia's Spartan
The Dawlish Chronicles, Volume 4
June 1859 and April - August 1882

Britannia's Mission
The Dawlish Chronicles, Volume 7
August 1883 - February 1884

Britannia's Gamble
The Dawlish Chronicles Volume 6
March 1884 – February 1885

Being accounts of episodes in the lives of

Nicholas Dawlish R.N.
Born: Shrewsbury 16.12.1845
Died: Zeebrugge 23.04.1918

and

Florence Dawlish, née Morton
Born: Northampton 17.06.1855
Died: Portsmouth 12.05.1946

Britannia's Amazon

Antoine Vanner

The Dawlish Chronicles
Volume 5

April - August 1882

(With bonus short story Britannia's Eye)

Library of Congress Cataloging-in-Publication Data:

Antoine Vanner 1945 -

Britannia's Amazon / Antoine Vanner.

(The Dawlish Chronicles Volume V)

ISBN 978-1-943404-08-7 (pbk.)—ISBN 978-1-943404-07-4 (Kindle)

Cover design by Sara Lee Paterson

This is a work of historical fiction. Certain characters and their actions may have been inspired by historical individuals and events. The characters in the novel, however, represent the work of the author's imagination. Any resemblance to actual persons, living or dead, is entirely coincidental.

Published by Old Salt Press

Old Salt Press, LLC is based in Jersey City, New Jersey with an affiliate in New Zealand

For more information about our titles go to www.oldsaltpress.com

Britannia's Amazon

Prologue

Thrace, West of Istanbul, January 1878

Last Weeks of Russo-Turkish War

Cold, sickness, hunger and exhaustion, not gunfire or sabre-cuts, were the killers now. The column had been seven days on the march, crawling eastwards, ever more slowly, through snow and mud and icy sleet towards the defensive lines outside the great city, each mile marked by the slumped bodies of those who had passed the limits of endurance.

The Russians had caught up the previous afternoon, light galloper guns dropping shells on the rear-guard to cover Cossack thrusts towards it. Smaller groups of riders darted in from the flanks to hit the casualty and refugee-laden wagons at the column's centre. They had been driven away – but only just – by rifle volleys from the remnants of the disparate and shattered Turkish units that had been somehow forged into a still-effective fighting force. It had lasted minutes only, though it seemed like aeons, when Florence Morton cowered beneath the cart in which Nicholas Dawlish lay unconscious as she tried to calm the terror of the women and children clustered with her. She could hear the crash of gunfire, smell the drifting smoke, hear cries of fury and hatred and agony, and yet she had no understanding of how the battle waxed and waned. She had reached a new depth of fear that she must not let others see, her hands trembling, her stomach knotted, her mind screaming incoherent prayers.

For deliverance. For Nicholas. For herself.

Now the Russians still followed, but on the column's flanks, a mile distant or more, dark shapes crouched over dark horses silhouetted against the snow behind, spurring forward at intervals to loosen off a few ineffectual shots, then turning back to get out of range again. This column might be the last remaining Turkish force that had any hope of reaching safety, the Ottoman officer, Adnan, had told Florence. The front had collapsed days since and only exhaustion that was scarcely less than that of those they harried was slowing the Russians' advance. Their victories in Bulgaria and Thrace in recent weeks had decided the war. Now the Russians were

1

pressing for the greatest prize of all – Istanbul, Byzantium, Constantinople, the Second Rome, the many-named capital that had been the focus of Muscovite desire for centuries.

The refugees were dying, more of them each day, the line of laden carts foul with the stench of gangrene and human waste as the wretched animals that pulled them plodded wearily through slush and mud. There was no time to bury the bodies, only enough to drag them to one side of the track and to strip them of any footwear or clothing that might be of value to those still-living. The food was all but gone, the only resource the scrawny meat hacked from fallen beasts and charred over inadequate fires during the nights' halts. Packed with the sick and the dying, with the oldest and the youngest, the carts were at the centre of the column, ahead of Adnan's rear-guard and following the naval brigade. The entire crew of an ironclad, seamen and marines, had been brought to bolster the collapsing Turkish front by the British officer who now lay in delirium in the bed of the cart Florence insisted on driving herself.

Nicholas Dawlish, worn out by weeks of exertion and combat, had collapsed five days since and had babbled about malaria before losing consciousness. Florence had forced the quinine she found in his pack between his teeth. It had done little good and now pneumonia too had taken hold. She and Agatha – no longer Lady Agatha to her, and now closer than a sister – took turns to tend him through the freezing nights, to soothe his ravings. They had risked their lives when they established a refugee-relief post a hundred miles to the west and if this man had not arrived in time they would never have left there. It had been close, closer than Agatha guessed, for only Florence had seen that the man whom the Turks addressed as Nicholas Kaptan had come close to shooting them both to save them from worse horrors.

His life is more dear to me than my own. And yet whether he lives or dies I'll lose him, even though I believe that he loves me as I love him. I can never be his wife. British officers, do not marry women who had once been servants. We'll part with embarrassed courtesy and I'll never see him again. But if he lives I can accept that.

She herself had killed, had had no option. The heavy Colt revolver she had used was still strapped around her waist over the thick army greatcoat she had acquired weeks before, a smaller pistol in one pocket. She would not rest without them until reaching safety. Necessity had found strength in her that she had never thought was there, and powers of organisation and leadership too. If she had not found them, even the remaining refugees might have been dead by now. A few days more, and they too might be dead, she knew, for she had little more to offer them now than encouragement and cajoling. She wondered if famished mothers still believed her as she told them for the hundredth time "Her adım şehre yakın bize getiriyor" - *Every step brings us nearer the city* – and urged "Umut pes etmeyin" – *Don't give up hope*. She might have given it up already had Nicholas Dawlish not been totally dependent on her.

The evening conference had become a ritual, she herself, the Turkish army officer Adnan and Dawlish's deputy Zyndram – now in command of the naval brigade. Both officers had come to treat her as an equal, accepting her management of the refugees as naturally as they accepted command of their own men. They did not disguise stark realities from her. Agatha had brought her on this mission of mercy, and Agatha still laboured tirelessly with the sick, but she had accepted – and probably welcomed – that it was Florence herself who was now the driving spirit. And each evening, colder and hungrier than on the previous, Florence crouched in the lee of a wagon with Adnan and Zyndram, warming themselves at a smoking fire, and discussed ever-increasing losses, ever-slower progress. Seven miles in fourteen hours' trek were a triumph, eight a miracle.

"How much longer?" Florence asked. She knew how far it was to the lines of entrenchments west of the city – eighteen, twenty miles – for she had come from the city six weeks before. But now distance was measured in time, not miles.

"Two days at this rate. Maybe longer." Adnan hesitated, then said, "The Russians won't give us that long. They're not as tired as we are, not as encumbered. They'll want another success before they're halted by our lines. They'll attack, no doubt of it. If not tomorrow, then the day after."

"We can't hold them if they do," Zyndram stated it without any hint of fear. "We've lost too many. And the ammunition is all but gone." This Pole in Ottoman service had inspired and driven the men of the naval brigade as tirelessly as Dawlish himself had done. Poles might often be beaten, he had once told Florence, but they were never defeated. Not even in death, which they were now facing.

"We're not leaving the women and children." Florence was alarmed by Adnan's use of the word 'encumbered'. She spoke with vehemence. "If you abandon them then I'll stay with them. Agatha too. If we can identify ourselves as British, then it might give some protection." She knew that it was a vain hope. Cossacks cared nothing for scraps of paper. Her hand crept to her revolver's butt. The last resort.

Adnan shook his head. "We must outrun them. The Russians won't expect it. They'll bivouac and we won't. We'll press on at dawn and we won't stop, not in the night, not for more than five minutes in the hour, not until we reach our own lines."

"It will kill half our people if we do," Zyndram said.

"It will kill them all if we don't," Adnan said.

A long silence, made yet more ominous by the distant wailing of a woman who had delivered in a cart three days before. She had realised only today that the child she had hugged to her ever since had been dead since birth.

"Florence Hanim?" Adnan used the formal address. He had recognised her fears.

Terrible as the cost must be, there was no alternative.

"We should press on," she said. "We should press on and leave nobody but the dead behind."

She turned away into the darkness, back to the typhus and pneumonia, to the wounded, to the starving women and shivering children, to the young seamen and soldiers rotting with gangrene, to the hopeless and broken-spirited who lacked the will to rise from the snow-free patches beneath the wagons. Back to where Agatha and a few loyal helpers were still doing their inadequate and pathetic best. And back to Nicholas Dawlish.

He was moaning in quiet delirium.

But he still lived. And that was satisfaction enough.

*

It took forty-two hours and it was the worst part of the entire nightmare. The snow was melting and the slush and mud made each step an agony. Long showers of sleet flayed their faces, soaked their clothing. Cart wheels sank in the mire and exhausted men threw themselves on the spokes to advance them a few feet at a time. Some vehicles sank so far as to be immovable and their freights of misery had to be transferred to others. The animals were dying as fast now as the humans and there was no bullet to be spared to end their

4

suffering, at best a blade drawn across a throat as bulging, innocent eyes pleaded for pity and release.

Florence, strong and healthy as she had been a month before, shambled now like an old woman, each step a misery, chewed and humiliated by the lice infesting the mud-smeared clothes she had worn for a fortnight, haunted by the awareness that if she were to collapse then Nicholas would die. She passed up and down the column from cart to cart, relentless in forcing dumping of the bodies of those who had died, heaping the clothing stripped from them on those who still lived to keep them warm, always encouraging, always feigning an air of confident cheerfulness she did not feel. Even from Agatha, who was still unrelenting in her attention to the sick, did she hide the increasingly grim prospects of deliverance that Adnan and Zyndram shared with her.

It was worst of all in the night, the darkness all but pitch, a misery of stumbling and falling and – for most – somehow rising again, each man grasping the coat-tails of the man in front, each leader of a horse or ox or mule hanging on to the tailboard of the wagon ahead. The rests were five minutes in the hour – too short to brew *chai,* if anybody still had it, but long enough for muscles to scream when it was time to move again. Each halt was marked by its own scattering of abandoned bodies, its own ghastly reminder of the fate that might be only hours away for those still living. The dawn brought no respite, only the prospect of a barren landscape and a leaden sky, and columns of smoke from burning villages to the rear marking the Russian advance. Progress slowed ever more through the day. Only the strong endured – and survived.

And at last it ended, salvation first-promised by an irregular scattering of low humps on the eastern horizon, then, as they grew larger, identifying themselves as earthwork redoubts bristling with cannon. These were the Lines of Büyük Tchemedji, the defences that stretched for thirty miles between the Black Sea and the Marmara, the last and perhaps impregnable barrier to the Russian advance. The grey afternoon light was fading, and the nearest redoubt still three miles distant, when a Turkish cavalry squadron came out to meet the column. The riders, and their horses, were ragged and emaciated enough to show that they too had reached here by retreat, but their protection, and the harnessing of some of their animals to the carts, eased the agony of this last stage.

Zyndram drew the men of the naval brigade into a semblance of proud discipline as they passed between the flanking earthworks and into safety. Nicholas Kaptan would have been pleased by them, Florence thought, but he still lay fevered and unknowing in the cart-bed behind her driving seat. Her mind was focussed now on getting medical help, even if it was only in some squalid barn converted to a hospital and packed with wounded. The slightest aid might make the difference between life and death for so many in this parade of misery. And yet, for all her concern, for all that she recognised that she would lose Nicholas Dawlish, even though she might save his life, she felt a glow of pride that she had somehow brought so many to this meagre haven.

Then, suddenly, a voice was crying out "Morton! Morton!" A voice querulous and demanding. A voice she had known when its owner was a boy and she a girl. When he had been the master's son and she a servant's daughter. She turned to see a burly figure mounted on a well-fed horse and urging it through a crowd of onlookers. He was enveloped in a thick woollen ulster, his red turkey-cock face half-hidden by a scarf, a fur kalpak on his head.

"Morton! Morton!" There was no joy of recognition in the voice of Oswald Kegworth, Lady Agatha's brother, First Secretary at Britain's embassy in Istanbul. "Where's my sister, Morton? You were supposed to take care of her! You haven't abandoned her, I trust?"

I'm a servant again, Agatha's – no, Lady Agatha's – paid companion.

"You'll find her driving the fifth cart back."

He lurched past without a word – he had never been an accomplished horseman.

Florence felt herself trembling with humiliation rather than from cold.

A servant still.

Then a surge of pride that cancelled all sense of degradation.

I have saved Nicholas Dawlish. Even if I must now lose him.

1

He had his heart's desire but, despite the pride she felt in his going, her own heart was already aching.

She was standing by the Square Tower at the entrance to Portsmouth Harbour, where for centuries families had stood to wave welcome or farewell to their menfolk. Now Florence Dawlish was doing so too on this morning of April 25th 1882, watching as her husband's cruiser, HMS *Leonidas*, gathered speed as she left the narrow channel astern. Some twenty other women were there also, some holding infants wrapped in shawls, many with older children clinging to their skirts. Most where poor, but respectably so, and few other than the three better-dressed officers' wives among them recognised Florence as wife of the captain of the ship they had come to see off. All were waving handkerchiefs and some were weeping.

"I can see him, Florence," her companion said, a large shapeless woman with a kind face and intelligent eyes behind thick-lensed pince-nez. She pushed her opera glasses towards her. "He's on the bridge. Look Florence! Perhaps he'll see you too!"

The magnification was low but still enough to identify Nicholas standing impassively among the other figures on the open platform. He would know that she was here – that Lady Agatha was too – even if he could not distinguish her from the throng about her. Even as she watched he turned towards her and raised his hand in salute. It was for seconds only, and then his concern was for his ship again, as it would be exclusively for the next six months and more. The newly-commissioned H.M.S *Leonidas* was building speed as she headed for the broadening waters of Spithead, the first mile of twelve-thousand that would take her to Hong Kong and back to test her engines to their limits. Lead-ship of a new class of steel-built cruisers, her command had been craved by many aspiring officers.

And Nicholas alone won it, Florence thought, *and I too played a role,* as the ache in her left arm reminded her. The wound she had suffered in Cuba the previous year had left a scar that she kept hidden from everybody but her husband.

The cruiser was receding fast, white foam in her wake as she passed the Spitbank and Horse Sand forts, past their grey bulk and dark gun muzzles, and soon she was would be lost in the morning's sea haze. The knot of women and children was dispersing and

Florence and Lady Agatha also turned to go. The walk back to the villa in Albert Grove in Portsmouth's suburb of Southsea would emphasise the separation even more, and Florence was determined to show nothing of the wave of loneliness that now washed through her. She saw now that Mrs. Edgerton, wife of *Leonidas's* executive officer, had been standing close behind with the wife of Tadley, the ship's surgeon. Ten years at least older than Florence, as her husband was at least five older than Nicholas, Mrs. Edgerton's sour expression confirmed her hostility as she exchanged frigid courtesies. She was not alone among the broad community of officers' wives in Portsmouth. Florence's youth, looks and marriage to an officer promoted faster than his contemporaries would always arouse resentment. The rumours – correct in fact – that she had once been servant gave a grim pleasure in maintenance of that hostility.

Florence recognised a friendly face, a heavy, homely-looking woman, neatly but not extravagantly dressed. A gangling youth of sixteen or seventeen stood with her. Lady Agatha saw her too and descended on her, taking her hands.

"So good to see you, Mrs. Latham! And how proud you must be of your husband today!"

He was *Leonidas's* staff engineer, a man who had worked his way to commissioned rank from humble beginnings.

"His mastery of such mighty steam power!" Agatha said. "Such expertise and dedication!" She had met the engineer's wife at a reception following the cruiser's commissioning and had taken to her warmly. So too had Florence– the petty slights she endured herself must be nothing compared to those inflicted on this kindly, dignified and poorly-educated woman.

"And this is your son? Benjamin, isn't it?" Florence was grateful that she had remembered the name and also what his mother had said of him. "And off to study in London soon!"

Blushing, the boy seemed tongue tied.

"To King's College, ma'am," his mother said. "Such a good and clever boy! None better!"

"Oh Ma!" the boy was even more embarrassed.

"What will you be reading?" Agatha was suddenly focussed.

"Chemistry, ma'am," he said.

"I can perhaps be of help when you're there." Agatha dug into her reticule and produced a card. Perhaps the only vanity she allowed herself was the addition of the letters FRS behind her name. As the first female Fellow of the Royal Society the pride was well justified. "You might like to meet some of my friends. Mathematicians mainly, I'm afraid, but the odd scientist too."

Overwhelmed, the youth mumbled thanks.

Only a few women now remained, several detained by children still waving handkerchiefs and refusing to leave. As Florence and Agatha moved through them a cleanly but poorly dressed woman, approached them. She was alone and her worn face could have been of any age between forty and sixty.

"Mrs. Dawlish," she said. The effort of approach had made her tremble.

Florence did not know her and her own expression must have betrayed the fact.

"My husband's on the *Leonidas*, ma'am. James Shepton, ma'am. Able Seaman."

He was one of two hundred and eighty men on board and Nicholas had never mentioned the name. There would have been no occasion to do so.

"I'm sure our menfolk will be back before we know it, Mrs. Shepton." Florence could think of nothing else to say.

"God bless you, ma'am," the woman said. "You and Miss Weston. All the work you've done at the Sailors' Rest."

It was a converted public-house, a duplicate of the hostel that the cheerful spinster Miss Agnes Weston had set up in Plymouth, where seamen ashore could get clean beds and simple meals without being fleeced by lodging-house keepers. Florence had spent long hours on its establishment and now devoted time to its running. It would be probably even more now that she was left alone.

"My Jem's not a bad man, ma'am. He was kind when the drink wasn't on him," Mrs. Shepton said. "Kind to me and the kids he always was, ma'am, but he was a demon when he was in liquor. But I want to thank you, ma'am, because since he's taken the pledge, an' it were you and Miss Weston as convinced him, ma'am, not a drop has passed his lips this twelvemonth. It's like I have the old Jem back."

It was a campaign that Miss Weston advocated relentlessly though jovially. Florence realised that she herself must have been present at one of the occasions when Miss Weston had administered the pledge and several dozen men had raised their hands in acceptance. Able Seaman Shepton must have recognised her, must have spoken of her to his wife.

"Your children are well, Mrs. Shepton?"

"Well, thank God, ma'am." She flushed a little with obvious pride. "An' my oldest, Andrew that is, is making something good of himself. He's on a training ship, the *Brahmaputra*."

"The *Brahmaputra*?" Agatha brightened. "My brother Oswald's on the board of directors. Your boy will be well equipped for a splendid career."

Florence had heard both Nicholas and Agatha speak of it, a Nelson-era hulk moored on the lower Thames where several hundred youths underwent Spartan-like training for careers in either Merchant or Royal Navy service. Many were orphans, others were directed there by the courts. The long-established enterprise was a private charity, well supported by socially prominent figures. It had recently attracted widespread praise in the newspapers when a man who had passed through a decade before had gained his master's ticket.

They parted with well-wishes for the boy's future, with the mother's repeated thanks.

"I'm so looking forward to meeting Oswald's future bride next week." Agatha had detected Florence's sombre mood and was determined to distract her. She herself was due to return to London that afternoon. "And an American too! I never expected it of Oswald. How happily that assignment to Washington turned out!"

Neither had Florence expected it. Women and girls had never interested him. No maid in Lord Kegworth's household – and she had once been one herself – had ever had to fend off unwelcome advances from His Lordship's heir.

"Such a pity her parents cannot come across immediately. Business concerns I understand," Agatha said. "She'll be travelling across with her brother Chester. Such an adventure!"

The fact that America's Leather King and his wife would arrive just before the wedding might be fortuitous, Florence thought. She had herself encountered a self-made millionaire in the United States who ate his food off his knife and spat on the carpet. However much their daughter might be bringing his son as a dowry, Lord Kegworth would be eager to minimise Hiram and Tabitha Brewster's exposure to British society.

"Such a beautiful girl," Florence had seen her photograph and it was true, even if there was a certain vacuity of expression.

"Papa has been so relieved," Agatha said. "He was afraid that Oswald might never marry, That the title might pass to…"

"No need to worry about that now." Florence forestalled any embarrassing mention of Godwin, Lord Kegworth's third son. There had been good reason to send him to Australia and to allow him a remittance on the condition that he did not return. There he had married a barmaid and already had half-a-dozen children. Nor was Cedric, the second son, likely to produce an heir. Almost as accomplished a mathematician as Agatha, his Fellowship at All Souls in Oxford prohibited marriage. The restriction did not seem to bother him.

"Oswald expects to be at the Foreign Office for the next two years," Agatha said. "Maybe there'll even be a little stranger in that time! And he's had hints that there might be an ambassadorship after that. Not a big one, not yet. But Copenhagen perhaps."

Agatha's pleasure was palpable. Other than his parents she must be the only one who ever cared for her stout, querulous and boorish brother. His devotion to her was perhaps his only admirable feature. It was hard to imagine anything other than his title being an attraction for a beautiful American heiress.

"Has Miss Brewster been in England before? Or her brother?"

"It will be the first time. Mamma has planned such a round of introductions for her. And Oswald is seeing to it that Chester has temporary membership at his club."

"Oswald will be overjoyed." Florence could not restrain the slight coldness in her tone. She had loathed him as a boy and later as a diplomat in Turkey and in the United States. He had never accepted her own elevation as Agatha's friend. Even marriage to Nicholas, and unavoidable cooperation with Oswald on that business in America the year before, had done nothing to reduce the mutual distaste.

They had reached Albert Grove. Time for a quick lunch and then a cab would carry Agatha to the railway station. Then the long half-year's wait for Nicholas's return would commence in earnest.

*

Florence knew that she must resign herself to time apart. *I'm twenty-seven and in the next twenty or thirty years there must be dozens of months I must spend like this.* For she was confident now that Nicholas would

11

advance to high rank – *if he was not killed first*, a small internal voice reminded her. Advancement would demand frequent absence, often long. *I must be busy – usefully busy – if the separation is not to destroy the love that Nicholas and I share. For I have seen it happen to others.*

She was glad of the Sailors' Rest, for it gave every day a focus. Miss Weston was back in Plymouth and though the hostel had a paid warden it was Florence who approved expenditure, oversaw accounts, inspected hygiene and cleanliness and planned the next expansion. The venture's success had stretched accommodation to the limit and she was now seeking additional premises. The company of other ladies who assisted was welcome – Mrs. Latham had proved a welcome and excellent addition – but the greatest challenge, and the most satisfying, was when she could help women with family difficulties. Her name had become known. Few approached her directly, but their friends often did so on their behalf. Within a mile of her comfortable home she encountered want and squalor as shameful as she had seen among refugees in Thrace. She did what she could but the knowledge that it was always insufficient depressed her.

There were private obligations too. She travelled to Northampton and stayed at a hotel where she met her parents and brothers. A friend on equal footing as she now was with Lady Agatha, she could not bring herself to meet them at their house on the grounds of the estate mansion where her father and Jack, her younger brother, were still Agatha's father's coachmen, where she herself had once been in service. Her elder brother's livery stables in town were doing well – Lord Kegworth, always a good employer, had advanced the funding to get them started – and he and his family had achieved modest affluence.

Her next visit was less pleasant, to Shrewsbury to meet the agent who managed Nicholas's farms. The revenues from the properties that supplemented his naval salary had shrunk to almost nothing. Produce prices for were low, had been so for years as cheap food flooded in from the colonies. She had often told Nicholas that he was too soft, that he should increase his tenants' rents, but now that she had authority in his absence, and was confronted with the reality, she recoiled from doing so. Once she had satisfied herself that the agent himself was honest – the Sailors' Rest had given her a proficiency in book-keeping – she realised that there was no more to be done. Her outgoings, such as they were, must be watched.

But there was bitterness too about the Shrewsbury visit. Nicholas's father, an established solicitor, had been pleasant enough and Nicholas's tiny half-brother Edgar had been ecstatic to see her again, but Nicholas's stepmother, little older than herself, had treated her with frigid politeness. There had been no invitation to lodge in the family home and she had stayed in a hotel instead. Most hurtful of all were the surreptitious glances at her waistline and the elder Mrs. Dawlish's obvious satisfaction that there was no hint of a rival for the inheritance that would one day be Edgar's. Not that there ever would be a rival, Florence thought. The miscarriage – she shrunk from the word – two years before had brought her and Nicholas even closer together through shared grief but its consequence would always be regret for what might have been. Doctors – several of them – had assured her that she could not now ever have children.

She returned to Portsmouth and Southsea, to the comfortable villa too large for herself alone where a cook and maid served her, where the Sailors' Rest demanded time and gave purpose, where she realised sadly that the injury to her left arm would always keep her from the proficiency she had hoped for when she had begun piano lessons. She persisted, but there would always be the unexpected odd jarring note that polite listeners would pretend they had not heard. There was satisfaction however in no longer needing other lessons. The elocution sessions that had remained unmentioned to Nicholas were no longer needed. She had the vowels of a lady now.

And yet the days dragged, the evenings even more. She took tea with the few ladies who accepted her easily, and they in turn took tea with her, and there was the occasional concert or dinner in which she made up a party's numbers. But there were always too many women in Portsmouth whose husbands were absent on service for her to be often needed on such occasions. In a naval town it was men rather than women who were lacking for the social round. She read until she was sick of reading and wrote numbered letters to Nicholas, careful always to withhold her true feeling of loneliness, to keep the letters light and cheerful so as not to burden him with feelings of guilt. The first batch would arrive at Port Said before him – they would go overland to Marseilles and then by sea to Egypt, but thereafter *Leonidas* would be faster than any mail-steamer. She sent subsequent letters to Hong Kong. The cruiser was to be dry-docked there for several weeks before her return to Britain.

She waited for Nicholas's letters in return. A half-dozen arrived from Egypt in mid-May – he did not write daily, as she did. He was well, *Leonidas* was performing even better than hoped, the crew was admirable and took willingly to its daily exercises, he was enjoying in his leisure moments the case of second-hand books she had sent on board for him, a rough passage through the Bay of Biscay had been made up for by a smooth one through the Mediterranean, he was not looking forward to the steam-bath ahead in the Red Sea. They were summaries of the unexciting, even dull, routine of life on a well-managed ship, punctuated by ponderous attempts at humour – for even Nicholas himself admitted that he was no wit – and yet they brought him close to her. As did the invariable last sentence. That he loved her.

*

Florence was writing to Nicholas one morning when Susan, the house maid, came to her.

"Ma'am?" The girl looked confused, even embarrassed. "I found something in a drawer an' I ain't sure what to do about it."

"Which drawer, Susan?"

"In that tallboy, ma'am. Where you keep…" she hesitated, "…some of your old underthings."

The girl had been sent to go through wardrobes and chests of drawers to identify used clothing which might be routed to some needy recipient. There were still even some dresses inherited from Lady Agatha and which had been modified for Florence when she had still been a paid companion. Only one did she intend to keep, that which she had worn on the morning off the Plains of Troy when Nicholas had first spoken to her. A sealed letter in her bureau indicated that when the time came she should be buried in it. The rest could go but she had not intended including undergarments in the donation.

"You mustn't be embarrassed to mention the matter, Susan," Florence said. "Everybody needs such clothing. It's just that we don't talk about it in public."

"It's not like that, ma'am," Susan said.

"Show me then."

And when Susan did it was not the tallboy that stood in Florence's dressing room, but another, in an unoccupied servant's room between Susan's and the cook's on the top floor. Florence had all but forgotten it and she realised even as she ascended the stairs what must have been found. Not just worn-our clothing that should have been disposed of long before. A reminder of the past.

Susan's removal of the underwear had revealed the small nickel-plated revolver and the box of shells that lay at the back of the bottom drawer.

"Is it dangerous, ma'am?" Susan spoke with pleasurable horror. "Is it the captain's"

"I'll see to this, Susan," Florence was curt. "And no need to talk about it. Not with anybody, not with Cook, not with anybody at all. Do you understand?"

Susan bobbed and left. She would probably talk of it, in awe, and a few might believe her. It didn't matter. It was legal for Florence to have it.

She picked it up and the memories flooded back. She had used the last of her money to buy it in Istanbul before she had left for Thrace with Agatha. Not just for protection but for... but for when the worst would be inevitable. As it nearly had happened in that besieged caravanserai. "No good. Too weak," Nicholas had said when he saw it and he had handed her instead a heavy Colt he had taken from a marauder's corpse. And she had used it.

In nightmares she could still remember the hate and lust-filled eyes of the Bashi Bazook who had tried to claw in through the window, the memory of herself raising the Colt and blasting a red crater in his face, of him falling back. And worst of all those minutes that followed when she realised that Nicholas himself was about to shoot her, and that she would be grateful to him for it, grateful that she would not have to do it herself.

She shuddered. She had hoped such days might never come again, and yet they had, in Cuba and...

The line of thought must be broken. She had glimpsed her future now and she must accommodate to it, a childless woman often necessarily alone as her husband built his career afloat. There would also be longer times together, she knew – shore appointments, or the opportunities Malta would offer were Nicholas to be assigned command of a ship in the Mediterranean Fleet – but the reality would always come back to separation. And worse perhaps. A chance might come again when some irregular service might claim him, as it did when she had first met him in Turkey, as had drawn him to

South America on some business he still refused to speak of, as had brought her with him to Cuba.

And dangerous as it had been, she wondered if she might yet hanker for the same again.

2

The day had started well with the unexpected, yet very welcome, arrival of a letter, this one sent from Suez as *Leonidas* passed out of the Canal. Florence read it over breakfast, spent most of the morning writing letters herself, had a piano lesson in early afternoon and left the villa at four o'clock to walk to the Sailor's Rest. It was fine May weather, though she brought an umbrella as a precaution, and the mile and a half stroll proved a pleasure. There were accounts for catering supplies to be checked and discussions with a builder about necessary roof repairs. She finished just before eight o'clock.

"Shall I fetch you a cab, ma'am?" It was a portly seaman with grey in his beard. The ribbon around his hat proclaimed that he was from the *Bellerophon*. The ironclad had recently returned from the North America station for a refit and many of her crew, without family living nearby, were grateful for the Rest's comforts.

"Thank you. I'd prefer to walk." Though it was dusk, the air was still pleasantly warm.

"We can't let Mrs. Dawlish go like that," another *Bellerophon* said. "It ain't safe. We need to look out for her. Ye're coming, Luke?" To Florence he said, "No offence, ma'am. Me an' Luke can walk a bit behind you, see that you get home safe."

It made sense. Several public houses lay on the way and drunken crowds sometimes spilled from them. Fights were not uncommon, garishly dressed women urging on the combatants with shrill obscenities. Seamen had previously escorted her and had tipped their hats at the corner of Albert Grove when she had reached her front door.

They set off and were soon almost out of the squalor of central Portsmouth. Florence strode ahead and the two men followed some twenty yards behind. As they came to a public bar, the Admiral Hawke, as proclaimed by a bewigged figure on the sign above the door, a seaman lurched out, red-faced and red eyed, the smell of alcohol wafting from him. He made to accost Florence but both her protectors grabbed him before he could slur more than a dozen words.

"One of the bleedin' *Glattons*, are you, matey? Always the bloody same!" Luke had him by the scruff of the neck. "That's a lady ye're talking to! What d'ye reckon we does with him, Tom?"

"A bloody good hiding." Tom was already balling his fist.

"It's been a misunderstanding." Florence did not want a fracas. "I don't think the gentleman meant any harm. He's going home quietly now, so all's well that ends well."

"Ye hear that?" Luke said to the seaman. "You're bloody lucky this time, mate – beg pardon for the language, ma'am – so on yer way!" He pushed the drunk away and kicked to speed him.

They walked on and had almost reached the street corner when they heard a woman's scream. Not anger, not drunken abuse, but rather one of genuine terror. Then men's voices, furious, the words unintelligible, and the woman screaming again, the cry suddenly cut off.

Florence rushed forward, heard Luke's and Tom's footsteps close behind. She rounded the corner and the street beyond was gas-lit, for it was almost fully dark now, and single-storied artisans' dwellings lined either side. On the near side of the closest lamp a closed cab had halted, one door hanging open. The driver on the box was trying to calm the single stamping horse panicked by the brawl alongside. With the light behind it was difficult to distinguish individual figures.

And again a scream, the single word "Help!" and another voice, male, shouting "Shut up! Shut up, you little whore!"

There were three of them, Florence saw as she dashed forward, two men in dark suits and a terrified girl trying to break loose as they dragged her back into the cab.

"Oh, God! Oh, God…" The girl's cry was silenced by a blow across the mouth.

"Help her!" Florence shouted, unnecessarily, for her two escorts were already rushing ahead of her. She realised that there would be no other help – this was an area where the residents knew better than to get involved in someone else's fight.

The men ahead were too intent on dragging the writhing girl towards the cab to notice the oncoming seamen but just as Tom drew level with the stamping horse it reared. He lurched away from the flailing hooves, caught his toe on a protruding cobble and tumbled down. Luke, fractionally behind, piled into him and went down too. The men with the girl had seen them now and were bundling her towards the cab's open doorway, each holding one of her arms. Florence saw that she was wearing a dress only, no hat or outdoor coat, and her hair was fallen in a tangle across her face. She was sobbing, despair and terror mixed, and her strength to resist seemed all but at an end. The driver had the horse under control again and once crammed inside the vehicle the girl would be beyond help.

From the corner of her eye Florence saw her two helpers struggling to their feet but she forged past them with only her umbrella as a weapon. A memory flashed into her mind of something Nicholas had once told her, that with a cutlass, point was more deadly than edge. Now there was no edge but the umbrella – a light, fashionable one, had a three-inch metallic spike at its end. Now she held the handle in her right hand, grasped the fabric body about half-way down the shaft with her left and drove at the nearer man.

It was his friend who spotted Florence. "Get back, you bleedin' cow!" he shouted and his comrade half-turned. Shocked, the man saw her and let go of the girl. He reached out to catch the umbrella spike but he miscalculated. Florence felt it impact against the hand, saw blood spouting from it, heard a howl of pain and even in the heat of this moment felt a surge of pleasure that she had hurt him. The bleeding man stepped back but his companion was throwing the girl against the nearest wheel and she crumpled, moaning, against it. Then he was making for Florence. "You cow! You bloody bitch!" he shouted and he reached for her. She parried with the umbrella but he was too close and he grabbed it, wrenched it from her and threw it down. His fingers locked on to her hair and dragged her towards him, his other hand drawn back to punch her in the face. She jerked and the blow shaved past. Swearing, he pulled back his fist for another blow but at that moment Tom impacted into him and sent him sprawling, Florence with him.

She struggled to her feet, saw that Luke too had risen and was plunging forward.

"Get back, ma'am," he was yelling. "Leave it to…" His words were cut off with a *Crack!* as the driver's whip tore a gash across his forehead. He froze in shock, a hand rising to his injured face and then a second lash caught the back of his hand and laid it open.

Florence's attention had been diverted from Tom's struggle. Now she half-turned and saw that he was on the ground and both men were above him and kicking. There was a terrible inertness about the way his slumped body accepted the impacts and he was offering no resistance. Behind them the girl was trying to lift herself by the wheel's spokes.

The man who had grabbed Florence saw her.

"Get back if you know what's good for you, you bitch!" Then to his companion, he said, "It's time to go."

And Florence realised that she had failed. She had nothing but her own fists now – she could not see the umbrella – and she knew she could no nothing with them. She stepped back and she saw them haul the dazed and sobbing girl to her feet and thrust her head first through the cab's door. One man followed inside but the other, blood streaming from the hand Florence had ripped was running back towards her.

"Leave her, Dick! Leave her!" The driver was yelling as a vicious slap caught Florence on her head's left side. Stunned, she was barely aware of falling and as she struggled again to her feet she saw the rear of the cab rounding the corner with a clatter of hooves.

It had been a kidnapping, not a brawl. Nothing remained to show that it had happened other than a badly battered seaman, another whose face and hand were bleeding profusely, and a dishevelled woman in torn clothing with a large bruise darkening on her face and a headache which she suspected would last for days.

*

Florence stayed with the half-conscious Tom while Luke went to the Admiral Hawke, the public house they had passed earlier, to get help. He returned with four tipsy seamen. Their immediate concern was Florence.

"She's the lady from the Sailor's Rest," Luke was saying. "Captain Dawlish's wife. Him of *Leonidas*."

"The bleeders! Hit a lady, did they?" Genuine outrage.

"Are you all right, ma'am?" Another said, a *Glatton* by his cap ribbon. "That's a nasty bruise, needs seein' to. We'll need to get you to the Royal. They'll help you there."

"No!" Florence's mind recoiled. The Royal Hospital in the Commercial Road was notorious for its Lock Ward where diseased women of the streets were confined. She would rather die than turn up there in her present bedraggled state. "It's nothing," she said. "It's Tom who needs help."

He was moaning, and every breath made him wince, but nothing appeared to be broken. They dragged him to his feet, supported him and began the painful steps back to the public house. The others helped Florence find her hat. It had been trodden out of shape but she still had to put it on and pile her loosened hair beneath it rather than be seen in public without one. She regretted that it had no veil to disguise her bruised face and her left eye that was almost closed by swelling. She found her reticule in the gutter, its strap broken but the contents safe. There was at least money enough to get home.

They brought her to the Admiral Hawke where the publican cleared the snug for her and brought a glass of brandy. She hesitated, then sipped but had no comfort from it.

"You shouldn't get drawn into this sort of thing, ma'am." The publican's wife had appeared. "There's always fights and such-like around here. It don't do no good to get involved. Especially not a lady. Just let them at it, says I, let them beat the living daylights out of each other for all that me or you should care."

"It wasn't a fight," Florence said. "They were trying to abduct a girl." She was surprised by her own vehemence, by the outrage that possessed her.

"Mrs. Dawlish's right," Luke said. His forehead and hand were swathed in none-too-clean handkerchiefs through which blood was seeping. He seemed proud rather than disconcerted, basking in the admiration of those around him. "I reckon that they'd had her in the cab already, that she managed to get out just as we got there. They were trying to get her back in."

"Not from round here then?"

"I don't think so." Florence said. Luke's assessment seemed correct.

"She might have been up to no good," the publican said. "Stole from her mistress maybe, or worse. Maybe she was being took into custody."

"No!" Florence was angry. She knew it hadn't been like that.

"You'll need your face treated, ma'am, get that swelling down" the publican's wife seemed no stranger to such injuries. "You need to be at the Royal. No? Then your own doctor? We can get a cab to take you there."

"I'll be obliged if you'll fetch one," Florence said. "But to the police station, not the hospital."

First things first.

*

Luke and Tom came with her but even in the first seconds when she stood before the police counter she realised that she would get little sympathy. The sergeant must have seen hundreds of bruised women accompanied by blood-stained men.

"Been in the wars then, love?" he said. "Been havin' a good time with these two gents?"

"You'd better keep a civil tongue," Luke said. "Her husband's captain of the *Leonidas*."

"And I'm the Prince of Wales," the sergeant said. The young constable at the ledger by his side laughed.

Two gaudily dressed women who sat on a bench behind had overheard. They seemed at their ease there, as if regulars. The heavy rouge did nothing to hide the age beneath. "Leave it to the professionals, missus," one of them called. The other laughed and said, "Did yer old man send you out?"

"Enough of your lip, Janey," The sergeant's tone was of amused tolerance.

Excitement and indignation had sustained Florence thus far but now the reaction was setting in. Her knees were trembling and she was fighting the urge to weep. She felt a sense of degradation now, was hurt by the sneering contempt for her battered hat, for her dishevelled hair, for the dress filthy from the street and the great rent torn at one knee. And most of all for the face she had been unable to bring herself to look at in a mirror at the Admiral Hawke. She did not trust herself to speak, lest she break down, but she fished inside her reticule and found a card. Captain Dawlish R.N. and the address in Albert Grove. She pushed it across the counter.

The sergeant took it, studied it, handed it to the young constable, who shook his head, took it back again. "Nice company for a captain's wife." He looked towards Luke's bloody face, towards Tom hunched in pain. "You're sure this lady is who she says she is?"

It was *lady* now, progress, Florence thought.

"She's the lady from the…" Luke began but Florence cut him off.

"I'll speak to your inspector," She had collected herself and her voice was steady. "And not here. In his office."

"But…" the sergeant began.

"Do I need to have one of my husband's brother officers to come here?" Florence looked the sergeant in the eye. He held his gaze for an instant, then looked away.

"The inspector's out," he said. "God knows when he'll be back."

"Come here and sit with us, dearie." Janey said from behind. "We can compare notes." Her friend cackled.

"Then I'll wait," Florence said.

The sergeant glanced at the card again, then sighed and said to the young constable. "Conduct the lady to Inspector Towton's room." He glared at Tom and Luke. "Not you pair. You wait here."

"Shove along the bench, Tilda," Janey said. "Make room for these two gents, all cosy like."

The constable led Florence through what seemed a labyrinth. She had never been in a police station before and the size surprised her, so too the feeling that she was soiled by just being there. She was repelled by the all-pervasive stench of disinfectant and vomit and urine mixed together, by the sounds of prisoners in unseen cells, of drunken singing and hysterical sobbing, of a woman screaming an obscene litany, of a voice shouting for quiet and getting it for thirty seconds before the cacophony commenced again.

The office was sparsely furnished but the constable lit a gas lamp so that she was not left in darkness. She saw that the desk was clear, all cupboards closed and probably locked, no sign of files or papers. The inspector must be a methodical man.

The wait was endless and as there was no fire in the grate the room grew cold and she began to shiver. It was important, she knew, to remember every detail of what had happened and she tried to do so despite the aching in her head. She wished that Nicholas was here, felt more alone than at any time since he had left, wanted to be gone from here and back in her own comfortable home. *Away from the miserable reality so close to you*, a small internal voice reminded her. The one image of the incident that was sharp in her memory was the girl's face, stark not just with terror or despair, but with awareness that she did not count, had nobody to turn to.

Except me.

The inspector arrived just before midnight. He radiated brusque impatience and a lack of sympathy that made the sergeant seem benign by comparison. He took her card, scarcely looked at it, handed it back. She had stood up when he had entered but he did not invite her to sit again.

"You'd better go home now, Mrs. Dawlish," he said. "I've spoken to those two men who were with you. They've told me all they could. I'll look into the case." His tone indicated that he would do nothing beyond noting the incident.

"A girl has been abducted, inspector."

"I doubt if a lady would know about what happens around here," Towton said. "Women of the street, men who control them, customers who get robbed or cut up rough or refuse to pay. There's always something of the sort going on. It was probably something of that nature." He reached for the door-knob and began to open it. "The sergeant will send for a cab, Mrs. Dawlish."

Florence sat down.

"I'm going to report what I saw, inspector," she said. "All I remember. You'll take it down and if you don't I'll be here tomorrow morning with my solicitor and a sworn affidavit."

He sat, unlocked a drawer, took out a notebook, a steel pen, and ink bottle, all in slow insolent silence during which he did not look at her.

"I understand that your husband is overseas," he said at last. "He'll be no doubt happy to hear of his wife roaming the streets with two common seamen."

She forced herself not to rise to his bait.

"I was doing some work at the Seaman's Rest," she began, and I left about..."

"The Seaman's Rest. Yes, Mrs. Dawlish, I've got that." He made it sound indecent. "I suppose that there are lots of officers' ladies to be found there."

Still she forced herself to be calm, told of the two seaman volunteering to accompany her, of the encounter with the drunk outside the Admiral Hawke.

"It's the kind of thing you'd expect round here, ma'am."

And then to the story of the scream, of the rush around the corner, of the cab and the stamping horse and the men struggling with the girl and...

It was all a blur, she realised, few concrete memories in a whirlwind of violence.

"How were the men dressed? Seamen? Civilians?"

"Civilians, dark clothes."

"Anything more specific?"

She couldn't say. But she remembered their bulk, their faces, the air of brutality.

"One was heavy and had a moustache."

"Like half the men in Portsmouth, Mrs. Dawlish. And you're going to tell me that the other was thin and clean shaven?"

She nodded, felt despair rising. "One called the other Dick."

At least he wrote it down.

"How old?"

It was hard to say. Not youths but not old either.

"And you assaulted one of them with your umbrella. You drew blood?"

"Yes." It was something to be proud of.

"Did it occur to you that these men might have been medical orderlies? That they might have been bringing this girl to an asylum? That she might have been a danger to herself?"

"It wasn't like that at all. She was terrified and they were handling her cruelly."

"And how old do you think she was?"

Now that she was put to it Florence found she could tell little. The girl might have been sixteen or eighteen and she was small, slight even, and she had brown hair and a dark blue dress.

"And that's all, Mrs. Dawlish?"

"The dress was plain. Very plain."

"Like a maid's?

Florence shook her head. "Like I think a woman might wear in prison."

"You've had experience of women's prisons, Mrs. Dawlish?"

"No, but…"

"You refer to the vehicle as a cab. You mean a hackney coach? A four-wheeler, a growler?"

"I just assumed that it was…" Now more than ever the events were a blur. "But I think that it was certainly a four-wheeler. Like a growler, but more closed."

"Assumptions and *I think* doesn't get us far, Mrs. Dawlish. Any markings? A crest on the door?"

She shook her head now and felt beaten. She knew that nothing would come of this. Only the card she had presented had guaranteed what hearing there had been.

"I'll have this report formalised, Mrs. Dawlish. We have your address. A constable will bring it round tomorrow for your signature." He moved again to the door and this time she let him show her out.

"If somebody reports a missing girl we'll be in contact with you." He did not give her his hand or accompany her to the front desk. At least Tom and Luke had waited for her.

In the hackney cab that brought her home she finally allowed herself to weep.

Not for herself, or for her face. But for the unknown girl.

3

Susan was already in bed when Florence got home. She did not awaken the girl to have water heated as it would take too long. The urge to cleanse herself was so intense that she bathed instead in cold water. By now the swelling around the left eye made it impossible to see from but when she probed her cheek she was relieved that no bone had been broken. The ache in her head was almost unbearable but she hoped that sleep might cure that. She debated with herself whether she should summon her doctor but instead decided against it. His genteel practice probably brought him little experience of such injuries and she hesitated to go to someone else. In the end she decided that she would treat herself in the coming days. She set her alarm-clock for her usual time of rising and tried to sleep with a wet flannel held to her face to keep the bruising down. She had little comfort from it. She kept wakening – her head still ached and her cheek was on fire – and the memory of the girl's futile pleadings haunted her. She worried too how Nicholas might take the news. He would have other cares and could do nothing anyway. Better, she decided, that her next numbered letter should say nothing of it Better to tell him about it only when he returned.

At breakfast she sat across from her usual place so that the maid could not easily see the injury. The *Morning Post* already lay on the table, as usual, when she sat down. When Susan entered with tea and toast Florence was already buried in it, her face all but hidden. It was of no avail.

"Oh Lord! ma'am!" Susan was genuinely concerned. "What happened to you, ma'am?"

The only explanation that came immediately to hand was unconvincing.

"I stumbled on the way home last night, Susan. I hit my head against a lamp post and my dress was torn." The dress was the least of it. She had found this morning that the cameo brooch pinned to it had also disappeared. The loss pained her. It had been a gift from her parents and brothers on her twenty-first birthday. Their love – and what had been a significant expense for them – had made it all the more dear to her.

"Shall I fetch Cook, ma'am? Shall we send for the doctor?"

"That won't be necessary." Florence found her pronunciation slightly slurred, as if her tongue was too large for her mouth. "And thank you, Susan. That will be all."

She wondered now why she still felt so... so degraded by what had happened. Not just the squalor of the incident and of her dishevelment in it, and the stench at the police station and the shrill women there and the studied insolence she had been treated with, but her powerlessness to help the girl. And there would be no hope of covering up the event either, even had her face not been injured. Tom and Luke would already be relaying the story and basking in admiration of their fellows for their heroic intervention. It would already be common knowledge at the Sailors' Rest – where she was to meet a builder this afternoon about its expansion – and it would be rippling outwards and gaining in the telling. She would gain respect for it from the Rest's guests and their families, but the respect would stop there. The memory of the inspector's words chilled her, that she had been roaming the streets with two common seamen in her husband's absence. If a journalist were to hear of it! What could be made of it! There were so many naval wives – Mrs. Edgerton most of all – who would seize on the incident with glee and put the worst possible construction on it. They would not be surprised however. Captain Dawlish could not have expected anything better when he had been unwise enough to marry a woman little better than a common servant. She herself would be an object of contempt and Nicholas one of ridicule.

Yet it was more than the risk to her own reputation – and Nicholas's – that worried her.

Inspector Towton's report would be a single line in a log book and that would be the end of it. She had been able to give him little enough to go on with, but go on he would not – she could see that clearly. She could imagine the sergeant and his sycophantic young constable joking about her with Janey and Tilda when they were next brought in. Her face burned now from more than the blow alone.

And then decision. She would not leave it at that. What had seemed even to herself an empty threat last night, to come back with a sworn affidavit, must give the affair some standing, would give some authority when she pressed for progress.

Before she went out she made up her face as best she could. It made little difference, but a thick veil on a summer hat did offer some disguising of what was now a dark blue bruise fringed with yellow. Then she set out for Carlton and Bagshot, Solicitors, in Palmerston Road. Nicholas's will was lodged with them and, though they were probably more familiar with conveyancing and trusts and covenants than with brawls, they must know about affidavits.

*

It turned out that there was no "they". Mr. Carlton had died in some indeterminate past but Mr. Bagshot, though old and white-haired, was still vigorous and apparently ran the business without any younger partner. Florence was hesitant to start but she found it surprisingly easy to tell him her story for he had a fatherly manner that inspired trust. He was even more outraged that Florence should have received a blow than that the girl had been abducted. The cat o' nine tails was too good for men who did such things and he would have no hesitation in wielding it himself were he to get the chance. He heard her out, then brought her back over the story with gently probing questions. His sympathetic manner elicited more details than the inspector had and within an hour Florence felt that a coherent narrative had been prepared which she could swear to in all conscience.

"My clerk will make three fair copies," Mr. Bagshot said. "Could you come back this afternoon to sign them and to take the oath?"

She could, but she suddenly felt a reluctance for the step that must follow. Mr. Bagshot noticed but did not allude directly.

"One copy for my safe and it might be better were I to deliver the others in person," he said. "First to my friend, Mr. Carson, the magistrate. Then to the police. With all due apologies to you as a lady, Mrs. Dawlish, the case might be taken a little more seriously were a legal gentleman be seen to be involved."

She was grateful for that. The idea of a return to the police station had repelled her. But another concern still troubled her and Mr. Bagshot seemed to sense that also.

"Is there something else, Mrs. Dawlish?"

"If this story..." she hesitated, "...if it were to be misconstrued. If the newspaper..."

The solicitor held up both hands and smiled, even beamed. "No conceivable public interest could be served by your name being mentioned. The editor of the *Portsmouth Argus* is a personal friend and I'll have a word. You may set your mind at rest on that score Mrs. Dawlish."

And so the rest of the day went well, despite the nagging headache which did diminish as time went on. She sent Susan to purchase arnica at the local chemist's shop and she rubbed it into the bruise. It seemed to have little effect and she was again veiled when she went to swear and sign the affidavit. She walked afterwards to the Sailors' Rest. There she acknowledged well-wishes and admiration with no more than a nod and concentrated on her normal responsibilities. Negotiating the builder's estimate down was a small but satisfying triumph. She allowed herself the small luxury of going home in a hansom cab and she felt content. Wounded she might have been, but not beaten.

Best of all, she knew that the girl's case could not be forgotten now.

*

Though Florence no longer feared mention in the newspaper she still scanned each edition eagerly for any mention of a missing girl. There was none. There was no news either about progress of the investigation.

"Mr. Carson is continuing to press the police about the matter." A week had passed and Mr. Bagshot had accepted an invitation to afternoon tea to discuss the matter. "With Inspector Towton's superiors too, as well as with that man himself. But there's nothing so far."

"A private lunatic asylums?" Florence had hung on to that idea as a last hope.

"All within thirty miles have been checked. And no, I fear, nothing." Mr. Bagshot's voice softened. "This business may never be clarified. Such things happen, especially in harbour towns. You've done your best, Mrs. Dawlish. If it's sorted out, then well and good. But if not, you really have nothing to reproach yourself with." He laid his cup down. "And is there news of Captain Dawlish and his great voyage to the gorgeous Orient?"

But there was another interview that week, less pleasant, a summons rather, that left Florence as angry and humiliated as she had felt on the night of the incident.

Lady Adelaide de Courcey was known to be more proud of her position as his wife than her husband was of his own as Port Admiral. She was treated with fulsome courtesy by many officers' wives and feared by all since it was rumoured that a word of her displeasure might well end a career's promise. Her family background – her brother was a viscount – was even more illustrious than the Admiral's only slightly humbler one and she did not hesitate to remind others of it. Florence had met her twice at official functions, but had been treated with the icy politeness she was by now so well accustomed to in Portsmouth society. There had been no invitation to Lady Adelaide's afternoon teas and Florence's own letter requesting patronage of the Sailors' Rest had elicited only a stiffly-courteous refusal. "It's water off the duck's back," Florence had said to Nicholas afterwards but the slight, like so many others, still hurt. It was therefore all the more surprising to receive an invitation – on a gilt-edged card with a family crest – requesting her presence at three o'clock on the afternoon of Thursday May 25th. No mention of tea, no RSVP, only the obvious assumption of compliance.

The left eye was fully open again and the vision was unimpaired, but a yellowing tinge showed the last remains of the bruise. Florence powdered it lightly and wore a veil when she set out. She was kept waiting in a small parlour, too small for the sort of gathering Lady Adelaide was famed for. Nobody else was present. Fifteen minutes passed, then twenty, the delay obviously intentional and calculated. When Lady Adelaide did finally arrive she made no offer of tea, no attempt at small talk. She was thin, gaunt and practically mannish in features.

"I understand you've been married to Captain Dawlish for four years." She made it sound like an accusation.

"Four years." Then, unwilling to be browbeaten, Florence added "Four happy years."

"And no children, Mrs. Dawlish?"

"No children, Lady Adelaide." *And none of your business.*

"Your husband is thirty-nine."

"No," Florence said. "My husband is not thirty-nine." *He's two years younger but I've no intention of discussing his age with you.*

"Young in any case for the command he holds. A rapid advancement despite…"

"Despite marrying a woman who was once a servant?" *There,* Florence thought, *I've said it first. Put that in your pipe and smoke it, madam.*

"That's not a subject to which I would wish to allude." Lady Adelaide showed no flicker of anger or emotion. Her voice remained cold. "You may or may not believe me, Mrs. Dawlish, but I'm talking to you in your own best interest. And in your husband's."

Florence remained openly calm but her heart was thumping.

"I was alluding to the fact that many resent your husband's early promotion. All the more so since there is widespread resentment about his promotion despite long absences from duty."

Absences, but not from duty, absences on tasks that had nearly killed him. And almost me too last year. The nation is in my debt as well as his. But bite your tongue, Florence, bite your tongue.

"It would be unfortunate if anything were to impair his future prospects, Mrs. Dawlish. Anything of a scandalous nature, even were he himself not directly involved."

"Like this, Lady Adelaide?" Florence lifted her veil and turned her head slightly so that the remains of the bruise was visible.

"Like brawling in the street, Mrs. Dawlish. Like consorting with common seamen."

"Like trying to rescue a girl, Lady Adelaide, who was being abducted by ruffians. A girl who was obviously terrified, and with good reason. A girl I was glad to try to help and I'm only sorry that I failed. And I'm proud of what I did and I know my husband will be proud of it also once he's heard of it. You're aware of course that he's at present on Her Majesty's service overseas."

Don't patronise me you old — even mentally she recoiled from the word and yet there was no other — you old bitch.

"So that's what you have to say, Mrs. Dawlish?" The tone had not changed. No rising to Florence's provocation. "And what have you heard since about this mysterious girl? Are you sure that she wasn't just some woman of the streets in altercation with her clients?"

Florence stood up. "I think it's time to leave, Lady Adelaide."

"I think it is, Mrs. Dawlish. The maid will show you out." Lady Adelaide left the room.

And afterwards, in the cab that took her home because her knees were shaking and she did not trust herself to walk, Florence realised that she might have destroyed Nicholas's prospects for ever. The snows and Bashi Bazooks of Thrace, the harried retreat to Istanbul, the charades in New York and Newport and Santiago, the murderous climax in Guantanamo Bay, dangers willingly shared. The price of his advancement which she had so willingly contributed to.

All now perhaps counting for nothing. Because of her own pride and for the sake of a girl whose name she did not know.

*

Another interview came before May's end, the most surprising of all.

Florence had been spending the afternoon at home, persisting with piano exercises, writing to Nicholas and now relaxing with a book over tea. She heard the doorbell ring, Susan going to answer it. The muffled sound of voices, then Susan entered.

"There's a gentleman at the door, ma'am. He said to give you this." She reached out a card.

Ludovic Gilpin. Lieutenant, Royal Navy.

The name meant nothing to Florence.

"Did he say anything about returning tomorrow perhaps?" Etiquette demanded that a gentleman present his card in advance of any later visit.

"He's still there, ma'am. He says he needs to see you today." Susan hesitated, then said, "He's seems to be a bit upset, ma'am."

Lieutenant Gilpin must be asked to leave. Florence had no intention of entertaining unknown gentlemen who turned up unannounced. But her interest had been aroused. "What way upset, Susan?"

"Pale like, ma'am. Very nervous."

"Please tell the gentleman that if he has anything to say to me he can put it in a letter. He obviously knows my address."

Susan was back a minute later. "He won't leave, ma'am. He says 'For God's sake', ma'am. Really upset he is, nearly crying. 'For God's sake let me speak to Mrs. Dawlish', he says. An' he said he'd known the captain at HMS *Vernon*, that he'd have spoken to the captain himself if he was here."

If an officer had displayed such a lack of dignity to a housemaid, then something serious was afoot. The man might not be what he said he was, might well be dangerous. At any other time Florence would have asked Susan to slip out to fetch a police constable but her recent encounters with the force dissuaded her. And curiosity was getting the better of her.

"I'll see him in the study, Susan. Just give me a moment."

And in that long moment she settled herself behind the solid writing desk. She put the paperknife in a drawer, away from temptation, and moved the heavy marble paperweight close to her right hand. If Lieutenant Gilpin expected a defenceless woman, then he would have a surprise in store.

But when he came in she saw that he was no danger. He might have been thirty, was thin, fair-haired and fair-skinned. The word that came to mind was not handsome, but beautiful. His clothing was civilian and obviously exquisitely tailored but the scent of eau-de-cologne that emanated from him was soured by the sweat staining the armpits.

"Thank you for seeing me, Mrs. Dawlish." The hand he reached out was immaculately manicured. "I must apologise, I must..." It was as if it had taken an immense effort of the will to get thus far and that he was now unsure how to continue. "In any other circumstances, Mrs. Dawlish..."

"Please be seated, lieutenant." Florence gestured to the chair across the desk from her. "Would you perhaps like some tea?" Brandy might be more appropriate, given his agitation, but she had no intention of offering it.

He thanked her but, no, he didn't want tea. And he didn't want to take up too much of her time. Then an uneasy silence.

"You served at *Vernon* with my husband?" Florence said at last. He had been an instructor at the mine and torpedo establishment at Portsmouth and, more importantly, had been involved in weapons testing and development. But she had never heard him mention a Lieutenant Gilpin.

He looked embarrassed. "Not quite, Mrs. Dawlish. But I attended a course that he lectured on. A very impressive man." He was struggling for words. "And very... very..."

She cut him off. "What you mean, lieutenant, is that Captain Dawlish probably wouldn't know you from Adam if he were to walk in this minute. He lectured to dozens, maybe hundreds of officers while he was at *Vernon*."

He dropped his head and would not meet her gaze. "I'm afraid that's it, ma'am." He was an object of pity now, perspiration streaming from his face.

"What ship at present, Lieutenant?"

"A shore appointment, Mrs. Dawlish. A staff position."

It seemed inevitable. It was hard to imagine this exquisite young man volunteering for Anti-Slavery Patrol duties in the Indian Ocean.

"So how can I help you, lieutenant?"

When the words finally came they did so in a torrent. "I believe that you're well acquainted with the Lord Kegworth's family... I mean that, no, no offence meant, ma'am, but that..."

"I'm a friend of Lady Agatha's," Florence said.

"I know," Gilpin said. "I know that she stayed with you some weeks ago. I nearly came to see her then. I should have spoken to her then but..." The words trailed off.

"But you lost your nerve, lieutenant?" Not too wild a guess, given his demeanour.

He nodded, shame incarnate.

"Why can't you speak to her now? She's in London at present. If you were to send her a letter first and..."

"It's too late for that." There was a depth of misery, even despair in his tone that was chilling. "If you could give her a message, Mrs. Dawlish. I'd be grateful, eternally grateful."

"You're sure you can't do so yourself?"

He shook his head. "I have to go away unexpectedly. For a long time. But if you could..."

Pity mastered her. "I'll relay any letter you have for her."

"No letter, Mrs. Dawlish. No need for anything in writing. Just a verbal message."

She could never have guessed what followed next.

"Her brother," he said. "Lord Oswald. She should tell him to be careful, that he can't be too careful."

"Lord Oswald is a friend of yours?" *And you're welcome to him.* "Why don't you tell him yourself."

"We had a falling out." Gilpin looked away. Every word was taking an effort. "But there's still regard. Deep regard. From his side,

I hope, as much as from mine. And I think he'll hear from his sister when it's unlikely he'll want to listen to me."

"So what's the message, lieutenant.?"

"Just that he must be careful in London. That he should stay away from Cleveland Street. And from the *Brahmaputra*." Then silence.

"The *Brahmaputra*?" The name was vaguely familiar.

"The training ship in the Thames, ma'am."

"And that's all, Lieutenant Gilpin?"

"That's all, Mrs. Dawlish. He'll understand. But he needs to know quickly, as soon as possible." He raised his head and looked her in the eye. "For God's sake do it, Mrs. Dawlish. I wouldn't have come here if there was any other way. Not letter, telegrams…" His voice trailed off.

"I'll do it," Florence said.

She thought that she was agreeing from regard for Agatha but as she saw him out – a beaten dog – she realised that it was also for pity of him.

4

It was easy to agree, much more difficult to do. Florence spent a day wondering what exactly she should tell Agatha – Gilpin's words were cryptic at the least – and how she could broach the subject. She realised then that the recent incident in the street might give an opening. Agatha would be concerned and would probably want to come to see her. Discussion of the implications of the girl's abduction might give an opportunity to drop in a casual reference to an acquaintance of Oswald's. The letter Florence wrote was carefully constructed to make light of her own injuries, while yet suggesting that they had been more serious than she admitted. Knowing Agatha, and the care they had taken of each other in Thrace, it was unlikely that she could stay away.

The reply came three days later. Florence's letter had been forwarded to where Agatha was accompanying Oswald's American fiancée on a round of introductory visits to relations in the north. They would be returning to London in the following week but Agatha was mortified that she could not come to Southsea. The wedding arrangements were demanding more time than anticipated.

But could Florence visit London, even if for only a few days, if she was fit to travel? There was a hint of pleading in the suggestion. Though Agatha said nothing overtly – and she was indeed incapable of unkindness – there was a hint that Miss Rebecca Brewster's company had been less than stimulating. Two letters followed and it was confirmed that Florence would come to London.

And no mention of accommodation, for it would be the same as on previous visits. Delicacy prevented Agatha ever inviting Florence to her father's Piccadilly mansion, nor would Florence have considered it if Agatha did. The fact that she had her once worn a maid's uniform there, and at the Kegworth country seat near Northampton, that she was known to many of the older servants, that her father and brother were coachmen there, made her shrink from the idea of entering. Even close personal friendship with Agatha and marriage to a Royal Navy captain would count for nothing in her own mind if she was to pass that door. And so Florence would lodge, as always, in the Charing Cross Hotel, at the front of the railway station and just off Trafalgar Square. Agatha would meet her there and they would make expeditions to museums and galleries together. Her heart rose at the thought as she wrote to book a room. Only now did she admit to herself just how hungry she had been for the company of an intelligent and generous-minded friend for whom her origins were immaterial.

She bought newspapers before her train left. The news from Egypt worried her as she read the national daily, the *Morning Post,* not because of the situation as of itself, but for what it might imply for Nicholas. The Egyptian army had taken over the government weeks earlier and were now threatening foreign interests. British and French warships were being sent to Alexandria to deter further menace – she recognised the names of the vessels, had heard Nicholas speak of some of their commanders. The situation seemed stable for now but the *Post's* correspondent was certain that nothing short of action would bring Egypt's new rulers to their senses. And action, Florence knew, meant ships in battle and chances for ambitious officers to distinguish themselves in the full light of press attention and public adulation. Careers could be made like this. But Nicholas was now somewhere east of Aden, on a worthy and necessary voyage, and might be missing the opportunity of a lifetime.

The *Portsmouth Argus* held no terrors for her. Mr. Bagshot must have been as good as his word, for no mention of the girl's abduction, nor of her own name, had appeared in its recent editions. She scanned it quickly – as so often, there was little of real interest – and she was about to lay it aside when a small item on an inner page caught her eye.

Tragic death of promising young naval officer.

She sought the name, found it.

Gilpin. Lieutenant Ludovic Gilpin.

Shocked, hands trembling, stomach hollow, she read on.

The coroner's inquest had taken place the previous day. The young man had been cleaning his revolver and had apparently overlooked the fact that it was loaded. To avoid distressing family members present, the coroner saw no need to go into detail. The single shot to the head would have meant that death was instantaneous. The servant who had found the body was commended for keeping calm in dreadful circumstances and for sending for assistance. The jury was recommended to ignore a statement by a housemaid, who was also a witness, that she thought that the gentleman had not seemed himself for some time. There could be only one verdict, and the jury agreed. Death by misadventure. The coroner knew that he spoke for all present when he conveyed sympathy to Lieutenant Gilpin's parents and regretted the loss to Her Majesty's Navy of a much-admired officer.

She stared blankly out the window, oblivious of the countryside slipping past. Gilpin had not seemed himself, the maid had said, just as Susan had noticed that he had been upset, just as she herself had seen that he was in despair. And no officer accidently cleaned a loaded pistol – she had cleaned her own before putting it away, had first checked twice over that the chambers were empty. Regret coursed through her that she might have been too brusque with him, that a word from her might have prevented… But no! She realised that he had been at such a pass that nothing she could have said would have changed things. He had asked a favour – perhaps his last favour of anybody – and she was fulfilling it now.

No matter how difficult, no matter that she did not understand the message, she owed the poor tortured soul that much.

*

Florence arrived in London at midday and by one o'clock was lodged and unpacked in her hotel. She would meet Agatha tomorrow – she was arriving home late that evening – and for now she had the afternoon to herself. Her original plan had been to visit the National Gallery across the square but the news of Gilpin's death had put an end to that. She went over his words again and again. The reference to the *Brahmaputra* might make some sense – Agatha had mentioned that her brother was on the board of the trust that ran that training ship – but the mention of Cleveland Street was more baffling. If she were to speak of it to Agatha, then she must first know something about it herself. She was not even sure where the street was and she hesitated to ask directions at the hotel reception lest it have some significance she did not know. Instead she borrowed a street map there and she pored over it in her room. It took ten frustrating minutes before she located Cleveland Street. It ran parallel to Tottenham Court Road on its west side and was intersected at right angles by several smaller streets. It was straight, about a quarter-mile long, but the map gave no indication of its nature. There was nothing for it but to investigate on foot.

The weather was warm, so she took a cab to the street's lower end, where it led north from Goodge Street. There was nothing surprising about it, nothing that made it significantly different from any other in the area. At its lower end was a four-storey red-brick block of apartments, the name "Cleveland Residences" over each of the three entrances. It could not have been more than a decade old, but obviously expensive, as confirmed by the presence of a smartly uniformed commissionaire who tipped his cap as Florence passed. Across the street was one wall of the Middlesex hospital – no entrance there, just windows. Beyond this point the three and four-storey houses from the last century lining most of either side looked prosperous and well-cared for. The area was obviously not fashionable but there was an air of solid affluence. The note that jarred did however come a little further on, where a public house on a corner marked the intersection with Foley Street to the left. Across from it, closed from the street by high walls, rose a massive and forbidding structure of soot-stained brown brick, many of its windows barred. A sign by the gate identified it as the Central London Sick Asylum. Even on this warm afternoon it seemed to exude a chill.

Florence walked on, saw here and there a brass plate identifying a doctor's or solicitor's practice, a large building that seemed to belong to London University, more well-maintained houses, still the impression of unostentatious comfort. The activity on the street was nothing more than might be expected – the occasional cab, several delivery carts, furniture being carried into an apparently empty house, a painter busy on a hall-door, maid-servants on errands, once a knot of boisterously cheerful medical students who nevertheless stood politely aside to let her pass. Further on was a cluster of buildings belonging to the Post Office. At the end, where Cleveland Street met Euston Road, she had a feeling of anti-climax. She had not known what to expect, but whatever it was, she had not found it. Vaguely irritated by herself – there must be something that she had missed – she turned to walk back.

A cab drew up by the asylum gate as Florence approached. The cabby got down to assist the respectably dressed man and woman who emerged. There was crying from within, pitiful, mumbling, incoherent, and then they were lifting down a child, a boy of ten or twelve, who was obviously terrified and whose head was lolling and mouth drooling. Florence stopped and was overcome by sadness and admiration as she saw how the parents – and they could only be the parents, for their faces registered misery as great as the child's – were trying to coax him towards the gate. The cabby seemed moved as he thanked the father for the fare thrust into his hand. The couple passed inside with the child and as Florence walked forward again – she felt tears welling in her eyes – the driver said to her "Most of us don't know how lucky we are, ma'am. We're never thankful enough."

"It seems a terrible place," she said.

"Bad now, but worse before. It used to be the workhouse, ma'am."

Depressed – and wondering if Oswald might have a link with this place, might be on its board of directors perhaps – she declined the cabby's services. She would walk on to the end she had started from. As she reached the next intersection – with Tottenham Street – she was almost blundered into by a boy hurrying from her left.

"Go easy, Alf!" a second youth yelled. He seemed more amused than concerned. "He ain't safe to be let out on his own, ma'am!"

"Hold yer row, Sid!" the first boy said, and then to Florence, "I'm sorry, ma'am. No offence, I'm sure."

They were both in tightly fitting page-boy uniforms, brass buttons gleaming down the front of their dark-blue jackets and their peak caps identifying them as telegram messengers, probably from the Post Office building further up the street.

"Are you looking for somewhere, missus?" Alf flashed a look towards his companion as he spoke, something like a smirk. "Maybe Mr. Dickens' house?"

"Mr. Dickens?" Florence was perplexed.

"The man as used to write books, missus. Used to live in Number 22 – over there, you see it? When he was a boy, a gentleman told me."

"He might have been a busy little lad too," Sid said, "maybe more than just writing." They both sniggered.

"I think you've both got work to go to." Florence sensed that she was being made fun of and she did not like it.

Sid nudged his friend. "Real hard work, ain't it Alf?"

"Give over," Alf said and they both sniggered again.

Florence ignored them and walked on, relieved, when she checked it, that her purse was untouched. She felt guilty for having suspected them, but she knew that a collision with a stranger in London was often a tactic of pickpockets. She paused at Number 22. It was a modest house, its doorway giving directly on to the street and she wondered if what the boy had said was true. Had Charles Dickens indeed lived here as a child? She had always imagined that he had lived in greater poverty than this. Then behind her, almost directly behind on the other side of the street, she heard a single rap on a door-knocker. She glanced around but the door was already closing. There was nobody else close by at this moment. Both telegram boys had disappeared.

Back then to the starting point on the Goodge Street intersection. Florence felt frustration rising. She had twice walked the length of the street and only the asylum had offered the chance of some link to Oswald. That, or the alleged Dickens house perhaps. Oswald might be associated with some literary society which might want its preservation as a memorial. In either case they would be worthy causes to be identified with and it was impossible to imagine why he needed to be warned to stay away from either. And yet each word had been an agony for the wretched young man who was dead so soon afterwards.

Troubled, more uncertain than ever how to raise the matter with Agatha, Florence walked back to Charing Cross. She missed Nicholas badly now, longed to share her doubts and worries, though she guessed that he might be as perplexed as she was herself. But in his absence there was one other source she might get insights from.

A hotel page-boy carried her note to the Piccadilly mansion. He had been instructed to wait for a reply and to bring it back as quickly as possible.

He was hot and panting when he returned – the promise of a sixpence had impelled him to run most of the way – and her name on the envelope she had sent for the response was in a hand she knew well. Her father's. It was a relief that he was in London and not at the Northamptonshire estate. He would meet her at the usual place.

Another sixpence sent the boy to a public house two hundred yards away, half-way down Villiers Street, immediately next to the hotel and station. The private upstairs room she had booked there several times before was available and food could be brought in from the chop-house next door. She needed it for an hour, the only time in which her father's note had indicated he could be free.

Florence waited until ten minutes after the appointed time to be sure that he would be there first. The thought of waiting alone disturbed her – it was bad enough to have to hurry down the street on her own, even it was for only for a hundred yards, a single woman eyed by loungers and inviting crude comments.

It pained her, as always, that he was now all but deferential to her, as if an invisible barrier had arisen since she had moved up into another social sphere. That she was now a lady, and he was proud of it, while he, however well paid and valued, was still a servant. When they usually met he would be in street clothes but this time he was in livery, splendidly impressive, his coat and breeches immaculately fitted, his boots gleaming, his hat alone worth a month of his salary.

He saw that she was surprised. "Lady Agatha's arriving at Euston Station at nine-thirty," he said. "I came with the clarence, we'll be going on there. Jack's driving. He's waiting with it outside your hotel."

She must have walked past him when she had emerged, and among the other vehicles on the cobbled forecourt she had not noticed the crest on the door of a closed carriage known as a clarence. Her brother would have seen her as he looked down from the box, had perhaps realised that for her – for a lady – he was as unlikely to draw her attention as were the two horses between the shafts. She felt a flush of shame that she had been so close to him and that she had probably looked past him without recognising him. However unwanted, however unintentional, the gulf between her and her family was widening.

"And Captain Dawlish is well? You have news from him?" Never Nicholas or Your Husband, always Captain, and with a hint of deference that was in itself upsetting. They had met only twice, son-in-law and father-in-law, both times in this room, and though they had striven to be affable neither man had been at his ease.

Then other family news, comfortable trivialities which in aggregate embodied happiness. The food came and as they ate Florence said, "I suppose you've seen a lot of Miss Brewster? I hear she's quite a beauty."

"Handsome enough," her father said, "but..."

Florence knew that hesitation since childhood. Her father had never criticised his employer's family in front of his own, would still not do so.

"... she couldn't hold a candle to my own girl. Not to you, Florrie."

She reached out and touched his hand, eyes suddenly brimming. She looked away and said, "I suppose she's been learning about England."

"We've been driving her all over, with Her Ladyship herself, and with Lady Agatha. But she don't seem all that interested. Not in the galleries and monuments and such like."

"I heard that her brother is here also?"

"He don't stay at the Piccadilly house. He's put up by himself at Brown's in Albemarle Street."

"I suppose they're good friends already, Oswald and – what's his name? – yes, Chester?"

"Not much love lost there, I'd say."

He was unlikely to say more. It didn't matter. Oswald had been brought into the conversation.

"Lady Agatha mentioned that when Lord Oswald got back from Washington he had taken private chambers in – where was it, she said? In the Albany, or in Cleveland Street, or was it in Cheyne Walk?"

"In Queen Anne's Gate," he said. "It's near enough for walking to the Foreign Office, not that Lord Oswald was ever all that keen on walking. But they'll be living in Cheyne Walk after the wedding – that's how you must've got the idea, Florrie."

Disappointment. Still no connection between Oswald and Cleveland Street.

"Are they very much in love, Father?" She knew the answer already.

"I don't see much sign of it," he said, "but then noble folk is different from you and me, Florrie. They've got other concerns an' other responsibilities."

Titles and land and tenants and money. And an heir was needed to inherit it all. Her father would never question it. They knew their place and he knew his, was proud of it, was of the fourth generation to drive the Kegworth's coaches, had come with the butler and the housekeeper to the apex of the servants' own aristocracy. And his own daughter had become a lady herself, even if at the price of a widening gulf.

It was time to go.

"I'll walk you to the hotel, Florrie," he said, "if…"

"I'd like that, Father." She embraced him and kissed his cheek. For she knew what the "if" implied. That he would not blame her if she were reluctant to be seen walking by the side of a coachman. She linked her arm in his.

Back in front of the hotel she walked over to where her brother Jack sat on the box of the clarence and talked five minutes with him, and asked him to come down and kiss her before leaving. She sensed that he was as uneasy as she was, as conscious of the incongruity of a coachman embracing a lady. And once more she felt shame, this time for the unworthy fear that some London acquaintance might recognise her at this moment.

She watched the coach sway away over the cobbles towards Euston, then turned back to the hotel, past the amused smirk of the commissionaire who had witnessed the scene and who opened the door for her with exaggerated, ironic courtesy. Back into the world she was now part of.

5

The coffee-room of the Charing Cross Hotel was as good as anywhere to meet – comfortable, central, large enough to give a degree of privacy for conversation. Florence's letter had suggested ten-thirty, as on previous occasions when they had met there. She had made it sound as if her visit to London was purely for pleasure and made no mention of a message. The reply, delivered to the hotel that morning, was a set-back. Agatha would bring Miss Brewster and had invited another lady too, an interesting woman, Florence would like her. There would be no easy opportunity to raise the matter of Gilpin's warning.

Florence was early for the appointment and she was sitting engrossed in the *Morning Post* – the situation in Alexandria was worsening by the day – when a voice said, "Mrs. Page, I believe?" The accent was American.

There was a blood-chilling moment before Florence looked up. She had used the name – just as Nicholas had been Mr. Page – a year before in New York and Newport. It had been more than a masquerade – she had lived the part – but it had been part of a larger deception that… that she had gone along with for Nicholas's sake. It had bought him the *Leonidas*. And almost nobody in Britain knew of it, should know of it.

Before her was a woman of indeterminate age in an obviously expensive but severely tailored and unadorned dress. She might have been good-looking had her face not been set in a permanent frown, a frown, as Florence remembered, not of hostility but of earnestness.

"Mrs. Bushwick," Florence said. "Mrs. Mabel Bushwick." The lady-journalist who had interviewed her in New York for the *Columbia Home Gazette*, whose work she had said was a sacred charge for the betterment of womankind.

"A pleasure to see you again, Mrs. Page. And I trust that Mr. Page is well?"

Florence glanced at the clock across the room. Ten twenty-five. Five minutes to get rid of this woman who had unquestioningly swallowed a stream of untruths that Florence had found amusing and essential at the time. And Mrs. Bushwick was showing no intention of leaving.

"I'll join you, Mrs. Page, if you don't mind." She sat down opposite her without waiting for a reply. She fished in her handbag and produced a small notebook and silver pencil.

"Are you travelling in Europe, Mrs. Bushwick?" Heart thumping, mind racing, possibilities of sudden stomach cramps, or light-headedness, of any other excuse to leave, were rapidly considered and as rapidly rejected. This woman would not let go easily.

"I'm here on an assignment, Mrs. Page." Her tone indicated that it must be another sacred charge. "The *Gazette's* editoress and I are interested in the phenomenon of American heiresses marrying into your British nobility. And all that it signifies."

Oh God! It can't be that...

"Viscountess Mandeville, of course, and Miss Jerome with the Duke of Marlborough's son, and Miss Work with Baron Fermoy..."

"You're interviewing these ladies, Mrs. Bushwick?"

"Just those ladies so far. And Miss Jerome – indeed I should say Lady Randolph, as she now is – was kind enough to see me yesterday and to show me her two angelic little boys. And now our latest dollar princess..."

"Miss Brewster?" Florence wanted to leave, but felt her legs weak.

"Yes! To be married to Lord Kegworth's eldest son. A splendid match." Mrs. Bushwick dropped her voice and spoke with awe. "Her father's worth thirty-one million in his hides business alone. But I'd value your views, Mrs. Page. About the infusion of fresh blood into an ancient nobility. And about the contrast of such wealth and privilege with the misery that is all so apparent in this metropolis, and indeed elsewhere I understand to be in..."

And then the terrible inevitability.

"Dear Florence!"

Agatha was manoeuvring her bulk between the tables, as always slightly dishevelled, delight written on her great, friendly face, eyes warm and kindly behind their pince-nez. No Miss Brewster followed.

"And Mrs. Bushwick got here early!" Agatha said. "And I can see you've made friends already! So glad you two have met, Mrs. Bushwick! Mrs. Dawlish is my oldest, closest friend."

Both Florence and the American had risen and Agatha was making to embrace them. Florence felt her face burn with embarrassment and saw Mrs. Bushwick step back.

"I understood that this lady was Mrs. Page." A tone of anger as well as of bewilderment,

"No! No!" Agatha alone was laughing. "Mrs. Dawlish. Mrs. Nicholas Dawlish."

"You told me that your husband's name was Fredrick. Mr. Fredrick Page of Silverbridge Court in Shropshire..."

44

"Oh what a misunderstanding this must be!" Agatha alone was laughing. "I'm afraid you're confusing Mrs. Dawlish with somebody else. And her husband is indeed Nicholas and…"

Mrs. Bushwick ignored Agatha so as to concentrate on Florence alone. "So that the Mr. Fredrick Page you were with in New York was not your husband!" She was genuinely outraged now. "That you were profaning the marriage bed at the very moment that you were lying to me! And that I published your opinions in the *Home Gazette*!" She turned to Agatha. "I suggest, Lady Agatha, that you do not introduce this person to Miss Brewster. Her purity of mind would be…"

And Florence felt something snap within. First the port-admiral's wife, and now this woman. She would not be lectured or harangued.

"Sit down, Mrs. Bushwick," she said. "You're starting to make an exhibition of yourself." As the American was, for her voice had been rising and heads were turning. "And you too, Agatha." Florence surprised herself by her own resolution, by her own air of authority that sounded more confident than she felt. It had grown, without her realising it, in restoring order in disputes in the Sailors' Rest, in interventions with drunken husbands whose wives had sought her help.

And both women sat down and were quiet.

"Agatha, will you accept my word if I tell you that I'm speaking the truth?"

"You know that, Florence."

She turned to Mrs. Bushwick. "I'm giving my word to my best and oldest friend, to a woman I came through suffering and death with, that what I will now say is true."

"But, Mrs. Page, the deception…"

"The deception was for a reason associated with the interests of my country. It had official support." *No need to mention that Oswald had been involved.* "The gentleman who accompanied me was my husband, Captain Nicholas Dawlish, who is equally respected by Lady Agatha. The deception, the charade, was for the noblest of motives but I am honour-bound to say no more." And to Agatha she said, "Do you believe me? Will you stake your honour on my word?"

"You know I do, Florence, but …" Agatha looked bewildered. "I knew you were in America but I never guessed that…"

"There's no need to guess anything, Agatha, no need to know anything either. But it was in our country's interest."

"Mrs. Bushwick." It was Agatha who now spoke. "I believe that this matter is resolved. We don't need to speak any more of it. That it remains confidential between us. And I trust that you'll accept Mrs. Dawlish's word no less than I do."

And, to Mrs. Bushwick's credit, she did.

*

Miss Brewster had been over-fatigued by the journey from the north — a glance from Agatha told Florence all — and she had regretted being unable to meet Mrs. Bushwick this morning. But Agatha had previously met the journalist and had liked her, and as the atmosphere thawed over coffee Florence found herself warming to her. She was a widow — the late Mr. Bushwick was mentioned only briefly, and did not seem deeply mourned — and what she referred to as financial exigencies had necessitated paid employment to support herself and two sons, by now grown-up and independent. The work as a journalist was onerous at first but now she felt she could not live without it.

Agatha mentioned the Sailor's Rest, the work Florence had done there — "No, my dear, don't underestimate your role" — and the conversation drifted to their time together in Thrace.

It seemed such an adventure in retrospect. *We remember the good parts,* Florence thought, *the companionship, the mutual support, even the occasion when I blackened the eye of that Turkish guard with a broom handle. And Nicholas's arrival most of all. And that we saved him as he saved us. But we're already blocking out the worst of it. As Cuba is also receding in my mind.*

"You should write a book about it," Mrs. Bushwick said. "As an inspiration to our sisters." Her frown of earnestness had not lightened once. It appeared too that her visit to Europe was not only to investigate the success of Anglo-American marriages.

"You had perhaps some impression of our social ills when you visited New York, Mrs. Dawlish? Poverty. Overcrowding. Drunkenness. Filth. Disease. Ignorance. Vice. And, above all, the degradation of our sisters." She seemed to take a grim pleasure in the litany.

Florence nodded. She remembered thinking that those who fled there from Europe must have left even worse behind if they considered the United States the promised land.

"I understand the problems to be no less here in London, and whatever solutions may have been found here I want to share with my readers. Your charitable institutions for example."

"Such as I've been associated with myself, and Oswald too," Agatha said. "Papa and Mamma have thought it time to pass the responsibility on to a younger generation. Mrs. Bushwick has already been talking to me about it."

"And your *St. James Fortnightly*!" Mrs. Bushwick said. "What a splendid organ of reform! How its revelations are awakening the conscience of your nation!" She dropped her voice. "It's my ambition, Mrs. Dawlish, to see the *Columbia Home Gazette* play no less a role in the United States!"

Florence knew of the *Fortnightly* and of its strident campaigns. Nicholas had decreed that no copy should enter the villa in Albert Grove. He had himself approved of the Navy's abolition of flogging – a formality, since it had been a dead letter for years – but he had been angered by the magazine's exaggerations about the extent of its previous use. The week after *Leonidas* departed Florence had bought a copy for herself. It was less lurid than she expected – and had hoped, she had to admit to herself. There was nothing in its revelations about conditions in slum areas that she did not know already. The outrage seemed somehow over-pious, too contrived.

"I will be meeting the editor this afternoon," Mrs. Bushwick said. "I wrote to say that I was visiting Britain and he was pleased to give me an appointment."

"And Mrs. Bushwick asked that I might attend as well," Agatha said, "and bring Miss Brewster, so she could learn more about British life."

"Such a pity she could not come today," Florence's suspicion was confirmed that more than fatigue had kept Miss Brewster away. "I'm sure she would have so enjoyed it."

"But you, Mrs. Dawlish," Mrs. Bushwick said. "You'll come, won't you? I'm sure Mr. Staveley would welcome it."

"Oh, Florence! Do come," Agatha said.

So Florence did.

*

They lunched at the hotel and a growler carried them afterwards not to Fleet Street, where Florence had assumed all journalism was concentrated, but to the dingy offices occupied by the *Fortnightly* in Farringdon Road. It was an area she did not know but obviously one where prosperity and major commercial activity were fading into squalor. A severe young woman with steel-rimmed spectacles – a Mrs. Bushwick in the making – led them through two small rooms closely crowded with desks. Two men and another woman looked up and nodded as they passed through. All were equipped with typewriters and one, a young man who looked consumptive, and who also wore round steel-rimmed spectacles – they seemed like a badge of uniform – was tapping noisily. Shelves of files lined the walls. The furnishings looked as if they had been bought second-hand. There was no smell of tobacco, as was so usual where men worked. Unassuming the offices might be, but there was an atmosphere of efficient concentration. The only note that jarred was the thickset man in a check suit who was slouched on a chair in one corner and studying a folded newspaper. He ignored the visitors. Florence glimpsed racing odds as she passed and saw that he had a broken nose and close-cropped head.

Walter Staveley was bent over his desk, writing, and he gave what Florence thought an unconvincing impression of surprise as the young woman ushered them into his small office, separate from the rest. He stood up.

"Forgive me, ladies." He gestured to his papers. "The deadline is a hard taskmaster! I've no doubt that Mrs. Bushwick will agree." His tone hinted at virtuous weariness.

Introductions. A hint of deference not only from Mrs. Bushwick but from Agatha also, to Florence's surprise. He seemed pleased by it.

"And this lady is…"

"Mrs. Nicholas Dawlish." She answered for herself. "A friend of Lady Agatha's." She did not elaborate. Nicholas would be furious if he knew that she was meeting this man.

"And also interested in 'The Social Question', Mrs… yes, Mrs. Dawlish.?"

"Who cannot be, Mr. Staveley?" She guessed that he was in his early thirties, long, lean, clean-shaven, sharp-featured, thin black hair slicked back and oiled, clothes immaculate and somehow out of place with the surroundings. His stoop reinforced the impression of weariness, of a great burden reluctantly accepted but patiently borne. Florence had read somewhere that he had been the youngest editor of a provincial newspaper in Britain and she suspected that the remnants of a Yorkshire accent had been deliberately retained. *I'm not one of you*, it seemed to say. *Take me or leave me. I am what I am. A plain, blunt man.*

Mrs. Bushwick had thawed, was almost girlish in her admiration for the *Fortnightly's* present campaign against slum-landlords. The names of eminent personages had been hinted at in recent editions, hints broad enough to make identity unmistakable.

"But do you not fear prosecution, Mr. Staveley?"

"For criminal-libel, Mrs. Bushwick?" He smiled, shook his head. "No, I'd welcome it. I'd welcome the opportunity to put certain persons in the witness box. Rich, influential people, members of Parliament, even peers of the realm." He looked to Agatha. "And no, Lady Agatha, rest assured that your father is not numbered among those of the nobility who derive profit from the rental of properties unfit for human habitation."

"You've checked, Mr. Staveley?" Florence asked.

"Oh I've checked, Mrs. Dawlish. All I've mentioned has been checked. Not just by direct ownership, but by intermediaries too. And the names would surprise you." He picked up a copy of a previous edition, flicked it open. "Perhaps the conditions we found in Lambeth were bad?" An engraving showed misery in some foetid court. He opened another. "And those in Hoxton?" Still another. "And in Whitechapel?"

"Appalling," Agatha said. "A disgrace to the nation."

"But I can show you worse, much worse, within ten minutes' walk from here."

"Mr. Staveley," Mrs. Bushwick's tone was almost humble. "If I were able to…"

And Florence could glimpse what Mrs. Bushwick herself most certainly did also. Articles, perhaps a series, in the *Columbia Home Gazette* – squalor in darkest London contrasted with the world invaded by dollar princesses, and guided through it by a journalist whose reputation was already international.

Staveley held up his hand. "Some scenes may be too distressing to your sensibilities, Mrs. Bushwick, and …"

"On no, Mr. Staveley" Mrs. Bushwick said. "The truth must be faced even if…"

"I've had some experience of the East End, of some charitable work there," Agatha said.

"And we're no stranger to Portsmouth, are we?" Florence suddenly felt revulsion at what she had just said, as if one misery was being played to trump another. She wanted to be gone.

"Ladies!" Staveley gestured for calm. "If you are concerned, genuinely concerned, I might make a suggestion. I have an appointment later this afternoon, a visit to a case not far from here, one so typical that it alone could stand as an indictment of the way we live now…"

"Yes!" said Mrs. Bushwick.

"Yes!" said Lady Agatha.

Florence took in their dresses, both expensive, Agatha's worth a housemaid's annual wage even if, as usual, it was worn untidily. She had once been glad to have been given one such dress and to have re-tailored it for herself. But now the plum-coloured travelling costume she herself was wearing had cost over twenty pounds. The gold brooch on her breast – she wore it when she could because Nicholas had given it – must have cost even more. The idea of flaunting such wealth, however unthinkingly, repelled her. She did not dress like this when she went to the Sailors' Rest, nor did Agatha, who was now beaming at Staveley. Florence decided she would make an excuse, go back to the hotel alone.

But Agatha forestalled her. "You'll come too, won't you, Florence?" She showed the same innocence, the same naive inability to comprehend reality that was so often the mark of the supremely intelligent, and had once brought them close to death – and worse – in the depths of a Balkan winter.

Florence had stood by her then. Agatha needed protection from the world.

"Of course," Florence said. "Of course I'll come."

*

The thickset man lurched to his feet and followed them when they left. He jammed on a billycock hat and picked up a heavy-looking stick, a so-called Penang lawyer. Florence guessed that its head was loaded with lead. Mr. Staveley was taking no chances. He noticed her appraisal and said, "Mr. Benton usually accompanies me."

Mr. Benton said nothing and walked five paces behind as they headed up Farringdon Road. It got poorer in the next two hundred yards and in as much again was wholly lined with run-down houses, the open hall doors proclaiming them as many-tenanted, the grimy curtainless or newspaper-covered windows indicating yet worse shabbiness within. The few miserable little shops must only survive by selling necessities by the pennyworth but even in mid-afternoon a garishly-adorned public house seemed to be doing business. Many of the children playing hopscotch on the pavement, or carrying infant brothers or sisters on their hips, were barefoot. Even in passing the sour stench of unwashed bodies and clothing was palpable. Several children came close – "Got a penny, missus?" – and a girl pulled at Mrs. Bushwick's skirt, but a growl from Mr. Benton made the child shrink back. Occasional cabs rattled down the centre of the street, a short cut from one business-area to the next for affluent passengers but a single wretched horse was slowly dragging a dray along one side, the driver calling listlessly for rags and bones.

They halted at a corner. Staveley swept his arm around, said, "Look around you, ladies. Look at the capital of the empire on which the sun never sets." Then he led them down a side street.

Florence could sense real poverty about her now, not hand-to-mouth survival but, glimpsed down side-alleys, the reality of hunger and privation deep enough to lead to death itself. She fancied that she saw grim exaltation on Staveley's face, disgust mixed with satisfaction on Mrs. Bushwick's – the promise here of a series of articles – and genuine pity on Agatha's. And she herself felt shame for coming. The people here were not animals in a zoo. She should have gone back to the hotel.

"This way, ladies."

Through a narrow archway that smelled of urine and into an equally narrow lane beyond, scarcely wide enough for two to pass. It was cobbled, dipping towards the centre and a thin stream – better not to look closely, better not to know – ran down it. Florence gathered up her skirt as far as decency would allow, indeed almost above her ankles, and so too did the other ladies. Filthy children shrunk into doorways before them and a small knot was trailing behind Mr. Benton. Drying rags hung on lines overhead and Florence resisted the urge – as Mrs. Bushwick had not, though

Agatha had – to press her scented handkerchief to her face. Had she done so she could not have looked in the eye the jaded women, most with babies, who came to the doorways to look on listlessly. A few greeted Staveley by name, but without any hint of warmth, and he acknowledged them only with a nod.

It led to something worse, a tiny courtyard with ordure piled in one corner and a gap where a door had once been. The sky was a tiny patch of smoky blue above, the walls gleaming with slime. They entered.

Up two flights of stairs, each more rickety than the other, and up a third that lacked a bannister. The stench was almost unbearable. A woman wrapped in a shawl – she might have been any age between thirty and eighty – stood in a doorway. "So it's you again," she said to Staveley and turned away into a room that seemed devoid of any furniture. There was an impression of others in other rooms, but nobody came out. A group of children had gathered in the entrance below, kept at bay by Mr. Benton,

They paused on a landing. Only the garret lay above and the ladder leading to it lacked several rungs. A child of three or four appeared in the half-light at the top. He – or perhaps she – was wearing a jute sack, head and arms thrust through holes, string tied around the waist, livid with spots and scabs.

"I can understand if you don't want to go up," Staveley said.

Heads shook. They had come this far and would not shrink from going the whole way. The silence of the child above, the blank look, the lack of any sign of curiosity, was chilling.

"Nine rooms are rented here," Staveley said. "Nine families, fifty-seven souls. And the lowest weekly rent is four shillings and sixpence."

Florence suspected that he could reel off similar information for a score of similar houses.

"Can anybody guess the ownership of this property?" His tone seemed to mix satisfaction and outrage. "Not just this house. Every single one in this entire block and for several blocks around? Every dwelling, every place of business you have passed almost since you left my office?"

Nobody could guess. Heads were again shaken. And still the child looked on in silence.

"His Grace, the Duke of Holderness!" Staveley paused, seemed to relish their surprise. "Seven times great-grandson of His Majesty

Charles the Second through an irregular union. An ornament of the Upper House, playfellow of the Prince of Wales, landlord to…"

"The duke!" Agatha was horrified. "His son is a personal friend, a perfect…"

"A perfect gentleman, I suspect you are about to say, Lady Agatha. And perhaps he is, and a man busy in his interests and well financed to indulge them. But does his eminence as an astronomer, as a Fellow of the Royal Society, absolve him of this? Should he perhaps not focus his telescope closer to home?"

Florence saw that Agatha's lower lip was quivering and that tears glistened behind her pince-nez. She had heard Agatha speak of this man with admiration, Nicholas too. His funding of a new observatory near Cape Town had received widespread accolades. It was time to break this conversation.

"I trust you'll lead the way, Mr. Staveley?" She gestured to the broken ladder. It was not going to be easy to get Agatha's bulk up it.

It was worse than she expected, worse than any slum in Portsmouth had prepared her for. The child in the sack stood aside as they mounted but a girl in a dirty dress and with matted hair emerged from a doorway – no door – to meet them. Her feet were in broken men's shoes, several sizes too large.

"Say 'Good afternoon' to the ladies, Maisie," Staveley said.

"G' afternoon, missus," Maisie's face was lost in the gloom. The only light was filtering through from a grimy pane set into the inclined and mildewed ceiling above. It had been broken, the jagged hole stuffed with rags.

"This is Maisie Webster," Staveley said. "Show the ladies where you live."

The floor was of bare boards, but wet, a gaping hole in the centre. A pile of sacking lay in one corner, spread out as if as a bed. By it, from the tea chest in which it stood, a baby began to cry as it saw them enter. Maisie picked it up and cradled it to her. Its dress had been fashioned from a threadbare shirt. The tiny legs and feet beneath were bare. The baby might have been washed at birth, but certainly not since.

"She's me sister," Maisie said. "She's Lucy. And that there," she pointed at the child in the sack, "that's me brother Bob." He made no acknowledgement, uttered no sound.

Florence was looking around. There was no form of heating and no obvious way of cooking, though a battered tin teapot, a single mug and two plates stood on an upturned box. A small pile of coloured cards lay next to them. No chair, no table, no jug, no ewer. A rusty bucket covered by sacking sat in the far corner. But what was most surprising was a bottle-crate set on its side, as if to make a seat and on one side was a column of women's straw hats, piled one above the other, with a similar column on the far side.

"Is this your work, Maisie?" Florence picked up a long coil of ribbon that lay on the box, a scissors, needles and sewing thread beside it.

"Yes, missus." She did not look up as if she was ashamed of what she was.

Another beaten dog.

"How much do you get, Maisie?" Florence saw that she had been sewing on ribbons, one column still without, the other with.

"Ninepence the gross, missus."

Twelve dozen to the gross. Seventy-two dozen to earn the rent alone.

"You do this every day, Maisie?"

"No, ma'am. The work ain't regular."

"Her mother died two months ago." Staveley spoke as if Maisie was not present. "In the charity ward. Delirium tremens." He picked up the cards from the box, handed them around. Each was a temperance pledge, dated first months, then weeks, apart, the signatures increasingly more shaky. "A hopeless case," he said.

Agatha had taken the baby and it calmed as she held it to her. She too had been looking around the bare room. "Where is everything, Maisie?" she asked.

"Pawned, missus."

"And that little boy, your brother. Does he go to school?"

"He don't have no clothes to go to school in." She laughed as if it was self-evident, as if the question was unnecessary. "They was pawned last week. Thruppence, and a ha'penny for the ticket. Tuppence ha'penny in me hand."

"Where's your father, Maisie?" Mrs. Bushwick was visibly moved.

"Fathers." Staveley did not drop his voice. "All different."

"Ain't got none." Maisie was clearly ashamed.

Florence felt as if something would snap within her. "May I speak to you just outside, Mr. Staveley?"

"Very well, Mrs. Dawlish." He must have detected the edge her tone and was obviously annoyed.

They stepped out on the landing.

"How long do you know about this case, Mr. Staveley?" she said.

"I was informed just recently."

"How recently, Mr. Staveley? A week? Two? Three? A month maybe?"

"Not that long, Mrs. Dawlish."

"How old is that girl?"

"Thirteen. Nearly fourteen." He made as if to go back into the room but Florence moved over to block him.

"There's going to be an article in your magazine about this case, isn't there? And we aren't the first people you've brought here? And you'll be bringing more?"

"I don't see that it's any of your business, Mrs. Dawlish."

She gave no answer, just turned and went back in. Mrs. Bushwick had her notebook out and was jotting down answers from Maisie. The baby was sleeping in Agatha's arms and the little boy, still silent, was now holding her skirt.

"Agatha," Florence said. "That charity your mother was associated with. I believe you've taken her place on the board."

"Rosewood House," Agatha said. "In Chigwell."

"Can it take these children?"

"Yes. Yes, it must be possible."

"You're on the board, Agatha. You'll make it possible. And we'll bring them there right now. They're not staying another night here."

Staveley was starting to protest – they had no right to sweep these children off to some home, no authority to act *in loco parentis* – but Florence ignored him.

"Straight to Rosewood! Right now, Florence!" It was the old indomitable Agatha of Thracian days. "You'd like to come, Maisie? Somewhere warm and clean and safe? For your little brother and sister as well as for yourself?"

"Yes, missus." Maisie was confused, overwhelmed. She began to weep.

"There must be a bath-house near here," Florence said. "We'll take them there first, Agatha." *They should not have the humiliation of arriving at Rosewood in this present state.* "And Mrs. Bushwick, you'll help, won't you? While we're getting these children clean can you find them clothes? Probably nothing better than second-hand to be found around here, but clean. You've had children yourself. You'll know what to get."

Mrs. Bushwick had put away her notebook. Her features had relaxed for the first time since Florence had first met her. "Of course, Mrs. Dawlish. Leave it to me."

Staveley's voice was full of anger.

"You can't just take these children away. The proper authorities…"

"Have signally failed in their duty." Florence cut him off.

"You could be prosecuted for this. A magistrate would have to be satisfied about this Rosewood place before you could take these children there. You're committing an offence by taking them without court approval."

"Just go ahead and alert the police, Mr. Staveley," Florence said. "I'm sure they concern themselves a lot with cases like this." She thought of Inspector Towton. There must be many like him.

"These hats," Staveley pointed to the two columns. "What's to become of them? Maisie has obligations to her employer."

"Just have Mr. Benton bring them back wherever they came from". Florence said. "It looks as if about half are finished. Tell the employer that he can keep the fourpence ha'penny he owes Maisie."

Staveley turned on his heel and left.

6

It proved more difficult, and took longer, than any of them had expected. A woman on a lower floor, sunken-cheeked, consumptive and furious, tried to stop them taking the children from the house. Her screams of abuse attracted several others, no less indignant, so that by the time they reached the squalid court a small crowd had gathered, men and children as well as women. It was not concern for Maisie and her brother and sister that moved them, Florence realised, but resentment, even outright hatred, of well-dressed outsiders whose charity mocked their misery. Long minutes passed – jeers and catcalls and abuse – before they managed to get away. Maisie's weak assertion that she wanted to go with them helped and one woman agreed to guide them to a public bathhouse.

The municipal authorities' provision of the bathhouse might have been well-intentioned, but the reality was foul – cold grey water, scum along the sides, the smell of carbolic insufficient to mask other odours, the grim-faced female supervisors who greeted their arrival with the children suspiciously. Mrs. Bushwick disappeared with the woman who had brought them there and who now assured her that clothes for the children could be bought nearby. Florence and Agatha refused the offers of several other women there to wash the children for them, though from them they managed to buy several of their own threadbare towels. A supervisor sold them soap. None of them was clad for the task in hand and there was nothing for it but to take off their jackets, roll up their sleeves and set to work. Florence felt a flush of affection for Agatha as they did, memories of dealing cheerfully together with lice-infested refugees in a refuge in Thrace. Agatha must have felt the same as she looked towards Florence, smiled in silence, and then returned to scrubbing Lucy, the baby. She and the boy were amenable, but Maisie, who had never been in a bathhouse, was reluctant to remove her clothes and needed patient coaxing. Her matted hair was infested. As Florence soaped it and rinsed and combed with the inadequate tortoiseshell comb she carried in her reticule she realised that some of the creatures had crossed to herself. There was no help for it. She had been lousy herself in Thrace, Agatha too, and they had survived it. As they worked, other customers stood watching, their remarks at first sarcastic, but then friendlier, even admiring, as their persistence and their disregard for their clothing became obvious. At last they finished and the children were wrapped in towels.

"What d'yer want to do with these?" A woman was greedily eyeing Maisie's discarded rags.

"We won't be needing them." *They belong in a furnace,* Florence thought. *But worth thruppence perhaps at the pawnshop.*

The woman scooped them up and hurried away before anybody else could claim them. Then there was nothing to do but to wait for Mrs. Bushwick's return. The offer of a half-crown bought them the temporary privacy of the supervisor's storeroom, a pot of weak tea, sugar in a twist of paper and half-curdled milk in a small rusting can.

"This is prime." Maisie's hands were clamped around a mug and she was savouring the contents. "Thank you, missus. Will it be like this in the place ye're bringing us?"

"Oh no, my dear," Agatha said. "It will be better, much better, and for your brother and sister too."

Maisie lapsed into contented silence. The boy had not spoken since they had first seen him but he seemed to have taken to Agatha and was standing close against her. She was holding the towel-swaddled baby and it was sucking sugar from her fingers.

"This Rosewood House," Florence said. "You hadn't been there when I last saw you, Agatha. What's it like?"

"I'd just come on the board then but I've visited since – most impressive, wonderful work," Agatha said. "Mamma wanted me to take her place as a director. She wants to step back slowly from her responsibilities. Just like when Oswald got back from Washington and Papa wanted him to take over his place on the board of the *Brahmaputra*."

Florence felt her heart thump. *Now's the time. But go slowly.*

"Nicholas has a very high opinion of the work which that ship does," she said. "How it's a blessing for so many young lads who might otherwise go to the bad."

"It works closely with Rosewood – such a good arrangement. The boys can stay there with their sisters until they're eight, just like little Bob here could do," – Agatha squeezed his shoulder affectionately – "and then they go to the training ship."

"A healthy life, I imagine," Florence said. "Education, discipline, good food, exercise in the open air, valuable skills to take into a future career. Pretty ideal for a young chap."

"Yes!" Agatha said. "That's Oswald's view entirely and …"

The supervisor was ushering Mrs. Bushwick in. The woman who had guided her was following with an armful of clothes. They were threadbare but reasonably clean.

"The shopman said they were second-hand," Mrs. Bushwick said, "but I guess that sixth or seventh-hand might be a better description. He said his wife had washed them herself. And these shoes! But they must do for now. I'd have preferred to go elsewhere but that was the nearest." She reached out to the boy. "Come here, young man! It seems like yesterday that my Lester was your age!" The boy shrunk back but she took him to her, cast off the towel and began to dress him. He had still not spoken but he seemed to relax as she drew on the tiny garments, naming them as she did, smiling, hugging him. The stern journalist of the *Columbia Home Gazette* was gone, replaced by woman who radiated patience and cheerful concern, joy even, as she sensed the child's trust in her growing.

Agatha busied herself with the baby but it was Maisie who gave the greatest problem. Florence had laid out the clean clothing on a chair in the corner for her and had discreetly turned her back to allow a modicum of modesty for her to dress. A minute passed and she called back "Is all well, Maisie? Do you like the clothes?"

No answer, but then the sudden sound of weeping. She turned to see Maisie still enveloped in a towel but her shoulders heaving, her head shaking in misery. Florence embraced her, held her close. "What is it, Maisie? What is it?" She looked back at her companions and shook her head slowly. *Leave this to me.* The girl's sobs were racking her and she clung to Florence, her face buried on her shoulder.

Maisie calmed at last but it took longer to determine the cause of her misery. The garments laid out for her – poor when made, thinned and ragged now along the edges – were a mystery to her. She had never worn either undergarments or stockings. It stabbed at Florence's heart, not just from pity, but for recognition of the joy she would have had in clothing this girl when she was little, of teaching her to dress herself as she grew older, for her own lack of the jovial confidence with which Mrs Bushwick was managing the boy. *As she must have been with her own sons, as I never will be.* But Florence made light of Maisie's concerns, joked as she helped her with each item, was pleased as the girl began to show delight. "Like a lady, missus," she said when at last Florence smoothed the skirts of the pathetic dress and tied the laces of the cracked and down-at-heel boots. "Like a real lady." The look on her pale pinched face was worth gold and Florence felt tears welling in her own eyes. "You are a lady, Maisie," she said. "A real young lady. A lovely young lady."

They found their way back to Farringdon Road, Agatha with the baby, Mrs. Bushwick holding Bob by her side, Florence behind with Maisie and trying to put her at her ease. She regretted that Mrs. Bushwick had failed to find her a hat. They should have brought one from the piles in the now-abandoned room. The payment foregone would have paid for six dozen.

*

59

A cab brought them to Liverpool Street Station and a train carried them to Chigwell. The boy showed no interest, no surprise, still did not speak, but Maisie was bewildered. She had seen trains in the cuttings and viaducts that slashed across the streets and alleys and courts of the only world she had known, but she had never been inside one. They had a compartment to themselves, a First Class one, which Agatha insisted on paying for.

Another growler took them from the station to Rosewood House. Florence had expected something stark and forbidding – like that asylum she had seen on Cleveland Street perhaps – but the reality could not have been more different. It lay three miles outside the village in semi-rural countryside, a large redbrick building, not quite a mansion, that some successful businessman might have built twenty years before. It seemed set in what must have been once part of a larger estate. There was woodland behind and the driveway that curved up from the gate lodge ran along the side of what was almost parkland. It was evening now, but still warm, and the grass had been mown for hay so that its fresh smell hung heavy in the air. It was hard to believe that the filthy courtyard was only two hours distant.

"It was Mamma who prevailed on my father to buy it for the trust." Agatha's pride was touching. "Some of Papa's friends – other directors of that Hyperion company he's involved with – suggested it to her and they've been contributing ever since to the running costs. Sir Herbert Mellish, such a good and generous man, and Mr. Reginald Whittier, the banker, and …"

The name Hyperion was familiar. Florence has seen it mentioned in newspapers, an entity– the word consortium was sometimes used – which was widely admired and she had read the stories only because she had heard from Agatha that her father was connected with it. She half-remembered that its shares had soared in price two years before and that some journalists had warned that the rise could not continue, yet she had heard nothing since then of any collapse. She had even suggested to Nicholas that they might have been a good investment but he had snapped back a "No!" with such vehemence that she thought it better not to raise the subject again. Not when he was in such a mood.

The cab drew up before the door. It was opened not by a footman but by a girl of perhaps eighteen in a plain dark-blue dress. She bobbed, led them into a parlour, more plainly furnished than a house of this size merited, and went away to fetch Miss Dorothy Braben.

The directress was perhaps fifty, plump, smiling, kindly eyes, wrinkles of mirth about her mouth and temples. Her dark dress might be severely cut, but it was of good quality and with a cameo fastened at her throat and a small gold brooch, a sunburst, on her left breast. The only indication of her responsibilities was the long silvered chain that looped from her belt to a pocket that must contain her bunch of keys. It was easy to like her even before she said that Lady Agatha and her friends was welcome at any time, however unexpected.

"If you'll allow me, Lady Agatha." Miss Braben took the baby from her. "Oh what a little lamb! And her name is?"

"Lucy."

Miss Braben raised an eyebrow, looked at Agatha and said, "The old story, I suppose?"

Agatha launched into a detailed account and it was plain that Miss Braben was looking for an opportunity to interrupt her politely. It came at last.

"We'll put them all together in the same room tonight, so they don't feel too strange here." She turned to Maisie. "You'd like that, Maisie, wouldn't you? To stay with your little brother and sister for now?"

The girl nodded. The enormity of being left here was still dawning on her and she was trembling slightly.

"There'll be time enough in a week or so to put them in the dormitories with others of their age," Miss Braben said. "It's better not to hurry these matters".

"You understand these things, ma'am, you surely do." Mrs. Bushwick was clearly impressed.

Miss Braben smiled, shook her head slightly as if the compliment was not deserved. "Have you eaten, ladies? You've had a trying day, I believe. May I offer you Rosewood's hospitality?"

Immediate assent. Miss Braben reached for a bell-pull. It summoned an older girl, eighteen, nineteen, a white apron over what was now obvious as the home's uniform, severe but of reasonable-quality serge.

"Kindly look after these children, Martha," Miss Braben handed her the baby. "A further wash, clean clothing, food, bed. In the

Lavender Room." To the visitors she said, "It's the room where we put newcomers whom we need to keep together."

They embraced the children and kissed them before they were taken away. The boy was distressed, and making noises for the first time, sounds rather than words He was choking with grief and fright and did not want to leave Mrs. Bushwick. Only when Maisie picked him up would he go.

Florence was moved, was fighting tears. "I'll visit you here, Maisie," she told her. "I'll come back. I won't forget you." *Had it not been for the two younger ones I could have taken you home with me. You could be like Susan. There's an empty room next to hers and Cook's. And Nicholas would not begrudge another twenty pounds a year. But I can't take you all, and I can't split you up.*

They ate in Miss Braben's own small dining room. The food was plain but well prepared.

"My staff and I eat the same as the children eat," she told them.

Mrs. Bushwick wrote it in her notebook. She kept up a flow of questions through the meal, apologised for her poor memory, for her need to take notes. And she hoped that Miss Braben would not object, nor Lady Agatha as a representative of the board? Neither did.

Afterwards they made a quick tour. The children's dinner was over and the refectory was empty but for several older girls sweeping the floors. They stood back and bobbed as the visitors passed. There was a roster for such duty, Miss Braben said, everybody took their turn. It was clean and airy and the windows were open to the scent of mown grass. A few biblical texts hung on the walls but there were other pictures, brightly coloured lithographs - the Queen, rural scenes, children playing, cottage gardens. The kitchen was spotless and the cook, a motherly woman, was still on duty and supervising the cleaning there personally.

The older girls had not yet gone to bed and were in a plain but comfortable common-room. They stood up and bobbed as the visitors entered and Miss Braben gestured to them to continue what they were doing. A few were reading, a few embroidering – they were doing it as a pastime for themselves, Miss Braben said – and most were just chatting.

The dormitories too were clean and airy, rows of single beds at adequate separation. It was past bed-time for the younger girls and for the boys, but many were still awake and rushed to get back to their beds when the door was opened.

"Up to your tricks again, Georgie!" There was no anger, even a touch of merriment, in Miss Braben's voice and there was a sound of tittering in the semi darkness.

The older girls' accommodation was even more impressive, small wooden cubicles open at the top but each with a door to afford privacy. Only one was closed. Miss Braben knocked once, then opened it. A girl was lying on the bed, fully clothed.

"Not moping again, Polly?" Miss Braben tinged concern with firmness. "This will never do! What will these ladies think? Go back down to the common room and have some fun with the other girls."

Polly mumbled something, bobbed and left. There was a deadness about her expression that Florence found unsettling.

"Some of these girls!" Miss Braben raised her eyes in mock exasperation. "They can be so moody! But it's their age and we must be patient, we must make allowances."

"Firmness too," Mrs. Bushwick added. "And especially so with boys. I speak as a mother. Sometimes one must be strict – not cruel – to be kind."

They declined the offer of tea before leaving. The cabby who had brought them had returned as requested. It was twilight as they rattled out the gate. Florence glanced back. The house seemed all the more charming for what she now knew was within and the scent of new-mown grass was still heavy in the evening air

If I had not met Nicholas, she thought, *if we had not married, if I had to live out my life as a spinster, I might have been content with Miss Braben's position. I would have enjoyed it.*

*

Even if Agatha had not fallen asleep in the train as it chugged back to Liverpool Street it would have been impossible to speak about Gilpin with Mrs. Bushwick present. There was however one topic that intrigued Florence and that could be discussed while Agatha slept.

"When you came to see me – or to see Mrs. Page – in that hotel in New York, how did you come to hear of me, Mrs. Bushwick?"

"A journalist's sources must be a matter of confidentiality, Mrs. Dawlish." The tone was simultaneously sententious and cautious.

The lamp in the compartment had not been lit and her face was in heavy shadow.

Florence made herself laugh. "But we're friends now, Mrs. Bushwick – I all but said Mabel. I would so like to. And you to call me Florence. As friends."

A softening of the tone. "I'd like that too. Florence." A sudden impression of loneliness under the chilly exterior of a woman who had been forced into a career, to all but invent a profession, to support two young sons.

"I'm afraid that Mrs. Page was less than truthful, Mabel. Neither she nor I ever met the Princess of Wales nor dined at Marlborough House. But I hope that she was of some value to you. I hope that your article was well received."

Now it was Mabel who laughed. "In our austere Republic there's an infinite appetite for the doings of British royalty and aristocracy."

"Like Lord Oswald? And his marriage to Miss Brewster?"

"Worth at least another twenty percent in sales of the edition it will appear in. But if the buyers read about that, they'll also read of what we saw today. Perhaps some financier's wife may prevail on her husband to endow a Rosewood."

"As Mrs. Page I met a man like that." *Careful now. However helpful he was to Nicholas, however charming when I masqueraded as his wife, however well he played his part in Santiago, he's dangerous.* "A Mr. Henry Raymond, a financier, something in banking. I met him at a dinner in Newport. He was talking about perhaps founding such a home." She had always assumed, and Nicholas too, that it was Raymond who had arranged the interview for the *Columbia Home Gazette.*

Mabel's laugh was unfeigned. "I'm not familiar with the name but he sounds worth interviewing. I'll need to run him down when I get back."

"As you ran Mrs. Page down, Mabel?"

"There was no running down needed, Florence. It's not just the *Gazette*, most other journals and newspapers too. We have little informal arrangements with staff in the better hotels. They let us know about interesting visitors. They get a dollar or two for it. Though in your case they didn't. Whoever it was in the Kennebec Hotel forgot to sign their name to the note they sent. But I followed it up anyway. I invited Mrs. Page to take coffee with me and she came."

There was no hint of dissimulation and Mabel had spoken without hesitation. She had been Raymond's unwitting tool. *A dangerous man, if a likeable one. I wonder if he's in London now, if he's consorting again with the Prince of Wales and his set? Nicholas had liked him too, but he had still been adamant that we should not meet him again.*

The conversation drifted into safer waters. Liking grew. They would see more of each other in London and Florence invited Mabel to visit her in Southsea afterwards.

They took a cab at Liverpool Street and dropped Mabel off at a modest hotel near the British Museum – it looked as if the *Columbia Home Gazette* was careful with expenses. It was almost midnight when Florence arrived back at the Charing Cross Hotel and Agatha went on to the Piccadilly mansion. Florence bathed, hoped that whatever had bitten her and left red blotches was buried safely in the clothes she bundled up and thrust in a laundry basket. Late as it was, she had a maid come to her room and take it away. Only the dress and jacket did she want back for she could not easily afford replacement. She could not bear to think of pulling on the underthings again, however well washed and ironed. A few years before she would have had no option but to keep them. She would have married Nicholas even if he had not a penny, but she was grateful for the modest affluence he had brought her.

Yet, for all that it had been a worthy one, this day had not furthered the purpose that had brought her to London – the late Lieutenant Gilpin's warning.

7

Florence had suggested on the way back that she and Agatha might again meet for coffee next morning at the Charing Cross Hotel. Afterwards they could go together to the National Gallery, have lunch and go on to take tea with Oswald's fiancée.

The visit to Rosewood House had given an opening. Florence used it when they met.

"Nicholas would be interested to hear about those young lads from Rosewood going on to that training ship. The *Brahmaputra*, wasn't it? I must mention it when I next write to him."

"Oswald is so impressed," Agatha said. "He speaks so warmly of it, about what fine young men it turns out."

It was hard to imagine Oswald ever speaking warmly about anything. Querulous, cowardly and demanding as a boy, he had been disliked by all the servants, not least by Florence herself. He had grown into a stout and surly man whose only saving grace was his affection for his sister. The need, for Nicholas's sake, to work closely with him in the United States the previous year had not lessened Florence's dislike of him, nor of his for her.

"It's quite a coincidence," Florence said. "A young officer in Portsmouth mentioned that ship too. And he said that he knew Oswald. A Lieutenant Gilpin." She paused, saw no flicker of recognition. "A tragic young man, I'm afraid."

"Tragic, Florence?"

"He died recently in a shooting accident."

"How awful!" Agatha's pity was unaffected. "I think he must have been mistaken about Oswald. I doubt if he knows many naval officers."

Florence felt a flush of anger. *I've more than once seen him as dismissive of Nicholas as he is of me. Dismissive of a better man, a far better man.*

"That's strange, Agatha! The poor young man spoke highly of Oswald's involvement with the Central London Sick Asylum. That place in Cleveland Street. He said such good work was done there." *A long shot, but worth trying.*

"He must have confused Oswald with somebody else. Oswald isn't involved with any hospitals or asylums. He can't stand the idea of illness. It's why his charitable impulses are concentrated on education. But perhaps Miss Brewster – I must call her Rebecca now – will be more interested in medical matters. The need is so great and…"

Florence was nodding but not listening. There was no option now but to be direct.

"Agatha. Dear Agatha." She reached across and took her hand. "Don't be offended. This young man came to see me unbidden, uninvited. He was upset, almost distraught. He knew your name. He asked me to pass a…" There was no alternative, the word had to be used. "…a warning, to you, for you to pass to Oswald."

Agatha withdrew her hand. Confusion, genuine bewilderment on her face. "A warning? How could that be, Florence? Why should he say that?"

"I don't know. But I think he did know Oswald, Agatha. He said they'd had a falling out but he still had regard for him. And he said that your brother might be more ready to listen to his sister than he would to him."

"And what was I to say to Oswald?" A chill in the voice. The cold logical mathematician who was the first woman elected as Fellow of the Royal Society, not the beaming, kindly, unaffected lady who had no hesitation in rolling up her sleeves to aid refugees and orphaned children.

"He said that Oswald must be careful in London. That he should stay away from Cleveland Street. And from the *Brahmaputra*."

"He must have been mistaken, Florence."

"I don't think so. And he said that Oswald needed to know as soon as possible. That's why I came up to London, Agatha. Specially to tell you that."

"You said that he was distraught, Florence. Unhinged perhaps? Deranged?"

"He seemed perfectly sane. But, yes. He was upset, badly upset. That's not the same as deranged."

"And the shooting accident was soon afterwards?"

Florence nodded.

"We're women of the world, Florence. You know as well as I do what 'shooting accident' usually means." Agatha was trying to inject warmth, understanding, in her tone, but she was failing. "At that extremity men can say anything, but it may count for nothing. He must have picked up some mention of Oswald in the newspapers, of his engagement to Miss Brewster perhaps. Who knows what goes on in a mind like that?"

"So you're not going to say anything to your brother, Agatha?"

"No, Florence. And I trust you won't say anything either."

"No, Agatha." *Not that he would listen to me anyway. I'm the last person he would accept it from. I've done my best for you, Lieutenant Gilpin. And I've failed.*

Agatha picked up her coffee cup, drained it and laid it back in its saucer. "It's time to be setting out for the Gallery. It was the Flemish art you wanted to see, wasn't it Florence?"

*

67

Tea that afternoon in Brown's Hotel in Albemarle Street was not a success.

It was only partly because Florence, no less than Agatha, was still trying to behave as if nothing difficult had passed between them during the morning. The feeling of tension, of caution around each other, was still there, something new, something threatening. Florence hoped it would not last. Other than Nicholas she felt closer to Agatha – almost her sister, from all they had passed through together – than to anybody else in the world. Agatha understood the difficulty of her social status, had encouraged and supported her on the journey from lady's maid to paid companion to officer's wife. And she in turn had guarded Agatha, not just against death and worse in Thrace, but in the long, slow decline into permanent spinsterhood that now stretched before her. Men might admire Agatha's intellect, but none would offer her marriage. Her bulk and clumsiness and her great benign sheep's face would see to that.

We need each other, though we'll never say it. We don't need to. But now this...

The stilted air, the long silences, that silent searching for some topic that might keep conversation going was due to neither Florence nor Agatha, but to Miss Brewster herself. Oswald's betrothed was beautiful – there was no gainsaying that – but she was either wholly bored, and making no attempt to disguise it, or she was very stupid. It was probably both, Florence decided. If she had indeed been born on the prairie in the back of a covered wagon while her father was shooting bison while her mother paused briefly from skinning them, as press coverage had admiringly claimed, then she had inherited neither's grit and energy. An origin that would have meant permanent social exclusion were she British was admired here because she was American – and wealthy. Agatha strove to elicit some comment on the recent visits made to Kegworth relatives, to raise some interest in outings in London, to evoke admiration for Oswald's achievements at the Foreign Office, but Miss Brewster's replies were monosyllables only.

She wants us gone, Florence thought, and *not us alone, but all England. The idea of a title may have attracted her, may have attracted the Leather King and the Leather Queen even more, but that's as far as it goes. Now she's facing the reality. Not that I blame her. Not with marriage to Oswald as the price.*

And still they sat around the small table with its white cloth, its triple-tiered stand of crustless sandwiches and tiny cakes, the silver cutlery, the delicate china cups, the choice of Chinese or Indian, the waitress hovering close by. Each lady's eyes flickered guiltily in turn towards the ornate clock in one corner, each estimating how much longer this torture must continue.

Relief – of a kind – came with the arrival of Miss Brewster's brother.

He might have been as handsome as his sister was beautiful, but already there was promise of unhealthy middle age. He was tall and well-built, but running to flesh. His neck bulged over his collar and his clean-shaven face was flushed and puffy. Agatha was telling an uninterested Miss Brewster about Rosewood House but he interrupted her without apology.

"It's time to go, Becky," he said. "We've got to be meeting those folks I told you about." Her two guests might not have existed. He smelled strongly of whiskey.

"Oh Mr. Brewster! What a pleasure!" Agatha was rising, innocent, unoffended, beaming. "I'm so happy you could meet my dearest fiend." Even though he had not looked directly at Florence, Agatha still made the introduction. "Mrs. Dawlish – Mr. Chester Brewster."

"Chester K. Brewster." He ignored Agatha as he corrected her but he was regarding Florence with something between a leer and a smirk.

Unmistakable. *Every woman has her price and I've got the money,* his eyes told her. She looked away and she hoped that he knew he was snubbed.

"It's such a pity if you have to go so soon Mr. Brewster," Agatha, herself incapable of inflicting pain, had not recognised contempt in his dismissal of her. "Mrs. Dawlish will have heard so much about you. Such a disappointment if you can't join us for five minutes!"

Miss Brewster sighed, said nothing but her brother looked again at Florence, then pulled over a chair, snapped his fingers at a waitress, pointed to a cup and sat down.

"Five minutes, Becky," he said. "Five minutes and then we're moving."

"Don't take on so, Chet," Miss Brewster sounded weary. "We've got time."

"I was hoping to ask you more about Harvard, Mr. Brewster," Agatha said. "Did you attend lectures from Professor Peirce when you were there?"

"Who?"

"Professor Benjamin Peirce. The mathematician. I'd corresponded with him before he died recently – such a loss! His work on linear associative algebra has been such a…"

"Never heard of him." Brewster sounded proud of the fact. "I'd better ways to fill my time at Harvard, hadn't I, Becky?" He winked at her and laughed as if at some private joke.

For the first time his sister showed animation, even if it was just embarrassment. "We need to be going, Chet, just like you said." She stood up.

After they were gone Florence saw that Agatha was upset, badly upset, by her dismissal. It was better not to allude to it, to turn conversation to the evening's dinner. And as she did she thought what she could never have expected herself to think of Oswald. *Miss Brewster's future husband is a better man than her brother.*

*

Florence wanted to be gone, had been depressed by the day's encounters, and yet the evening proved enjoyable, much as she had dreaded it. Agatha's friend Dr. Pauncefote, a philologist, had been happy to include her in an invitation to dinner. There would be a small group, Agatha said, friends from the Royal Society, university people, scholars, scientists, who dined monthly in rotation in each other's houses. The list sounded intimidating, a Sir Alfred Greenway who was coming down from Cambridge and whose name Agatha assumed Florence should know, though she did not, and a Mr. Dodgson, a mathematician from Oxford and a Major Chalmers who was apparently renowned for his translations from Sanskrit. There would be others, some with their wives, most of whom sounded accomplished in their own right. Florence's own efforts in self-education seemed trivial by comparison. And there had been another reason to hesitate, one that Agatha had recognised but had not alluded directly to.

"Can you be ready at the hotel at seven?" she said. "I'll come with a hansom. They're so much more airy on these summer evenings."

70

No need to say more. A rented cab, not one of Agatha's father's coaches. Not one driven by Florence's own father or brother.

The house was in Russell Square, large and imposing without, untidy, cluttered and yet comfortable within. Mrs. Pauncefote, a somewhat dishevelled lady of middle years – herself no mean philologist, Agatha had said, though self-taught – welcomed Florence warmly. Her husband was no less cordial as he introduced her to his guests. To be a friend of Agatha's seemed to guarantee instant acceptance. No two present seemed to have exactly the same interest and the best approach proved to be to ask them exactly what they did. None exhibited the arrogance Florence might have expected and several proved fascinating. This was a world that Nicholas would enjoy, she thought, and its easy assumption of worth seemed far removed from the petty snobberies that strove to humiliate her in Portsmouth. When dinner was announced she was sharing memories of encounters with Ottoman officials, and laughing over them, with a wife who had supported her husband during excavations in Cyprus.

There were sixteen at table, ten of them male, Florence and Agatha seated with men who had come alone. The old gentleman on Florence's left was deaf on that side but the guest to her right was no older than Nicholas and strikingly handsome to boot. He had arrived late and she had not caught his name. Now he gave it.

"Count Sergei Ivanovich Livitski. I'm attached to the Imperial Russian Embassy." There was only the slightest hint of an accent, the faintest scent of eau-de-cologne. In a gathering in which concern for fashionable clothing seemed minimal he stood out for elegance.

"I imagine you're a friend of Dr. Pauncefote?" Florence said.

He shook his head. "Not quite a friend, not yet at least, but I hope to be. I had an introduction to him when I came to London. We have shared interests." He said it in such a way that curiosity did not seem impolite.

"And those interests are, Count Livitski?"

"Central Asian languages, Mrs. Dawlish. Turkic languages in general, Uzbek and Karakalpak in particular."

"Ayrıca Türkçe biliyor musun?" Florence could not help flaunting her ability, limited as it was. *Do you speak Turkish also?*

"Yanı sıra ben İngilizce konuşurken, Florence Hanim." He had picked her name up on a single hearing. *As well as I speak English, Madam Florence.*

It was better now to continue in English only. The little Turkish Florence had picked up in soup kitchens and refugee shelters was inadequate for table talk. But she had obviously made an impression and it pleased her.

"And how did you come to have such facility in…" she searched for the word, remembered it. "In Uzbek?"

"Languages interest me. And in my days as a soldier I served in Turkestan. I was with Skobelev at Khiva and Kokand."

The Russian general's name might have meant nothing to any other woman in the room other than Agatha, but it chilled Florence. Skobelev had burst like a whirlwind through the Turkish defences in Bulgaria and Thrace four years before and she, and Agatha, had been in its path. The terror of the refugees fleeing through the winter snows before the unstoppable Russian onslaught, the nightmare retreat towards Istanbul, the columns of flame and smoke behind marking some new Turkish defeat, all came flooding back. And Nicholas in fever on the bed of a wagon, unconscious of the Cossacks snapping on the column's heels as the *Mesrutiyet* brigade died one by one in its defence. And the small revolver that now lay in a drawer in Southsea but which she then had in her pocket and had touched a dozen times a day to reassure her that there was still one way of escape. *First Agatha. Then myself.*

"And you, Florence Hanim?" Livitski used the Turkish form of address, at once familiar but respectful. "How did you come to learn Turkish? Though with somewhat of a Bulgarian intonation?"

She told him, but only briefly, mentioned only the feeding centre near the Spice Market in Istanbul, Agatha's role as well as her own, said nothing of Thrace. The refugees she had picked up the language from were Bulgarian Turks. That was the source of the intonation.

"Bad times, Florence Hanim. You were lucky you were just in Istanbul. It was bad in Bulgaria, worse in Thrace. I served under Skobelev there also. With His Majesty's Sumskoi Hussars."

"I understand that it was bad there," Florence said. "I heard stories. Dreadful stories." *And I lived through them. Just. And could this man have been in that Russian force I saw shredded by Nicholas's guns along the River Tunca? Better not to ask. Better not to know.*

Pride in Livitski's voice, but a hint of regret too. "Hard fighting, Florence Hanim, terrible events. But the blame must go to those who initiate such wars, not those who fight them. Let's be glad we've put such days behind us."

Nicholas would like this man, two of a kind, ruthless perhaps, but decent. And… and I like him too.

To change the subject, she complimented him on his English, asked how he had become so fluent. He too seemed glad to change. He had spent a year at Oxford, still had friends from that time, had been an honorary equerry when the Queens's son, Prince Alfred, had married the Czar's daughter. The prince was still a serving officer of the Royal Navy, Florence said, just like her husband. And no, she didn't think he knew the prince other than by reputation.

"Your husband isn't here tonight, Florence Hanim?"

"He's at sea. But I'm looking forward to him coming home soon."

"I've no doubt that he is too, Florence Hanim. A lucky man."

Soon after Mrs. Pauncefote invited the ladies to withdraw. Once more Florence felt herself comfortable in the group and was grateful that disparate interests rather than shared gossip formed the basis for discussion. She liked her hostess, and even more the wife of Major Chalmers, and she was invited by both to call on them when she would again come to London. In the dining room the men would be passing the port in an atmosphere which she suspected would be one of companionable regard.

The gentlemen re-joined them some forty minutes later, some a little more flushed than before. Dr. Pauncefote must have been told by Count Livitski of Florence's familiarity with Turkish because he cornered her to speak of Turkic languages. She did not have to say more than *Yes* or *No* or *Indeed*, for she saw that he was a bore, if likeable otherwise, and like all bores had no interest in hearing his listener. Across the room she saw Agatha in lively discussion with Livitski and wondered if she too was being as reticent as she had been herself about her experiences in Thrace. Knowing Agatha, probably not.

Dr. Pauncefote was deep in the complexities of Karakalpak subjunctives when Agatha came sailing across the room, Livitski following.

"It's such a delight to talk to the count." Agatha's pleasure was, as ever, unfeigned but guileless. "And do you know that we cannot have been more than a couple of miles apart when we were at the caravanserai at Ljubimec? And Count Livitski assures me that he would have guaranteed our protection if Nicholas had not reached us first!"

There had been little protection for Bulgar women and children though. The Czar's Cossacks had been little better than the Sultan's Bashi-Bazooks. For all this... for all this attractive man's charm, those atrocities could not be forgotten – or forgiven. At least I had my revolver. Those Bulgar women had not. And not just the women either, but the young men and boys who were violated just as savagely.

"And the count has made a splendid invitation, Florence!" A child could not have been more innocently elated. "He'd like us to join him for an outing in the park tomorrow morning"

Livitski was smiling. "A new equipage, a new matched pair also, greys. Nothing too special, ladies, but I am rather keen to show it off. Especially with two such lovely passengers."

"Oh how splendid!" Agatha said. "Oh Florence! Do come!"

"But I'm going back to Portsmouth tomorrow, Agatha." Florence saw how Livitski was looking at her, could read his thoughts. *Do join me, Florence Hanim. You know you would like to.*

"But you said that you would be leaving in the afternoon, Florence," Agatha said. "There's time enough."

As Florence agreed she told herself that it was only to please Agatha. Not herself. And certainly not to please Count Livitski.

*

The open landau was magnificent, the horses more impressive still, but it was Livitski's driver in traditional Cossack costume who turned heads. It had joined the stream of scarcely less splendid vehicles moving slowly along the South Carriageway of Hyde Park. This stately progress, no less than the groups of elegantly dressed riders on the Rotten Row bridle path to its side, was as much a social occasion as a ball or a banquet. Whether in delicate summer dresses and sheltered beneath parasols in the carriages, or on horseback in elegantly trim riding habits, this morning promenade was the fashionable woman's hour of glory. And Florence, dressed even as she was in her best, felt dowdy and insignificant by comparison with so many expensive beauties. Agatha nodded recognition of gentlemen's hats tipped to her, of ladies' heads inclined, but when Florence asked who they were Agatha did not know. Her pince-nez allowed her to detect outlines only, not faces, but she was still as innocently happy as a child on an outing. She laughed about it, Florence and Livitski too. He was sitting across from them, elegant in a white linen suit. Conversation with him was easy as he identified men who greeted him, several of them contemporaries of his at Oxford, he said, and he spoke too of his pleasure in breeding horses on his estate near Orel. He listened, with interest that Florence suspected was feigned, but well and politely so, to Agatha's account of the good work at Rosewood House. Russia was backward in such things, he said, but there was so much to do and one could only trust in the future. Florence said little, though all the time she saw Livitski's gaze returning to her. Admiringly, yet not in a way that gave offence.

Livitski had turned to look forward and now he called out in Russian to his driver. The landau came to a halt and now another – considerably less modern, less luxurious – that was coming from the opposite direction drew level. Florence's father was driving. He caught her eye for a moment, saw Agatha by her side, then looked impassively ahead as he drew rein. Oswald was sitting on the rear seat, Miss Brewster by his side – a vision in white – and across from them her brother Chester. They looked as if they had been in glum, bored silence. The ride was clearly an obligation, not a pleasure.

"Lord Oswald! An unexpected delight!" Livitski was on his feet, sweeping off his hat and bowing. "And your lovely fiancée, I presume. I look forward to meeting Miss Brewster on another occasion!"

"Dear Oswald!" Agatha called. "And Rebecca! How lovely you look today!"

Oswald was no more gracious in his response than Florence had ever seen him be. Yet she had no care for that. More painful was the sight of her father sitting stiffly on the box, not acknowledging her – not from resentment but from love, to avoid embarrassing her as she sat as a lady in another carriage. She looked away herself, heart thumping, mouth dry.

Miss Brewster had all but ignored the greeting and her brother, sunk back in the cushions, face red and bloated, might have been oblivious of it, for he said nothing. Livitski was undeterred, was enquiring how Miss Brewster was enjoying London, and all the while Oswald was looking more like what Florence always thought of him as, a querulous and pompous turkeycock. She had never liked him but in the next instant that dislike was transformed into hatred.

He looked her in the eye, nodded and then called up to her father "Drive on, Morton." He did so unnecessarily loudly, intent on her hearing it. She felt tears starting to her eyes as the unsmiling, forward-staring figure on the box urged the horses forward.

She sat in silence as Livitski's landau also moved on. It hurt all the more that Agatha had seen what had happened and was ashamed for it. She felt Agatha reaching for her hand and pressing it. *Like sisters.* The exchange had meant nothing to Livitski. Florence was grateful for that, and then felt guilty for feeling it.

Suddenly the carriages moving in both directions were pulling over to leave a clear run between. Another landau was approaching and passengers in the other vehicles were rising to their feet to get a better view of it as it passed. A murmur rolled along the onlookers as the carriage drew level, not of cheering, but of quietly expressed admiration. Gentlemen were sweeping off their hats and ladies were bobbing curtseys even in the confined spaces available

Four figures reclined in it, two gentlemen looking rearwards and their faces as yet hidden, but looking forward was a portly, florid man whose features simultaneously radiated some kindliness but even more self-indulgence. The slim woman by his side made Miss Brewster's beauty seem commonplace.

Florence rose to her feet as Livitski cried "Bravo!" and, with Agatha, Florence also curtseyed. The Prince of Wales acknowledged with a wave and Princess Alexandra – it was said she had a lot to put up with – inclined her head.

But as the Prince's carriage passed it was another face that now became visible, one of the gentlemen with their backs to the driver. Smiling, relaxed and welcome in this august company, he was as confident and urbane as when Florence had played the role of his wife in Santiago de Cuba, as chastely as if he had been her brother. He was a man whom both she and Nicholas liked, a man of courage and ingenuity. They had almost died with him. *But he could be trusted only up to a point, Nicholas had said, though it was unclear what that point might be.*

He had seen her and he was raising his hat to her and smiling in obvious pleasure as the carriage receded.

Henry Judson Raymond.

To the world, to the heir to the throne himself, he was a rich American expatriate who like so many of his kind had tired of the vulgarity of his native land and had chosen to live as an English gentleman.

A man, Nicholas had said, whom we should never meet again.

8

It was good to be back in her own home in Southsea, to look forward to immersing herself for a few days each week in the running of the Sailors' Rest, to continuing lessons at her own piano, to dining at her own table and to writing to Nicholas at her own desk. Mabel Bushwick's visit was to be looked forward to in the following week and she was already planning what places to bring her to. And yet, as she went to bed on her first night home, one thought nagged. Her conscience was clear, she tried to assure herself, as regards her promise to the unfortunate Lieutenant Gilpin. She had delivered the warning to Agatha, had done to the letter what had been asked of her. It was up to Agatha now how to proceed. And yet she knew that Agatha would not do anything, that whatever message had been intended for Oswald would never reach him. No matter how much she disliked the man she should have done more.

She returned from her morning walk next day to find Susan and Cook both excited.

"There's been a man here for you, ma'am. Came in a cab, he did, all to himself and for what he'd brought for you! And I didn't know what to do and…"

"What sort of man? What did he bring?"

"It was so lovely that I didn't know what to do and…" Susan was flushed with delight.

"I heard her taking on, ma'am, the silly girl, so I came out myself. And 'twas good I did." Cook had an air of pride in a job well done. "They was so lovely that I had him put them in the drawing room, ma'am. I thought you'd like that."

"Show me." Florence pushed past them.

It was more than a bouquet, an arrangement that was almost as high as Florence herself even though the ornate basket that contained it was standing on the floor. The greenery looked luxuriant and all the flowers must have come from a hothouse – there were even what Florence suspected to be orchids, though she had never seen one. The room suddenly seemed shabby by comparison with this glory. The scent was exquisite, all but overpowering, as Florence reached out to take the envelope nestling at its centre. It carried only the name *Mrs. Nicholas Dawlish* in italic script on thick yellow paper. She turned it over. An embossed crest on the back.

She guessed who it was from even as her trembling hands tore it open.

A card bearing only the words *In admiration.* And the initials. *S.I.L.*

No need for more. Florence felt a surge of pleasure mixed with shame. Cook and Susan were crowding close, entranced by the blooms, intoxicated by the scent. She knew that the blood was draining from her face, that her knees were trembling, that they had not noticed her discomfiture. To disguise it she said, "What sort of man brought it?"

"A shopman," Cook said. "From a place in town that sells flowers. He said the order had come by telegram, that he didn't know who sent it. He got that envelope an' a postal order in the mail to pay for it." She paused, obviously aware of Florence's confusion, then said. "Is it from Captain Dawlish, ma'am?" She must know it was not, must know it from the envelope's crest. A glance passed between her and Susan. The girl smirked.

"That will be all, Cook. You can go back to the kitchen. And Susan – please fetch a cab." Florence gestured to the flowers. "I want you to go with the cab and take these flowers in it to the Sailors' Rest. To be put in the Reading Room. You understand? In the Reading Room."

"Yes, ma'am." Susan looked elated by the prospect of the adventure. Not just a ride in a cab but this wonder in her charge. "Is it some sort of mix-up, ma'am?"

"It's some kind of mix-up, Susan," Florence said.

But as she went to her room to compose herself she knew it was not. Livitski must have gone to considerable effort to find her address. She regretted now that she might have been too easily familiar with him, innocent as it had been. He must have misinterpreted it and her feeling of shame that he had done so was strong. His admiration was flattering but she was not tempted. Nicholas would never have thought of such a gesture as these flowers, but he was a better man.

Her husband, now and forever.

*

A letter arrived from Nicholas. It had been posted in Singapore during a brief stop to load coal before pressing on to Hong Kong. It was affectionate but dull. The voyage was going well, engines and boilers were exceeding expectations, crew and gunnery exercises were satisfactory and the officers, including a secondee from the Imperial Japanese Navy, were meeting and exceeding expectations. He was enjoying the books she had selected for him and accommodating the isolation of command. Only one sentence saddened her, a reference to the escalating crisis in Alexandria, to the concentration of naval forces there and to the possibility of action. There was no hint of self-pity and yet she knew that missing the opportunity to play a role there would hurt him keenly. The safe and even boring time he could expect in the Far East would be no substitute. At least, she thought, he would be far from danger.

But other reading angered her. The outrage in the *St. James Fortnightly* had seemed contrived when she read it previously, but now Staveley's latest outpourings disgusted her. The misery of the crippled cardboard-box maker and his wife and five children in a single room in Bethnal Green, the privations of a consumptive widow in a garret in Poplar, the despair of the father of seven in Bermondsey whose wife had died in childbirth and who had been workless for months, were all no doubt true. So too, no doubt, was the squalor which was described in almost loving detail, so too the fact that all lived in properties owned by a minister of the Crown whose identity was unmistakable even if not spelled out. But Florence suspected that Staveley would have brought others to view these unfortunates just as she herself had been brought to that terrible attic in Clerkenwell. He would have put these people on display, like animals in in a zoo, and for all his righteous ire he would have done nothing to aid any of them as individuals. His virtuous fury, Florence suspected, was aimed more at boosting circulation than at curing ills.

Three days after her return Florence was leaving the Sailors' Rest in late afternoon when a woman waiting by the door approached her hesitantly. She recognised her as the seaman's wife who had also watched HMS *Leonidas's* departure and who had been so grateful that her husband had been prevailed upon to take the pledge.

"Mrs. Shepton," Florence smiled, took her hand. "How good it is to see you! And perhaps you've received news from your husband? From Singapore perhaps?"

She had – a shipmate had written at his dictation. He had not touched a drop and *Leonidas* was a happy ship.

But it was obvious that Mrs. Shepton had not come here just for that. There must be more and she looked uncomfortable about where to start.

"It's a fine evening, Mrs. Shepton," Florence said. "Perhaps we can walk a little together?"

They lapsed into silence, as they walked, for all Florence's efforts to start conversation on neutral topics proved ineffective. At last they came upon a bench sited to look out across the harbour. At Florence's suggestion they sat.

"I think there may be something bothering you, Mrs. Shepton," Florence said.

"Oh ma'am." Suddenly she began to weep. "I don't want to…"

"Just take your time, Mrs. Shepton. Take as long as you like." Florence produced a clean lace-trimmed handkerchief, folded and ironed, and handed it to her.

"I don't know who to talk to, ma'am." A sob. "I don't know what to do and Jem's so far away with your husband. If he'd been here…" Then more sobbing.

Florence reached for her hand and held it.

"Is it about your children, Mrs. Shepton?"

"It's me eldest, ma'am, Andrew. A lovely lad, ma'am. I told you about him before."

A half-forgotten memory stirred.

"The boy who's on that training ship, on the *Brahmaputra*?"

And other memories too. *Gilpin. Oswald.*

"He's gone, Mrs. Dawlish. He's gone without a word."

"He's not on the ship?"

Mrs. Shepton reached into her pocket and handed Florence a crumpled letter. There was a small stylised image of a ship on the letterhead, the name underneath, the date two weeks before. It was signed by the vessel's captain. Andrew Shepton had been absent for a five days. Did his mother know of his whereabouts? There would be serious repercussions if he did not return.

"It was the first I heard of it, ma'am. We hadn't seen him."

"Did he seem unhappy when you last saw him? Anything unusual?"

"No, ma'am." She said it too quickly.

"So what did you do then, Mrs. Shepton?"

"In such a state I was in myself then! A friend helped me to write a letter back and I heard no more from them." Sobs racked her. "And then I got this, ma'am."

A cheap envelope and inside it a lined page ripped from a copybook. Much of it had been blurred, almost certainly by Mrs. Shepton's tears. No date, a few sentences only, no punctuation, the hand that of someone unused to writing but signed "your loving son Andrew". He had had enough of the ship and had come into some good fortune and now he was going to America. He would write from there and hoped that this letter would find his mother as it had left him, well.

"Did he speak about America before, Mrs. Shepton?"

"No, ma'am. Not a word. Not ever."

Florence was looking at the envelope. The Post Office's franking of the stamp confirmed that it had been sent from London six days before. Later than the letter from the *Brahmaputra*.

"Is this your son's writing?"

"I don't read much and he never wrote often. But Mrs Jephson – she's my neighbour – she reads for me and she thinks it is."

"Would he have had enough money to pay for a passage to America?"

"He could never have had more than a shilling to two, ma'am. The boys don't get much on that ship. But he…" Mrs. Shepton hesitated, was perhaps wondering if she should say more.

"When exactly did you last see him, Mrs. Shepton?"

"About a month ago." She was avoiding Florence's gaze. "He said he had permission to come to see his dad before he left. We was wondering how he got the money for the train but he said he'd been given it by the ship. And he had good clothes too."

"New clothes?"

"Smart. Very smart. An' a watch too, ma'am." She was weeping again. "His dad wanted to know where he got it but he wouldn't say. There was a terrible row, ma'am and he left without saying goodbye. But he's a good boy and me and his dad thought he'd be back to say sorry."

Florence tried to disguise her rising excitement. *There's something here.*

"Did he ever mention anybody called Gilpin, Mrs. Shepton? I seem to remember hearing somebody of that name being associated with the *Brahmaputra*."

"Andrew never did say, about him nor anybody else. It was his dad who heard about the ship and thought it was a good chance for him."

And his father was this minute on the far side of the world.

"That lady that was with you the day the ship sailed," Mrs. Shepton said. "She said that her brother knew about the *Brahmaputra*. Maybe he might know something, ma'am. If it would be too much to ask, ma'am? He's still a boy, ma'am, and a good boy too and…"

"I'll look into it," Florence said. "I can't promise anything, But I'll so my best."

And as Mrs. Shepton thanked her Florence knew that no help would be forthcoming from Oswald's quarter.

*

The meeting with Mrs. Shepton had troubled Florence deeply and when she got home she consulted the copy of *Kelly's Handbook of the Titled, Landed and Official Classes* that Nicholas kept in his study. She knew that its contents were broader than the name implied, for it was also an exhaustive listing of business and trade addresses. She had never had reason before to consult it previously and so it took ten minutes' perusal of small print before she located the *Brahmaputra*. She assumed that the Captain J.A. Wilton (Retd.) who was listed as superintendent had been a merchant rather than a naval officer for there was no proud R.N. after his name. It was to him she wrote on behalf of her friend, asking for information on the last known movements of her son, Andrew Shepton. Was there some reason why he wanted to leave? Had he spoken of America to other boys? Did he appear to have come by money in some way to pay for a passage? The more she wrote the more Florence feared that the reasons might be very simple – theft, fear of discovery, hiding in London's teeming warren, America beyond reach for lack of passage-money and mentioned only as a blind. After the letter had been posted next morning there was nothing to do but to wait, for Florence had dismissed the idea of raising the matter with Agatha.

The answer came almost by return. Captain Wilton was writing in sorrow rather than in anger. The Shepton boy had been quiet, but attentive to his duties. He had been popular with his fellows and well regarded by his instructors. He had never mentioned America, nor should he have had any money over and above the few pence of pocket-money per week the boys were given. The possibility of accidental drowning had been considered but neither the coastguards nor the port-pilotage service had found any evidence to support this theory. The youth had been in no trouble previously but as he had disappeared wearing clothing belonging to the *Brahmaputra,* to the value of fifteen shillings and eightpence-ha'penny, that could be construed as theft. As it was not a naval ship there was no question of desertion in the legal sense but it was a strong offence in terms of honour and morality. Should Andrew Shepton reappear he would not be welcomed back. Captain Wilton remained Mrs. Dawlish's obedient servant etc. etc.

She had drawn a blank.

As she had done in every line of enquiry she had followed since Nicholas's departure.

*

It was not easy to break the news to Mrs. Shepton. Florence visited her in the three rooms she occupied with five children. Plain and sparsely furnished they might be but they were spotlessly clean and so too were the children. Her husband's signed pledge of temperance hung framed over the mantelpiece. The other tenants of the house seemed equally dedicated to preserving standards and their decent frugality – their straitened circumstances rather – was a world removed from the squalor from which Maisie and her brother and sister had been rescued.

"I can't bear to think of me lad alone in them heathen places." Mrs. Shepton was weeping softly and the other children were looking on in silence. "Is there any hope, ma'am?"

Florence realised that the distraught mother had placed more confidence in her ability to resolve the problem than had been justified. She felt guilty when she said, "There's always hope" because she knew there was little. But there was nothing else she could have said.

And yet, and yet... This boy, Gilpin, Oswald, the *Brahmaputra*...

It was dusk when she emerged, would be dark when she reached a main thoroughfare. She would allow herself the luxury of a cab to take her home. She passed down a narrow street, the poor but decent occupants gathered on doorsteps in the evening warmth for women to gossip and for men to smoke pipes. Children playing hopscotch on the pavement parted to let her past. There was no hint of threat or of resentment of her presence.

She turned into another street, a narrower one and all but deserted, lit only by a single weak gas lamp half-way along. And suddenly she heard footsteps close behind, light but steady. She did not look back but she quickened her pace. So too did the footsteps. She slowed, the footsteps also. Frightened now, she shifted her parasol into her left hand – ever since that scuffle in the street she had gone nowhere without a parasol or umbrella – and she grasped the handle in her right hand. *Better to act too soon than too late…*

Heart thumping, mouth dry, she spun around and crouched, the parasol's spike extended like the bayonets Nicholas had once shown her seamen exercising with. The figure before her – slight, face in shadow, but clearly female – froze and stepped back.

"You'd better go home, my dear," Florence said. "You don't want to get in trouble."

"I am in trouble, ma'am." A sob. She came closer. "You saw me before, ma'am. When you tried to save me. You was good to me."

Her features were just discernible now in the distant lamppost's light. Unmistakable. Last seen as she had been pushed, sobbing and distraught, into a cab.

Florence advanced, dropping the parasol to hang from her wrist and embraced the girl. To her surprise the dress felt smooth to the touch – good quality, perhaps even silk – and though the girl's hair was dishevelled it was clean and scented. There was a hint too of a heavier perfume. Long seconds passed, the girl – little more than a child – clutching fiercely as great sobs raked her. *I remember girls being like this in Thrace after they had been used by troops and irregulars, girls who…*

"God bless you, ma'am. God bless you."

"You can come home with me," Florence said. "You'll be safe at my house." She could hail a cab in a street or two. Within twenty minutes Albert Grove's comfort and serene respectability could envelop them.

The girl shook her head violently. "No, ma'am. I'm going somewhere else."

"Walk then with me a while, my dear." Better not to press her yet. "Just to the next street." She reached down and took the girl's hand in hers. It was trembling. They began to walk. The girl was calming but there was a deadness about her calm. As they neared the lamppost Florence saw that the dress was low-cut and dark red. No shawl, no hat. A livid bruise on one side of the face. Like she had received herself on the night she had first seen this girl.

"My name's Mrs. Dawlish. But if you like you can call me Florence. What's yours, my dear?"

"Dorcas." A hint of Cockney in the low voice. "Dorcas Hayward, ma'am."

"Do you have a family near here, Dorcas?"

"Ain't got no family, ma'am."

"Where have you been, Dorcas? Since that night I saw you.?"

"In a house, ma'am. In the house they took me to." She was weeping quietly now.

No need to ask what had happened in that house, what had been happening since.

"Do you know where that house is, Dorcas? Could you find it again?"

"No, ma'am." The question had frightened her. "I won't go back there, ma'am." She tried to pull away.

Florence did not let go of her hand. "Nobody's going to take you there again, Dorcas. You can come with me. You know what I tried to do for you. You know you can trust me."

A nod. Unbidden, the girl embraced Florence, did no let go. They stood together in silence.

At last Florence said, "Where were you before that, Dorcas?"

"At an orphanage, ma'am. Since I was little."

"Were you happy there, Dorcas?"

"I was, ma'am. Until… until…" She began to sob again.

"Until what, Dorcas."

"It was Mr. Whittier. When Mr. Whittier used to visit."

The name vaguely familiar, then remembered with sudden clarity. A banker. Agatha had mentioned him. Florence felt a chill wash through her and recoiled from what she must ask.

"Was the orphanage called Rosewood House, Dorcas?"

The girl was shaking her head. "I'm not to say that, ma'am. They told me not to say that."

"I've been to Rosewood, Dorcas, I've been there and …"

The girl shrunk back. "I'm not going back there, ma'am. I'm not going back."

"How did you get here, Dorcas? To Portsmouth? Who brought you?"

"It don't matter now, ma'am. It don't matter no more."

"You can come with me, Dorcas. To my house. You'll be safe."
Florence tried to hold the girl, draw her close to her, but she was
wriggling free.

"I ain't going with nobody no more! I'm going on my own,
ma'am." She was violent now, catching Florence's wrists and pushing
her arms free from her.

"Dorcas, listen to me, we can…"

Florence did not expect it, and so she fell when the girl pushed
her backwards to send her sprawling on the pavement. As she strove
to rise she saw the girl turning away and running. By the time
Florence had regained her feet, if not yet her dignity, Dorcas had
disappeared into some side alley. Ten minutes of fruitless searching
followed, made worse by that single word gnawing in Florence's
mind.

Rosewood.

*

Once more the police station, the counter, the stench of disinfectant
and vomit and urine, the same hysterical sobbing in some unseen cell
and again some woman screaming obscenely in another. No Janey
and Tilda this time – they must be at work or in gaol – but it was the
same sergeant, and no more sympathetic than before.

"Been fighting in the street again? Mrs. Dawlish, ain't it? We've
been rescuing again, have we?"

Florence followed his gaze. It was fixed on her sleeve, a long
rent.

"I want to speak to Inspector Towton please."

The same exchange as before, the same studied insolence. The
inspector wasn't here, wouldn't be until later. Florence was willing to
wait. She wouldn't leave without seeing him. She was once more
brought to Towton's office to wait by the bare desk and closed
cupboards and with a single lamp to light the darkness.

When he did arrive Towton offered no welcome and listened
with undisguised irritation.

"So this Dorcas was wearing a red dress, was she?" He was
going back over the details he had jotted in his notebook.

"Red," Florence said. "Dark read. Good material, maybe silk."

"Her hair was clean? And she was smelling of some perfume?"

"That's right, inspector."

86

He leaned back in his chair. "I don't need to tell you what this sort of thing means, Mrs. Dawlish." Condescension, mock-patience in his tone. "There are plenty of these sorts of women in this city. They're always involved in scenes like this. But they'll be back with their menfolk, and willingly too, before morning, and back then to their old ways until it's the next time."

"So no likelihood this time of an asylum? No possibility of medical orderlies?" Florence could not keep the sarcasm from her voice.

Towton did not rise to it. "We can't rule anything out, Mrs. Dawlish. But it's probably unlikely. She didn't want to go with you, did she? Girls like that don't really want to leave the life they lead. She won't be much different."

"Thank you, inspector." Florence stood up.

"You can depend upon it that you'll hear from us if we find something, ma'am." The words brought no assurance. At the door he said, "Can we expect another sworn affidavit, ma'am?"

"I'll consider it," Florence said, but she knew it would be as useless as the first.

And in the cab on the way home her mind was focussed on one fact only, one she had decided not to mention to the police.

Rosewood House.

Towton might have noted it if she had, but he would not bother to follow it up.

But she herself most certainly would.

9

She missed Nicholas very badly now, not just for himself, as she always did, but for the opportunity to discuss her doubts and concerns with somebody she could be wholly open with. Miss Weston would have heard her patiently and have been a source of common sense, but she was in Plymouth, heavily concerned with the original Sailor's Rest there. It was to Agatha that she would normally have turned in such a case – they had few secrets from each other and though Agatha was so often impractical her invariable kindness made her a tolerant listener. And that was all she needed now, Florence thought, somebody who would listen, would not dismiss her concerns as those of a naïve woman for whom altruism was becoming an obsession. But now, the more she thought of Rosewood House, and of Agatha's favourable reference to Mr. Whittier – she seemed to imply that he was involved with that Hyperion company – the more reluctant she was to mention the matter to her friend. The chill in Agatha's voice when she had refused to consider relaying Gilpin's words to Oswald had told that there were limits even to friendship. Florence thought too of speaking to Mr. Bagshot, the solicitor. The copies of the earlier affidavit he had personally brought to the police, and to his magistrate friend, had led nowhere, though he had been effective in ensuring that Florence's name was kept from the press. But, however well-meaning, he was an old man, unsuited to any more active role.

There's nothing for it but to go to Rosewood House myself. Miss Braben, the matron, is capable. She'll have good records. And she seems the sort to be discreet about my enquiries.

Yet Florence still hesitated. The girl might turn up again – she looked for her on the two following evenings in the streets near the Sailors' Rest though women she approached on doorsteps during their evening gossips had not seen her. It was better not to be precipitate, Florence told herself – Inspector Towton's words might have a grain of truth in them, for all their cynicism. She would put off going to Rosewood House until after Mabel Bushwick's visit. And then? She could not decide without more information how much further she should get involved.

As she waited at the station for Mabel's arrival from London, she bought a copy of the *Portsmouth Argus*. She leafed through it idly, passed quickly over notices of social occasions, news of warships arriving and departing, preparations for arrival of a minor royal personage to attend commissioning of a new vessel. She began to fold it as the train drew slowly in, steam and smoke-wreathed, but as she did a small item at a page's bottom corner caught her eye.

Tragic discovery off Spitbank Fort.

A body had been recovered, apparently that of a young woman. The "apparently" warned, without being explicit, of its condition. It had most likely have been in the water for some days, carried out from the harbour with the tide. Nothing to identify her, but she had been wearing a red dress. No report had been received by the police of a missing person fitting her general description. There was no evidence of injury inflicted by a third party. The inquest had been brief and the coroner had indicated to the jury that death by misadventure might be the appropriate ruling. There were many quaysides in Portsmouth that had unguarded edges and it was not difficult to make a mistake. The jury had agreed.

Florence felt suddenly faint, her knees shaking, her hands trembling.

Death by misadventure. It guaranteed her a Christian burial that a certain other verdict would have denied her. But it did not alter what must have really happened.

"Florence? Are you well? You're so pale!"

She had not noticed the train stopping, the passengers disembarking. Mabel Bushwick was regarding her in alarm.

"I've had a shock. Something dreadful. Something…" Her voice failed.

Mabel led her to the Ladies' Waiting Room and sat her down.

"Is it your husband, Florence? Some news about his ship or …"

Florence shook her head in mute misery.

I failed her. I failed Dorcas. Perhaps if I had gone to Rosewood House and…

Mabel was drawing her close, embracing her, not pressing her for details.

At last Florence spoke, an act of will. She was forcing her hands not to shake, was telling herself that she must not fail again. "It's not my husband. But it's bad, something very bad." She glanced around the bare waiting room. "We can't talk here, Mabel. There's a hotel close by." Relief and gratitude flooded through her that this self-reliant, quietly decent woman was here, that she had at last somebody to share her concerns with.

They settled in a corner of the deserted hotel parlour. Mabel produced smelling salts but Florence refused them. Mabel ordered coffee. She had not asked questions as they walked here but now she said, "You need to tell me the whole story, Florence, no matter what it is."

Dorcas's face when Florence had last seen her was foremost in her memory and yet she thrust it aside. It was better to tell all she could remember and in the strict sequence it had happened. Mabel did not interrupt and at the end she made no comment. She reached into her bag and produced her notebook. She saw Florence's look of alarm and said, "I'm not a journalist now, Florence. I'm your friend. But it's best that I take notes. Best for our poor lost sister also."

"Thank you, Mabel." *Thank God she is with me when I need her.*

89

"I want you to start again, Florence. From the very beginning. And this time I'll ask you questions. You won't mind that, will you?"

Mabel's interrogation proved more thorough than either Inspector Towton's or Mr. Bagshot's. She took her time, was persistent without being intimidating, returned several times to answers Florence had given earlier to clarify points that seemed to have become more relevant later. Under her gentle probing Florence found herself recalling more than she could ever have remembered on her own.

"Do you know if she's been buried?" Mabel asked at last.

Florence did not, but suddenly the idea of an unmarked pauper's grave repelled her. If Dorcas had had nothing in life, then she deserved more in death. She said as much to Mabel, wanted to go at once to find out, though she was not sure where to go.

"Somebody from this hotel can find out," Mabel said. "You sit here. I'll see to it. And then we'll have lunch together. You'll feel better for it. Afterwards we'll follow up the matter together." She left, was back five minutes later. "The manager has sent a porter to the police station. An older man, trustworthy I'd guess. He'll find out."

The visit Florence arranged to the *Victory*, Nelson's own flagship, moored proudly as a memorial in the harbour, would have to wait. The hero himself would have agreed that there was a higher priority now.

*

The smell of formaldehyde was not strong enough to mask the yet more ghastly odour in the mortuary. It was warm, foetidly warm, in the corrugated iron shed in the hospital grounds and there were three bodies. That two were male made it unnecessary for the attendants to draw all the covers back but even though Florence had steeled herself for what was to come she had not anticipated the full horror of what was revealed. She choked, thrust into her mouth the folded handkerchief she had guessed she would need, and spun around. Mabel, who had not flinched, but who was also now looking away, took her in her arms and held her.

"Is it her, Florence?"

"It's her. It's Dorcas." Even without the scraps remaining of the red dress she would have been recognisable despite all the indignities that Nature had inflicted on the poor body.

"Can you identify her, ma'am?" The attendant had mercifully drawn the cover again.

"I only know her name. Dorcas Hayward."

Then afterwards an endless round of seeking officials, of waiting in dingy offices, of explaining again and yet again that Florence had encountered Dorcas only twice ever, and that there was no evidence that this had indeed been her name. Only Mabel's quiet but firm support, her unwillingness to be deterred by petty functionaries who found it a burden to do their jobs, sustained Florence through the long, depressing afternoon. The coroner was not available, would not be officially reachable for two days more, but Mabel's persistence elicited his home address and to there they went, to a comfortable house in Southsea.

"This adds nothing concrete to the case, Mrs. Dawlish. It's a common one, by the way, not unusual with this class of women." The coroner had received them with bad grace. "Without confirmation that the name she gave you was real..." He raised his shoulders and shrugged. "I'll see that your information is filed of course, if you'll leave a statement at my office. But even then she'll have to remain recorded as an unknown female."

Florence was on the point of mentioning Rosewood House, then suddenly thought better of it. Whatever information came from there would not interest this official. He clearly regarded his responsibility as discharged and wanted to be rid of these two importunate ladies. Had they been less well dressed they would not have passed his threshold, would not have been granted even this much-begrudged hearing.

I want justice, I want retribution and neither this man nor any of his kind will bring either.

What lay on that slab had once been Dorcas. That was all that mattered for now. Investigation and reckoning must wait. It was more important first to arrange decent burial.

"I want to claim the body," Florence said.

The coroner shrugged again. "It's not in my jurisdiction, ma'am. If you go back to the mortuary they'll tell you what to do. And now, ladies..." He stood up, ushered them to the door.

The pauper's burial had been arranged for the morrow and there was no time to be lost. Offices were closing by now and only judicious offers of half-crowns induced surly caretakers to reveal further home addresses. Florence and Mabel had retained a hansom and they lapsed into depressed silence as it carried them from one house to another to meet refusal at one, bored indifference at another, outright suspicion at a third, unfeigned sympathy at a fourth and at last the necessary signature on a release document. On then to catch an undertaker before bedtime, to offer a premium for quick action and, yes, Florence was prepared to pay for a good coffin, not the most expensive, but respectable, and the plot's location must be far from the pauper's trench in a corner of the cemetery. Nicholas would have no hesitation in approving such expenditure. He was always generous but never ostentatious in his charity.

It was almost midnight when they reached the villa in Albert Grove and both women were exhausted.

"I didn't invite you here for this, Mabel," Florence said. "I wanted it to be a pleasure."

And only then did she begin to weep.

It was good that Mabel was here. A rock.

*

They alone stood by the graveside. The coffin was covered with flowers ordered from that same shop from which Count Livitski's tribute had come and Mabel had insisted on paying for them. The young curate whose presence had been secured at such short notice read the service with a depth of feeling that Florence found moving. She had outlined the circumstances to him and when he spoke of *Our Dear Sister Dorcas* he did so with sincerity. After the coffin had been lowered he asked them to cast some earth on it. It fell with a chilling rattle, a reminder of the unescapable, of shared destiny. A layer of straw was thrown on the casket to deaden the sound and the two gravediggers began to fill. Florence and Mabel stood by until the final slight ridge had been patted in place and they laid the flowers on it. They returned to the villa in silence.

They walked along the Esplanade in the afternoon, all but silent, their conversation forced and quickly dying, and looking out towards the Solent and its island forts and the ships moving there. Florence did not identify the fortification on the Spitbank near where Dorcas's body had been found. By unspoken but mutual consent neither mentioned what had happened. That would come, Florence knew. There would be no visit to *Victory,* no crossing to the Isle of Wight. Mabel told her without being asked that she would be ready to come with her to Rosewood House, and not as a journalist either. If they started early next morning they could get to Chigwell and back within the day.

As they turned for home they heard indistinct shouting. Drawn by it, others were hurrying past and gathering in a knot a hundred yards beyond. As they moved away again, open newspapers in hand, Florence saw that it was a newsboy who was crying out. He was clutching a flapping poster with the words *"Alexandria – Victorious Bombardment"* and this too was what he was calling out. Under his other arm was a sheaf of papers. Florence hurried up herself, plucked a paper from him and pressed payment into his hand. It was a single sheet, a special edition of the *Portsmouth Argus* and it was obviously copying – possibly pirating – material from larger newspapers which had correspondents on the spot.

She took it to a nearby bench, sat and began to scan it. The columns of type were broken into separate sections by bold headings – *Admiral Seymour Triumphant, Fortifications Levelled, Lord Charles Hero of the Hour, Fort Mex Silenced, HMS Invincible lives up to her name, Scenes of Destruction, French nowhere to be seen, Relief of Foreign Community, Dread Power of Modern Cannon, Few British Casualties, White Flags Fly over Egyptian Batteries.* It was obviously a crushing victory and much of the population of Portsmouth must have menfolk who were present. It was no wonder that the newsboy was already sold out and that copies were now passing from hand to hand between strangers.

"Is your husband there, Florence?" Mabel asked, concerned.

Florence shook her head. He must be in Hong Kong by now, the *Leonidas* perhaps already in dry-dock for inspection before her return home.

"Oh, thank God!" Mabel said. "He is safe then!"

But Nicholas would not thank God for this, Florence thought, would regret this lost opportunity to the end of his days. She recognised the names of ships, *Temeraire, Monarch, Penelope,* others she had seen at anchor here or had heard mentioned by Nicholas. The names of officers too. Captain Fisher of the *Inflexible* had apparently distinguished himself. Nicholas had spoken well of him, had known him since he was a boy in China. He had been scarcely older than

Nicholas but he had carried himself there like a hero. He was marked out for great things, and he deserved them, Nicholas said, and yet for all his genuine admiration Florence detected a note of unease. Nicholas had risen almost as quickly in the Navy and, though he would never say it, he must recognise Fisher as a rival. And so too must he regard another officer of his age who had been singled out for praise. Lord Charles Beresford had taken HMS *Condor* in close under the Egyptian guns and had single-handedly silenced a fort. Florence knew of him not just through Nicholas alone. Beresford's social prominence, his friendship with the Prince of Wales, the political career he maintained in parallel with his naval service, all brought him frequent mention in the newspapers. Florence had never heard Nicholas speak ill of him though he had once remarked that Beresford was known as "a sailor in parliament and a politician in the navy." Now, like Fisher, he had become a national hero while Nicholas was occupying himself with calculations of coal consumption and improvements in boiler efficiency.

"And those unfortunate Egyptians," Mabel said. "Benighted as they may be, they must have mothers, wives, children. It's too terrible. It's…"

Florence did not hear her. *It's Nicholas's trade,* she thought, *his life, the focus of all he has wanted since childhood. And without it, what can I be to him, no matter how much he loves me?* She remembered the uncle whom he had told her of, the officer whom consumption had forced to retire young and live out the brief remainder of his days at a spa in the French Pyrenees. Nicholas had spent time there as a boy, had loved that uncle and had inherited his Shropshire farms from him. And he had grieved for this uncle, as he had told her, not just for his early death but for the career that had eluded him. *Don't let it be like this for Nicholas. May I never see him decline into frustrated old age.*

And then suddenly she felt guilty. The memory of that remnant in the mortuary, of the graveside with just two mourners, one who had met the dead girl but twice, the other who had never seen her, was a sudden reproach. Dorcas's life had been short – how long? Sixteen, maybe seventeen years? She could have known no modicum of the happiness that Florence herself had known, would still know, and Nicholas too, even if all he strove for was to crumble to ashes in mid-career. Dorcas might have lived into some unimaginable future, to a barely conceivable 1940 or 1950, to contented old age, to be loved by children and revered by grandchildren. All dashed away, all

94

hope, all modest aspiration, all innocence, all trust, even the face that had had some beauty in it gnawed away by some foul creature of the sea.

A memory flashed of atrocities in Thrace, of blank-eyed women and girls who shrank from any touch, however merciful and kind, of young men who had been outraged just as viciously. And she remembered too the fatal vengeance that Nicholas had allowed to be inflicted on a perpetrator of such outrages, a retribution that he still believed she had not witnessed and which she had never alluded to. She had seen it from a window, looking out over earthworks in which artillery was embedded, and across a river swollen with melting snow, to where justice, brutal and merciless, had been done.

And justice was what she craved now, what Dorcas deserved even in death.

Justice and retribution.

10

Even with an early start it was midday when they reached Chigwell. Time had been lost by the need to travel between railway terminuses in London by underground railway and it had left their hair and clothing smelling of smoke. There was no cab immediately available at the Chigwell station and it was well after one o'clock when they arrived at Rosewood House. Children were playing on the lawn in front and older girls were sitting chatting in the sun. Miss Braben welcomed them, was delighted they had been able to come back, was sorry that they had missed lunch. Something could be easily arranged for them however. They might care to sit with her in an open-sided summerhouse overlooking the lawn and the field beyond – the children had an hour's break at this time and it was good to watch them making best use of the sunshine. Florence had agreed with Mabel that it would be better not to mention Dorcas immediately. The purpose of the visit was ostensibly to be to see how Maisie Webster and her brother and sister were settling in. An older girl was sent to bring them.

Maisie bobbed. The boy would not look them directly in the face. The baby was walking unsteadily and clutching her sister's hand fiercely. All three looked healthier, less pinched and gaunt, than when they had last been seen. Good food and clean surroundings had seen to that, Miss Braben said. They were still sharing a room

"Tell the ladies about Bob, Maisie," Miss Braben said.

"He called me by me name." Smiling. Joy incarnate. "He called me Maisie, ma'am."

"Not once either, was it Maisie?" Miss Braben said. "Several times now."

"Bravo!" Florence said. She felt tears starting to her eyes and knew she must resist the urge to hug the boy and the baby to her. She must not give too much affection, perhaps arouse hopes, if she could not fulfil the promise.

"And I'm sure you like it here, Maisie?" Mabel said.

"Yes, ma'am. And they're teaching me to sew. Real good like. Proper clothes, not just like them ribbons on to hats."

A bell sounded. The break was at an end.

"You must go now, Maisie," Miss Braben said. "Say goodbye to the ladies. And Bob too, and Lucy – can you say goodbye too? Can you wave?"

Maisie bobbed again, held Bob's arm and made him wave, then picked up the baby.

"I'm sure the ladies will come back to see you another time, won't you, ladies? And you'll look forward to that, won't you, Maisie? Now run along!"

Tea and delicately-cut cucumber sandwiches arrived on a silver tray, covered by a crisply- ironed linen cloth. The older girl who brought it set out the porcelain cups and plates and saucers, dispensed napkins, asked for preference of Chinese or Indian, poured tea, added milk, dropped sugar from a silver tongs, offered sandwiches from a three-tiered cake stand. The refreshments had been served with a grace and elegance that would be expected in a luxury hotel.

Miss Braben was regarding the performance with obvious pride. "Thank you, Jenny. That will be all." She waited until the girl was gone before speaking again. "We train the girls for good positions. Not just to be scullery maids or maids of all work. To be proper housemaids from the start, to be placed with the best families."

"It must take a lot of effort to place them well," Mabel said.

I too once waited like that. Florence thought. *Until Agatha made me her lady's maid. Until she lent me books, until I became her paid companion. And then Istanbul and Thrace. That changed everything for ever.*

"We take the greatest care," Miss Braben said. "It's not always easy. It's a great responsibility. But well worth it."

"I hope the girls are grateful," Mabel caught Florence's eye for an instant. Her tone hinted at sternness, that benevolence should only go so far without due acknowledgement. "Given the backgrounds some of these unfortunates come from, I guess the odd one doesn't count her blessings. I've seen as much in the States. Even cases of girls running away. Sad. Very sad."

"There's never been such a case here," Miss Braben said. "We can't create a full family atmosphere but…" she paused, an instant only, but a slight sound had attracted her gaze towards the gate lodge a hundred yards distant. She looked quickly back to Mabel "…we do our utmost to create the next best thing."

A carriage was visible outside the gate. The lodge-keeper had already swung one side open and was busy with the other. Florence glimpsed two black horses.

Miss Braben stood up. "I've a little business to attend to. If you don't mind, ladies, I'll bring you to the parlour and leave you there for ten minutes. I'll be with you directly thereafter."

She ushered them to the front steps – somewhat hurriedly, Florence thought – and at the door handed them over to a supervisor, a Miss Watson, an older, unsmiling woman, whom they had met previously. Three girls were standing behind her and were dressed identically in what looked like a Sunday version of the usual uniform.

"Wait here, girls. I'll be back directly." Miss Watson spoke to the girls. One was Polly, the girl who had seemed so morose when she had been found in her cubicle during the previous visit. She looked no happier now but the other two looked in better spirits, as if anticipating some treat. Miss Watson gestured down the hallway "And if you'll follow me, ladies? The parlour is this way."

Florence glanced back. The carriage – a landau, with its hood raised – was drawing up outside and Miss Braben was advancing to meet it. A fleeting glimpse of white hair indicated an older man inside.

The parlour was at the rear of the house. Its open French windows looked out into a walled garden, flowers close by, fruit trees beyond and a long, glassed hothouse along one wall. Some older girls were working there, broad-brimmed straw hats shading their faces. Several had been chatting pleasantly but they stopped and laughed a little guiltily, and then bent again to their tasks with exaggerated attention as they saw the visitors looking towards them.

"It's not how I imagined an orphanage," Mabel said. They had declined the offer of more tea and had been left alone. The scent of flowers was strong.

"It's not how I imagined it either," Florence said.

Miss Braben joined them five minutes later and apologised for the delay. She was fully at their service now. They might perhaps like to see the vine in the hothouse?

"Was that Mr. Whittier I glimpsed just now?" Florence said. The name mentioned by Agatha had suddenly come back to her. An outside chance, but worth taking. "Mr. Whittier the banker? I met him at a dinner. A friend of Lady Agatha's. Such a kind man."

The slightest flicker of surprise in Miss Braben's eyes. "No, Mrs. Dawlish. Not Mr. Whittier. But another of our benefactors. Sir Herbert Mellish."

"Ah! That must be it! I think he was also present that evening – Lady Agatha mentioned his name – but I didn't speak to him. How silly of me to get the two gentlemen confused."

"We couldn't keep this establishment running without their support." A hint of caution in Miss Braben's voice. "And Lady Agatha's family also. Always so generous."

Hyperion.

A glance, an instant only, between Florence and Mabel.

"I guess that Sir Herbert takes an interest in the running too," Mabel's accent was more American than before, her tone earnest. "It's good to see him turn up like this. Some of our richer men in the States, business barons, captains of industry as we call them, are taking a more active interest in philanthropy than before. I'd be so glad to meet Sir Herbert. I'd value any advice that he might give that I could carry home. I know several ladies who'd like to pass it on to their husbands."

"I'm afraid that won't be possible, Mrs. Bushwick. Not today. I understand that he's in a hurry. He just drops by sometimes if he's in the area." Miss Braben's smile seemed just so slightly forced. "As a hard-headed man of business, even if he has a kind heart, I suspect that Sir Herbert likes to see his money spent wisely." She stood up. "Perhaps you'd like to see the hothouse before you go? We have grapes this year! Could you believe that?" She moved towards the French window.

She wants us gone.

"Maybe we can stay here a little longer?" Florence said. "There's another matter."

Miss Braben's glance flitted from one to the other.

"I understand that there was a girl here called Dorcas Hayward," Florence said

"Yes, Mrs. Dawlish. Dorcas Hayward. She was here until recently. A splendid girl. She had come from another orphanage. I seem to remember that she was a foundling. Such a sad beginning." Miss Braben spoke without hesitation. "But she became the sort of girl we're proud of at Rosewood House. I've been assured that she's doing well since she's been placed. Have you met her, Mrs. Dawlish?"

"And when did she leave Rosewood?" Florence ignored the question. She hoped that her surprise at the mention of assurance was not obvious.

"It would have been in March. I'd have to check the records but I think it was late March, certainly before Easter."

"You said she was placed. Where, Miss Braben?"

Again no hesitation. "In Portsmouth, Mrs. Dawlish. But of course! I think you mentioned before that you lived there yourself. So you met Dorcas there, did you?"

"I met her," Florence said. "Only briefly."

"So you're a friend of her mistress!" Miss Braben's hesitation was a fraction of a second only, but it was unmistakable. "You must know Lady Adelaide! She was so appreciative of Dorcas when she wrote to us. That she had settled in so well, had given such satisfaction."

Florence was suddenly cold, felt her heart thump, flushed with nausea. *Lady Adelaide de Courcey*. The contemptuous words on the day of that dreadful interview. *"Are you sure that she wasn't just some woman of the streets in altercation with her clients?"*

"Are you well, Florence?" Mabel had noticed that she had paled and was already groping for her smelling salts.

"Do you need a glass of water, Mrs. Dawlish?" Miss Braben's solicitude seemed unfeigned.

"Just a little lightheaded. Such a warm day. It's passing. I'm better now."

"You saw her at Lady de Courcey's, Mrs. Dawlish?"

"No, Miss Braben. I'm not acquainted with any Lady Adelaide. I was walking along the Southsea Esplanade one afternoon. About a month ago. I hadn't noticed that I'd dropped a glove until a girl who had picked it up brought it to me. A lovely girl. She told me her name was Dorcas Hayward but she didn't say for whom she worked. I gave her sixpence in thanks."

"And how did Dorcas seem to you, Mrs. Dawlish?" The tone conversational. No hint of doubt or alarm.

"Dead, the second time I saw her."

"That's impossible!" Miss Braben sounded shocked.

"I accompanied Mrs. Dawlish to identify her," Mabel said. "The poor girl had drowned."

"When?"

"Perhaps a week ago, nobody could say for sure. She was buried yesterday. We read in the newspaper about the body being found. It seemed so dreadful that any girl should have a pauper's grave. And Mrs. Dawlish thought it was an act of Christian charity to pay for a decent one – no, Florence, don't be so modest about it. It was a generous impulse and you'll be blessed for it."

"It was the girl I'd met before," Florence dabbed her handkerchief at her eyes. "I'm sure it was the same girl. I'm certain it was Dorcas Hayward."

"It can't be," Miss Braben was emphatic. "Lady Adelaide's letter arrived only yesterday. She was so complimentary. It must have been some other poor girl. Some awful tragedy."

Florence did not know what to say but Mabel did.

"I guess you might be right, Miss Braben. The face was... you'll understand. She was a long time in the water. But, just to put all our minds at rest, could we see Lady Adelaide's letter?"

"Of course, Mrs. Bushwick." No hesitation. "I'll have to ask you to follow me to my office. The records are there."

The office was as well-regulated as everything else at Rosewood House, shelves of ledgers and other files identified and arranged by number, several closed cabinets. Miss Braben's own desk, an in-tray with a few papers on one side, an out-tray with as many more on the other, a spotless blotter pad between, inkwells, several pens on a silver tray, a graceful oil lamp. A horseshoe swivel chair behind, two uprights for visitors before it. A delicate scent of lavender. It was easy to imagine Rosewood House being managed briskly and efficiently from here.

Miss Braben asked them to sit, then opened a cabinet with a key from the bunch on its silver chain. Rows of brown cardboard folders, names on the spines, probably arranged alphabetically since Miss Braben had no hesitation in reaching straight for a single file. She brought it back to the desk, sat down, opened it. Papers within, separated by dividers.

"That girl you saw can't be Dorcas." She was frowning slightly as she hooked a finger under a divider and flipped it over. The first document visible was headed with a crest. She took it out, scanned it, and shook her head slightly. "It's like I said, it can't have been Dorcas. Lady Adelaide dated her letter two days ago." She reached it across to Mabel.

A single sheet, heavy cream paper, creased halfway to fit in its envelope. A crest – Florence had seen it before on a gilt-edged card – at the centre of the letterhead. A single paragraph, handwritten, a signature beneath. Mabel read it in silence, then passed it to Florence without comment.

The address in Portsmouth was the same that Florence remembered with anger and embarrassment. The hand was fluent, elegant even, the script of somebody for whom correspondence was a social courtesy rather than a business need. A half-dozen sentences. Confirmation that the decision to accept a girl from Rosewood House had been a wise one. Dorcas had not just met expectations but had exceeded them. Not just the writer but Mr. Quentin, her butler, whose standards were even more exacting – a hint here of humour and affection – considered Hayward a valuable member of the household, reliable, courteous and ever-cheerful. A compliment about the training Miss Braben had been responsible for. There would be no hesitation in advising friends to accept other girls from Rosewood House in the future. A ten-pound note was being enclosed as a small recognition of the meritorious work done there for the most unfortunate in our midst.

The signature. Confident, a statement of pride. *Adelaide de C.*

Florence's hands trembled and she hardly heard Miss Braben's words.

"You can see that it must have been some other poor girl, Mrs. Dawlish Perhaps somebody who met her and admired her. A girl who might from affection have chosen to use her name. You know how strongly young women can feel for each other at that age."

"I'm sure you're right, ma'am." Mabel's accent yet more strongly American. The impression she wanted to give was clear. *We Yankees are direct people and persistent too. I'm not familiar with all the social niceties here. If I'm giving offence, then it's from ignorance.* "And I guess that Lady de Courcey was mighty impressed when she visited here before."

"Oh, but Her Ladyship has never been here. She heard of us by repute and she contacted us. You'll see ..." Miss Braben riffled further in the file. "Yes, here it is."

The same crested letterhead and as brief as the first. Mabel took it, read it, handed it to Florence. "March 15th," she said.

And the same address, the identical signature. A friend had mentioned Rosewood House to Lady Adelaide, had praised a maid she had secured from there. No mention of the friend's name. There was a vacancy for a housemaid in the de Courcey household. Could the writer's butler, a Mr. Quentin, visit Rosewood House to interview possible candidates? Ideally in the coming week, in view of the demands on domestic staff that entertaining obligations would impose in the coming months.

"I answered by return." Miss Braben was nodding towards the letter. "And I got a reply by return also." She reached across another sheet. Same paper, crest and signature. Mr. Quentin would be at Rosewood House at one o'clock on Tuesday March 21st.

"And he came?"

"I spoke to him only briefly. I was somewhat indisposed that day. But Miss Watson dealt with him. Perhaps you'd like to speak to her?" She did not wait for an answer but reached for a bell-pull to her right. A girl appeared almost instantly and was directed to fetch Miss Watson.

As they waited Miss Braben said, "That other poor girl, the one who drowned, can't have been Dorcas. How terrible! And how dreadful for her parents, never knowing what became of her."

"Probably the old story, I'm afraid," Mabel said. "The old, old story. We're women of the world, Miss Braben. We can guess what was involved. So many girls in the same old trouble, and feeling they have nobody to turn to. And the men, the men responsible..." She held up her hands, as if speechless.

Miss Braben was nodding grim agreement as she put the documents back into the folder and closed it. Florence caught Mabel's briefest nod towards herself, the slightest glint of conspiracy in her eyes. *Watch out.*

A light tap on the door and Miss Watson entered. As Miss Braben looked up towards her Mabel's glance shifted towards the folder on the table, then back to Florence. Again a tiny nod – *it's important, we need it* – and almost imperceptible shake of the head – *not you, I'll do it.* In that instant Florence realised what was wanted from her.

"These ladies have some questions about Dorcas Hayward, Miss Watson," Miss Braben said. "About how she was selected to leave here. I remember that you handled the matter."

"With that gentleman who came for Portsmouth?" Miss Watson's sour expression did not change, did not reflect surprise or curiosity. "Whose mistress wanted him to see five or six girls and choose the best?"

"That gentleman, Miss Watson. Mr. Quentin. Lady de Courcy's butler."

Miss Watson remembered him, elderly, fine manners, a firm but kindly way with the girls. He had seen five in total – she recalled their names – but it was Dorcas who had made the most favourable impression. He would recommend her to his mistress.

"She didn't leave with him?" Mabel asked.

Miss Braben was aghast. "Certainly not, ma'am! It could hardly be seemly. He would not have proposed it and we would not have consented if he had. But he did arrange for Lady de Courcy's housekeeper, a Mrs. Tonge, to come to collect her the following week. And she did."

"And very proper too!" Florence's tone implied disapproval of her American friend's unfamiliarity with decent British standards.

Mabel faced Florence, away from the others. "I think that settles it, my dear, doesn't it? Whoever that girl we saw was she can't have been Dorcas Hayward." Her expression said it all. *Do it! Now!* She pulled her watch from her pocket. "Good heavens! What time it is! We need to be getting back to…"

Florence lurched forward in her chair, her head almost hitting the table before it. She clutched her stomach, groaned, then made a retching noise. She clapped her hand to her mouth and rose, eyes wide in panic of embarrassment as if she was about to vomit. She swayed, dropped back in the chair, struggled to her feet again, jerked as if another spasm hit her.

"Oh Florence, Oh my dear! Not again, Florence!" Mabel had an arm around her to steady her. "Miss Braben! Is there a bathroom? Quickly!"

Florence was retching again, so convincingly that she feared she might indeed vomit. She staggered towards the door and Miss Braben and Miss Watson caught her arms to either side. She made as if her knees were giving away as they brought her out. Down a corridor and past several doors. Her gasped apologies and thanks were cut off by another apparent surge of pain. They reached a door, saw a floor with black and white chequered tiles. Mabel caught up with them.

"It's better I stay with her, Miss Braben," she said. "It'll pass." She dropped her voice as if revealing a secret. "My friend may be in a certain condition. She wasn't sure but this may prove it. I'll look after her." She had charge of Florence now, was pushing her gently into the bathroom, was closing the door behind them and leaving the others outside. She shot the bolt.

And as Florence gasped and retched loud enough to be heard outside Mabel whispered in her ear "I have it."

The professional from the *Columbia Home Gazette* had triumphed.

*

They had asked the cab to return at three-thirty. For fifteen minutes they waited on the front steps in an agony of fear lest the theft be detected. Florence claimed to be much better now, that the fresh air was doing her good. She had had several such bouts recently, mainly in the morning, and the reason might well be a happy one. Mabel kept up a continual stream of questions and observations about the orphanage that kept Miss Braben from going back inside. At last – five minutes late – the cab reappeared at the gate. It seemed an eternity before it drew up before the door and until they were ensconced and on their way again. There would be a train just before four and Mabel promised the driver an extra shilling if they could catch it. Miss Braben's obvious efficiency made it possible that she might check the contents of the folder left on her desk before putting it away. Until they were on the train the possibility of pursuit could not be ignored.

Neither spoke as they bowled along, the horse at a smart trot. They were still a little outside Chigwell and trees and hedges in full summer leaf lined the narrow roadway. Suddenly the cab was slowing, drawing over to the left so that foliage brushed against the side. It moved forward at a slow walk. Florence, alarmed, looked out. A carriage was approaching from the opposite direction, also at a walk, carefully negotiating passage. Two black horses. Behind them was the landau that Miss Braben been identified as Sir Herbert Mellish's. As it edged past Florence saw that the coachman on the box was sitting rigidly, his face wholly expressionless, neither acknowledging the cabby's greeting nor shifting his gaze from some distant point before him. He might have been a waxwork.

And for all that the day was hot, windless and humid, the vehicle's hood was still raised and curtains had been drawn at the sides to close off the interior.

*

The journey back to Portsmouth was a misery. There were others in the train compartments on all stages and so there was no opportunity to talk openly. All that Florence knew was that Mabel had the letter fixing the time for the butler's visit. The fear that the theft had already been detected worried her. She had read of telegraphed warnings streaking ahead of fugitive criminals, of detectives waiting at stations or ports to effect unexpected arrests. She could visualise grim men in long coats and billycock hats waiting by the Liverpool Street station's ticket barrier. That there were none did not ease her fear. They might yet be waiting at Portsmouth.

The enormity of Lady Adelaide's involvement, if such there was, frightened her. It would be essential to meet her, tomorrow perhaps, to determine if the signature was hers – but no, better to talk it through first with Mabel, to tread carefully. The memory of her previous encounter with the admiral's wife frightened her, for the implied threat to Nicholas's career could not have been stronger. If she were now to blunder into a situation that might well have an innocent explanation, then the consequences could only be disastrous. If Nicholas had been here she could have… but no! He wasn't here, would not be for months, and yet the matter could not be let rest. That body in the morgue had been Dorcas's, she was sure of it. There must be justice.

No police awaited them at the Portsmouth barrier – Florence had had a frightening vision of Inspector Towton's mock civility as

105

he led her off to share a cell with Janey and Tilda. Relief now flooded through her as she walked towards the standing row of cabs for hire.

"Just a moment, Florence," Mabel gestured towards the W.H. Smith newsstand. "We need something here."

She bought a packet of brown manila envelopes. Before they reached the cabs she said, "You told me you had an attorney here who'd helped you, Florence. Do you trust him?"

"My solicitor, you mean? Mr. Bagshot? Yes, I trust him."

They drove home by his house. The evening's light was fading and he had not yet gone to bed. He took charge of the sealed envelope – there were documents inside about her husband's farms in Shropshire, Florence said – and he would lodge it in his personal safe this very evening. And the unexpected visit of Mrs. Dawlish and her charming companion was no imposition, was indeed a pleasure.

Albert Grove at last, and the villa with its promise of rest and privacy, of opportunity at last to pour out and discuss all that had happened this day and what must now happen.

Susan opened the door. She looked excited.

"There's a telegram for you, ma'am. It came this morning after you'd left."

Florence shuddered as she took it. Telegrams were seldom good news. *Oh God! Not Nicholas!* She tore it open, scanned the pasted strips.

FOR GOD'S SAKE COME AT ONCE STOP PICCADILLY STOP ROOM BKD CHARING X. STOP I NEED YOU FLORENCE.STOP.

And at the end the sender's name.
AGATHA.

11

They travelled up to London together, silence again imposed by the presence of other passengers. They had discussed the Lady Adelaide letter only briefly over breakfast but in the light of Agatha's telegraphed cry for help it was obvious that any approach to her must be deferred.

"I've no doubt you can manage on your own," Mabel said, "but it's better if I go with you when you face that woman. She sounds like a termagant. I'll join you as soon as I can, as soon as this other matter of yours is sorted out."

It's not my matter, it's Agatha's, Florence wanted to say. *But I owe her so much, I can't refuse her, whatever it is.* Instead she said, "I'd value that, Mabel."

Mabel was returning to her lodgings near Russell Square. She had some writing to do and appointments in connection with her Dollar Princess articles would involve travel to the provinces in the coming week. She would forward her contact details to Florence by post.

They parted at Charing Cross station. At the hotel there Florence found that what was booked for her was a small suite rather than a room and more opulent than she could afford. She was about to go back to reception to request a move to more modest accommodation when she saw the envelope addressed to her on the writing desk. A note inside from Agatha. Not to be offended that all costs would be covered. A week's accommodation had been paid for in advance. But come quickly. For God's sake.

She had dreaded what she must now do, and that dread – too embarrassing to admit to Mabel – had grown worse each minute since she had left Portsmouth. She had hoped and prayed that this day would never have to come. She had vowed that she would never enter the Piccadilly mansion in which she had once been a maid, where her father and brother were still servants. There, for all Agatha's friendship and present regard of her as an equal, the glances of those she had once worked with would challenge her present status as a lady and imply that it was a sham. Only Agatha's plea could have brought her to do it.

I survived Thrace, she told herself. *I came through New Haven too, and Santiago, and that hell at Boquerón. This is nothing by comparison.*

But it was, as a hansom whirled her up Pall Mall and St. James's Street and along the edge of Green Park, lush and shady in the summer sunlight, and her heart was pounding, and the nausea she had feigned yesterday threatened to be real today. The gates of the semi-circular driveway were open – one in, one out – and on the pavement to either side several men who seemed to have been standing there in boredom came to sudden life as the cab swung in.

"Any news about him, ma'am?" one shouted and she realised that they must be journalists.

She turned her face away, wishing that she had worn a hat with a veil, but even as she did a voice rang out. "Hey! Mrs. Dawlish! What can you tell us? The people have a right to know!" She caught a glimpse of a young consumptive-looking man with round steel-rimmed spectacles, who seemed familiar. She had seen him before and – Yes! – she was sure he had been in the outer office of the *St. James Fortnightly*. Whatever was afoot, Walter Staveley's journal was interested in it.

The cab pulled into the driveway and halted before the Kegworth mansion's steps. Her knees were weak as she dismounted and reached payment up to the cabby. Behind her somebody was shouting "It can't be covered up forever!" as the great front door swung open.

She recognised the footman who ushered her in – she had known him as a page, Tommy Hopkin, but now he was a tall and handsome man with an impassive face – and hurrying from behind was a man whom she had once, and maybe still, respected and feared. As butler, Mr. Pollock, had had a dignity – and, for the servants, a power – greater than Lord Kegworth himself. His face was a mask and he said, "Lady Agatha is expecting you, Mrs. Dawlish. I'm to bring you to her directly."

She thanked him just as formally, then followed him through the hall, past the wide staircase, along a short corridor that she had so often swept and towards what she knew was Agatha's study. Just before the door Mr. Pollock stopped and when he turned to her he was smiling.

"You're so welcome here, Mrs. Dawlish. Not just for Lady Agatha, not just for her father. For all of us. We're proud of you, Mrs. Dawlish, so proud of you."

She felt tears rushing to her eyes even as the door was thrown open. Agatha had obviously heard the voices and she all but pulled Florence inside. She had obviously been weeping, for her face was swollen and tear-streaked, and her red-rimmed eyes told of a sleepless night.

"I don't know what we're going to do, Florence. I really don't" She seemed half distraught as she lifted piled books off a chair and laid them on the floor. The study was as untidy as it had always been – it was when Agatha had found Florence leafing through a book here one day when she should have been cleaning that their friendship, and Florence's transformation, had begun. On the desk was a silver-framed photograph, one taken in an Istanbul studio four years before. She herself and Agatha stood on either side of a gaunt Nicholas whose Ottoman uniform hung so loosely on him, still recovering from the fever they had saved him from as he had lain delirious in the bed of a jolting wagon on that nightmare retreat across Thrace. She had a copy of the photograph herself but she was touched and surprised to see one here.

Agatha eased her bulk into her swivel chair and suddenly began to sob. "It can't be any worse, Florence. We're at our wits' end, Father and I. And it will kill Mother, I know it will. And you're the only one I can turn to, Florence. You're so practical and I know I'm not."

Florence went to her and embraced her, herself overcome with emotion. That this clever and indomitable woman had faced Bashi Bazooks with fortitude made this collapse all the more moving. "There, Agatha," she said. "There, there. We'll handle this together." *Whatever it is.*

Agatha at last shook free and reached for a bell pull. "I should have offered you something, Florence. Tea, coffee, lunch, whatever you want. You've come so far, and so quickly…"

"Later, Agatha. Just now tell me what has happened. Tell me slowly. All you know." Florence settled back in her chair and remembered how expertly Mabel had jogged her own memory. Patience was the key.

"Oswald. Two nights ago," Agatha was forcing herself to speak calmly. "He came here about ten o'clock. He was bleeding. His poor face was cut and he could hardly walk. He collapsed in the hallway and Pollock fetched Father and me directly."

"Had he been robbed?"

Agatha shook her head violently. "It would have been better if he had been. He'd been beaten. Beaten with a horsewhip."

"Where did this happen?" Florence was aghast. Not just pain. A horsewhip implied contempt, degradation, humiliation.

"At his club. On the steps outside as he was leaving. Oh poor Oswald, poor, poor Oswald." Agatha was sobbing again.

Florence felt anger, no matter how much she might dislike the man. He was not somebody who could easily defend himself physically. "Who could do such a cowardly thing?"

"Chester Brewster."

The name fell like a thunderbolt and yet it was instantly easy to imagine that arrogant, insolent lout setting about a weaker man.

"He knocked him down, Florence, he thrashed him without mercy. The doorman came out to stop him and he got beaten badly himself. Chester was gone when Oswald's friends came out and found him. Two of them brought him here."

"What did the police do?"

"He didn't want the police involved. Because of... because of the shame of it."

"Does Miss Brewster know?"

"She's gone. A note was delivered from her brother yesterday morning. From that Chester. Father would not let me see it. There were words in it that no lady should see, he said. Words a lady would not understand. But Chester said that he was taking his sister back to America immediately. That the wedding was off and that..." she began to weep again. "That it wouldn't stop here. That he'd see to it that everybody in London would know what Oswald was. That no decent man would shake his hand."

Florence was trembling herself now. *Gilpin's warning*. Whatever was involved it would mean scandal, ostracism, a reputation besmirched, rumour and suspicion that could never be lived down. A half-century before men had fought duels and killed each other over lesser insults. Even Oswald would have preferred to sight along a pistol barrel at dawn in some chilly meadow rather than face this.

"Is Oswald here now, Agatha?"

"He's not here, and not at his chambers either – Pollock sent somebody to check. We don't know where he is. He wouldn't let Father send for a doctor. He wanted to be gone. And about midnight – he was still bleeding – a friend came and took him away."

"Which friend?"

"We're not sure. It was a private carriage and the man didn't come out and Oswald insisted that we stay inside. But Pollock, and Hopkin, that young footman, they thought it could be Lord Arthur Kidderminster. They think they recognised the coach. Or perhaps a Mr. Billing, a Mr. Hesketh Billing. They've both been at receptions here though I can't remember them. So many guests come here."

"Those people outside now, Agatha – you've seen them? They're reporters. One's from the *St. James Fortnightly*. How do they know about Oswald?"

"There's worse." A deadness now in Agatha's voice that was sadder than any tears. "Three policemen came just after Oswald left. One was in uniform but the others were detectives. I went with Papa to meet them – Mamma was too distraught. We thought they'd come about the beating but..." She began to cry again in great, shuddering sobs.

"But what, Agatha?"

"They wanted to arrest Oswald, Florence. They had a warrant, they said. They handed it to Papa and when he read it he got weak and I had to help him sit down. But he wouldn't let me read what it said and he told me to go. He was starting to weep. He said that men got sentenced to hard labour if they were caught for... for this sort of offence. I wanted to bring him brandy but he wouldn't hear of it. And one of the detectives also said that it was better that I shouldn't see it, that I shouldn't stay. That it was nothing for a lady to hear."

"Did they talk to anybody else?"

"To Pollock and to Hopkin. They asked them if they'd known where Oswald had gone. And Pollock told me that neither he nor Hopkin said anything about whom he might have left with."

Florence was not surprised. The Kegworths had always been good employers. It was time now to display loyalty.

"One of the detectives told Pollock that the ports were being watched," Agatha said. "That it would be better if Oswald was to give himself up. That they'd find him sooner or later."

"Where are your parents now, Agatha?"

"Papa insisted that my mother go to the Northamptonshire house. She went with her maid yesterday. They took the train. Your brother went with them as an escort."

Jack would be well capable of seeing off any importunate reporters, Florence knew. That Agatha had referred so casually to her brother as a Kegworth retainer, without her usual sensitivity to Florence's feelings, was a measure of just how distraught she must be.

"And then Papa – you know his heart isn't good, don't you?" Agatha rushed on. "He had such palpitations when he saw the journalists outside that I feared apoplexy. I sent for the doctor. He's been put to bed and he's been given medicine to calm him. But I do so worry about him."

Florence saw that it was on Agatha alone that the family burden had fallen. Her brothers would be of no help. Cedric, the Oxford don, focussed on his mathematics to the exclusion of all else, would be useless. Godwin might have known better what to do – he had some personal experience of police attention – but he was in Australia. The eldest son of the half-dozen children his barmaid wife had given him might now look forward with confidence to future inheritance of the Kegworth title.

"Have the police been back, Agatha?"

They had been, on three separate occasions. They had spoken to each servant individually. Lord Kegworth's indisposition had saved him from questioning but Agatha had not escaped.

"They kept asking me about Oswald's friends," she said. "They mentioned the gentlemen we thought he might have gone with and others besides. The names meant nothing to me."

The warning that Oswald had never received began to have some significance now.

"Did they mention the name Gilpin, Agatha? Remember – that naval lieutenant I told you about. The young man who died tragically."

"No. They'd didn't mention that name." The answer came too quickly.

"Did they say anything about that training ship, the *Brahmaputra*?"

Agatha shook her head. Too violently.

"Or about Cleveland Street, Agatha?"

Another shake of the head and then, in mute misery, a reluctant nod.

"Did they say why they were asking about those places?"

"They didn't say. But there was something terrible about the way they asked their questions. A coldness, no sympathy."

It's worse than I ever feared, Florence thought. She remembered the refugee boys she had helped treat in Thrace, as foully abused as the women. And Nicholas had once mentioned that certain things sometimes happened in the Navy, behaviour he hinted at but was unwilling to talk about in detail, activities that were always punished with great severity. And the more senior the person convicted, the greater that severity. Nicholas had said too that in civilian life the penalties were no less draconian. *Now I'm as reluctant to talk about it as Nicholas had been.*

"What am I going to do, Florence?"

I want no part of this. And what could I do anyway?

"Florence. For God's sake Florence, you're the only one I can rely on."

Rely on for what?

And the small internal voice answered. *Anything. She's your sister. Anything.*

"We're going to find your brother, Agatha," Florence said. "And only when we've found him will we know what to do next."

If the police and the newspaper reporters had not yet found him she would have little chance herself.

But she would try.

*

The police enquiries could only be spreading and the half of the London that mattered must know it already – Oswald's superiors and colleagues at the Foreign Office, probably the Secretary of State, possibly even the Prime Minister himself. Lord Kegworth was himself a well-known political figure in the Tory opposition to the Liberal government and there were many who would take ill-natured delight in the disgrace of his son. They had done so when Godwin's misdemeanours had caused so much embarrassment before he was shipped off to Australia. But this was worse, far worse. And somebody had alerted the press – some informant within the police no doubt – and already the *St. James Fortnightly* was on the scent. Walter Staveley's preoccupation with abuses by the wealthy, powerful and titled would guarantee that there would be no let-up.

Florence did not know where to start and she longed to have somebody to confide in, somebody not personally involved as Agatha was. Mabel would be ideal – they had acted together so conspiratorially, so successfully, at Rosewood House the previous day and ...

A truth hit her.

Mabel could not be neutral in this. The collapse of Oswald's engagement to Rebecca Brewster, the cancellation of the wedding of the season between an English earl's son and the daughter of an American millionaire, the drama of Oswald's horsewhipping and his subsequent disappearance, all made a story a journalist might dream of. The series of articles Mabel had come to Britain to write about Dollar Princesses would now have an appeal far beyond the pages of the *Columbia Home Gazette*. The scandal would be a goldmine and she could not be blamed if she were to exploit it.

There could be no support from Mabel, no contact even.

Florence could only rely upon herself.

*

It felt strange to pass through the house she had once helped clean, where she had once feared the slightest frown from Mr. Pollock, where she had stepped back and bobbed respectfully at the sight of her employer and his wife, where she had felt guilt when Agatha had first discovered her with a book. It was now to her that girls who had not been here then bobbed as Mr. Pollock led her through the kitchen – where the cook, older now, beamed at her arrival and addressed her as ma'am – and out into the mews at the rear.

Her father's back was turned and he was finding fault with the gleaming brass of a carriage lamp that a hapless young groom had polished inadequately. He must have recognised her step and his face showed mixed delight and concern when he turned to her. They embraced.

"It's about Master Oswald's trouble, isn't it, Florrie?" He knew that she had vowed never to enter this house. "We'd better talk in my rooms."

"I'll have tea brought up," Mr. Pollock said, then left them.

Her father's accommodation above the coach-house was spacious and comfortable, his home in the periods the Kegworths were in London. Florence's mother always remained at the Northamptonshire estate and never joined him here,

It was a terrible thing for the family, he said. His heart went out to His Lordship, even more to his wife. The whole household felt the same. There must have been some mistake. And beyond that he could tell her little more than Agatha had. He had not seen Oswald arrive or depart.

"But them reporters," he said. "They was here at crack of dawn. God knows how they got to hear of it so soon. One even got into the mews and offered Jeb Thomas – one of the grooms, young, you wouldn't remember him – ten bob if he'd anything to tell about Master Oswald. A good lad too, Jeb is, came straight to me and I saw that this reporter chap was seen off an' told not to come back or he'd know what for."

114

Florence was not surprised. It must be common for policemen to be remunerated for alerting journalists. But it was unlikely that the assault at the club was unconnected with the police visit, even though it had occurred before it. Either somebody in the police had contacted Chester Brewster, or he had contacted them.

Cleveland Street. Brahmaputra.

"Father…" Florence hesitated, embarrassed by what she knew she could not avoid saying. "Father, I'm a married woman. There are things I know about which I'd never have mentioned to you when I was little, but…"

He was reddening with discomfort. "It would be better, Florrie, if you was to talk to your mother about …"

She shook her head. "Nothing like that, Father. It's about Master Oswald."

"What about Master Oswald, Florrie?" He looked away from her.

She remembered the tone from childhood. *End of discussion, nothing more to be said.* But she was no longer a child.

"When I was small I used to hear jokes about Oswald, Father. And that there'd been some trouble one time with a stable boy. I remember that you boxed Jack's ears one time when he repeated something he'd heard."

"It was all sorted out." Obvious irritation at the persistent questioning. "Me and Pollock went to see His Lordship about that matter. He was good enough to hear us out. He said he'd talk to Master Oswald, and that it wouldn't happen again. And it didn't. That was the end of it."

A maid arrived with tea. Her father might often have it brought to him by less senior servants but Florence guessed that this time the silver tray and white cloth and bone china were for her benefit.

After the girl had left, Florence said, "Have you heard of anything like that in recent years? Since he came back from America perhaps? Anything that Miss Brewster's brother might have got to hear of? Anything about…" she hesitated, "…anything about young men?"

"I don't listen to no rumours, Florrie. Never have, never will, and me and your mother raised you to do the same."

And the moment came that she suspected would come to every adult. That she indeed knew better than either of her parents.

"I don't like him, Dad. I know you don't either, nobody does, maybe not even his mother and his father, nobody except Agatha. But the family's always been good to us and I want to help – and I know that you do too, and Mr. Pollock and all the rest here do as well – but I can't help until I've seen him, until I know what's going on. So I've got to find him."

He nodded. She sensed something of relief.

"I heard the names of two friends of his," she said. "One of them might have taken him from here last night. A Mr. Billing. Or a Lord Arthur Kidderminster. They'd dined here at some time." She paused, was unsure how to phrase it. "Are they a certain sort of men?"

Blushing, he said. "Yes, Florrie. They might be."

"Are there any others like that you might have heard of? Come on, Dad, Mr. Pollock would know and you and he have always been thick as thieves. He'd have told you."

And within thirty minutes she not only had half-a-dozen names but had also found their addresses in the copy of the *Kelly's Handbook* in Mr. Pollock's care.

Time to start the search.

*

At four o'clock a page was sent out on to Piccadilly and he ignored the reporters' badgering as he hailed a cab, a growler. It swung in before the mansion. A housemaid of Florence's size and build and clad in her dress and hat, but now with one of Agatha's veils shielding her face, boarded. A trunk was loaded, one large enough to carry the clothing and necessities a gentleman might need for a long journey. As the vehicle rattled away several of the waiting reporters rushed out and hailed cabs themselves. Watching through a chink in curtains on an upper floor Florence noted with satisfaction that the man from the *St. James Fortnightly* was among them. When he reached Euston Station and saw the girl board the train there for Northampton he might realise he had been on a wild goose chase. But maybe not. At best he might suspect that Oswald had gone to ground at the Kegworth country seat. He might even follow the girl there.

It didn't matter. Now wearing the same maid's own cheap but respectable walking-out dress, Florence could slip out unseen through the mews to walk back to the hotel by a circuitous route.

Nicholas, she thought, could not have handled it better.

12

It was too late after she had got back to the hotel, and had changed there, to go far that evening. But one address, one of a name on the list that her father had given her, was close by. Its location had obvious significance.

When she emerged from the hotel it seemed as if every eye on its forecourt was turned to her but she composed herself walked some distance up the Strand before hailing a closed cab. Agatha had pressed twenty sovereigns on her – "For expenses, dear, and don't you argue!" – and the luxury could be afforded. The vehicle deposited her outside the Central London Sick Asylum in Cleveland Street and she hoped that she made herself look suitably sad as she paid the cabby. She scanned the street – no sign of another cab, no indication of being followed. Had she any suspicion of it she would have gone inside the building on the pretext of making a donation. She remembered the house-numbering and walked southwards.

It was as she had guessed. The Hon. Gabriel Foster's residence was in the Cleveland Residences, the block of four-storey red-brick apartments across the street from the Middlesex Hospital. She pulled the bell and the door was opened by an elderly one-armed man in a commissionaire's uniform. There were two campaign medals on his chest. She asked if Mr. Foster was at home.

"Who might you be, ma'am?" Both tone and question were disrespectful.

"I'm Mr. Foster's cousin, from Taunton." She had prepared herself for this. "I'm just briefly in London, on my way to Scotland and…"

"Wrote ahead, did you, ma'am?"

"Yes," Florence said. "But I couldn't be sure about…"

"There ain't been no letter come here for a month," he said. "I'd ha' seen it if it had. And I'd ha' forwarded it to him."

"Mr. Foster isn't here then?"

He ignored the question but she sensed sympathy when he spoke. "You've got a son, ma'am? Is that it?"

She shook her head. "I've no children. But I'd like to know where Mr. Foster is."

Sympathy faded. Caution replaced it. "He's in France, ma'am, been there since April, and he don't want nobody to know his address there. He likes to be private-like." He made to close the door. As his hand rose Florence pushed a shilling into it.

"Are any of his friends staying here?" she said.

"Two bob, ma'am."

It was humiliating to stand on the doorstep, rummaging in her purse to find more coins. She felt polluted as she passed them to him.

"There ain't nobody here, ma'am. It's been shut up."

She reached over and touched one of his medals, a round one with the Queen's head at the centre and hanging from a red and white ribbon. "On your honour as an old soldier?"

"On my honour, ma'am." Her question had clearly embarrassed him.

"There's another shilling if you let me see his rooms."

And, as he had said, the apartment had indeed been shut up. It was airless, the curtains closed, the carpets rolled up. The dust sheets prevented closer examination of the furniture but Florence sensed elegance. The large painting on one wall – two naked boys beside the ruins of a Greek temple – might have been a copy of some master's work that she did not recognise, but it was in genuine oils.

As they went out she nodded towards the empty sleeve pinned just below the medals. "Where did it happen?"

"At Magdala, ma'am. In '68"

She gave him two shillings.

*

Florence had four different newspapers sent up to her room with a breakfast tray. Three had short items about a fracas on the steps of a club – not named, but clues enough for the knowing to identify it. The victim was the son of a noble lord and himself held a responsible post in the Foreign Office. The perpetrator was rumoured to have been the brother of the victim's affianced bride, a young American lady, but it was understood that the engagement had been broken off. The victim's whereabouts were unknown but it was understood that the police wished to speak to him on another matter. One of the papers – a bastion of the Liberal Party – was unctuous in its mention of widespread sympathy for the victim's father, an ornament of the Upper House and well respected in political, commercial and philanthropic circles. No names mentioned, but no names needed to be. There were leads enough for political and fashionable London to identify the parties. Only the *Morning Post*, Tory in sympathy, and probably reluctant to report anything embarrassing about a pillar of the party, carried nothing. The *St. James Fortnightly* would not appear until the following week, but that could be to its advantage – there could be more, much more, to report by then.

There was worse in the personal columns of all four papers, announcements in the names of Mr. and Mrs. Hiram Brewster of St. Louis that the forthcoming marriage between their daughter Rebecca and Lord Oswald Kegworth would not now take place. Nothing more. There were probably similar announcements in another half-dozen newspapers.

Mr. Hesketh Billing's address was in another block of gentleman's chambers, this one in South Kensington, a more imposing edifice than that in Cleveland Street. Following her experience on the previous evening Florence had filled her purse with shillings at the hotel, but in the event the commissionaire needed no inducement to bring her to Mr. Billing's door. And there she found disappointment. Mr. Billing had left for the Continent on the previous morning. His final destination was not yet settled but he would be providing notification on arrival so that mail could be forwarded. Mr. Billing had travelled alone and no, none of his friends had lodged here the previous night. The manservant who had been left in charge had a smug assurance about him that indicated that he was telling the truth. *Doubt me if you like, madam, but it won't help you.*

One of the strongest leads had brought her nowhere. Now for the next.

The residence in Ralston Street, in Chelsea, was an impressive four-storey redbrick terraced house with a basement area to the right of the front steps that seemed large for a single occupant. *Kelly's Handbook* had however indicated that Lord Arthur Kidderminster was the sole resident. Sole, Florence thought, except for the six or seven servants who would sleep in cramped rooms on the low-ceilinged top floor and the scullery maid who probably had a pallet in the kitchen. She knocked and the door was opened by a young footman. And yes, Lord Arthur was at home. And no, she wouldn't state her business. She handed the man her card. She must see his master and that was all she would say.

She was not ushered into a parlour to wait but was left instead on an upright chair in the long, tiled hallway. There was elegance here – and more, luxury – not just in the furniture and the still-life paintings on the wall, but in the scent of the three separate arrangements of hothouse flowers on low table against the walls. The Albert Grove villa was a hovel by comparison.

Lord Arthur was perhaps only her own age, but he was already balding and he had a pallor that indicated little time spent outside. He was sweating profusely and though it was almost midday he was enveloped in a silk dressing gown and his bare feet were thrust into slippers. He apologised for his appearance, said that he was a little indisposed and hoped Mrs. Dawlish would pardon him. He begged forgiveness for her being left in the hallway but renovations were in progress in other rooms. He was sure she would understand. How could he be of assistance?

And all the while Florence saw that he was frightened, the brow wet, the slightest tremor in the voice, the ingratiating tone. He knew something. *Time for the direct approach.*

"I've come here to speak to Lord Oswald," she said.

A second, two seconds. Terror in his eyes. Florence feared that he might faint. "I don't know... I'm..." He collected himself. "Who are you? Why do you want to see him?"

"I'm his sister's friend. He knows me and I know him for twenty years or more. He may not believe it, but I'm here to help him if I can."

She knew for certain that he was lying when he said, "Is there some sort of trouble?" and failed to look innocent.

"I'm asking you again to let me see him."

"He's not here. If he was here I'd tell you, Mrs. Dawlish." The words came in a rush. "I assure you that he isn't here. And I haven't seen him for at least a month. Maybe longer."

Oswald's here right now, he's hiding in some upstairs room and he must be desperate. This man is just as frightened. He doesn't know what to do and he's got no good reason to trust me. And pressing him will make him more cautious still.

Lord Arthur was not looking her in the eye now and he edging towards the door. "I hope you'll find him, Mrs. Dawlish and now…"

She ignored him and moved to a semi-circular table bearing a vase of flowers. From her reticule she took out a silver pencil and another of her cards. On the back she wrote five words. *Istanbul. Basilica Cistern. East Egg.* Places where she and Oswald had once been at the same time, even if not always amicably. Proof of her identity. She handed it to Lord Arthur. "If you should perhaps see Oswald then please give him this. Tell him I'm here not just to help him, but to help his family too. For his parents' sake. For his sister's."

He took the card and thrust it into a pocket.

She moved to the door, paused there. "I'll call back in an hour," she said. "You might have some news for me then."

He was starting to protest but she ignored him and let herself out.

*

The day was uncomfortably warm. The certainty that Oswald must be near had increased her fear of being followed but Florence resisted the urge to look back as she walked. She had been in this area once before, though she did not know it well, but she recognised the Royal Hospital as she walked past for she had visited it with Nicholas. On benches in its grounds she saw the bright scarlet tunics of the army pensioners living there, some bent, some white-bearded, some still retaining with pride their soldierly erectness. She had heard that there were still a few who had been at Waterloo and wondered if some of them were among those dozing in the sun. They had known what seemed now like another world, one without steam-ships or telegraphs or railways or anaesthetics, one impossibly different, and she wondered if the reality of her present world might seem equally strange if she were to reach such an age herself.

She walked on and, though she hesitated to ask anybody for directions lest she draw attention to herself, found herself at last in Sloane Square. A tea-shop there offered respite and time to scan later editions of the newspapers which she had read earlier in the day. It was a good sign at least that the articles she sought had not been updated. As she sat there the enormity of what she was doing began to oppress her. She knew the expression *"accessory after the fact"* from newspaper accounts of criminal trials but she was vague as to the exact legal meaning. But now, depending on what Oswald was wanted for by the police, the term might be applied to her present actions. She knew the penalties could be serious – she had fleeting visions of herself in a sacking apron and scrubbing stone floors in prison corridors under the baleful gaze of grim-faced matrons. Worse still, what might befall her would destroy Nicholas's career also. And all the worse since he had never liked Oswald.

But I owe everything I have to Agatha, even Nicholas himself, for I would never have met him without her. I'm the only one she can rely on at this moment and I cannot fail her. Risks must be taken.

When she returned to Ralston Street the door swung open with her first knock, as if the footman had been waiting there for her. She stepped in and it closed quickly behind her.

"Lord Arthur…" she began.

"Begging your pardon, he left this for you, ma'am"

An envelope, sealed with a wax straggle that indicated haste.

"I want to speak to Lord Arthur personally."

"He's left, ma'am. Ten minutes ago, you just missed him."

"When is he coming back?"

"He didn't say, ma'am."

She was ready for something like this. She pressed a shilling into his palm.

"I don't think he'll be back for a while, ma'am. He packed a bag himself, hurried like, didn't want no help. Took just the one bag with him."

"Where has he gone?"

"Don't know, ma'am. But maybe one of them foreign places he likes."

She turned away from him and ripped the envelope open. A single sheet of paper. An address. No signature.

"Has somebody from here been to Redburn Street today?" she asked.

He coloured, then shook his head. Not a shilling this time, a half-crown.

"Sally. The scullery maid."

"She went there after I had left?"

He nodded.

A wise choice. A poor little slavey would attract no attention as she went to and fro.

"And Lord Arthur left after she came back? She had some message for him?"

Another nod. He obviously wished her to be gone but he gave her directions nonetheless. Not far, two or three minutes' walk

The house in Redburn Street was only slightly smaller, but here also she was invited hurriedly inside, clearly expected. She was asked to wait in a parlour. Again the sense of opulence, of luxury, the air heavy with the scent of several vases of lilies. Her heart was thumping. Now that her search had almost certainly been successful she was unsure what she must say.

Oswald looked worse than she could ever have imagined, not just the swollen face and the two black eyes but the obvious pain with which he moved. Normally plump, he seemed already withered inside clothes too large for him. When he saw her he said, "Thank God" and then he began to weep. He held his hand – it too was swollen and livid - across his face and he started to sob.

Pity overcame her. She took his elbow, guided him to a chair, helped him sit down – the effort brought a sharp intake of agonised breath. "Thank God we've found you, Oswald," she said. She had never used his name before but it felt right to do so now. He took her hand and pressed it to his cheek. She felt it wet with tears but did not remove it.

"Agatha is concerned for you," she said at last. "Your parents also." She paused, then said what she could never have imagined herself saying even a day before. "I too." In the face of such misery two decades of resentment counted for nothing.

He was calming now and trying to thank her. She broke free and sat down opposite him.

"Whose house is this?" she asked.

"A friend's. He's not here now. He's left already."

The packet-ferries to France must be thronged with his friends, she thought.

"What happened, Oswald? Why do the police want to arrest you?"

He shook his head, would not look at her.

"If we don't know, we can't help you."

Silence.

"Is it some sort of mistake?"

When he finally spoke he would not meet her gaze. "It wasn't anything bad. But people – most people – don't understand that. They can't imagine what it's like…" His voice trailed off.

"Is it to do with Cleveland Street?"

He started, looked up. "Who told you about Cleveland Street?"

"And about the *Brahmaputra* too, Oswald?" She tried to mix severity as well as sympathy in her tone. "About…" she paused, then knew the word was inevitable "…boys."

No denial, but he seemed to slump into yet greater wretchedness. "How do you know, Florence?" He too was using a Christian name for the first time.

She told him of Gilpin's visit, of his despair. She tried to avoid mentioning that Agatha had been unwilling to pass it on but he pressed her. He groaned when she admitted it. "It was for the best," she said. "She would never think anything bad of you." Even as she spoke she knew that her words were ill chosen.

"It isn't bad," he said. "It's not a weakness. It's just the way that some fellows are. Decent fellows, most of them. People never understand." His tears were welling again, were running down his cheeks. "Gilpin was a good man. He was well thought-of and brave – your husband will tell you that. He'd have gone high in the Navy if … if it hadn't turned out as it did."

"How did you know Gilpin?" It didn't seem a likely acquaintance. Florence remembered Nicholas's resentment of slighting remarks Oswald had made about naval officers when they'd been at that house in East Egg.

"We met in Cleveland Street. There's a house there that… a house that many men go to. Well-connected men too. Names you'd never suspect. That's why it was safe."

All she had seen there made sense now. She felt distaste but there could be no holding back. "Telegraph boys?" she said.

He looked away again, then nodded. "They were all willing," he said. "Most of them liked it. All of them liked the money. Nobody got hurt. Not there."

"But one of them must have been pressing Gilpin," Florence said. "Could he have been made to pay somebody to stop them talking? Maybe one of those boys?"

"We didn't know. If we had, then some of us could have helped him – we support each other. Gilpin didn't have much money. A good family but he was a third son. When we heard about what happened, we knew it wasn't an accident. We hoped it would end there, that he was the only one being threatened. And some of the others who go there… No, you don't need to know the names."

"But somebody told Chester Brewster about that place in Cleveland Street?" She could see from his misery that he had passed some boundary of self-imposed secrecy, that it was a relief now to confide. "Somebody you didn't want to pay yourself?"

He shook his head. "They didn't want money. If it was, I'd have paid."

"Was it something to do with the *Brahmaputra*, Oswald? You're on its board of directors, aren't you?"

"Yes." The word scarcely audible.

"Did you and your friends use it to meet boys?" She did not want to think about it but knew she could not hold back now.

Silence. Guilt. Shame. He seemed even more shrunken now inside his clothes.

"We need to know what happened, Oswald. We can't help you otherwise."

"You still want to help me, Florence? Even after I tell you this?" Surprise and gratitude and pleading in his tone.

"If I can." She knew that Nicholas would have told her to be gone from here by now but she could not resist this misery, this collapse.

"It was going on before I came back from America. Some of the other *Brahmaputra* directors used to bring boys to London to see the sights. It… it wasn't badly meant. Most of the boys liked it. They were glad to come again. Sometimes here, at this house. Sometimes at Billing's. They were given presents. They were mostly orphans, you know. Nobody had ever given them anything before and they were grateful. And they were never hurt."

He had mentioned *hurt* before, had been eager to emphasise it then also.

"But somebody did get hurt, Oswald, didn't they?"

Silence, eyes closed, his face a mask of misery and despair. There must be more than *hurt*. Much more.

"Was somebody killed, Oswald?"

"A boy." He said it with what sounded like relief. "A boy called Jemmy Gleason."

"Did you…"

125

"No!" He shook his head violently. "No, Florence! I couldn't do that sort of thing!"

"But you were present?" She felt her hands shaking, disgust and horror rising.

"It was… there was a visitor. An eminent one. I had been helping with official arrangements for his time in London and he indicated that he liked… that he liked certain things. I didn't expect what happened, that it would get out of hand. None of us present did."

"Nobody contacted the police?"

"We couldn't. This man was… he was important. It couldn't be known."

"Who, Oswald?" She felt almost sick now. It was worse – more dangerous indeed than she had steeled herself to expect.

"He's… he's a member of a royal house in Germany. A minor one, but the complications would still be intolerable. Not just diplomatic, but links to..." His voice trailed off. No need to be more specific.

"There must have been a body, Oswald." She remembered them in Thrace and Cuba, slumped like piles of discarded clothing, pathetic remnants crying out for decent burial.

Oswald looked away and began to sob again, his shoulders heaving, head downcast.

"What happened to the body, Oswald?" A dreadful fascination, horror and pity mixed.

A full minute passed before he was calm enough to say "It was taken away. In a carriage."

"And then?"

"It was put in the river. Downstream of the *Brahmaputra*."

"And when it was found it was assumed that he had fallen overboard and drowned?" Florence could not keep contempt and anger from her voice.

His nod seemed more terrible than any words.

"That boy must have had a family. They must have asked questions."

He shook his head. "The boys were always orphans. Chosen because they had no known families. Gleason had a sister but I was told she'd disappeared. But there was a mistake. The other boy there that night did have a family."

She knew with sudden certainly who it must have been.

"Was it Andrew Shepton?"

He looked up, surprise – and a suggestion perhaps of hope too – on his features. "You know where he is? Do you know how to find him, Florence?" And only then did he realise the import of what she had said. "How do you know about him?"

"His mother came to me for help. His father's on the *Leonidas*. On Nicholas's ship."

He blanched visibly. Nicholas's name seemed to frighten him, as well it might. Nicholas was known for standing up for his men. Oswald's discomfort was an advantage for her and she pressed her questions. Facts emerged slowly, painfully, reluctantly. Andrew Shepton had been guaranteed money, clothing, a new life in America. He had been grateful. He had been kept at a certain house in London. And just before he was due to leave the country he disappeared.

"So he too was murdered?"

Oswald shook his head. "That wouldn't have been permitted. Not by… not by certain influential people. It was difficult enough already. But he just disappeared."

"And then?"

"Somebody approached me. He spoke for some group that had Shepton hidden somewhere. Maybe not even in London. They'd already got to know about my friends. Maybe through Cleveland Street. God knows what they'd offered Shepton but he'd told them all he could. Everything except the identity of the man from Germany. But the boy knew me, and he knew that I must know who His Highn… who that man was."

"Did they want money?"

"Not money. Information. Not just the name of our visitor, though that alone would have caused endless embarrassment for the government. But information. From the Foreign Office. Sensitive information I have access to, that I must deal with every day. Secrets, things vital for this country. It was not to be for just once only. There was to be no end to it. They'd contact me whenever they'd want more. And if I didn't cooperate…"

"…they'd inform the Brewster family." Florence completed the sentence. It all seemed so obvious now. "They'd inform them about Cleveland Street. About the *Brahmaputra*."

"I couldn't do it." For all his misery, there was a hint of pride in Oswald's voice. "I couldn't do it. I couldn't betray my country. Better this…" He spread out his hands as if to embrace the entire avalanche of shame and despair that had engulfed him.

"Do you know who they are, Oswald?"

"I've no idea. One accosted me on the street at night. A scarf over his face. Well dressed, but by his accent not a gentleman. I didn't know him. And again three nights ago. My last chance, he said. That a letter was already written, was ready for delivery to Chester Brewster. That it was my last chance."

"And you didn't take it, Oswald?"

"I didn't take it, Florence. I couldn't. A fellow can't be a traitor."

He was no longer weeping. She sensed the pride that a man might take as he listened to a sentence of death and accepted it willingly because of loyalty to a cause. There was something admirable about him too, something never discernible in the long years of his complacent assurance. But she felt fear as to what he might do. There must be razors in this house, curtain cords, belts, innumerable ways for a ruined and despairing man to make the ultimate escape. And it would kill not just him but his parents and Agatha too.

"What do the police want to charge you with? Is it…" she was reluctant to say it. "Is it the boy's death. The murder?"

The word made him wince. "Not that. But other things, things the courts deal with mercilessly if they get that far. Things that happened in Cleveland Street. Some of the boys who go there might have been glad enough to talk if it was made worth their while."

It was only too easy to imagine the Sid and Alf she had encountered there being glad to say anything if the price was right.

A long silence, he gazing into space in numbed exhaustion, she fighting a raging inner fear.

"I'll help you, Oswald." Florence said at last. "I don't know how. But I'll help you."

She pushed from her mind any consideration of what Nicholas might say or do. She alone must decide.

An accessory after the fact.

Yet she could make no other choice.

13

The return to the hotel was a nightmare, the fear that she might be followed growing, the urge to look back constantly all but irresistible.

She should have worn that maid's dress she had borrowed yesterday, she told herself, for even though she had left the Redburn Street house through the garden at the rear, the presence of a well-dressed woman in the alley it gave on to would have aroused suspicion had she encountered anybody there. Her knees were trembling as she walked towards the river and along the Chelsea Embankment, where she hailed a cab, and the full enormity of what she was doing weighed ever more strongly. The latter part of the meeting with Oswald had been all but business-like, as if all emotion, all shame, all fear, had been spent and they discussed alternatives and possibilities with the same detachment as if their concerns were of others unknown to them. Oswald could not remain in their house indefinitely, ideally for no more than a day or two longer – the reliability of the servants could not be guaranteed as the likelihood of an early return by their absent master diminished.

Oswald had spoken of France and of Italy – he had friends living there, in some luxury, Florence gathered – and officialdom there was more tolerant of activities that caused such outrage here. He mentioned names – Lord Arthur would be in Paris by now, and Billing in Nice and there were others also at Menton and Capri. Any one of them would accommodate him discreetly until he could make other plans.

But only if he could cross the Channel. And Florence knew that a detective had said that ports were being watched. Immediate flight was obviously out of the question, but Oswald's remaining where he was could be almost as dangerous. And neither he, nor Florence, knew where he might safely move to. But somewhere must be found quickly.

I'm a conspirator, she thought, as the cab bowled eastwards, *but a conspirator without a plan.*

She dared not go to the Piccadilly mansion again – the reporters and detectives would still be there – and she shrank from the idea of telling Agatha what she had learned from Oswald. And even worse was what that reality might mean for Oswald's parents. Shame and social ostracism could kill as surely as apoplexy. Better that they might convince themselves of the truth of some future fiction that Oswald's health demanded that he live out his days in the comfort of a Riviera villa. Her agony of mind was all the worse for awareness that Nicholas would have disapproved of every step she had taken up to now, that knowledge of whatever she would now do would enrage him, might drive a wedge between them. Nicholas's opinion of what men like Oswald did, his dislike, almost contempt, for Oswald personally, all would infuriate him however well this business might pass off. And she could see no way to make such a positive outcome happen.

It got worse at the hotel. A message was waiting for her, a note from Mabel Bushwick stating that she would come by to take tea at half-past four. It was ten minutes to that time already. That Mabel was in London was ominous – she should have been interviewing a happily married dollar princess in Cumberland by now and only one thing could have brought her hurrying back. There could be no avoiding her. Florence hurried to her suite, took off her outdoor hat and put on one more suitable, splashed toilet-water on her temples and neck and hands and went down to be ahead of her visitor in the tea-room.

Embraces, pleasantries, and yet a cautiousness on both sides. Mabel had returned because Lady Seymour Harley – née Susannah Hickson of Omaha – had been struck down by a summer cold. Florence spoke only of the discomfort of London in the hot weather. She could sense Mabel's frustration rising. Better to get it over with.

"I saw Agatha," she said. "She's so upset. You know that the Brewster engagement has been broken off?"

Mabel knew, looked as if she was itching to produce her notebook.

"The whole family is upset," Florence said. "It's understandable, and it's so embarrassing. But it's for the best. I really do believe it is. She wasn't the girl for Lord Oswald. A lovely girl, but not – how shall I put it? – not really his intellectual equal. And that's what he needs of course. Some bluestocking, some friend of Agatha's who can discuss Greek translations with him and would like to hear him pontificate about border readjustments in the Balkans. It's really for the best and the whole family will come to see that a few months from now." She smiled, the smile she hoped of a settled matron viewing with tolerance the follies of youth. "And it's best for Rebecca also. She'll be no sooner back in America than some lucky young financier or steel baron will be winning her heart."

"You're too clever to talk like that, Florence." No anger or animosity in Mabel's tone, even a hint of amusement on her features. "And I'm too smart to be taken in. So just tell me what happened. It will come out sooner or later. So tell me now."

Knowing it before anybody else might set you up for life, would be a just reward for years of striving to support two children alone. Newspapers and magazines in the United States could publish what they like, could name names, without fear of litigation. And I've come to like this woman, almost as much as Agatha.

"I'm not going to talk about it, Mabel. Let's speak of something else."

"Somebody beat him up," Mabel said. "On the steps of his club. Beat him badly."

"I can't say, Mabel."

"It was Chester Brewster, wasn't it?"

Florence stood up. "I'm not going to continue this conversation." It was hard to say it, bitterly hard to choose between two friendships. She was afraid that she was going to weep, that all the pent-up fear of the last twenty-four hours was going to overwhelm her. Guests at other tables were looking towards her, then turning away discreetly.

"Sit down, my dear." Mabel was reaching out and taking her hand. "Sit down, Florence. We won't talk of it."

She sat.

"You know I'll follow this story," Mabel said. "I'll do it to the limit of my abilities. But I won't involve you, Florence, I won't press you, I won't trade upon our friendship." She produced a card from her reticule, wrote on the back of it, passed it across. "That's where I'm staying. If you need me, if you need help with that other business, with meeting that admiral's termagant wife, with anything but this matter of the Brewsters, then contact me."

No more was said of it. They talked about London sights, about what Mabel had seen of the North, about the inconveniences of train travel, and though it was artificial it was also somehow comforting. They embraced when Mabel left. Her agreement to exclude this matter from their relationship was a proof of true friendship.

And that, at this moment, was more valuable than diamonds.

*

It was more dangerous to do nothing than to act. Boldness was an ally when there was no other, Nicholas had once told her, and so it had proved when she had rescued him at New Haven. The problem now was rather to know how to act. She was reluctant to be seen again in the hotel restaurant – the sense of being hunted was growing

– so she had a tray sent up, although when it came she found she had little appetite. For all its opulence, the suite was beginning to feel like a prison cell. It was at the front of the hotel, looking out on the railway station's cobbled forecourt with the tall Eleanor's Cross monument at its centre. The light of the late summer evening revealed it to be still thronged. Between the cabs and carriages and passengers coming or leaving there were individuals or small groups that were obviously waiting to meet somebody. The obvious family groups gave her no concern but men who were alone seemed possible threats until some innocent meeting brought them away. It was the half-dozen or so seemingly bored men who leant against walls, or who slouched by the monument, smoking or reading newspapers, who worried her. From behind the window curtain she scanned each face for some resemblance to a confused memory of the swarm outside the Piccadilly mansion. Most drifted away but a few still remained after the gas lamps were lit and she fancied that one or two were glancing at intervals towards the hotel entrance. There was a terrible fascination in watching them – it would be bad enough if there were journalists among them, but detectives would be incomparably worse, and the uncertainty, perhaps the probability, that they were neither was no comfort. All the time her feeling of despair was growing. If Nicholas had been here... but no, that would have been no help. She needed counsel, she needed help from someone else, someone eminently practical, someone at home in the world as it was and not how it should be, someone who understood human weakness and was prepared to accommodate to it and make use of it.

Then the memory of a face recently seen came to her, smiling, confident, urbane, a man of courage and ingenuity. And one who already knew Oswald even though he might not necessarily like him. But he was a man who could be trusted only up to point and it was unclear what that point might be. *A man, Nicholas had said, whom we should never meet again.*

But now there was no alternative.

She went down to the reception and borrowed its copy of *Kelly's Handbook*. She found the address she needed, a villa on Clapham Common, one she had once heard lovingly described on a calm evening on the afterdeck of a steam yacht ploughing southwards towards Cuba.

Before she lay down she went one last time to the window. The forecourt was all but empty now. The newspaper-readers were gone but two figures were slumped against the Eleanor's Cross, perhaps derelicts sunk in drunken sleep.

Or perhaps not.

*

The night gave no respite, and little rest either, for the knowledge she now had was a sleep-banishing torment. It was still not too late to step back from... from this business. She was risking too much, much more than Agatha might ever have expected of her, and for a man who... who did things she recoiled from imaging even if he was not guilty of far worse. Had Nicholas been here he would almost certainly have approved of Chester Brewster's action. And yet, a small voice reminded her, even Nicholas would have grudgingly admired Oswald's deliberate choice of ignominy and ostracism, the risk of hard labour in prison, rather than betray his country. Courage manifested itself in different forms and Oswald was demonstrating it in a way that could never have been expected of him. Gilpin's death made sense now also. It might not have been money that had been demanded of him, as Oswald had imagined, but perhaps information he was privy too. He had mentioned that he had attended one of Nicholas's courses at HMS *Vernon*. She knew little detail of Nicholas's work there, other than it was associated with torpedoes and that even to her he never spoke of it except in general terms. There must be secrets there also, secrets no less valuable than those Oswald was charged to guard at the Foreign Office. Gilpin, trapped, had made a heroic choice.

And yet for all her pity for Oswald, for all her unexpected respect, the misery of someone else troubled her even more. Mrs. Shepton, must have endured years of wretchedness but had come at last to believe that a future of modest happiness was within her grasp, gratitude for a drunken husband turned from drink, pride for a son training on the *Brahmaputra*. Her heart had been broken by that boy's vanishing – it was distressing to remember her anguish – but her worst fears could not have encompassed the reality, not just of degradation, but of danger. A boy had died – apparently when Oswald had been present – and the stakes were high enough for many who were involved in the affair not to stop at another death.

When Florence had promised to look into Andrew Shepton's disappearance she had envisaged nothing like this. That youth's father was even now serving somewhere in the Orient on HMS *Leonidas*. Nicholas would expect loyalty to the death from that humble seaman and she knew that in return Nicholas would pledge his reputation and his life for him, as for any member of his crew. Nicholas might step back from helping Oswald but there would be no limit to what he would undertake for Mrs. Shepton. His loyalty to *Leonidas* and her crew – and their families – would be no less absolute than hers to the Kegworths.

Dawn came, daylight filtering through the curtains, the noise of iron tyres on stone cobbles growing outside, the promise of a new day. She pushed her doubts and fears aside. She had survived worse and would not shirk this challenge. Oswald, contemptible in privilege, had gained stature in adversity, for all that he would be greeting this same dawn in shame and fear. Mrs. Shepton, poor and simply good, deserved her modicum of happiness. And so Florence rose and bathed and removed all traces of powder from her face and rubbed her cheeks until they were almost raw. She pulled back her hair and wound it into a tight bun and put on the servant's plain dress she had borrowed, then stripped her hat of its decorations, twisting it slightly out of shape. It was somehow disappointing when she saw her reflection in the wardrobe mirror and recognised that it had been so easy to transform herself into what she had so fortuitously escaped becoming, a frugally respectable working woman. For all Nicholas's assurances she knew that she was not beautiful – her face was too bony, her mouth was too large – and it was sobering to realise how it was prosperity alone that helped disguise the fact. A maid she rang for brought a breakfast tray and while she waited she yielded to the temptation she had resisted to look outside. It was as she feared – and expected. There were still men waiting, men loafing, men reading newspapers. They might be innocent. And they might not.

A shilling for the maid when she returned for the tray bought an exit through the hotel kitchen. As she took the coin the girl's cool appraising eye told that she was not unaccustomed to surreptitious exits by apparently respectable ladies. Florence found herself in Villiers Street, the narrow thoroughfare sloping down towards the river, on her left the shops and houses and the public house where she had met her father, on her right the station's brick walls. It was busy, as it always was, but she forced herself not to look behind her or to search in faces for signs that they might be seeking her. She walked on calmly to the Thames Embankment, then up the steps to the narrow footpath leading along the downstream side of the railway bridge there. There were, as always, wretches crouched there, begging, and it pained her that she must look away as she walked past. A woman like she now impersonated could afford little charity. Below her the water ran foul and yellow, the last terrible refuge, she knew, of so many Dorcas Haywards.

Waterloo Station lay on the south bank, the terminus for the lines to Portsmouth and the south-west. The multitudes thronging it might hide a score of pursuers but Florence felt pride in the subterfuge she had planned to frustrate any such. Only when she came to the ticket booth did she realise that she had overlooked one detail.

"First Class, you said?" The clerk had taken in the plain dress, had seen her for what she had striven to be. "Are you sure you want First Class, Miss?" The tone was kindly, the intent to avoid expense for some simple girl unfamiliar with travel.

There were others in the line behind her and they must have heard, must also have thought the request anomalous. She must do nothing to attract attention to herself, yet now she had done just that.

"That's right," Florence dropped her voice, relapsed deliberately into the regional accent she had done so much to lose. "My mistress gave me the money for it." She reached it across, enough for the return ticket to Portsmouth, enough to buy a place in a compartment reserved for ladies. "Me mum's sick," she said, "and me mistress wanted me to go in comfort. She's a kindly one, she is."

"Go third-class and you'll have enough left over to buy your mum some flowers," the clerk said. "But if it's what you want…" He took the money and pushed the ticket and the change to her.

"Some of these women are getting above themselves," a lady's voice said from behind and another agreed. Blushing, Florence ignored them and hurried away.

And into the arms of Count Sergei Ivanovich Livitski.

Intent on the clock overhead, concerned to be as soon as possible on the train that was waiting to depart in ten minutes, she had blundered into him. He steadied her, stepped back and bowed.

"Florence Hanim! Mrs. Dawlish! An unexpected pleasure." He was in the same light linen suit he had worn on the carriage drive, a diamond pin in his cravat, a scarlet rose on his lapel. He looked exquisite and he was beaming.

"Count Livitski." She did not know what to say and she hoped that the sudden terror coursing through her was not showing. *Foreign Office. Secrets. Russian Embassy.*

"You're no doubt travelling back to Portsmouth, Mrs. Dawlish."

She saw that he had noticed the plain dress that now proclaimed subterfuge rather than anonymity.

"I'm travelling to Portsmouth myself," Livitski said. "I'll be there only briefly, alas. I need to cross to the Isle of Wight – arrangements about the Cowes Regatta at the month's end. The Embassy is inviting guests." He had touched her elbow and she found herself being steered towards the ticket barrier. "Are we perhaps on the same train, Mrs. Dawlish? The nine eleven?" He spoke as if he was genuinely glad to see her.

"Yes. The nine eleven." She was too flustered to think of saying anything else.

"And your luggage, Mrs. Dawlish? My man can have it loaded for you." He nodded towards a burly figure in a dark suit standing behind him and carrying two large valises. Florence saw that the man was looking intently at her, as if to memorise her features.

"A porter loaded my things already." She could see that he did not believe her.

They were at the ticket barrier now and Livitski stopped. He gestured to his man to step back.

"A word, Mrs. Dawlish." His voice had dropped and he suddenly seemed less assured. "It would be unseemly for you, for a married lady, to travel with me. I understand that. But if I might call…"

"No," she said. Her heart was pounding.

"If you might care to join the party at Cowes, Mrs. Dawlish." He was obviously conscious of her unease and yet he seemed hesitant to exploit it. "A perfectly proper invitation, Mrs. Dawlish, one that could include your friend, Lady Agatha, if you wish. Several eminent guests, British and French as well as Russian and you would…"

"We need to hurry, count," Florence moved towards the barrier. "Five minutes to go and I haven't yet found a compartment." She reached her ticket to the collector. Livitski followed her, his servant also.

The ladies' carriage was the one from the end of the train. There was no connection between the individual compartments, each with seating for six. Florence hurried past three empty ones before finding a compartment already occupied by two ladies, one old enough to be the other's mother. She reached for the door but she felt Livitski's hand on hers, staying it.

"Mrs. Dawlish." There was nothing menacing in his tone, in his glance either. "You know of my admiration. I have no desire to offend you. Nothing could be further from that. But certain circumstances have to be taken into account and..."

She pulled her hand free from his, then wrenched the door open.

"Goodbye, Count Livitski." She did not look him in the face as she stepped inside and slammed the door closed behind her.

The older lady was alarmed. "Is that man bothering you, my dear?"

"It was a misunderstanding," Florence said. She settled back in a forward facing seat. Her knees were weak, her pulse racing. She could see Livitski and his man moving on up the platform. They passed quickly out of view and might well have boarded the next carriage. She knew that they would be looking out for her at every stop.

"Would you care for some smelling salts, my dear?" The younger woman was reaching them to her. She took them gratefully, noticed suspicious glances passing between the women. She was too frightened to care. A man who had commanded Cossacks in Bulgaria and Thrace would stop at nothing.

The train drew out, wheels clacking over the succession of points as it passed over the wide swathe of parallel and merging tracks and headed towards Clapham Junction. There it stopped to collect passengers coming down from Victoria Station and though Clapham itself was Florence's destination the thickly crowded platform made it too easy for her to be followed unobserved should she alight. There was no option but to remain on board and to hold to the plan she had made for shaking off pursuers. It seemed a desperately inadequate one now.

But there were a dozen stations or more between here and Portsmouth and there must be some opportunity...

14

She needed a station platform that would be all but empty just as the train was about to depart and, as it was a stopping service, she should find several opportunities. Both ladies in the compartment alighted at Surbiton, and nobody entered, but sufficient passengers had left the train to make it possible that Livitski and his man might have mingled between them to watch her compartment, then board the train again as it departed. As it drew away Florence took a small hand-mirror from her reticule.

The Esher stop came ten minutes later. She lowered the sash window but did not get out. Passengers were disembarking, a dozen or more. She cupped her left hand around the mirror and rested it on the window's still, concealing it as much as possible and angling it so that she could see along the side of the train towards the locomotive. The passengers were dispersing but a head and shoulders were leaning from a window two coaches ahead and looking back. She could not be sure if was Livitski but she had to assume it was. The station master's whistle shrilled and the train lurched into motion again.

The next station was Weybridge – no opportunity there either, but once again her mirror indicated that somebody was leaning out and looking back as the alighting passengers moved away down the platform. She was beginning to feel panic now. The stratagem of leaving the train at some station and getting another back towards London would be compromised if another lady should enter the compartment – as must happen at some stop – and make use of the mirror difficult. The next station, Woking, would be a busy one, a junction, where more than one unaccompanied lady might be expected to board.

The train slowed and as it drew in she saw that the platform was thronged. She again lowered the window and stood, trying to look as if she was scanning the crowd for a familiar face, yet still keeping her head and shoulders inside. Her mirror was again in surreptitious use but with so many disembarking and embarking it was impossible to discern any one figure looking back from a window. A lady with three young children approached and reached for the door.

"This compartment's reserved, ma'am," Florence was waving an open hand in a gesture of denial. "An old lady and her nurse will be getting on at the next station. She's quite ill and …"

The woman turned away to seek a place further along the carriage.

The crowd was dispersing. No sign of Livitski or his servant on the platform and the train was about to leave. The mirror revealed a single figure leaning from a window ahead – she could not be sure that it was the same window, or if it was whom she feared, but she had to assume the worst. The whistle blasted and the train lurched. Florence knew that this was her opportunity. A last glance in the glass told that the figure was still leaning out but it was unlikely that he would expect her next action. The train was gathering speed – less than walking pace still, but it would be more rapid in seconds, and the end of the platform would soon approach.

She swung the door open, stepped on to the running board outside, faced forward, and half stepped, half-jumped on the platform, somehow slamming the door behind her. The impact was more violent than she had expected and she stumbled, all but falling. Behind her the quickening rhythm of bogies clacking on rail joints told of the train accelerating away.

And nobody between her and the platform end. Livitski, surprised, had not managed to get off himself. She looked back and saw an irate-looking station master hurrying towards her as fast as his stout bulk would allow. Some bye-law must have been breached by her sudden exit but she had no intention of arguing the case. Another train, heading towards London, was drawing in to the platform on the other side of the double tracks. She rushed for the connecting bridge, gathering her skirt as she raced up the steps, and almost falling as she descended on the far side. The train was disgorging passengers as she reached the platform. A knot of poorer-looking people were heading for what must be a third-class carriage. Florence saw a shabby and weary-looking woman carrying a baby and simultaneously lugging a bag and dragging two small children.

"Let me help you with that, ma'am." Florence reached for the bag and saw gratitude on the woman's face. She pushed forward into an already crowded hard-seat compartment, drew up the children behind her, and helped the woman herself to board. She crouched down as if to reassure the children so that a press of bodies hid her from sight from the platform. Her heart was pounding, fear rising that the portly station-master might view her misdemeanour seriously enough to delay the train to find her.

Long seconds passed and then relief flooded through her as the whistle screamed and the train juddered into motion.

She was headed back in the direction she had come from.

Towards Clapham.

*

Florence alighted and hurried from the station. A furtive backwards glance assured her that she was not being followed – *probably* not, she told herself, for vigilance could not be relaxed. She walked for five minutes in a generally southerly direction before going into a newsagent's shop and asking for directions. Another five minutes brought her to her destination.

She had heard its owner once describe it as a villa and the word had conjured an image of a larger version of her own residence in Southsea. But the house that looked out over the park that was Clapham Common was a mansion, bigger, more grand, more opulent than she had expected, the very embodiment of solid wealth and propriety. The prosperity was genuine but the respectability was a mask.

A footman opened the door, more formidable-looking than those she had encountered in recent days and Florence suspected that he was capable, when needed, for other duties than this. He might have directed her to the tradesman's entrance – she saw that he was appraising her plain dress – had she not pushed her card towards him.

"Give this to Mr. Raymond," she said. "He knows me. He'll see me immediately if he's here." The thought that he might not be was frightening. She had no idea what to do otherwise.

In the hallway, in the parlour where she was asked to wait, there was some indefinable quality about the décor that indicated a woman's touch. She wondered who she was – his wife, or perhaps someone else's, a confederate in his schemes or an innocent who knew him only as a rich expatriate who preferred British society to American. For all that she had worked so closely with this man – had indeed almost died in his company – neither she nor Nicholas knew anything of his domestic arrangements. And it was clear that that was what he preferred.

The wait was no more than two minutes and when Henry Judson Raymond entered there was a broad smile on the otherwise clean-shaven face on which the moustache curved up to meet the side-whiskers. Even before he spoke the dark, clever eyes beneath thick eyebrows conveyed warmth and humour that might have been genuine.

"Mrs. Dawlish – a pleasure. I was expecting you." The accent of a cultured American.

It was how he had always addressed her in private even when he was calling her Florence, and My Dear, in public when they had impersonated man and wife a year before. The subterfuge had been carried off well enough to convince a Spanish provincial governor and the upper echelons of Santiago society but back on the steam-yacht on which they had occupied separate cabins he had been scrupulously correct. "Is he a criminal?" she had once asked Nicholas. He had answered "Only part of the time" and had refused to say more.

"I knew you'd turn up, Mrs. Dawlish." He gestured for her to sit. "But I wasn't sure when and I was starting to get worried."

"Why do you think I'm here, Mr. Raymond?" Unease growing. *A man who could be trusted only up to a point though it was unclear what that point might be. Yet Nicholas and I entrusted our lives to him and he did not fail us.*

"We've got friends in common, Mrs. Dawlish, and one friend in particular. A certain gentleman who helped with our arrangements in the United States last year."

Memories flooded back. Oswald, then at the Washington embassy, had been the link between Raymond and Nicholas on the one hand and a certain figure in government in London on the other. The business they had been engaged in – into which Florence herself had been drawn – had been illegal in America and almost fatal in Cuba.

"Who are you talking about, Mr. Raymond?" *I should volunteer nothing yet.*

"Lord Oswald. Mrs. Dawlish. Not the easiest of men to like, I admit, but one whom neither of us would like to see chained to an iron ball and breaking stones in a quarry. He's in trouble, and he's missing, and not even my people have been able to locate him. But I thought you would. You're the only friend the Kegworths can trust to the limit at a time like this."

"How… how can I…"

He cut her off. "How can you trust me, Mrs. Dawlish? There's sentiment in the matter, I admit it, but it's in my interest too. A certain friend – your husband knows him – would also like to help him, and I'm somewhat beholden to that gentleman."

And if it was whom she guessed, then Nicholas was beholden to him too. She had met him once, on a rainy night in Southsea, even knew his name – Admiral Sir Richard Topcliffe – and for all his outward charm there had been something chilling, even reptilian, about him. He had the power to send Nicholas to accomplish tasks he would be disowned for if he failed. Tasks that had almost killed him – and her too – but tasks which when successful had ensured early promotion to captain and command of HMS *Leonidas*.

"Are you telling me that this gentleman's interested in Lord Oswald's wellbeing?"

"Not just that gentleman, Mrs. Dawlish. Other persons too, persons that gentleman is in close contact with. Highly placed persons who can't afford a scandal but who would like to see Lord Oswald in comfortable exile. Persons who cannot afford to be suspected of complicity in his escape."

"And persons whom you would find it expedient to assist, Mr. Raymond?"

"We understand each other, Mrs. Dawlish. Persons whom your husband would also find it expedient to assist, despite any personal likes or dislikes, were he here."

"And you're aware of the offences for which an arrest warrant has been issued?"

He held up his palms in mock exasperation. "We must live in the world as we find it, Mrs. Dawlish. And these highly placed persons – whose names are in some cases household words – cannot be seen to be opposing arrest efforts since the substance of the allegations is already known to certain journalists who cannot be muzzled without drawing further attention to the matter. But these persons would like to see Lord Oswald safely away from Britain. And that gentleman to whom I am beholden has entrusted the matter to me."

"But you haven't been able to locate Lord Oswald, Mr. Raymond?"

"I would have, in time. Certain of my associates have established some leads. But it's taking too long, and time's running out. But I guessed that as Lady Agatha's friend you too might have been busy. I know that you're a resourceful woman."

"And what if I have located the unfortunate gentleman, Mr. Raymond?" *I'm talking in circumlocutions already but it seems natural when with this man.*

"He would be assisted to France initially, Mrs. Dawlish. My yacht – the *Shamrock* – has been anchored for days in the Solent with steam up. Our friend could be across the Channel within hours. And thereafter he could be helped onward. Switzerland, Italy, perhaps further East. Places where somewhat Grecian tastes are discreetly ignored. I have associates across Europe who could facilitate the process. And in time the present business would be forgotten here and he might return."

The prospect might not be unwelcome to Oswald, Florence reflected. It might indeed mean welcome liberation from a life that for years must have demanded so much subterfuge, so many lies. The family pressure for an heir must have been irresistible. It might not be Rebecca Brewster alone who would ultimately profit from the current nightmare. But first he had to be got out of England.

"Are you going to tell me where he is?" Raymond said.

She avoided the question. "Have you had somebody following me, Mr. Raymond."

He laughed. "Not very effectively. I had a man outside the house on Piccadilly. He saw you go in. He missed you going out again – I presume you wouldn't have remained there. But I was right in assuming that you would be willing to help your friend's family. And you know that I'm probably the best man in England to help in such a matter."

"Were I to tell you where he is, would you be able to assist immediately?"

"Measures are already in hand. He could be in France thirty-six hours from now. All we now need is the man himself. And some help from yourself."

"More help?" The relief that she had felt was replaced with sudden fear. She had though it would be enough to hand the matter over to Raymond, to walk out the door here as if she had never been involved, to return to Portsmouth to consider her next actions. For there was also still Rosewood House.

"Help for just a little longer," Raymond said. "A little masquerade. Somewhat like you and I carried off in Cuba, Mrs. Dawlish. But for a few hours only."

"No!" *I've done enough. More than enough.*

"He'll be frightened, Mrs. Dawlish. Highly nervous and badly frightened. And frightened men make mistakes. They don't trust others easily either. He'll need somebody with him whom he can trust implicitly. Somebody he'll know won't betray him if they come to take him from his hiding place. Somebody he would travel with – part of the way only, no more."

"No!"

"Somebody who would lend normality to his travel. For that's the best disguise of all."

"No, Mr. Raymond." She stood up.

He made no effort to bid her sit again. "Was he frightened when you left him?"

"Yes," she said. *He was terrified.*

"Do you think he could be a danger to himself?"

"Yes." Said reluctantly.

"I don't need to tell you how such cases often end," he said. "Despair can make a man irrational. They can think no further than the present moment, see no other way…"

"You're doing this for a price, aren't you, Mr. Raymond?" She could see her way ahead now. "For you everything's always for a price, is it not?"

He was not offended. "You know me so well, Mrs. Dawlish."

"I've got a price too. I'll help you in return for your promise that you'll pay it."

"And your price?"

"A boy called Andrew Shepton. A promise that you'll find him if he's alive, find how he died if he's already dead."

Raymond shrugged. "I've got no choice, Mrs. Dawlish. You've got my word."

Florence sat down.

"Just tell me what help you have in mind," she said.

.

*

The details were agreed as she lunched alone with Raymond. The meal was superb and he mentioned, when complimented, that his chef – apparently not a mere cook – was a Frenchman. It could be another two hours at least before the maid sent by cab to the Charing Cross Hotel could return. She had with her a note from Florence that authorised her to pick up a valise and some specified clothing.

"Could she not be followed?" Florence asked.

Raymond smiled. "She won't be followed. She's reliable. She knows her business."

The furnishings gave every indication of female taste. Whoever Raymond had sent, Florence thought, it was not a maid. Raymond had made no mention of any lady in the house but that meant nothing.

"Tell me about this Andrew Shepton," he said after coffee has been served. "Tell me everything you know about this affair."

She did, starting with Gilpin's warning. He heard her patiently, interjecting only the odd question, though then a penetrating one. She had an impression that he knew much already, especially as regards Cleveland Street, but it was impossible to gauge from his calm, steady drawing of information from her just how much that was. Andrew Shepton's name seemed new to him, but then it would have been unimportant to him up to now, just as was the identity of the dead boy. To those who wanted knowledge of this matter efficiently supressed neither youth was more than an embarrassment to be forgotten. He took no notes but she had the impression of every fact being filed systematically in a mental archive.

"You may wish to lie down until your things are here," he said when she finished. "It's going to be long evening."

A maid brought her to what appeared to be a guest bedroom, as richly furnished as what she had seen of the rest of the house. Now that action was imminent, that she had support from a source she trusted, she felt more relaxed than she had for days. Once the curtains had been drawn she dropped off almost instantly into dreamless sleep.

No time seemed to have passed before she was woken by knocking on the door. The maid who had conducted her here was now holding her valise. "Mr. Raymond asks if you can join him in half-an-hour."

It took shorter than that. The costume she had chosen was the practical skirt and jacket she had travelled between Portsmouth and London in – dark plum, linen, severe in design, cut and tailored for comfort rather than ostentation. Ideal for her purpose. The messenger who had been sent to the hotel – whoever she was – had returned, as directed, wearing Florence's broad-brimmed straw hat adorned with artificial flowers. The valise also contained a silk shawl, underwear, a nightdress, various necessities, enough for an overnight stay. She viewed herself in the room's long mirror before she went below and saw the solidly respectable wife of some successful but unpretentious professional man. *As I am,* she thought. There would be no great call for acting.

Raymond saw her off. There were half-a-dozen stables and a coach-house in the large yard behind the house. Two beautiful matched bays stood harnessed to a gleaming black clarence. The liveried driver took her bag and loaded it – he looked as formidably capable of looking after himself as the footman who had admitted her – and Raymond handed her in. He nodded to the curtains and said, "Leave them open, Mrs Dawlish. If they're closed they'll attract attention." She settled back on the padded seating, composed herself.

"You're in good hands with Staunton." Raymond nodded towards the coachman. "And there'll be others on hand. You won't notice them, but they'll be there. You'll need to impress that on our friend also. Tell him above all that he's to behave normally."

He stepped back and closed the door. The coach lurched into motion and passed through the rear gates. When it reached the roadway bordering the Common the driver urged the horses into a fast trot. Florence had never sat in anything so well sprung – she might have been borne on air – and in any other circumstances the motion, and the regular clatter of hooves, and the scented breeze wafting in from the parkland, would have been a delight.

But not now.

For there could be no legal defence now, no denial, even to herself. Murder had been done even if Oswald was innocent of it.

An accessory after the fact.

15

Oswald only agreed to go because he was more terrified of staying than of leaving. The mention of Raymond had calmed him somewhat – "He's a good fellow, a damn good fellow," he kept repeating, as if reassuring himself. Yet even after he had assented to the quickly-summarised plan, Florence feared that he might still reconsider. She had entered the Redburn Street house as she had left it previously, via the rear alleyway and the kitchen. His relief on seeing her had been pathetic to see, for he had taken her hand and held it to his cheek and gasped "God bless you, Florence. I knew you'd come, I was sure you would, but if you couldn't…" His voice had trailed off, tears brimming.

They had to be gone in fifteen minutes, must exit the way she had come and meet the clarence at the point where she had been set down at the end of the alleyway. In the meantime it was driving around the area – in this fashionable district its opulence would not make it seem out of place – but the faster they could be gone the better.

"One bag, Oswald," Florence was relaying Raymond's instructions to the letter, "and a travelling suit. But be fast! No – I mean fast, quick! Anything else you need will be on board."

He protested. A fellow couldn't leave just like that, there were things he'd need, his valet was not here to help and the servants in this house didn't properly understand his needs.

"One bag," she repeated, "and change for travelling as fast as you can. If you're not back down here in ten minutes I'll come to dress you myself." She tried to sound jocose but was all the time conscious of time slipping away.

When he returned she saw that he had done his best, even if his tie was awry and needed her to adjust it. The bruising around his eyes was less pronounced now, green drifting into yellow, his face slightly less swollen but still livid. The single leather bag looked as if it had been crammed to bursting and closed with difficulty.

"Have you got money?" she asked.

He had. Ninety pounds, sixty-five of them in gold sovereigns.

"Give twenty to the cook, another twenty to that man who opened the door. Tell them to divide them among the other servants." *Most of them won't get more than a sovereign or two, but it would not matter.* "Tell them that you'll be back in a month. That you'll be relying on them to keep quiet. That there'll be more when you get back."

"But I won't be coming back."

"They won't know that. It's enough if they stay quiet for just another day or two."

"I need more money. I can't just go to the bank."

"Raymond's arranging for that. Now we must go!" She caught him by the elbow and steered him towards the door, along the corridor, down the stairs to the kitchen. He complied as a child might. He seemed tongue-tied with the servants and it was she who took the money from him and distributed it. A gleam of greed in a human eye was never pleasant but was welcome now.

When they emerged from the garden into the alleyway there was no sign of the clarence at the end but, as they hastened on, it emerged into view and drew to a halt. The timing had been perfect on both sides. The coachman remained on the box. Florence pulled the door open, took Oswald's bag and heaved it inside, then pushed him in ahead of her. She slammed the door closed, the coachman cracked his whip and the clarence sped westwards.

*

The coachman was skilled in such work, Florence realised. The pace was fast, but not so excessive as to attract attention. As the clarence passed through Chelsea it took a succession of turns, some which seemed to bring it back on itself, making it impossible to guess its heading other than by reference to shadows. Following the vehicle would have been difficult, guessing its overall direction all but impossible. And that direction was not southwards, over the river, as Florence had anticipated, but westwards, towards Putney, where it at last swung south and crossed there. It was late afternoon now, near many businesses' closing times, and the traffic was denser than earlier. But progress never slowed, the coachman swinging effortlessly down side streets, turning, turning again, outflanking any blockages, never obviously hurrying and yet always maintaining a smart pace. Florence found it easy to look relaxed as she had never been in this area before and the sights, such as they were, attracted her attention. She smiled at children and their mothers waiting to cross and when the vehicle was detained briefly at one intersection she called over a woman with a baby who was begging there and gave her a shilling.

Oswald was sitting on her right and thus further from the pavement. He calmed slowly – he had been shaking when he entered and his naturally florid face was wet with sweat. He obeyed her orders not to slouch low but when she made conversation, remarks about buildings passed, questions about the area, comments about the day's heat, his participation was like an automaton's. She remembered Nicholas telling of her of men who had never recovered from the horror of combat, who even if not wounded themselves had remained haunted by the death and mutilation of comrades. A return to normal life offered little solace, he said, either for themselves or for their families. She wondered now if Oswald was just such a case, whether the querulous, arrogant, unfeeling character she and so many others had loathed would ever return. Unpleasant though it had been, it had been somehow better than this empty husk of a man who blanched at the sight of a policeman.

They passed through the outer suburbs, patches of greenery, even in places open fields between the clusters of houses. Closer to Surbiton they passed several modest villas of the sort that might be occupied by a married couple of the professional class, such as they now looked. As planned, the coach drew up at the station just before six o'clock. It was a modest stopping place, a more unlikely point of departure than either Waterloo or Clapham Junction as might be guessed by anybody assigned to following Florence. With luck Livitski's man – perhaps men – might still be keeping up a lonely vigil outside the Charing Cross Hotel and wondering whether others loafing there might be detectives or journalists. And another possibility was worrying her too, that a similar watch might be kept on her home in Southsea.

The coachman leaped down and swung the door open. As Florence alighted a ragged man, dishevelled, dirty, toes showing through a broken boot, hurried towards her.

"Carry your bag, ma'am. Just carry your bag. And the gentleman's also." He smelled strongly of alcohol.

Oswald stepped back, clearly disgusted. The coachman raised his fist. "We don't want no help from yer sort! Be on yer way!"

The man cringed. "No offence, ma'am. An old soldier, sir. Just an old soldier."

"Let the poor man be," Florence said. "Let him carry the bags."

The coachman handed the luggage over with obvious reluctance. The derelict staggered slightly as he carried it towards the entrance hall. As he set the bags down Florence pressed a shilling into his grimy hand. As she released it she felt the tickets he had transferred to her.

First Class.

To Swanage, on the Dorset coast.

*

They changed to a fast train at Woking, a few stops down the line, and several passengers – a clergyman and his wife, two old ladies, a single gentleman – boarded and left at intermediate stations, nodding briefly as they entered, sitting quietly and leaving without ado. A lady with a little boy boarded for two short stages only.

"You mustn't stare, Arthur," his mother whispered. "It isn't polite." He was clearly fascinated by Oswald's bruised face.

"He means no harm," Florence said. "Do you, Arthur? My poor husband was thrown from his horse. Would you like to ride a horse when you're older? What a sweet boy you are!"

Oswald was trying to smile genially, and failing. Embarrassed, the lady thanked Florence, hoped that her husband would be well soon and got off shortly after. The exchange had pleased Florence. It had been unforced, natural, all she could hope for.

The ten-minute wait at Woking gave her time to purchase magazines at the news-stand, behaving as normally as she could while Oswald stood fretting behind her. She resisted the urge to scan any of the others waiting on the platform to identify the escorts Raymond had promised. On the next stage, almost an hour's run to Winchester, they had the compartment to themselves.

It was after seven now, the sun still high in the west, the fields lush, cattle browsing happily, the air still warm, even the scent of the countryside somehow perceptible despite the smoke drifting back from the locomotive ahead. Oswald was quiet and when he took the copy of the *Strand Magazine* that Florence reached across to him he did so mechanically. Sensing that he did not want to talk, she buried herself in the *Illustrated London News* and its account, and its correspondent's drawings, of the occupation of Alexandria.

Florence glanced up as she turned a page and saw that tears were running down Oswald's face. He was looking out the window and she got the sense that all he saw was suddenly very valuable to him. A condemned man on the way to the gallows might feel like this also, she thought, simple beauty previously overlooked or underestimated now priceless as it slipped away. For Oswald was already in a certain way all but dead, dead to his family, to the society which had given him purpose, to the career he had aspired to, to that nation he was choosing to flee rather than betray. Years, decades, maybe a lifetime of luxurious, aimless sloth might lie ahead, villas where local youths might take the place of Cleveland Street's telegraph-boys, Riviera hotels where previous acquaintances might cut him dead, once-agreeable leisure interests a torment when they alone remained to satisfy his ambitions. His father – even if the shame did not kill him – might never bring himself to see him again. Agatha, and perhaps his mother too, might visit him, their awkward conversation avoiding all mention of what had exiled him.

There had been a time – no, her whole life, right up to the moment of that last crass humiliation in Rotten Row – when she had resented and despised him. She was not alone in suffering his petty humiliations, his callous disregard for the feelings of those whose continued employment made it essential to endure. Even Nicholas, a thousand times a better man, she believed, had been subjected to Oswald's slights. Yet all that seemed as nothing now as resentment was reproached by pity, and as pity turned to mercy.

She reached out and took his hand. He did not resist but he did not look at her – she realised that he could not bring himself to do so.

"You're not a bad man, Oswald," she said. "You must remember that. You're not a bad man. If you were then you would not be on this train now."

A long silence before he spoke

"I loved some of those boys," he said. "Even though I knew they only wanted money. But I hoped that at some time one of them would…" He shook his head. "I can't talk to you of such things, Florence. You'll never understand. No lady, not most men, ever could. And I don't want you to despise me. Not after all you've done for me."

"I don't despise you, and I can't. Not a man who stands by his country as you do."

She withdrew her hand from his and sat back. The evening light was golden now, the landscape almost Arcadian, Winchester and a five-minute halt there now close.

"I would have had an embassy in two years." A voice of infinite sadness. "A smaller one, Copenhagen or Brussels or maybe The Hague. Almost certainly a larger afterwards. I'd always hoped to get Constantinople, I loved the city and I wanted to return. I'd kept up the Turkish I had learned there. And now…"

They sat in silence until Winchester. Nobody entered their compartment and passengers who hurried past along the platform did not glance inside. Raymond's men must be among them. The

151

shadows were lengthening and an attendant boarded briefly at the stop to light the compartment's inadequate oil lamp. Less than two hours remained and Florence knew she would never see Oswald again. He was calm now, resigned, and this was her last chance to pump him for what she must know. It seemed easier to do so in semi-darkness and it was best to be direct.

"That captain of the *Brahmaputra* – Wilton, isn't it? – was complicit in supplying the boys, wasn't he?" she said.

An almost imperceptible nod.

"And it wasn't the first time?"

"No." A very low voice. "It had been going on for several years."

"How did you find out about it? How were you drawn in?"

"I encountered one of the other directors at that place in Cleveland Street. We were both surprised, embarrassed by meeting each other there. But when he knew of… of my interests, he invited me to a party soon after. With boys from the ship and…"

"Was there any other death?" *No, not just death, for that comes naturally to all of us. Use the right word.* "Any other murder?"

Hesitation. He looked away, then shook his head. Reluctantly, she thought. The word was one he had shrunk from.

"Any murder before you came back from America? One you were not linked with?"

"There was talk. Jokes that boys could fall overboard and drown. Somebody mentioned a boy called Willie Burton. It might have been a normal accident for all I know, a trip in the night."

And now the hardest question of all, because the man it referred to was one who had been a friend to her family all their lives. Yet it must be asked.

"Did your father know, Oswald? He was on the *Brahmaputra's* board of directors. You took his place."

She had been prepared for indignation, for blustering defence, but what came instead was a sob, shame incarnate. Not for his father. For himself.

"Never," he said when he composed himself. "I don't think he knows such things exist. My father's naïve in some ways. Dale used to joke about that, said my father would never guess in a million years what was going on. And now he knows about me, about Cleveland Street. It will finish him. I'll have killed him." A pause. "And Mamma also."

Now she had a name.

"Who's Dale?"

"You'll find out anyway. Rear Admiral Dale. He's been retired for years."

"Who else on the board?"

He was obviously unwilling to say more.

"It went beyond... beyond whatever you did with those boys." Florence felt herself past pity now. She must force her advantage. "Two boys are dead. Willie Burton, before you came back from America. And the one you know about. He had a name – you told me it, Jemmy Gleason – and he once had a sister. He had nothing but his life and that was robbed from him. His body was dumped in the river like offal. It's got to stop, Oswald, there can't be more like Willie Burton or Jemmy Gleason. You've been foolish but you didn't kill those boys. But those other people did. And you'll be gone and it will happen again. Who are those vile men?"

He yielded. "Sir Charles Pugh. The ship-owner. Of the Atlantic and Occidental Line."

"And?"

"Wigworth. Lord James Wigworth."

She knew the name. He had held office – she could not remember as what – in the previous government. Nicholas had spoken admiringly of him because of his support for increased Naval Estimates.

There were major stations ahead, Southampton perhaps ten minutes away and Bournemouth beyond. The chances were high of other passengers boarding. Raymond had stressed that trying to deter entry would only draw attention. Ten minutes remained for pressing Oswald to the limit.

"Where was Andrew Shepton kept afterwards?"

"A place in Lambeth. Poor but decent. The house belonged to the brother of one of Wigworth's servants. Shepton was frightened of course after that other boy had died. He was well looked after, he was happy about going to America. He'd been given money before. He was eager for more."

"But then he disappeared?"

"He was taken, kidnapped. In the early hours. Two men. Great bruisers by what we heard – they beat the house owner and crammed the boy into a coach."

"Just like that?"

"It's a rough area. The police don't get involved more than they have to."

The train was slowing.

"Who were they?"

"I don't know. And it was after that when I was approached for information. When I was threatened. It wasn't only about the... the incident, that Shepton knew about. He'd heard us talk about what went on at Cleveland Street. And that's what the police came for me about."

The train was slowing.

Southampton.

*

There was no time to talk thereafter, not on the stage to Wareham, or on the branch-line to Swanage that they changed to there, for other passengers now also occupied the compartment. It was dark, but still warm and with a clear, starry sky and a full moon when they alighted at the small seaside town. The other passengers alighted, Florence and Oswald waiting until last.

"I'll carry your bag, ma'am." A cabby's dress and demeanour. "There's no other baggage, is there? The hotel's close." The wording agreed with Raymond.

Florence said nothing to Oswald and left him as if he had been some unknown traveller with whom she had briefly shared a compartment. She passed along the platform, the man with her bag preceding her. She glanced back as she entered the ticket hall. Oswald was following at a distance, a respectably dressed man by his side and another behind, carrying his bag. All exactly as planned. He was out of her hands.

She was at the hotel within five-minutes, an expensive place where wealthy families might holiday. It was impressive that a room had been found at such short notice but she guessed that if it had not been at this place then Raymond's people would have located something similar elsewhere. The booking for Mr. and Mrs. Lacy was for a week. Her husband – such a thoughtful man, she told the receptionist – had sprung a surprise on her because she had perhaps overtaxed herself when tending to his mother when she was unwell. He had asked a friend living locally to arrange the holiday. It was such a pity that an unanticipated business matter in London had delayed him there at the last minute. Mr. Lacy was apparently as conscientious in his commercial dealings as he was attentive domestically. He had pressed her to go on ahead and would follow tomorrow. Florence signed the register, as instructed, as Mrs. Norbert Lacy and she went straight to her room.

It looked out directly eastwards across the bay. Moonlight reflected on barely rippled water. There were stationary lights a mile or two from shore – Raymond's steam-yacht, the *Shamrock*, summoned at high speed from the Solent. Florence saw the dark mass and single light of a fishing boat creeping towards the loitering vessel. The two shapes merged briefly and then the lights separated, the single heading back to shore, the yacht's masthead and green starboard lanterns pinpricks that moved away at speed. Florence watched until it was hidden from view by a headland. She had kept her promise to Agatha and Oswald's exile had begun.

The elation that a weight of responsibility had been lifted from her, the surge of pride that she had carried the business off successfully, did not last. She slept badly, troubled by the doubts that she had supressed until now about helping the escape of a man who had been associated with such enormities. There was another task ahead of her now. There was still justice to be done. For Willie Burton. For Jemmy Gleason. For Mrs. Shepton.

And for Dorcas Hayward.

She was at breakfast next morning – it was a beautiful one, and she would have willingly stayed here for a week – when she saw a flurry of activity at the dining room door. The manager was there, a telegraph boy hovering behind him, and the waitress was indicating where Florence was sitting. It was as planned, the excuse for her quick and apparently unexpected departure.

The manager approached and holding an envelope. "There's a telegram for you, Mrs. Lacy." His manner was apologetic, even sympathetic, as if he feared it might contain bad news.

RETURN IMMEDIATELY. REGRET MOTHER DIED IN HER SLEEP STOP HEARTBROKEN STOP NORBERT

Florence hoped she looked sufficiently shocked.

"How soon can I get a train for London?" she asked.

16

The temptation to leave the train when it stopped at Southampton was almost irresistible. A half-hour would bring her to Portsmouth, as much again to the calm normality of her own Southsea home. She wanted to shut from her mind, even if only briefly, the squalor she had been confronted with, had been indeed part of, in the last days. And then it struck her that there was no normality at home either, would not be again. Everything had changed – and still suppurated like an open wound – since she had encountered Dorcas Hayward. It was perhaps as much to delay addressing that outrage as much as loyalty to Agatha that kept her on the train to London.

Newspapers bought at the stop contained no mention of Oswald's beating, of the arrest warrant or of the disappearance. Without an actual arrest any mention of his name might well run a risk of action for libel. It was a first step perhaps to the entire affair fading in prominence. As the train neared London Florence felt less sense of being hunted than before, not just because the inconspicuous guardians Raymond had provided were still near but for the knowledge that even if Livitski and his men should corner her there was nothing to hide. Oswald must be in France by now – where exactly, she did not know. Revealing as much, if she had to, could do no harm.

She took a cab from Waterloo Station to the Charing Cross Hotel and entered it by the front entrance. It amused her to imagine that there might still be some spy among the loafers on the forecourt outside. There were welcome to see her now. Her suite was as she had left it and she had a light luncheon sent up while a messenger carried a note from her to the Kegworth mansion. He returned a half-hour later. Agatha was at home and would be happy if she could come at once.

The journalists who had previously congregated outside the mansion had given up. A single figure reading a newspaper and leaning against a lamp-post across the street might have been a detective. Florence was admitted by the butler himself, Mr. Pollock, and she suspected that he had been waiting specially for her.

"His Lordship is very low, Mrs. Dawlish, very low indeed." The greeting formal but respect beneath. "If it weren't for Lady Agatha..." The shake of his head conveyed all.

The meeting with her was hard. It was better to say no more than that Oswald was already in France, was being protected, was perhaps already on his way to somewhere safer still. That he would write as soon as possible – though Florence doubted if, once safe, his concern for his family would be greater than pity for himself. She made no mention of how or where she had found him, nor of Raymond's assistance.

Agatha kept her composure and heard her out in silence. She only spoke when Florence was finished.

"He won't be coming home, will he?"

"No, Agatha. He won't be coming home. Not for a long time. Maybe not ever."

"You know why, Florence, don't you? You know but you don't want to say it. But I think I do know why. And Father does too." The great thick lenses of her pince-nez magnified the tears welling in her eyes. "It's to do with that that warning you brought, isn't it? From that poor young man who killed himself?"

"It was about that. I think you guessed that your brother is… that he is not like most other men."

Agatha looked away but nodded, tight-lipped.

"He was being blackmailed, Agatha. I understand that men like him often are." No need to mention the full horror, the dead boy, the eminent figures involved. Not either the time to talk of the *Brahmaputra*. "They didn't want money, only government information that he couldn't in honour disclose. When he refused they informed the police, and Chester Brewster too."

"He… he would not betray his country?" A tremor of hope in Agatha's voice.

"He could never do that, Agatha. He's an honourable man. You must remember that." *The only consolation now and in the years of shame to come.* "You must be proud of him for that, even though nobody else may know it. You must be proud. And your mother. And your father."

Agatha left briefly to convey the news to her still-bedridden father. She was profuse in his thanks and hers when she returned.

"One word of advice, Agatha. From a friend of Oswald's and of your father – no, he doesn't want to be named." Florence repeated what Raymond had suggested. "Behave as if nothing has happened. Go out. To shop, to a gallery, to take tea, to meet your Royal Society circle. No true friend will mention the matter or think you the less of you for it. The journalists have gone and if that one man still out there is a detective then he and his masters will soon recognise that they'll gain nothing by watching this house." She picked up a newspaper she had brought, folded back to see the theatre announcements. "Look here, Agatha – the Lyceum. Mr. Irving's playing in *Much Ado about Nothing*. We can enjoy that, can't we? And you must be seen when we're there. You must greet any friends you meet as if nothing has happened."

But though they did see the play, from a box in which Florence ensured they were conspicuous, they enjoyed it little. Both knew, though neither said it, that for now only misery lay ahead.

And Florence knew too that there were duties she could not with honour shirk.

Andrew Shepton. Willie Burton. Jemmy Gleason. Brahmaputra.

Duties she knew she was ill-equipped for.

And one most of all.

Dorcas Hayward.

*

Florence returned home the next day, a Saturday. It chilled her that there were once more flowers awaiting her there with a card from Livitski. Two words only. *In admiration.* And once more the flowers were sent to the Sailors' Rest, leaving her with unease that she had refused Raymond's offer to provide continued protection. It was to him that she sat down to write – a summary, with names, of all that Oswald had told her on the train to Swanage. She did not sign the letter, did not need to. When she finished writing – it was just after nine o'clock, still bright, and there were enough respectable neighbouring couples returning from evening walks for her to feel safe – she posted the letter in a pillar box three streets from the villa. Despatching it brought a feeling of relief and she slept well.

The Sunday was difficult, for all that she tried to make it normal and ignore for one day only what she knew now lay ahead. She went to service at her local church, St. Jude's, but had no comfort from it. The sermon irritated her, benign platitudes that reflected no real awareness of cruelty and degradation, no recognition that mild altruism alone could never be sufficient for confronting evil. Now more than ever she felt that she had been plunged into a sewer in which she was still trapped and feared that is foulness would pollute her for ever. She fell silent half-way through the Lord's Prayer, unable to ask forgiveness because she had none to give for those who trespassed. *Against the weak and innocent. Those women in Thrace, those villagers in Cuba. Dorcas. Those wretched boys. Trespass against them is trespass against me.* The thought troubled her as she walked home, that she was not leaving vengeance to the Lord, that she had taken it on herself, that it might consume her, might wither and embitter her heart. The long hours afterwards were empty, a review with Cook of kitchen expenses, warnings to Susan about falling into conversations with strangers, however charming, lunch eaten alone, an afternoon stroll along the Esplanade that would in any case have felt lonely without Nicholas but was now doubly so. She would have welcomed Miss Weston's company but problems at the Rest in Plymouth would detain her there for weeks. And Mabel – only now did she realise how much she had enjoyed their brief friendship, how much support she would have had from her were they to confront Lady Adelaide together.

Now she must do so alone.

*

"A trustworthy photographer?" Florence's query had obviously surprised the solicitor. "I doubt there is any other sort in Southsea, Mrs. Dawlish." He was looking at the brown manila envelope he had just returned to her, obviously curious but unwilling to be direct "But Mr. Simpson in Marmion Road – you may have seen him in St. Jude's – could indisputably be described as trustworthy." He gestured to the silver-framed studio portrait of a frowning woman on his desk. "My dear wife's picture was captured by him last year."

"Thank you Mr. Bagshot." She stood up to go.

"If I may intrude, Mrs. Dawlish – a private matter perhaps, but you'll forgive me – if you require a fair copy of the document my clerk can be relied on for absolute discretion."

"That won't be necessary, sir. But thank you again."

The day was uncomfortably warm and it added to her unease as she walked the quarter-mile to the photographer's studio, the envelope secreted in an inner pocket. The arrival of Livitski's bouquet had unsettled her and the same fear that had dogged her in London was beginning to gnaw again.

She realised that she knew Mr. Simpson by sight and that he knew her. An impeccably dressed bald-headed man, slightly smelling of chemicals, he was solicitude itself. Of course Mrs. Dawlish could be present while the photograph was taken and he would hand the document back to her immediately thereafter. He brushed away her suggestion that she might pay extra for fast development. He would personally undertake the process. And as to content there would be no fear that the document, or the copy, might be read. Florence saw the gleam in his eye, the hint of prurient suspicion of some adulterous intrigue. *Let him read it. He'll be disappointed.*

The photographic plate would not be ready until mid-afternoon but it was not too soon to send a letter to Lady Adelaide to request an interview as soon as possible. She hesitated to hint at the reason for it but settled at last on asking for advice on matters previously discussed. Unsure how to conduct herself when they met, she rehearsed in her mind a dozen openings, as many speeches, was satisfied with none of them. Her unease drove her to walk again along the Esplanade after lunch, endlessly churning over wording, occasionally glancing back to see if she was being followed. The sight of nursemaids with children, of a father holding up a boy to show him a warship nudging from the harbour and heading out to sea, made her feel lonely, even bereft. Nicholas's absence hurt.

"You have my word as a gentleman that confidentiality has been respected," Mr. Simpson was unctuous when he handed over the plate.

She held it against the light, saw the letterhead and crest sharply delineated in white against black, the handwriting too and the flowing signature, *Adelaide de C.*

"I look forward to seeing you on Sunday, Mrs. Dawlish." He was ushering her to the door. "And perhaps… perhaps you might like to take tea with Mrs. Simpson one afternoon."

She recognised that acquaintance with a captain's wife was to be valued by the mournful woman whom she had seen in church and whose husband was on the knife-edge between a trade and a profession. Respectability mattered.

"Yes. Mr. Simpson. We must arrange it sometime." She saw that he knew that she did not mean it but his manner never faltered as she left.

Back then to the solicitor. The photographic plate, enclosed in a large sealed envelope, was locked in his safe.

The letter itself she kept with her and would remain beneath her pillow when she slept.

*

Lady Adelaide's reply arrived by the second post two days later. She would be available – she did not say pleased – to receive Mrs. Dawlish for thirty minutes in mid-morning on Thursday. The days between seemed interminable, the urge to contact Mabel Bushwick and plead for her support almost irresistible.

Florence perused the newspapers in detail and there was still no reference, however guarded, to Oswald's case. There was none either in the *St. James Fortnightly* when it came on sale on the Tuesday. It contained yet further revelations about slum conditions, this time in Stepney, dwelt almost lovingly on details of squalor and privation, and demanded, as it seemed to do in every edition, establishment of a Royal Commission to investigate such matters. The main article was on another topic however, one that Staveley as editor proclaimed would be the start of what he termed a *New Crusade*. He named a name, a recently ennobled peer, and challenged him to deny his allegations. Lord Allingham of Thanet, formerly Mr. Stanley Allingham and known as "The Lucifer King", had blocked installation of improved ventilation in his match factories. Florence, sickened, had to look away from the engravings showing women afflicted with phosphorous poisoning, their lower jaws hideously deformed, teeth and gums exposed. Worst of all was depiction of a girl – name, Mary Pickering, age twenty-three – whose jaw had been surgically removed to save her life. Others were identified, a girl of nineteen, a mother of thirty-four and another of forty, whose deaths had been attributed to handling phosphorous. Lord Allingham's lawyers had argued successfully at inquests that all reasonable precautions had been taken, that violation of the working rules by the women themselves had been responsible. Small ex-gratia payments, one as much as twenty-five pounds, had subsequently been made to family members. Lord Allingham had refused to meet the *Fortnightly's* editor to discuss the matter and he was now holidaying with his wife and daughters at Monte Carlo.

The article was long, four double-column pages of small print, but Florence had the impression that every fact had been checked to incontestability. Statements were quoted not only from the wretched women's fellow workers but from doctors and clergymen likely to be trustworthy for the very reason that they were outraged enough to speak out against a powerful man. Further revelations were promised for the following edition. The article concluded with a challenge by

Staveley to debate the matter publicly with Lord Allingham. The crusade had commenced and would not slacken until justice had been done.

Having met the man, it was easy to imagine Staveley's smug righteousness as he had overseen the investigation and penned the article. But yet...

The man was effective.

At least one landlord of slum properties – an eminent lawyer and Member of Parliament – had embarked on improvements to his properties and had been awarded grudging credit in the *Fortnightly* for it. Shaming was effective where conscience was not. And Staveley was fearless, unhesitant to confront the powerful and the wealthy, and he could be so because of the impeachability of evidence systematically gathered. Depending on what might transpire around Dorcas Hayward and Rosewood House he might yet be useful, as useful as Raymond had been and might be again. It might well be wise to build bridges to him, possibly through Mabel Bushwick.

But first must come the interview – the confrontation rather – with Lady Adelaide de Courcey.

And Florence dreaded it.

17

Florence was shown into the same small parlour in which she had previously met Lady Adelaide. She was made to wait longer this time, thirty-five minutes beyond the appointed time, and there was no book, no magazine, to ease the boredom and the anticipation.

"Well, Mrs. Dawlish?" No greeting, no extended hand, no welcome, when the admiral's wife entered. She sat down but did not invite Florence to do so after she had risen to meet her.

Florence sat anyway on the settee she had been on.

"You've asked to see me, Mrs. Dawlish." Spoken like an accusation. Lady Adelaide glanced down at an ornate watch hanging from a chain around her neck.

"I want to talk about Dorcas Hayward." Hours of preparation for this moment, consideration and rejection of a dozen possible approaches, rehearsals of wording, had convinced her that her opening should be direct, should perhaps provoke Lady Adelaide into some blurted explanation.

And instead she looked not just surprised, but blank.

"Who are you talking about, Mrs. Dawlish?"

"Dorcas Hayward, Lady Adelaide. Dorcas Hayward, the girl I had seen abducted in the street. The girl I mentioned when I was last here. The girl who drowned herself in the harbour two weeks ago." She paused, hoping for some reaction but saw none. She kept her voice low, her tone measured, even though her heart was thumping. "The girl who was in your employment as a housemaid, Lady Adelaide. The girl who was brought here by your butler, Mr. Quentin, and by your housekeeper, Mrs. Tonge."

"Are you insane, Mrs. Dawlish?" No sign of anger, only of controlled alarm. "Are you well, ma'am?" A hint even of sympathy when she said, "Are you perhaps in a certain condition, Mrs. Dawlish? The burden of it while your husband is away can be heavy – I understand it, Mrs. Dawlish. I'm a naval wife myself and a mother too."

Florence was trembling now. She had been prepared for fury, for vehement denial, even for sly evasion. But not for this. The woman was more formidable than she had ever anticipated.

"Dorcas Hayward, Lady Adelaide. Are you telling me that…"

The woman had come to her feet, was stepping across with arms outstretched. Florence flinched, braced herself to strike back if necessary. But Lady Adelaide had dropped to sit by her side and was drawing her towards her. "It's not easy, Mrs. Dawlish. It's not easy, but we must bear it. We owe our husbands that." Her voice was gentle now, as reassuring as a parent's when comforting a child woken by nightmare. She drew Florence's head towards her shoulder, felt resistance and said, "It's not wrong to be like this, my dear. It takes all of us women differently. You should have come to me before." Her voice seemed to convey genuine regret when she said, "I was too hasty with you when you were here last, Mrs. Dawlish. I was too hasty and I apologise."

This woman is more dangerous than I ever could have feared and I don't know how to deal with her. But she cannot deny knowing Dorcas.

Florence pulled away towards the further end of the settee.

"I've got evidence that you knew Dorcas Hayward, Lady Adelaide, hard evidence. And even if you deny it then Mr. Quentin and Mrs. Tonge might be more forthcoming. Especially when they're questioned in a police station."

Lady Adelaide made no attempt to reach out again but her voice was calm, even soothing. "There's no Mr. Quentin here, Mrs. Dawlish, No Mrs. Tonge either."

"But… your butler, your housekeeper?"

"Mr. Quentin died three years ago. And Mrs. Tonge went to Australia shortly afterwards to live with her son there. My husband and I still miss them."

"I can't believe…" Words failed.

"I can ask my butler to come here, Mrs. Dawlish. His name is Withers. My present housekeeper too, Mrs. Avery. You're welcome to question them."

"That won't be needed, Lady Adelaide." Florence was feeling foolish now. The affair was deeper, wider, than she had ever conceived.

"And that unfortunate girl you mentioned. There was never any girl called Dorcas here." She settled back. "But I believe you must have known such a girl, that perhaps you tried to help her too. So tell me about her. I won't interrupt you, Mrs. Dawlish." Again that look of concern, as if for Florence, not herself. "But before you start some tea perhaps? Might that not help a little?"

Florence shook her head. *All I can do is behave as if this woman is as harmless as she wants to appear. Tell her the story and watch her reaction.*

Lady Adelaide listened. She frowned and pursed her lips at details of the brawl in the street and of the abduction. She shook her head in what seemed like exasperated indignation when Florence told how she had been treated at the police station. At several points she seemed about to interject a question but held back. Then came the story of how Florence had met the girl again, only hours, minutes perhaps, before she died. She felt tears gathering as she told it, even if this woman knew already of that pathetic girl, and blinking through them she saw no sign of guilt, rather one of shock. Silently, gently, Lady Adelaide reached a lace-edged handkerchief towards her. Florence took it and dabbed her eyes.

It was hard to tell of the identification in that squalid mortuary, harder still to force herself to describe exactly what she had seen there, so as to confront her hearer with the outrage of what had been done to that frail body. Lady Adelaide flinched, but stayed silent and it seemed the silence of horror and pity rather than of anger. She reached out and took Florence's hand and squeezed it. And it was comforting.

A long pause before Florence could continue. The desolation by the graveside with its two mourners was dreadful to recollect but somehow it was told of. Afterwards she began to weep.

"I didn't know this girl, Mrs. Dawlish. I declare before God that I never knew the poor creature." Lady Adelaide was visibly moved, had tears in her eyes also. She drew Florence towards her again so that her head rested on her shoulder. "You're a dear, good, Christian woman, Mrs. Dawlish. And I... If I had known more, if I had not been so hasty, so... so unthinking, I hope I could have helped. May God forgive me that I misjudged you..." Her voice was breaking.

There was comfort in her words, in her embrace, and yet still there must be caution. This woman might be clever, very clever.

"I went to Rosewood House, the place Dorcas had come from." There had been no flicker of recognition when the name had first been mentioned. "They knew about her there. She was a foundling, had no relations. And they told me your name. That you had written to the place, had heard of it from a friend."

Lady Adelaide was pushing her back, involuntarily it seemed. Her face had blanched. "I can't believe it. The wickedness of it! Oh, the wickedness!"

"That you had written on headed paper with your family crest. That you wanted a housemaid from there. That you had sent your butler and your housekeeper to bring poor Dorcas here. That you sent Mr. Quentin and Mrs. Tonge."

"Dear God! The wickedness! That poor, good Mr. Quentin's name be used like that! And Mrs. Tonge's – such a kindly, motherly woman!"

But the advantage must be pressed.

"I've got a letter here, Lady Adelaide. A letter in your hand."

"There can't be!" Bewilderment rather than surprise.

Florence produced it, the original, not a photographed copy. She handed it over without comment. Lady Adelaide took it and began to read. She got to the end, shook her head, then seemed to go back over it again. Then she held it up, the paper shaking slightly as her hand trembled.

"How did you come by this?"

"My friend manged to secrete it when we were at Rosewood House. From the office of the matron."

"It's not my handwriting. It's our notepaper – no doubt of that. But it's not my handwriting, Mrs. Dawlish. It's some disgraceful forgery." Then her face flushed and there was suspicion in her voice. "Are you trying to blackmail me, ma'am? Is this some criminal swindle?"

Keep calm, Florence. Keep calm but don't yield. Press your advantage. But a small voice also reminded her that Nicholas's career could end this minute. *This woman can have him broken, have me in a police cell. But the only way is forward.*

"Can you show me that the writing isn't yours? This is no blackmail, Lady Adelaide. If the writing isn't yours then you're as much a victim as that poor girl."

"How dare you come here and…" Lady Adelaide stopped, was obviously trying to control her anger. She stood up. "Follow me, Mrs. Dawlish."

She led her along a corridor to a small study, its décor obviously feminine, a writing desk in one corner, the scent of potpourri, a French window giving out on to a garden beyond. A half-completed letter lay on the blotting pad and a small pile of what looked like addressed envelopes by one side, unused crested writing-paper on the other. She picked up the letter and thrust it towards Florence.

"Look at this, Mrs. Dawlish. You can read it if you wish. There's nothing confidential, just a letter to my son. He's a naval officer himself" A hint of pride. "He's serving on the *Victoria and Albert.*"

The royal yacht. Assignments to it were keenly sought and were often stepping stones to higher things, Nicholas had said. Even being considered for such a posting demanded family connections he did not have himself.

Florence looked at the handwriting. It looked broadly similar to that on the document from Rosewood.

"And here, Mrs. Dawlish, look here." Lady Adelaide was picking up an addressed envelope. It was already sealed but she ripped it open and thrust the note inside to Florence. A cheque fluttered from it as she unfolded it. "A settlement with my milliner. And there – you see my signature. Does it bear any resemblance to that paper you brought me?"

Florence felt embarrassment, foolishness, and urge to apologise. *Don't yield.*

"Let's lay the letter I brought alongside your writing, Lady Adelaide. Let's compare them in detail."

An angry look. "If you insist, ma'am. If my word is not to be doubted." But the sheets were laid side by side.

And there was no doubt that the writing was different – similar, perhaps in another feminine hand, but definitely different.

"It's a forgery," Florence felt cold, her stomach knotted. "As you said, Lady Adelaide, it's a disgraceful forgery. I'm sorry that I doubted you but in the circumstances… because of poor Dorcas, I had to be sure."

The older woman gestured as if to wave the apology away. "You did right, Mrs. Dawlish. I hope I'd have done as much myself. But who could have done this? And why?"

"Are you sure that this is your writing paper?"

A nod. "No doubt of it."

"Is it always left like this on your desk? Where anybody who comes in might take a sheet?"

Another nod, a slow one, the significance clearly dawning, the realisation of treachery. "It's always here. We trust the servants, all of them. I could not imagine one of them doing this."

"Bear with me, Lady Adelaide." Florence took the forged letter and laid the cheque on top, manoeuvring the position until the signatures were roughly aligned. She went to the window, held them up against the sunlight. The outline of the forgery just showed through the cheque's paper. She adjusted the positioning further until one signature overlay the other directly. They were indeed different, but somebody had made a very good imitation of Lady Adelaide's hand.

"It's somebody in this house. Oh God! Somebody in this house did this."

"Did any of the maids here come from Rosewood House? Or any other orphanage?"

"I never heard of the place. And no servants came from any other place either. The same families have been with us for generations. People my husband's family or mine have always trusted and always will."

As my family served the Kegworths. As I too could have been described.

"Who else lives in this house?"

"Only my husband and myself. My son is on the yacht and both my daughters are married."

"But considering your husband's position there must be much entertaining here. And you yourself perhaps receive ladies?" The reference was embarrassing, to those tea-parties from which Florence knew she had always been excluded. "Could somebody have sneaked in here and…"

"No! Mrs. Dawlish! No! Nobody who comes here could do such a thing!" Then a pause, reluctant consideration, acceptance not easy. "But yes. It could have happened. It's always possible. Unlikely, but it could happen. But I can't imagine who might do it."

"A girl is dead, Lady Adelaide. And she was… was used badly before she chose to take her own life. Somebody has tried to link your name to hers. Somebody very wicked, somebody very clever. It's even worse than I thought before I came here."

"It's a matter for the police. We need to contact them immediately and…" Lady Adelaide stopped, face even whiter than before. "The shame of it! The very association with such a thing! My husband's position! The scandal!"

The police will be as useless as before They'll find cold trails and give up too easily. They'll smirk at this woman's discomfiture and promise everything and do nothing. They must be kept out of it for now. Better to feed this lady's doubts and fears.

"My experience is that they're insensitive in such matters," Florence said. "Very insensitive. And they have such close contacts with the more sensational parts of the press. I've heard that the more scurrilous journals even pay them for information."

"I've understood the same, Mrs. Dawlish. But we can't let this matter drop."

Florence felt a surge of respect – and something like liking. She had no doubt now that this woman had been innocent in the matter.

"I won't let it drop, Lady Adelaide." The vehemence in her own voice surprised her. "It's so clever, so clever that I wonder if you're the only one whose name has been used like this. If that's so then there may be other girls involved, girls who might yet be saved. I'll find out what's happening at Rosewood and … yes, I'll be careful."

"And I, Mrs. Dawlish? Can I help?"

"For now, one thing only. Question your servants, every one of them. Do it quietly, one by one. I've no doubt they're as good as you indicate but some of them – younger ones, silly young men or women – might see no harm in taking a few sheets of paper to give to somebody who'd asked for them. It could be the follower of a maid or some dubious girl whom a gullible footman might be consorting with." Florence had known such cases in her own days below stairs. "They might have been told it was for some practical joke. And they might have spoken innocently, with affection even, of Mr. Quentin and Mrs. Tonge. So their names too got used."

"But other visitors to the house?"

"Not a word, Lady Adelaide. Any enquiry, however cautious, might raise alarm too soon. But if you'd be kind enough to let me know about your questioning of the servants – yes, thank you. Perhaps we might speak when I know more about what happened at Rosewood?"

"You'll always be welcome here, my dear. You should…" Lady Adelaide's voice was tremulous. "You should have been welcome here before. I judged too easily, that you were… no, you're as much a lady as I am. And your husband – he's been sent to China, has he not, he and his fine ship? You must be proud of him and yet you do not wish to see him go. And we women must never let our men know it, that we begrudge every hour the Navy takes them from us, and yet that we are so grateful for them for what they do. I thank God each day for the splendid man I married, that I could support him in gaining all that he has achieved. I think that you must do the same."

"Yes." Florence's eyes were filling. An avalanche of memories. The caravanserai where Nicholas had arrived with his men when hope was all but gone, yet how she had known that he would come no matter what. The declaration of love in a boat gliding on an underground cistern in Istanbul. The desolation when he had disappeared in New Haven and her own role in his rescue. Shells from a Spanish gunboat falling around a fleeing yacht when only Nicholas's willingness to sacrifice himself could save her. And that nightmare miscarriage that had ended all hope for children, and the love he had shown then, the love that grew yet more intense because of that shared tragedy.

"Yes, Lady Adelaide. I thank God for it."

"Could you stay to lunch with me, Mrs. Dawlish? It's almost time."

She could, and she did, and when she left the house – she had refused the offer of a carriage – she felt she had another friend, however unlikely.

Agatha. Miss Weston. Mabel. Now Lady Adelaide as well.

She was not alone.

*

"There's a woman here to see you, ma'am." The clerk who oversaw administration at the Sailors Rest stuck his head in through the door of Florence's small office there.

"I think you mean a lady." His wording had irritated her. "I've told you before, Mr. Bolton. Every woman is a lady until she proves herself otherwise. Who is the lady?"

"She's been coming here nearly every day for the last week to ask for you. A Mrs. Shepton, ma'am."

"Please bring her up." Florence laid her pen down and supressed a flicker of annoyance at the intrusion. The prospect of an afternoon spent here reviewing expenditure and accounts, evaluating bids from three tradesmen for repair of the guttering, approving a contract worth ten pounds or less, had been attractive, the very mundaneness a brief relief from the awareness of evil that oppressed her. For evil was what it was and…

"Thank you for seeing me, ma'am."

All irritation vanished on seeing Mrs. Shepton. Her features seemed more haggard than before, their hue more pallid. Florence bid her sit and dreaded what she knew was coming.

"Did you hear anything of my boy, Mrs. Dawlish? I thought that perhaps while you were away you might have…"

"No Mrs. Shepton. I've heard nothing." The lie was merciful but it was bitter to utter. *Even if he's found alive she must never know the full truth of it.* "But we shouldn't give up hope. I'm sure he'll contact you when he can."

"He's such a good boy at heart. And we miss him so." A sob. "It's not knowing that's worst. And if he's already gone to America without seeing me I don't know what I'll do."

No word from Raymond about his investigations. Whatever he and his people find it's got to be broken to this wretched woman by me. And how I fear it…

They spoke for five minutes more, enquiries about the other Shepton children, assurances that they were well, each recognising the hollow conversation as a necessary formality and glad when it could be ended.

Oppressed, Florence chose to walk home along the Esplanade, the park to one side, the sea directly on the other. The sun was shining, the day warm, children playing on the grass, mothers sitting on rugs with the younger ones around them, nursemaids tending babies. A father was making ineffectual efforts to get an obviously home-made but ill-fashioned kite aloft but his failure did not lessen his small son's delight. The breeze was light, the water barely rippled, and an ironclad was steaming slowly towards the open sea, black hull glossy, upperworks brilliant white, funnel and masts deep yellow. And yet Nicholas had told her that despite many captains' obsession with smartness – some sought every reason to delay practice-firing lest it scorch and begrime the paintwork – rats might swarm and teem down in the bilges.

She stopped, chilled by a possibility she had not considered before. She had assumed, naively so perhaps, that Miss Braben had been taken in by a clever forgery, had taken the bogus Mr. Quentin and Mrs. Tonge at face value. Miss Braben had not questioned the story of Dorcas picking up Florence's glove and returning it on Southsea Esplanade. She had seemed genuinely shocked by the news of the girl's drowning. She had not hesitated to show the correspondence now known to be fake. Her deputy, the sour-faced Miss Watson, had collaborated the story. Miss Braben had given every indication of being as much a dupe as Lady Adelaide herself had been.

And yet…

Those three girls waiting in the hallway, two of them happy at the prospect of an outing, the third glum, unsmiling. The carriage – a landau, with its hood raised. A glimpse of a white-haired older man. And afterwards the encounter with that same carriage, hood still raised and curtains drawn, the coachman's face wholly expressionless.

As it might be with that ironclad, gleaming paintwork perhaps masking horror in her bilges, so too might it be with Rosewood. And, if so, the foulness there would be of a yet more terrible order, planned and executed with pitiless cunning. The forgery had proved that.

Florence was angry with herself now that she had been so easily impressed when – the recognition horrified her – she had helped place Maisie at the orphanage. The girl was little younger than Dorcas had been when … Her mind recoiled. Some things could not be imagined. Maisie might even now be at risk. She walked on, brooding, knowing that she must proceed with infinite caution. If Miss Braben was what she feared she might be then a direct approach would be futile. The enquiries she and Mabel had made about Dorcas would be too fresh in that woman's memory, even if the disappearance of the forged letter had not been noticed.

But someone else could go there, someone whose position justified enquires and whose impression of naïve benevolence might allay suspicion.

Agatha.

A telegram could bring her here tomorrow.

18

"Is there word of your brother?"

Florence had met Agatha at Portsmouth station and a cab was carrying them to the Albert Grove villa. It was to be a day-visit only, returning to London in the evening.

"A telegram. From Milan. It said he was well but was travelling onward. It didn't say where to." Sadness in Agatha's voice, acceptance that the long exile had begun. "Mamma was pleased, but Father wouldn't talk of it. He's gone back to Northamptonshire and…" she dabbed her eyes, "…I doubt if he'll come to London soon again. Perhaps never. He hasn't been to his club since… since Oswald went away."

They reached the villa and sat under sunshades in the garden at the rear. Susan brought them iced lemonade. It was another glorious summer day, bees nuzzling among the flowers, the air scented, the noises of the street outside muffled almost to silence. And now evil must be spoken of.

"Rosewood House," Florence said. "Something very bad may be happening there."

"Rosewood?" Shock.

"Something terrible, Agatha, though I can't be sure. I didn't speak to you of it before. You had worries enough. But now it can't be allowed to rest. What I've found out – with Mabel's help, she's been invaluable – may be worse than you can image. It's to do with that poor girl I saw being kidnapped."

"Tell me from the start, Florence." No longer the slightly flustered Agatha whom the commonplaces of daily life so often perplexed. Instead was the calm, measured voice of the intellect that had won Agatha the first female fellowship of the Royal Society.

She made no notes, but Florence sensed the facts being filed away as efficiently as if they had been in a shelf of files. There was no need to dwell on what might have happened to Dorcas – they had both tended women, and boys, who had been brutally used in Thrace, knew the full horror of it – but Florence sensed growing outrage.

"This letter, this forgery, Florence. May I see it?"

She fetched the photograph of it. The original was back in Mr. Bagshot's safe.

Agatha held it close to her pince-nez, examined it minutely.

"This Lady Adelaide, Florence. Do you believe her?"

"Yes. I didn't like the woman at first, nor she me. But I trust her now. And I think her now a much better person than I had thought. As she perhaps thinks better of me."

"And you now distrust Miss Braben? Why?"

Florence had left out one detail, the sight of Sir Herbert Mellish and his curtained landau. The man was on the board of the orphanage, helped with its running costs, had every right to visit there. She knew that he was a friend of Agatha's father, a fellow director of the Hyperion company. And Agatha had spoken of him with respect. Better to say nothing yet.

"Why do I distrust her? I'm not wholly sure if I do. But I have an uneasy feeling – you know the sort of thing. It's hard to explain but… yes, maybe because she seemed so calm about it. But if I'm right," Florence was speaking with vehemence she could not control now, "then Dorcas may not have been the only one. And the same might happen to other girls. Even Maisie. We can't take that risk."

"So what should we do, Florence?"

"We need more evidence. More like that letter. And I can't be seen going back to Rosewood, nor Mabel either. It will raise suspicion because we've no official standing there. But you have, Agatha. You're on the board of directors, you have the right to visit, to see records, to make it seem natural and innocent that you should, to seem naïvely pleased by what you find, to go away happy." Then the practicality hit her. "But we can't risk stealing another document. Notes would be needed, and making them would arouse suspicion and …"

"Trust me, Florence." Agatha was smiling and tapping her finger on her forehead. "Mathematics improve the memory. I'll manage."

Work at the Sailor's Rest was a welcome distraction for Florence until Agatha had made her visit to Rosewood. It must not seem urgent, should rather be a dutiful inspection by a new board member who had been impressed by what she had seen already and who wanted to know more. And Lady Agatha would like to meet Maisie and her dear little brother and sister again – they must be so happy now in their new home. A telegram from Agatha confirmed that she would visit on the coming Tuesday. Florence came up to London the day before and lodged again at the Charing Cross Hotel. She felt a flush of pride as she looked out on its forecourt from her room. Anonymous men had watched for her there and she had outwitted them. With Oswald long gone by now there was nothing more to fear.

Agatha dined with her at the hotel that evening, then came up to her room. They found nothing to add to the list of questions they had developed together a week before but being together felt somehow reassuring. They parted early. Florence would have welcomed seeing her father but he too was back in Northamptonshire with His Lordship, leaving only her brother Jack to provide transport for Agatha. She had told him to take the evening off, because he should be rested for the drive to Chigwell in the morning, but Florence suspected that it was to spare her the embarrassment of seeing him waiting patiently outside.

The next day passed glacially. She walked up the Mall and through St. James's Park. It was depressing to see so many homeless people sleeping on the grass there, even at midday, like bodies scattered on a battlefield, misery in the midst of power and plenty. After lunch she visited the National Gallery, yet there, as elsewhere, the thought of Agatha at Rosewood allowed her neither ease nor pleasure. She fretted that she should be there herself, knew that she would be a better match in guile to Miss Braben than Agatha could ever be. There was so much that could go wrong.

But nothing did.

"That woman thought I was a fool," Agatha said. "As so many people do, Florence. You've seen that so often. So I asked every stupid question I could think of."

"And a few others besides?"

"Quite a few others. And I got answers too."

They were in Florence's hotel room and the maid who had brought coffee had just left. Agatha was buoyant, flushed with the joy of a new purpose after the miseries of Oswald's disgrace.

"So Miss Braben saw nothing strange in the visit?"

"None that I could see. I was shown around again – and Maisie and her brother and sister seem to be happy there – and it was as spick and span as you could ask for and of course I was impressed by all I saw and I told her that. Not once either. And I asked all sorts of questions about the price of milk and the cost of bed linen and whether gas lighting could not be substituted for oil lamps because it's better for the eye-sight. I was most particular about the quality of the beeswax polish used on the furniture and whether Rhode Island Reds were better egg-layers than Black Minorcas – they've got a big chicken coop there, did you know that? – and I recommended that Miss Braben should consider keeping rabbits too, delights for the younger children to pet and good eating also."

Florence laughed. It was the Agatha she loved. "And the teaching of mathematics? Surely you had something to say about that?"

"My dear! How could you doubt me? I don't think Miss Braben knows who Pythagoras was or is, but she should know from me by now that no girl should leave Rosewood House without a close acquaintance with him."

Then, suddenly, the merriment was gone.

"It wasn't really fun, Florence, for all that I think I took Miss Braben in. It all seemed so happy there – just as on that day we brought Maisie there. I stopped and talked to many of the girls – Miss Braben was beaming like the Cheshire Cat beside me, and she told them who I was and I played up as Lady Bountiful – and I made silly little jokes and they laughed and seemed pleased to see me. But several older girls seemed so... so miserable, so withdrawn. And I thought I saw hatred in the looks of two of them when they were told who I was. Not the sort of resentment that people like me so often meet from those who envy our wealth. Something worse. As if I had injured them myself."

"Was one of those girls called Polly?" *Three girls dressed in what looked like a Sunday version of the usual uniform. Two looking forward to a drive in a landau. The third as morose as when she had been glimpsed once before, alone in her cubicle.*

"I believe she was. Yes. Polly was her name. We saw her on our first visit."

Florence let it go. *For now.* "But you did see the books?"

"An hour's interminable examination of accounts. I'm not a book-keeper but I got a strong impression that there was nothing amiss in that area. I doubt if the purchase of single cake of soap or box of lucifers hasn't been listed or that a penny of expenses hasn't been justified. But I shouldn't have been surprised. One of the other directors, Mr. Whittier, oversees financial matters. Miss Braben said that she valued his advice. She joked that he helped keep her on the straight and narrow and that she welcomed his visits."

"Mr. Whittier, the banker? Your father's friend?" *Dorcas had named him with terror.*

"Yes, Florence. He's a Hyperion director."

As is Sir Herbert Mellish.

"And do the girls welcome his visits also?"

Agatha looked surprised. "Yes. Miss Braben said they did. He likes to bring them out in his carriage for little treats."

Florence let it pass. "And you saw the registers too?

"Last of all. Miss Braben – that woman is arrogant, you were right to distrust her – she was so pleased that I'd been impressed by the accounts, and that I'd asked so many silly questions about the prices of cloudy spirits of ammonia and of starch and of cream of tartar that she could hardly contain her amusement. So she had no hesitation in letting me see the registers." She reached for her reticule and took out a notebook. "I made myself remember only the important points and I wrote them down as soon I could on the way back."

Florence would have been surprised had she not known Agatha so well. There were several pages of notes, and memorisation of what they contained, and her ability to recall it, must have demanded concentration of an all but inhuman order. Scrawled in a swaying coach, all but unreadable to anybody but the writer herself, they embodied a mass of detailed information that Miss Braben could never have imagined being carried away.

"Thirty-four children came to Rosewood in the last two years, twenty-six of them girls. Three were foundlings, thirteen had lost parents and their relatives couldn't afford to support them and the rest were put in by parents themselves – mainly widows and unmarried women. Eight children were removed by parents when their fortunes improved and eleven boys went to the *Brahmaputra* when they were twelve."

A first step towards use by those whom Oswald had consorted with.

"Twenty-five girls left in the last two years. Three were sent to a mental asylum – they seem to have had breakdowns – and twenty-two were placed in service." Agatha was not looking at the notes and probably had no need of them. "The youngest was fifteen and the oldest seventeen. They've all gone as maids to what seem like respectable households – doctors, clergy, lawyers, a mill owner, two maiden ladies, a general's widow, a member of parliament."

"How many had families, Agatha?"

"Sixteen. The rest had been foundlings, or the parents were dead, or no other relatives had ever come forward. One did have a brother but his whereabouts were unknown."

"And one of them was Dorcas Hayward?"

Agatha nodded. "Yes. And I memorised the names of the others and as much of the addresses they have gone to as I could manage."

A sudden inspiration, a shot in the dark. "What was the name of the girl who had a brother?"

"Emily Gleason."

Gleason. The name of a boy whose body had been cast into a river estuary. Florence was back in the house in Redburn Street with Oswald. Jemmy Gleason had a sister but she had disappeared, Oswald had said.

"Did the Braben woman say if he had been on the *Brahmaputra*? Or if he'd gone there from Rosewood House?"

"I never asked her anything at all. She thought that I was just leafing through the register. I complimented her on how neatly it was kept – and it was." But Agatha was suddenly looking alarmed. "The *Brahmaputra*? That training ship? You mean that there might be…"

"I'll explain later. Tell me first about those six girls." Florence had her own small memorandum book out now, its silver pencil in her hand.

Agatha looked embarrassed. "Other than Dorcas Hayward I could only remember four with confidence. And not the full addresses either. Just the towns or villages."

"Never mind, Agatha. You're working wonders already."

Emily Gleason, sixteen, was listed as furthest from London, at Christchurch in Dorset, in the household of a Dr. Henry Longworth. Rachel Barnes was a year older and had gone to the Misses Lily and Lydia Scott at Bentley in Hampshire. Mary Flood was at the home of a retired General Addis near Godalming in Surrey. Lucy Manners was in the service of the Reverend Charles Hurd, rector of the Sussex parish of Tamridge. Agatha was mortified that she could only remember that Rose Church was in Wimbledon but she could not recall for whom she worked.

"Did Braben say how these people knew of Rosewood?"

"She didn't say and I didn't ask. I didn't want to alert her. I just closed the register and started asking her whether she could be sure the mutton supplied to the pupils had been humanely slaughtered and whether the Sabbath was being strictly enough observed. I'm sure she thought I was a genuine fool. I can imagine her laughing about me with Miss Watson after I'd left."

Respectable-sounding homes. Miss Braben's files might well contain letters on headed paper arranging the employment, signed letters as convincing as those which purported to have been written by Lady Adelaide de Courcey. It was unlikely, almost unthinkable, that anybody might ever enquire about these girls who lacked all family and, even if they did, such letters would assuage all concern. Each of those girls might have been exposed already to the degradation from which Dorcas Hayward had fled. Some might yet be saved.

"We've got to go to each of those addresses." *It must start again. Fear of being followed. Evil that does not stop short of violation and murder. The confidence of so many involved that they are above the law.*

"You and me, Florence?"

But Florence was remembering the article about the phosphorous-poisoned match-girls in the *St. James Fortnightly*. It was fearless, accurate, well-evidenced enough to resist in court a charge of libel. She might not like Walter Staveley but he would know how to trace these orphan girls, to follow every lead, to delve into the rottenness at Rosewood, to confront and shame the arrogant and criminal, irrespective of who they were. He might not do it for the girls' sake, but he would most certainly do it for circulation. Florence was about to say as much when she remembered the earnest young *Fortnightly* journalist hovering in the street before the Kegworth mansion, hungry for news of Oswald's whereabouts. She could not expose Agatha to that.

"Yes, Agatha. You and me." Time enough to approach Staveley once more facts were known, once Oswald's disappearance was stale, forgotten news. "And not just you and me, Agatha. Mabel Bushwick too if she has not already gone back home."

For she too was a journalist, as wise and resourceful in the ways of investigation as Staveley himself. Resolute and capable, she would be an invaluable ally.

*

Agatha had not been easily convinced about involving Mabel. She only agreed if there should be no enquiries about Oswald, nor his thrashing and disappearance nor, most of all, about the Brewsters and dollar princesses. Florence went to see Mabel.

"Those are the terms," she said. It sounded too absolute for friendship but there was no avoiding it. She found it comforting to see Mabel again, to sense her strength and resolution and self-reliance, and she hoped it could continue "But this Rosewood business, it may be a story that could be of value to you as a journalist and…"

"No, Florence. Not as a journalist. I was with you in that mortuary, when we saw that girl, that poor defiled girl. I'm no more willing than you are to let it rest."

"How much longer will you be staying in England?"

"I'm booked from Liverpool in little more than two weeks. I've all the material I need for the articles about that subject that brought me here."

"We should be finished long before then." *But I don't know what 'finished' means.*

Mabel's hotel was clean and comfortable but certainly not luxurious. It seemed to cater to prosperous but not wealthy provincial families. It would be a less conspicuous address than the Charing Cross, and cheaper too – it would be wrong to allow Agatha to continue to cover costs. It seemed a good idea to transfer there and Florence did so that afternoon. They met Agatha there that evening to agree their division of work. The conversation was stilted at first, both Mabel and Agatha avoiding any reference that might lead to the undiscussable. Florence pretended to ignore their unease and produced the *Kelly's Handbook* she had borrowed from the hotel receptionist.

"Agatha has done so well," she said. "And now we can find the exact street addresses and house-numbers."

The atmosphere thawed as they searched the book. Only the Misses Scott could not be located but Bentley did not seem too large a place and it must be possible to find them by local enquiry. Florence would go there herself. General Addis and the Reverend Hurd might be impressed by a title of nobility and Agatha – Lady Agatha – and Mabel would visit them over the next two days.

"I want to investigate Emily Gleason myself," Florence said. "I'll travel to Christchurch tomorrow – it can be done in a day." She hoped she would find the girl unharmed there but a small, cowardly, unworthy fear nagged her. If she was there the girl might know nothing of her brother's death and yet it might be necessary to question her about anything he had ever told her of the *Brahmaputra*. It would be an agony to break the news, worse still perhaps to withhold the information should that seem expedient.

I've begun to lie easily, perhaps even to live a lie myself and to find it easy.

And there was no option. Not if justice was to be done.

19

Waterloo Station seemed an uncomfortable place when Florence took the train the following morning. The smell of the coal-smoke hanging against the roof and the press of bodies around the ticket-counter windows brought back the memory of blundering into Livitski. She realised that her fear of being followed had lain dormant but that it was as strong now as before. She wondered if it would ever leave her. The journey to Christchurch covered much the same route she had taken with Oswald and memory of his squalid confessions disturbed her. It had seemed right at the time – though barely so – to aid his escape but now she was doubting it.

An accessory after the fact.

The enormity of what Oswald had been involved with seemed far worse when focussed on the single name of Gleason. Her brother had been all that Emily, the girl she was hoping to find, had had in the world and he had been taken from her. The splendour and innocence of the countryside sliding past, the ripening corn, the cows chewing their cud in the shade of trees, a mare and her foal grazing close together, their tails lazily swishing flies, a wain glimpsed making its slow way along a dusty road, were all mocked by the vileness that had brought her on this journey.

It was past midday when she reached Christchurch but her heart was thumping and she knew she could neither eat nor rest. A cab brought her from the station to a narrow street that led directly into the sunlit churchyard of the medieval priory. *It's like a scene from Trollope, troubles always decorous, even the villains gentlemen. And yet so too in the world's eyes are those responsible for all the evil that has brought me here.*

The brass plate by the door of the pleasant Georgian house identified the practice of Henry Longworth M.D. Florence rang the bell and asked for the doctor when the door was opened by a middle-aged parlour maid.

"Oh, ma'am! Don't you know about the poor man? That he died a fortnight since, all sudden like?"

Another death.

"May I speak to the lady of the house?" Florence gave her card and was conducted into what must be the waiting room. It was oppressively warm and airless, clearly unused for days.

"Mrs. Dawlish?" The woman who entered was little older than herself. The widow's weeds looked inappropriate for her age, even if her face was wan and the eyes red-rimmed.

"I didn't know about your husband. I'm sorry to intrude. It must be so terrible."

"It was too cruel." Mrs. Longworth was close to weeping and she showed no curiosity about Florence's presence "Harry was so young! Not yet forty! And it was his goodness that killed him. He came back soaked that night. It had been wet and cold all day. But he went out again directly when a message came about a difficult confinement. He wouldn't listen to my pleas for him to change his clothes first and he came back chilled. His poor chest was never strong and when pneumonia set in…" She began to sob. The handkerchief she pressed to her eyes was already sodden.

Florence put her arms around her. The woman yielded to her and she sat her gently on a chair. *Is this how I might be if I lost Nicholas? Would I give myself up to grief like this? I can't be the first stranger she has broken down to like this. And there's nothing suspicious about this death.*

181

"My dear mother, not three years ago! And Harry's father a year before that. And my only brother is in Australia and my three little children are without a father. What can I do, Mrs..." She blinked through her tears at Florence's card. "Mrs. Dawlish." She collected herself. "Were you a patient?"

"No. And I'm afraid I never met your husband. I can see he was such a fine man, that your loss must be so tragic."

"But it is, Mrs. Dawlish! It is!" She began to sob again.

It took Florence another ten minutes before Mrs. Longworth was calm enough to hear the explanation for her visit. She had rehearsed her story on the train, that she had come to enquire about a girl from an orphanage she supported.

"St. Ursula's, in Clapham – and so badly needed. So much poverty, today! So many dangers and temptations for young women and so many who fall! And at St. Ursula's we place such importance in placing our girls in good families and we keep track of them afterwards. But the girl I've come here about left her place – it was in Brighton – after two months. Not a word to anybody! Then only last week we had word from another of our girls, a friend of hers, that she'd heard that this girl had found work at a doctor's house in Christchurch. She didn't know the name. And so the governing committee asked me to visit all the doctors in this town. Your husband and Doctor Beamish and Doctor Killigrew and Doctor Enfield and Doctor Transept." Florence had checked the names of the local practitioners in *Kelly's Handbook*.

Mrs. Longworth shook her head. "There's no young girl here. Just Cook and Sarah. They've been with the family since long before my marriage." She had not asked the girl's name, had shown no sign of suspicion.

"Perhaps I could speak to those two ladies," Florence said. "You know how it is with servants. They hear things. They might know of the girl being at some other doctor's." She sensed now that Mrs. Longworth wanted her gone, not from any guilt but rather from embarrassment for her unbridled grief.

"I'll ask them to come in. I'll leave you with them. Sarah will show you out."

Sarah, the housemaid. was at least fifty, the cook little younger. Neither had heard of Emily Gleason but they couldn't answer for all the doctors in Christchurch.

"Doctor Longworth seems to have been a very good man," Florence said.

"One of the best, ma'am. And his father before him, James he was too, like his son. Good Christian men – you'll never meet their better. Never took a penny, neither of them never did, from them as couldn't pay them, nor delayed a moment day or night if there was call for them, fee or no fee. They're missed, ma'am, they're surely missed!"

The respect and grief was obviously unfeigned. *Servants know people as they really are.* Yet somehow the late doctor's name had been appropriated.

Now for the most difficult part.

"I don't know the town well. I wonder if you could help me with directions to the other doctors?" Florence opened her reticule, made a show of rummaging, of seeming more fluttered as she did. "Oh, bother!" I do believe I've left my notebook at home." It was not, but rather in her pocket. "I remember the names but I needed to note down the addresses. And now I've lost them." She looked appealingly at the women. "It's so embarrassing! Could I trouble for a piece of paper? Anything, a blank page, a sheet of notepaper?"

The housemaid disappeared, was back quickly with a headed sheet. "Oh, Thank you so much, Sarah!" A glimpse of the lamented Doctor Longworth's name, the address beneath, as Florence folded it. She jotted down the other addresses on the back and the directions she received were as confusing as such instructions always were – turn right, second left, no! third left, then right – but she noted them solemnly. She made light of neither woman being able to remember the exact street where Doctor Killigrew lived – they knew it was on the far edge of town and somebody at the other addresses would know. When Florence left she gave each woman a shilling.

Back to the station, she drank a cup of coffee and nibbled a tea cake before her train arrived. She tried to ignore her growing sense of dread that this quest might be futile. There was no reason whatever to doubt what the mistress or the servants had said. Emily Gleason had never been with the Longworth family, had perhaps already disappeared for ever.

She scrutinised the sheet of headed notepaper again, admitted to herself that it could tell her no more. But there was almost certainly a similar sheet in the files of Rosewood House and written on by a hand closely approximating that of one of the Longworths, father or son. It would not have been difficult for some patient – a trusted social acquaintance perhaps – to snatch a sheet during an examination when the doctor's back was momentarily turned. And prescriptions would provide samples of handwriting and signature.

It could have been any of dozens, maybe of hundreds, of patients.

And she would never know which.

*

They gathered in the hotel again that evening. Agatha's and Mabel's expedition had been no more successful. General Addis had retired to the Italian Riviera – damp British winters had made his rheumatism unbearable – and had not been home for over four years. His unmarried daughter occupied the large house near Godalming on her own.

"She paints," Mabel said. "Not too well either, as far as I can judge – still-lifes and landscapes in oils – and she treats the whole place like one big studio, and an untidy one at that. But she was friendly and she invited us to come back. I think she hopes we'd buy some of her work. I can't think of anybody else doing so."

"Did she know of the girl – what was she called? Yes, Mary Flood."

Agatha shook her head. "No, and I believe her. The servants have been there for years – the cook's husband is the gardener. He's an old soldier who was in India with the general. The housemaid's younger but even she has been there for a decade."

"Headed paper?"

"I couldn't find an easy way to ask," Mabel said. "But if there is – and the place is so untidy, a chaos I'd say, that reams of it might be lying about anywhere – there would be no difficulty in filching some. And there appear to be visitors coming there often. Other artists who stay for a few days – a 'meeting of minds and talent', Miss Addis said. She didn't mention names and it was difficult for us to press for them."

So Mary Flood was as untraceable as Emily Gleason.

Florence told her story. For all their attempts at cheerfulness she suspected that her two friends shared her fear that what they had undertaken was impossible.

There was nothing for it but to press on.

Another morning departure from Waterloo, but the journey this time took little over an hour. The Bentley station was no more than an isolated halt and lay amid rolling countryside, cornfields and hop-gardens and patches of woodland. The village, Florence learned, was over a mile away. There was no cab for hire and she had resigned herself to walking there when a smart-looking trap arrived to pick up another lady who had also alighted from the train. The driver, a respectably dressed middle-aged man who might have been a squire, and was obviously the lady's husband, noticed Florence and asked if they could help. She said that she was seeking two sisters, the Misses Scott.

"Poor dears," the lady said. "So sad. But Miss Lydia bears up so heroically. A tower of strength."

It was not far out of their way, the gentleman said. They would be glad to drop Florence off there. She climbed in and a flourish of the whip set the trap off at a spanking pace.

"You know the ladies well, ma'am?" The wife was clearly curious.

"Not at all, I'm afraid" Florence dropped her voice. "I'm afraid it's rather a delicate matter."

Propriety discouraged further enquiry even if the answer had piqued it. Florence commented on the richness and beauty of the countryside and they agreed. Yes, they were lucky to be living here.

They reached the village and bowled along the single dusty street and on into the countryside beyond. Another mile brought them to a large half-timbered house set in a well-tended and luxuriant garden. Maiden ladies the Misses Scott might be, but there was clearly no shortage of money.

Florence was set down.

"I can call later to bring you back to the station." The husband had noticed that Florence had no baggage and had been glancing admiringly at her as he drove.

"That won't be possible, Matthew," the wife said." We've got that matter of the timber sale to discuss." She looked at Florence. "But we can send the stable boy to collect you, ma'am. At what time – two o'clock? No inconvenience at all, ma'am. He'll be here."

The old house's interior was immaculately clean and splendidly furnished, the impression given of a home dwelt in for generations by the same prosperous family. Florence was received by Miss Lydia in a wainscoted parlour with a now-cold inglenook fireplace and several portraits darkened by age.

"You'll have to make do with me, Mrs. Dawlish." She must be nearer ninety than eighty, and bent, and dependent on a cane for support, but she still radiated energy and indomitability. "My sister's bedridden. So what can I do for you – but no! I'm being a bad hostess. Would you like tea? Coffee? Lemonade if you like it."

It was uncomfortable to lie to this woman, to use the same story as the day before, the fictional St. Ursula's orphanage, the mythical friend who had heard that the missing Rachel Barnes had gone to work for a family called Scott in Hampshire. Florence realised that her delivery was nothing like so fluent as she had managed with the doctor's widow. She had seen the names of the Misses Scott in *Kelly's Handbook,* she had...

"None of this is true, is it, Mrs. Dawlish?" Miss Lydia interrupted and was looking at her with amused contempt rather than with anger. "Just because I'm old doesn't mean I'm a fool."

"It's not... not really..." Florence stammering, shocked, lost for words.

"Some form of swindle, I'll be bound. Can you guess how many families are called Scott in Hampshire? Dozens, hundreds maybe. And in this obscure village my sister and I are supposed to come first on the list of Scotts?"

"It's because it's on a direct rail-line from London, Miss Scott and ..."

"And I'm to hear a cock and bull story and to make a substantial donation before you leave? Or perhaps you'd like me to change my will?" The old lady was all but laughing. "You'd need to do better than that, Mrs. Dawlish, so you'll understand if I wish you 'Good day' and good hunting." She pushed herself to her feet with her cane. "There's the door, Mrs. Dawlish."

"Five minutes," Florence said. "Five minutes. Bring the Good Book and I'll swear on it if I must. Hear me out. I'll tell you as much as I can safely can." *This woman is palpably honest and too clever to hoodwink. I've got to risk trusting her.* "A girl's future, maybe her life, is at stake and..."

"I'll drink my coffee as you talk, ma'am." Miss Lydia sat down again.

"There's no St. Ursula's orphanage," Florence said. "But there is one in Chigwell called Rosewood House. Your sister's name and yours are in a register there. It indicates that a Rachel Barnes came here last year as a maid."

Miss Lydia's smile had disappeared.

"There's no Rachel Barnes here I've never heard the name before. And I've never heard of that place – what do you call it? Yes, Rosewood – and I doubt if my sister has either. We can ask her if you wish. I'm not even sure where Chigwell is. It's mentioned somewhere in Dickens, I recall, but that's as much as I know of it."

"It's possible that there's a letter there also, a forged letter, maybe even more than one, purporting to be from you or your sister. I can't be sure of that – I only know about the register – but it's quite likely."

"Is this some sort of blackmail, Mrs. Dawlish?" The voice icy now. This woman must have been fearsome in her prime, seemed formidable still.

"My husband is an officer of the Royal Navy. He's serving the Queen in China at this moment, at the risk of his life for all I know. Even if I was so wicked as to dream of blackmail I would never do anything that could be detrimental to his career or his honour." Florence fought to control the passion in her voice. "Do you think I would ever risk his reputation? The best man I've ever known? The man whose wife I'm proud to be?"

A long pause

"No, Mrs. Dawlish." The slightest smile. "But how can I believe a story so preposterous? How can you believe it yourself?"

Florence told the story. She did not mention Lady Adelaide by name and she did not mention Agatha's either.

"If you need corroboration then I'll identify these ladies. You could speak to them."

The old lady shook her head. That would not be necessary.

"Somebody used your name, just as the other lady's name was used," Florence said. "Somebody who knows you, perhaps well. Can you trust your servants implicitly?"

"With our lives. They've grown old with us."

"Do you used headed notepaper for your correspondence?" Florence asked.

A nod. "I can show you." Miss Lydia heaved herself up and went to a roll-top bureau in the corner. She pushed the cover up – it was unlocked – to show a large blotter pad, pens and ink by it, and small pigeon holes behind, each with its neat pile of writing paper or of envelopes of various sizes. "Here, ma'am." The sheet's heading, bore the two names and the address, Yewbank Cottage, near Bentley, Hants.

"Do you entertain many people here, Miss Scott?"

"Not any more, Mrs. Dawlish. Most of our friends have passed on, though their children are polite enough to invite us to social gatherings now and then. But I can't easily leave my sister and so the invitations get fewer by the year. The old get forgotten, Mrs. Dawlish, especially women. You'll find that when your own time comes."

"But family members perhaps come to visit?"

"Rarely, too rarely. My nephew is a judge in India. He's dutiful, but we only see him once in every few years. Two nieces, one married in Scotland and the other's husband has an estate in Ireland. And our cousin Reginald of course. He comes twice or three times a year."

The only relative living in England. It's worth probing. Think quickly!

"Sir Reginald Scott, you mean? The surgeon?" Florence tried to look surprised as she improvised. "What a small world! I met him once at a dinner. A fascinating man!"

"I fear not, Mrs. Dawlish. Reginald is on our dear mother's side. Reginald Whittier."

The link.

Florence's heart was thumping hard, her hands trembling. Miss Lydia's voice seemed distant.

"Dear Reginald. More like a younger brother than a cousin – he came to live with us after his parents died. And then he went into Tellson's bank, and was so successful there…"

Banker. Hyperion Director. Oversees financial matters. Miss Braben values his advice. The girls welcome his visits. And Dorcas had named him.

"…and later in other business also. He's too modest to admit it but I've heard that his name on a shares prospectus is as good a guarantee as the Bank of England itself."

"It must be trying looking after your sister, Miss Lydia." *Lead away from Reginald Whitter, don't let her see my interest in him.* "Trying, but rewarding. There can be few loves to match a sister's."

Miss Lydia insisted that Florence stay for lunch. That she was not invited to meet Miss Lily hinted that the lady's incapacity might be mental as well as physical. Florence made no further allusion to what had brought her here but spoke instead of the Sailor's Rest. Miss Lydia herself was still active in good works – there was more poverty among the farm labourers and cottiers than a visitor might suspect, she said. Before Florence left – the stable boy was back with the trap at two o'clock, as promised – she was bought out to see the garden. The beds there were thick with columbine and mallow and irises and tall blue delphiniums bowing under their own weight. Bumble bees bustled from flower to flower and burrowed among the petals. The scent was heavy, the summerhouse in one corner ideal for whiling away long, luxurious afternoons. A paradise.

One in which the serpent was a regular guest.

*

Agatha and Mabel's story was quickly told that evening. The Reverend Charles Hurd had never heard of Lucy Manners, nor had his wife either.

"He's an antiquarian," Agatha said. "We couldn't get away from him. He clearly loves an audience and we'd still be hearing about Anglo-Saxon barrows if we hadn't mentioned another appointment. They're all he cares about and I doubt if his duties as rector of Tamridge have bothered him much. We gathered that his curate does most of the work."

"Headed writing paper?"

"There was a half-written letter on his desk," Mabel said. "It was headed. And there were files and papers everywhere, piled on chairs and shelves and even on the floor. We could have picked up anything ourselves without him noticing."

"I've never seen a more untidy study." If the Reverend Hurd's was worse than Agatha's own then it must be chaotic.

"So no success?" Florence had hardly dared hope, yet some had remained.

Mabel was suddenly beaming. "We've kept the best for last. The curate arrived just before we left. A Reverend Martin Thursley, a consumptive-looking man, thirty-five or six I'd say. He wanted to leave when he saw that the rector had visitors but we kept him talking about the parish. I didn't like the look of him and I asked him outright if he'd heard of any Lucy Manners who might have come in service for a parishioner."

"He went pale," Agatha said. "I thought he'd drop. Then he flushed and said he'd never heard of such a name."

"Frightened," Mabel said. "Badly frightened. He had to rush off, he said, he'd forgotten an appointment to pray with a sick old lady. But before he did I asked if he'd heard of Rosewood House and the splendid work done there."

"And he hadn't?"

"He hadn't. But he all but choked getting the words out."

Two names, two links.

Progress.

20

The links were convincing, but tenuous, and Whittier was a sufficiently reputable figure to shrug off any accusations. Mention of his name had horrified Agatha – her father had always spoken so highly of him but she accepted reluctantly that his involvement looked suspicious. More evidence was needed and neither Mabel nor Agatha nor Florence herself could imagine what that 'more' should be. Even more perplexing was to know what action to take once the facts were better known. Florence's experiences with the police had left her with little confidence that they would press an investigation with any vigour. Mabel was in favour of seeking advice from Walter Staveley – the *St. James Fortnightly* was adept in exposing abuses – and Florence was also inclining to the thought. *But not yet*, she thought. Raymond might be an even more astute adviser. Information – any information, she guessed – was his stock in trade and he had already agreed to trace young Shepton. The Rosewood affair would surely interest him. She would not yet mention him to her friends, all the more so since it would be difficult to explain who or what he was.

They reached no conclusion even though they talked late into the evening. All that was agreed was to meet for lunch in a restaurant in Old Compton Street the following day.

Florence and Mabel found Agatha beaming when they found her there already.

"There's something wonderful, Florence!" She seemed bursting with impatience but she had to wait to say more until the waiter had left them in the private dining room she had engaged. At last they had the room to themselves.

"Rose Church," Agatha said.

"Rose Church?"

"The girl in Wimbledon. The address I could not remember! I made myself think about it before bed last night – it sometimes helps with mathematics! I wake in the night and know the answer, so why not this one also?"

"And it worked?" It seemed too much to hope.

Agatha said nothing. She had laid a notebook before her and she flipped it open at a page marked by a ribbon. She reached it across.

The writing was spidery, almost unreadable, but Florence knew it of old.

Bury. Copse Hill.

And the precise time. *03.47.*

"The notebook's always by my bed and I scribbled it down immediately!" Agatha was beginning to babble with mixed delight and pride. "Amazing how the brain works! It was the association, you know! Rose Church! Church – you see it? Church! Churchyard! Like a graveyard! And Bury! What you do with a corpse! And 'copse' so like that! Copse Hill!"

"We need the *Kelly's*," Florence was already on her feet, heart thumping. "We need to know the number!" She did not voice the fear that it might all be an illusion. "Let's get back to the hotel. We can check it there."

They hailed a cab outside. The short journey seemed endless, Agatha still chattering enthusiastically about the mysterious functions of the mind and Mabel silent like Florence and probably also not allowing herself to hope too much.

Florence's hands were shaking as she took the *Handbook* from the receptionist and she resisted the temptation to open it at C and to search for Copse Hill as she carried it to Mabel's room.

And there it was.

Bury, Frederick Thomas, b. 1821, M.A. (Oxon.)

And the house number. And the profession. Stockbroker.

It was still early afternoon and Wimbledon was less than an hour away.

"There's a good chance of finding at least his wife at home." Florence knew that any longer wait would be unbearable. "And better just two of us. Please don't be offended, Agatha dear, if you stay behind. I'm sorry to say that I can fib better than you and Mabel can look innocent while I do. We can meet here in the evening."

*

It was a big house, three stories, but there was an unwelcoming chill about it from the moment that the maid opened the door. Mrs. Bury was at home and she would see them. Florence disliked her immediately – her demeanour and manner identified her as the type of sour, mean-spirited, cheese-paring mistress that servants feared and despised. Florence launched into the story she had told before, though this time St. Ursula's had moved further afield, to Birmingham. The orphanage had found a good place for Rose Church in Coventry but she had disappeared recently after telling another girl that she had found better employment with a family called Bury in London. Such girls were in more danger than they ever guessed and the directors of St. Ursula's were keen to find her before the worst should befall her.

Mrs. Bury heard Florence out without comment but with ill grace. At the end she said she had never heard the name, knew nothing of any such girl. In any case she would never take an orphanage girl into her house.

"There's too much sympathy for women of that type. Decent people end up paying for them and for another generation born out of wedlock." She stood up, making it plain that the interview was at an end, and jerked the bell-pull to summon the maid to see them out.

Florence had expected this moment, had thought of ways to play it and each one was a gamble. *Two links, Whittier the banker and Thursley the clergymen.* There was only one chance but the banker seemed the better bet.

She smiled sweetly as she thanked Mrs. Bury. "It's somewhat of a coincidence meeting you," she said. "It must be your husband whom I heard my dear uncle refer to so."

"Your uncle, Mrs. Dawlish?"

"Mr. Reginald Whitter. Of Tellson's Bank. I heard him mention another banker he regularly did business with. He spoke highly of a Mr. Bury, and I do believe he mentioned Wimbledon."

No look of surprise nor of guilt either.

"Not my husband," Mrs. Bury said. "He's a stockbroker. Mr. Whittier would have been referring to my brother- in-law, Henry.

He's the banker of the family. He's a close friend of Mr. Whittier and he brought him to dine here several times. A charming man."

The third link.

*

They had agreed to meet Agatha at the Kegworth mansion on Piccadilly since absolute privacy would be assured there. Florence felt no embarrassment in entering it now. Most of the senior staff had returned to the estate in Northamptonshire to where Agatha's parents had both retreated. The sense of triumph carried the three women through the dinner served in a small dining room but it faded afterwards as they debated what to do next.

Suddenly Agatha began to weep, tears running from beneath her pince-nez, her face flushed, great shudders rippling through her bulk. Florence threw herself on her knees beside her and drew her head to her shoulder.

"There, Agatha. There, there." It made it worse that Florence had never seen her break down like this, not even in Thrace when death and worse had been imminent.

"It's the shame of it," Agatha sobbed. "That the family's been associated with it! Mamma on the Rosewood board before I replaced her. And Mr. Whittier! A director of Hyperion, just like Papa. The shame of it will kill him and Mamma too. First Oswald, now this. It's too much!"

It's even worse than you think, Agatha. Sir Herbert Messish, your father's other fellow director of Hyperion is also involved. But better to say nothing yet. Florence held her close, rocking her, and nodded to Mabel not to intervene. Agatha was strong and would be her herself again.

But not tonight.

Better to let her sleep it off, to resume the discussion the following day, to let the sharp, logical brain that had won her fellowship of the Royal Society assert itself over fear and sorrow. She was already calm, but still tearful, when Florence and Mabel took their leave.

"It's dark outside," Agatha said. "Piccadilly is no place for ladies to pick up a cab." It wasn't. Women of the street thronged its other end and the night business of many cabs moving along it depended on men accompanying them to their lodgings. "Florence, dear," Agatha was pressing her hand. "You won't be offended if I ask your

193

brother to take you and Mabel to your hotel? It's embarrassing for you I know but…" She paused, guessing most likely that Florence had never told Mabel that her brother was in service here. "…it's because I care for you and all you've done for us."

"It will be fine," Florence said. "Jack won't be embarrassed and I won't either. He's always been a good brother." She saw the surprise on Mabel's face but explanation could wait.

Jack must have been put on notice in expectation of assent, for the clarence was waiting outside the front door. He smiled down from the box as a footman helped them in. "Good evening, Mrs. Dawlish!" He touched his whip to his temple in salute. "And the American lady too! A fine evening for a drive!"

Mabel was impressed when she heard of the relationship. "You're a lucky woman to have such a brother, Florence! What a splendid-looking man, and such an accomplished driver, and no sense of stigma about honest toil. He'd do well in the States."

And he was to do well outside the hotel.

*

The street was deserted when the clarence drew up before the hotel steps. Jack had locked the brake and had swung himself down to open the door and had helped Mabel out. He now stretched his hand out to Florence. One foot only had reached the ground and he was saying "Always a lady, Florrie, you was always a lady to me." His words touched her heart.

And then the cry.

"Mrs. Dawlish! Mrs. Dawlish, you bitch!"

She spun about. A burly figure was rushing from the shadows, his face muffled in a scarf. His right hand was drawn back and a reflected gleam from a street light told that it held a bottle.

"Take this, you bitch!"

It flew from his hand and in a dreadful moment of terror Florence realised what it must be. She screamed, but already Jack was throwing her to the ground and shielding her with his body even as he tried to drag Mabel down also.

An aeon passed, sight blocked by Jack's bulk, gut-wrenching horror – *O God! Not that, not Jack nor Mabel either, not…* Then the sound of glass shattering on the iron-bound wheel and an acrid, throat-searing stench as Mabel shrieked and Jack gasped and writhed in pain.

Florence heard running feet as Jack heaved himself off her. She sensed another coach drawing up down the street, bodies spilling from it, a figure collapsing beneath them, but it was remote, as if in a distant universe, and hers was filled with Mabel's jerking body and her screams of pain.

"Vitriol!" Jack was pulling Florence to her feet and then dragging off his coat as wisps of white vapour rose from scattered points on its sleeves. Then he was ripping Mabel's shawl off – it was already half-eaten by the acid – and tearing away her linen jacket. Mabel was trying to rise to her feet and Florence saw – *Thank God! Thank God!* –that her face was untouched but that the blouse was smouldering on the right shoulder and the white skin beneath was bubbling. Mabel was thrashing in agony and fear as Florence ripped away the garment.

The hotel porter had emerged on the steps above and Florence shouted "Get her inside! Get her to a bathroom!"

Jack was trying to lift Mabel but her spasms were tearing her from his grasp. Florence bent to help, her words of comfort futile, Mabel's terror-filled eyes a horror never to be forgotten. And suddenly somebody else was beside her.

"Step back, Florence Hanim. I can do this better."

And Count Sergei Ivanovich Livitski scooped Mabel up in his arms as Jack strove to calm her and together they rushed up the steps, through the doors the porter had thrown open for them.

"Show us to a bathroom," Livitski yelled and the porter scurried on ahead. Florence glanced back before she followed. The other coach was forty yards away, a dark mass silhouetted against the glow of a street lamp behind. Two men were bundling a third into it. But that was of no concern now and only Mabel mattered.

They were ahead of her on the staircase. Mabel's cries were now moans that seemed more fearful, more pathetic than her former screams, as if a proud strong woman had been degraded. Livitski cradled her to him as Jack kicked open a door the porter was gesturing to and then they were inside. Mabel was already in the bath when Florence entered. Water was gushing from the tap and Livitski was scooping it in his hands and dashing it over the great red patch on Mabel's shoulder as Jack held her still. Her chemise had been ripped away, exposing her breast, but Florence's heart soared as she saw that the vitriol had not run down so far.

"Is there a doctor near?" Livitski shouted at the porter. "Yes! Then bring this man to him!" He nodded to Jack. "Drive like the wind but get the doctor here no matter what it takes." Jack bundled the porter before him as he left.

The housekeeper had arrived, two maids, all but paralysed by the sight.

"You've got laudanum here? Yes! Bring it! As much as you can!" Livitski's words sent them rushing away.

"Is it bad?" Mabel sobbed. "Oh Florence, tell me it isn't bad." She could not bring her terror-filled eyes to look at the injury.

"It's not bad, Mabel, it's not bad at all." Florence, like Livitski, was still pouring water over the blotch. Skin had shrivelled and the flesh was raw beneath, and obscene blisters clustered at the edges, but the patch was smaller than it might have been, six or eight inches across the shoulder and collar bone. *It was meant for my face*, Florence thought. The realisation that there could be so much evil, so much hate, chilled her. She was trembling herself now.

"You were not hurt yourself, Florence Hanim?" Livitski had noticed her hands shaking and she sensed a kindness in his voice that she could never have expected.

"No. I'm not hurt." Only now was surprise dawning on her that Livitski should be here and that they were working together in this nightmare.

"I didn't see him until too late," he said. "A moment later and I could have..." He broke off as the housekeeper arrived with the laudanum.

"Here, this will ease it, dear." Florence held the bottle to Mabel's lips, saw her swallow, knew that the mouthful was many times what should normally be administered. "It'll be easier now, Mabel, and it will heal, and nobody will ever see the scar." She eased the bottle from the clenched teeth.

Mabel calmed and her eyes glazed.

"We can take her to her room now," Livitski said. "Show me the way, Florence Hanim" He told the housekeeper to follow with bowls of water and towels.

"Should we call the police, sir?" The porter had been hovering in the doorway.

"No police!" Livitski was adamant. "You understand? I'll settle this business myself!"

The porter stammered compliance.

They laid Mabel on her bed. Her clothing was saturated. "Can you strip her as best you can, Florence Hanim?" Livitski said. "Cover her then, keep her warm. Keep bathing the burn. I'll wait in the corridor." He turned to the housekeeper and porter. "No word of this outside, you understand? You'll be rewarded. Do everything that Mrs. Dawlish tells you."

Jack arrived with the doctor soon after. Mabel was all but asleep. She jerked but calmed again as a salve was spread on the scorched area and a dressing applied.

"She'll need a nurse to stay with her," the doctor said. He scribbled a note for a reliable woman who lived not far off. Jack was sent to fetch her. Florence accompanied him to the entrance.

"You weren't burned, Jack, were you?" Her eyes filled up.

"I got the jacket off in time, Florrie. Just you worry about that poor American lady."

She watched from the steps as he drove away and saw too that the street was empty. No second coach.

"Florence Hanim." Livitski was standing behind her. "We have the man who did it."

His words hardly registered but now the strangeness of the count's presence struck her.

"You were following us," she said.

"I was following you. For days. If I wasn't then one of my people was. Christchurch, Bentley, Wimbledon today. You'd grown careless, Florence Hanim."

"Why?"

"Your friend's brother. I was sure that you'd bring me to him sooner or later." No hint of menace in Livitski's voice. "I'd still like to make him a certain offer though I doubt you'd tell me where to find him."

"I couldn't." She found herself starting to laugh, a sudden release of the tension that had gripped her since the attack. "He's gone. I helped get him away. He's in Europe, somewhere. Not even his own family know where he is. But why do you still want to find him?"

"He knows certain things that my government would like to know. And a bitter man who's been shamed and driven into exile is often glad to reveal such matters."

She felt a surge of indignation "He's not a traitor," she said. "He's loyal to his Queen and to his country no matter what. Would you betray your Czar if you were in a similar situation, if you were shamed as he has been?"

He shook his head. "Either a bullet in the head or silence in exile. I would see no other choice."

"Neither did Oswald." She had never expected she would ever defend his name.

He showed no anger and she felt no threat. The camaraderie that had carried them through the last hour was still strong.

"You were following me when you approached me at Waterloo Station."

He shook his head. "No. I was surprised to see you there – it was purely accidental – but I was glad too. I had been hoping that..."

"You should not have sent those flowers, Count. Let's not talk of admiration. There's only one man I love or ever will. I'm a wife and I'll never be a mistress. So please, no more of it."

"You looked beautiful that day even though you were dressed like a servant." A hint of wistfulness. "It was only then I realised that you were playing some game. I knew of Lord Oswald's disappearance, knew too of your friendship with his sister. It wasn't hard to guess what you were involved in. And I became sure of it when you left the train at Woking. I lost sight of you there. It was well done there. Very well done."

So he doesn't know of my visit to Raymond and it's better that it remains so.

"Since when have I been followed?"

"Since you left Southsea. But you would never have been harmed. You must believe that, Florence." He had dropped the *Hanim*.

The clatter of hoof-beats on cobbles, the clarence swaying into sight from around the corner, Jack in his shirtsleeves on the box. The nurse was arriving.

"So who did this – this awful thing – tonight, Count?" Florence asked.

"I don't know." The tone suddenly chilling. "But we'll find out. We have the man, the animal. And if you'll trust me, Florence – and you have my word that you can in all honour and safety – you must come with me. Your life and your friends' lives are in danger otherwise."

They left Mabel sleeping, the nurse by the bedside, the doctor pledged to return in the early hours, the porter and the housekeeper and the maids bound to silence by gold sovereigns pressed into their palms.

Jack, now in a coat borrowed from the porter, carried Florence and the Count westwards in the clarence.

Towards the Russian Embassy.

21

They entered not through the front entrance but from the mews, to where Livitski had directed Jack. Despite his English clothing Florence recognised the man who led them along a passageway and down steps as the driver whom she had previously seen in traditional Cossack costume. She could not understand his answers to Livitski's brief questions, only the deferential *Da* and *Nyet* that she knew to be Yes and No.

They stopped outside an iron-bound wooden door.

"This will not be pleasant, Florence," Livitski said. "Would you like your brother to be with you?"

"No." For all that she had trusted herself to the count she would feel more secure if Jack remained in the yard and knew where she was. In the worst case…

Livitski pounded on the door, spoke in Russian. The sound of bolts drawn. It swung open.

The cellar was large, well-lit by gaslight and its walls whitewashed. Wooden boxes were piled against the rear wall and the two small windows high on one side were heavily barred inside and covered with dark-painted glass on the outer side. But it was to the figure tied to the single chair in the centre of the room that Florence's gaze was drawn, shirt ripped away from the huge, flabby and blood-striped torso, the face dark with bruises and one eye lost behind a huge swelling. Two men, one with Asiatic features, an Uzbek perhaps, stood by him and bowed as Livitski approached. He spoke and was answered with a single "*Nyet*".

This is the man who tried to disfigure me, who scarred Mabel for life. Florence felt the same cold loathing, the same lack of sympathy as when she had once pushed a revolver into a Bashi Bazook's face and pulled the trigger.

Livitski reached out and lifted the bound man's chin. "You can hear me? Good. And you can see me?" He gestured towards the brick arched ceiling above. "And you can see what's up there too, I believe?"

The man moaned as he looked up to the iron ring set in the stonework above.

"We won't be needing it if you're willing to talk." Livitski's voice was soft. "But you'll start by apologising to this lady."

The man mumbled something. Livitski nodded to the Uzbek who balled his fist and drove it hard into the man's stomach.

"Louder," Livitski said. "The lady didn't hear you."

A stammered, meaningless expression of regret when the prisoner stopped retching. It left Florence cold.

"You know that you're in sovereign Russian territory. No British power can save you here. and there" – Livitski gestured to the barred windows– "are two layers of glass that nobody will hear your screams through. So I think you're going to answer my questions, aren't you?"

A weak nod, and a mumble that might have been assent.

"What's your name?"

"Sankey. Peter Sankey."

"Why did you attack this lady?"

Hesitation, then flinching as a nod from Livitski brought the Uzbek closer.

"It wasn't my idea, it wasn't..."

Another blow to Sankey's stomach. He jerked and vomit ran down his chest.

"Somebody paid you?"

"I didn't take money. It was for old time's sake."

"Who? I want a name. I'll have it from you if it takes all night."

Hesitation before he said it in a whisper. "Dolly Braben."

"Does the name mean anything to you?" Livitski turned to Florence.

It's even worse than I could ever have thought.

"It does," Florence felt fury now. She leant over and looked Sankey in the face. "Miss Dorothy Braben of Rosewood House?"

"She's still the same Dolly. Like when we was working together." The admission seemed to have loosened Sankey's tongue.

"Me and her and old Jenny Coleman that was. In Jenny's place in Lord North Street. Plenty of fine gentlemen clients. Some of the very best." A hint of pride even at this extremity. "Dolly got respectable and …"

"Respectable? How?" Florence said.

"Some gentlemen who used to come to Ma Coleman's. They wanted Dolly to manage that home for girls in Chigwell for them."

"And that woman gave you my name?"

"Mrs. Dawlish, that's what she said."

"When?"

"This morning. She came to see me. She'd had a telegram the night before… "

It could only be from that curate, Thursley, the Reverend Martin Thursley. He had only met Agatha and Mabel but when Miss Braben had been notified she must have seen me as leading the hunt.

"…she was leaving immediately, she said, her and that Watson woman who helps her. But Dolly said she wanted to leave you something to remember her by."

At Livitski's nod the Uzbek struck Sankey again.

"Where's she gone?"

"Antwerp." The word almost inaudible. "She'll be half-way there by now. She sailed this morning."

"Why Antwerp?"

"We did business there. We sent a lot of girls there after Dolly passed them on to me."

"So you're still working with her?"

A moan that seemed like confirmation.

"Emily Gleason," Florence said.

The name seemed to shock Sankey – he clearly recognised it – but he dropped his head and shook it.

"Mary Flood." All the names were clear in her mind. *Nobody spoke for them, but I will.* "Rachel Barnes. Where are they now?"

He would not look her in the eye.

"Lucy Manners. Rose Church."

Livitski grabbed him by the hair and dragged his head back. "Mrs. Dawlish wants an answer."

"I don't know. They wasn't our business after we got them to Antwerp." Sankey was sobbing. "People we did business with there sent them on, Germany, Belgium, France, God knows where."

"People you sold them to? Like cattle?" Florence had never felt anger so cold, so merciless as she did now.

"I was only the middleman. Dolly was the one who…"

"Dorcas Hayward."

His eyes darted in terror from Florence to Livitski and back again. "Never heard of her. God's honest truth, ma'am. I never heard the name."

Livitski released his head and said something to the Uzbek. The man moved to the stacked boxes and lifted a coil of rope that lay on top. He walked back and with a single fluid, practiced motion cast the end upwards. It snaked through the ring in the ceiling, hung swinging on the other side. He reached up and pulled it down. Sankey's eyes were locked on it and he moaned.

"The lady asked about a girl called – what was her name, Mrs. Dawlish? – yes, Dorcas Hayward." Livitski's hand moved to the rope end.

"She was a special case." Sankey's words were a whisper. "The girls didn't usually stay in England. But somebody in Portsmouth must have been glad to pay for a girl like Dorcas."

"Who in Portsmouth?"

"I never knew. I just brought her there and handed her over." His eyes were locked on the rope end. "I'd tell you if I could, as God is my witness I would. But it was night and it was dark and the men's faces was covered and they never said their names. It was Dolly who'd organised it, only she would have known who they was. That girl must have been wanted in some flash place in Portsmouth. Dolly knew people all over. She made her own deals."

Livitski swung the rope end slowly, like a pendulum. "You'll tell the truth sooner or later."

Sankey was sobbing now, collapsed within his bounds, a dark patch spreading around his crotch and liquid pooling on the floor beneath him. "It's true," he gasped. "On my oath it's true. I wouldn't lie to you. I wouldn't be such a fool. If I knew who them people in Portsmouth was I'd tell you."

"I've some more questions," Florence lowered her face to look directly into his. She saw dread incarnate and felt no pity. "More names. Do you know them? You'll answer me truthfully."

"As God is my judge, ma'am."

"Lady Adelaide de Courcey."

No flicker of recognition. A mumbled but convincing denial

"General Addis."

He shook his head.

She ran through the other names, Dr. Longworth, Miss Lydia Scott, the Reverend Charles Hurd, Frederick Bury. He said he knew none of the names and she saw that he was too terrified to lie. Miss Braben must have played her cards very close to her chest. Sankey was her thuggish lackey, but little more.

And then the two names she had been holding back for last.

"Sir Herbert Mellish. Reginald Whittier."

He hesitated before he answered, then said, "Yes. They used to come to Ma Coleman's. Dolly was their favourite, she was for both of them."

"And they got her to manage the home for girls?"

"It was her idea but it was them as set it up, paid for it, put her in charge. Them and some friends of theirs. I don't know who, and that's God's truth"

And they drew in Agatha's mother as a board member. As unwitting cover for their own private brothel. One they could share with others of their type.

"You'd testify to this?"

"It would be my word against theirs. Nobody's going to believe me."

We're no further forward. Miss Braben's gone and all the blame can be laid on her. No court would accept Sankey's word against the words of Mellish or Whittier. And there's no hard evidence.

"You'd get the cat and ten-years hard labour at the least for the vitriol attack," Livitski said. "We've witnesses enough to swear to it." He turned to Florence. "A word with you in private."

Outside the door he said, "There's another way. No police, no reporting of the attack, no prosecution, no matter what he deserves. He'll pay for that with a signed statement, all he told us, maybe more, and witnessed by the solicitors who handle our routine business. It wouldn't stand up in one of your courts of law but if delivered to some influential people in government it might get results." He smiled. "Unofficial results, Florence, but all the more effective for that. I'm sure Lady Agatha's father would know who to speak to."

Not Lord Kegworth. Somebody much more ruthless. Raymond. No need to mention him to Livitski.

"You can hold this man here, count?"

"Oh, yes." He smiled. "We can keep him here as long as you like."

She had an immediate impression that it was not an unusual occurrence.

"You're not just a diplomat, are you, Count?"

"You've guessed the answer to that already, Florence. I guard my Czar's interests no less than your husband does your Queen's."

"Why are you helping me now? This affair is of no interest to you. You know that I love my husband. You know that Oswald is already gone, that I would never tell you where to, even if I knew. What do you want of me?"

"Nothing." Sadness in his voice, sincerity also. "That man in there, that animal, tried to destroy the beauty of a woman I admire. That's reason enough to help all I can." He looked away.

An awkward silence, seconds only, yet it seemed like hours. Florence broke it.

"I want a signed confession." She tried to sound brisk, business-like. "All he told us, all he's probably holding back still. Thorough, witnessed by those solicitors you mentioned. To be delivered to my hotel – no, wait, better to my address in Southsea. You can do that for me, Count?"

Livitski was no less brisk and business-like. "Mr. Sankey will be most cooperative in helping me arrange that, Florence Hanim."

And Florence felt no pity in her heart as Jack drove her back to the hotel where Mabel lay in drugged stupor.

As we forgive those who trespass against us…

The hardest commandment of all.

*

Florence stopped at the hotel only long enough to satisfy herself that Mabel was well attended to. More salve had been applied and the wound had been lightly covered with gauze. The doctor arrived back while she was there. And yes, it would be safe to move Mabel in the coming day, though she must be sedated, and yes, he could arrange for yet more nursing care. Then Florence left Mabel in her drugged sleep and had Jack take her to the mansion on Piccadilly. A sleepy footman whom their knocking had aroused admitted them.

"Agatha, Agatha dear," Florence had gone directly to her friend's room and was shaking her into wakefulness. "Something's happened. Something very bad."

The full horror of what might have been, of what had been so narrowly averted, oppressed her as she spoke. Which was worse, she wondered, the vicious malice of the attack or the long squalor that Mellish and Whittier and Braben – and perhaps many more as yet unknown – had engineered. She held nothing back from Agatha, not Livitski, not what had happened in the cellar, nothing but one last detail. But at the end of her account she broke down, the tension she had controlled all night suddenly unleashed. Agatha held her tight and rocked her.

"I'll go to Mabel immediately," Agatha said. "You stay here and rest. You've done enough for now, Florence. And that doctor said she could be moved? Carefully? Yes? That's good. We'll bring here as soon as possible. She can have every comfort, every care, and she'll be safe."

"Wait Agatha. There is more you must know." Florence had hesitated to mention it before, but now there was no option. "It's about a colleague of your father's."

Agatha blanched when she heard about Mellish's involvement.

"Papa always spoke so highly of him." She was brushing tears away. "He regarded him as a friend and…" Then stopped, her face a mask of agony, too frightened to voice the fear now rising in her.

Florence took her hand. "Your father is a good man, Agatha. There's no mention of his name. If he has a fault it's that he was too pure-minded and trusting ever to suspect such men."

"Thank you, Florence. God bless you."

"There's something else, Agatha, and we can't ignore it. Rosewood House. There's nobody in charge there and before we know it Mellish and Whittier will have another creature of theirs installed there and doing their bidding."

"But the board, Florence! The Rosewood directors must approve!"

"There's no time for that, and God knows who else on the board may be in league with Mellish and Whittier. You may be the only director who isn't. You could be outvoted and they'll be clever enough to portray you as – forgive me, Agatha, but I've got to say it – as an eccentric spinster whose head had been turned by mathematics and scientific theory. If they're ready to destroy my face they won't hesitate to ruin your reputation."

"What then?" Agatha was no stranger to ridicule. It was cruel, effective, and it hurt.

"You must go to Rosewood today, Agatha." As Jack brought her here Florence had realised that there was no alternative. "You must take charge yourself. You must bring Mabel with you – she'll be able to travel, the doctor says. It'll be painful, but she's strong, and she'll have a nurse with her and we can have a second sent on afterwards. Jack will bring you, and he can take a footman with him. They can stay there, they'll be your protection."

"But I won't know how to start! The organisation! The books!"

"Remember Turkey, Agatha? Remember Thrace? The refugees, the hunger, the cold, the fear? How we somehow fed them and nursed them and got those Bulgarian girls to help us? How you coped then? Even when all hope was lost. I could not have borne it were it not for you."

"And I could bear it only because of you, Florence." Tears glistened in Agatha's eyes and trickled down the kind, sheep-like face. "If you could come with me to Rosewood then I'd …"

"Mabel will be more than enough. It may even help her recovery to keep busy. And once you're there – and they won't expect you being there if you act quickly – you'll be able to keep Mellish and Whittier at bay until…"

"Until what, Florence?"

"I don't know." Her mind was numbed by the complexities and uncertainties. She felt an enormous evil weighing upon her, a knowledge of wickedness she did not want to know existed but could not ignore, a fear as to how far the network of corruption extended. And, worst of all, recognition that those involved would not shrink from extreme violence.

Agatha must have seen it too and she hesitated before she answered. "I'll go to Rosewood. I'll do it."

"One more thing," Florence said. "You must contact your father – no need yet to tell him the details. Just say you're needed at Rosewood. But ask him to send a gamekeeper to you – Fred Marlow would be ideal – and have him bring three shotguns with him."

"Three?"

"For himself. One for Jack – he knows how to shoot. And Fred can instruct the footman. They'll need to keep watch night and day."

"And you're not coming, Florence? You're sure?"

"There are things I can only do alone."

With help. And not from Count Livitski alone.

*

It was better not to be in London for now, not again until she had Sankey's confession, not until certain other arrangements were in hand. She waited until she had seen Agatha and an obviously pain-racked but stoic Mabel set off for Rosewood in the clarence driven by Jack. A powerfully built footman sat by his side and they had cudgels close to hand under a rug. Then Florence packed her trunk, paid her hotel bill and had a cab bring her to Waterloo Station. It seemed even more threatening than when she had been there last. Sankey might not have been acting alone. She now knew that a vitriol attack was easy and saw that the press of people before the platform barriers could give easy cover for another attempt and for escape in the confusion thereafter. Her hand was trembling as she handed over coins for a newspaper and she did not feel fully safe until she was settled in a compartment with two other ladies and the train was pulling out.

The news she read would be painful for Nicholas. Praise was being heaped on Lord Charles Beresford for his imposition of order in Alexandria – he had been appointed city governor and had not hesitated to back up martial law with several hangings. Captain Fisher of the *Inflexible* had won admiration for his ingenious improvisation of an armoured train, manned by bluejackets and armed with weapons from his ship, and for its use against Egyptian forces outside the city. They were opportunities Nicholas would have relished – and which would have improved his prospects – but instead he was on the far side of Asia, engaged in a worthy but unexciting mission that could bring no prospect of action or advancement. It was a comfort to know that he was not exposed to danger, and yet danger, and that alone, was what could earn him the advancement he so fiercely craved. It was ironic that he was now safe, as safe as a naval officer could ever be in peacetime, and that it was she now who was at risk at home in Britain.

The villa in Albert Grove felt like a safe haven. She slept for an hour directly after she arrived and it was only afterwards, in the evening's fading light, that she addressed herself to the small pile of letters that had accumulated in her absence. Most were routine – personal bills, correspondence relating to the Sailors' Rest, a letter with little news from her own mother in the painfully exact script that must have cost hours of effort.

And at the bottom of the pile was an envelope written in a hand she did not recognise.

It proved to be from the man she had intended to contact.

Henry Raymond.

22

She was to meet Raymond in Winchester in two days' time, not only, she suspected, since it was a half-way point, but because neither would be seen at the other's house. He had reserved a private dining room at a hotel. His letter said nothing more, but unless he had something to report he would not have contacted her.

A package arrived by registered mail just before she set out. Florence's hands trembled as she tore it open to find what she expected, no note or letter from Livitski but three copies of Sankey's confession. She locked one in her desk, sealed up the second in another envelope and had Susan bring it to Mr. Bagshot for him to lock in his safe. The third she took with her. She did not read it until she was alone in a first-class compartment on the train.

Sankey must have been tougher than he had appeared when she had seen him in the embassy's cellar. What he had held back then was revealed now and she flinched from imagining what measures must have wrung it from him. The straggling signature on each page, stamped and witnessed by a representative of an impressively named firm of solicitors, told its own story.

Whatever faint pity she might have felt evaporated as she read. Only girls who had no family – foundlings or absolute orphans – had been traded on, but she had known that already. But it was others, who had relations, but who kept little contact with them, who were made available – the exact term used – when certain gentlemen came on visits. All named. Not only Whittier and Mellish, but over a dozen more, two lawyers and a judge, another banker, two army officers, an archdeacon and three clergymen – including the Reverend Martin Thursley. Two doctors who also performed abortions when needed, an actor-manager whom Florence had once seen perform in Shakespeare, a member of parliament whose name was vaguely familiar and another five described only as businessmen. These girls, whom relations might at some time in the future enquire about, were routed to domestic service in households with no other connection to Rosewood than that they had approached it to find maids. Most, probably all, of the girls would be too scarred by their experiences ever to speak of them later.

And there was worse. Livitski must have pressed Sankey hard for he had admitted that somebody had already been suspicious of Rosewood. Contact had been established and names passed, a few only, against payment, generous payment. Only Braben and Sankey himself had been involved, a small profitable business for them both. He could not identify the contact – he was always met in a cab at night and he kept his face well muffled. Florence believed it. If Sankey had known any more, then Livitski's interrogation would have wrung it from him.

She sat numbed when she finished the document, oppressed even more than before by awareness of evil, by the insolent and boundless wickedness that was so confident that it was beyond the reach of justice or retribution. As it might well be still. She longed now for Nicholas to be with her, not just to discuss with him what might follow now, but to share the burden of her awareness and depression.

The hotel was only minutes from the Winchester station and she found Raymond there already, soberly dressed like an attorney who had come to meet a client. He had coffee sent in – they could have lunch later.

"You have news of Andrew Shepton?" She had decided to say nothing yet about Rosewood.

"It may be nothing, Mrs. Dawlish, but it could be a lead."

"Tell me." *O God! Let it be so for that poor mother.*

"I'll not burden you with details that a lady would most surely find offensive but I know that you're aware, that you know only too well, of the activities Lord Oswald was associated with. And we referred to an establishment in Cleveland Street when we spoke before, one which he visited at intervals."

She nodded. *The telegraph boys, The depravity of it.*

"There are other places like it, patronised by men just as rich and powerful. They know that they're taking chances of exposure and disgrace but they rely on their support for each other. They mostly succeed. Only the odd one or two of them are ever subjected to blackmail. And even for that there can be decisive solutions. Though not often."

"Oswald wouldn't pay." For that she would always remember him with respect.

"But most do. Especially if the others they associate with advise them that it's the less dangerous course. That happens too. So the blackmailer is always on the watch and always keen to find yet another boy who's prepared to talk, to name names, to give day and date and circumstance and what was done. And that's what Shepton most likely is, a living goldmine who was worth kidnapping and hiding until his testimony can be used. It'll be made worth his while and he's probably quite happy wherever he's in hiding. So to find him we need to find a blackmailer. Not a petty one either, but somebody operating on a large scale, and fearless about whom he targets."

"But where can you start, Mr. Raymond?" She felt soiled by hearing of it.

"We've already started. My associates have identified four establishments where boys have been approached for information, where money has changed hands even for listening. One of the lads was prepared to admit as much when one of my people met him. He's greedy, he's stupid enough to think that he can play one bidder against the other, and he's prepared to cooperate."

"And you can trust him?"

"No. But we can use him."

His use of "We" offended her. *I'm above this. I cannot be part of it.* And then she remembered Mrs. Shepton. *He's such a good boy at heart. And we miss him so.*

"How could it lead to Andrew Shepton?"

"Because the same person is seeking informants at so many locations. He knows the business, has probably been blackmailing already, and doing it successfully. There's a chance – and I emphasise that it's a chance only – that he already has young Shepton in his pocket and needs more like him."

"How will you ... use that boy you mentioned?"

"We'll pay him to contact the person who first approached him and to say he wants to discuss terms. He'll be told where to meet, most likely in some public place to put him at his ease. We'll be watching. And afterwards we'll follow whoever meets him." Raymond spoke as if it were a routine undertaking, nothing out of the ordinary.

Florence was not surprised. His business – and she had decided before now that she did not want to know what it was – seemed built on information. Any information.

"I want to be there," she said. "I want to see it happening."

Nicholas's words. That this man he could be trusted only up to a point, though it was unclear what that point might be.

"Why?" Surprise in Raymond's voice and face. "Why? You've nothing to contribute. You'd be a hazard, Mrs. Dawlish."

"Bear with me. I want to watch, listen if I can, no more. I played my role well enough when I took Oswald to Swanage. I can do as much again." She could not say what she feared. *Depending what he finds Raymond may well want keep it to himself for his own reasons. I need to be there. I may not get anything otherwise.*

"We made a bargain before," she said, "that you'd find me Andrew Shepton if I helped Oswald's escape. And I'll offer you another bargain now if I can witness that meeting."

"What are you offering, Mrs. Dawlish?" His eyes cold even if he was still smiling. That they had worked together before, had almost died together, counted for nothing. This was business.

"Other information," she said. "About another matter, but just as bad. Important people who'd want nothing known of it." She mentioned several of their professions and positions but she did not identify them by name.

"A judge, you said?"

"A senior one. Very senior."

Eyes narrowing in what seemed closer to hunger than to greed. "You're sure? The MP also? The banker too? And two colonels, you said?"

She nodded slowly.

"Your source is reliable?"

"You'll be surprised when you find out, Mr. Raymond. Probably more reliable than yours. You can have everything once I've witnessed that meeting."

A long silence. His face was a blank but the brain behind must be churning furiously.

"You'll need to borrow clothes from your maid," he said at last. "It's unlikely that the appointment will be in the West End."

*

It was two days before she heard from him and they felt like a century, for all that she flung herself into business at the Sailors' Rest, fearing all the time that Mrs. Shepton might again come by. She was however cheered by a letter from Agatha. Mabel was still in pain, but she was on her feet, and together they had Rosewood House in hand – Agatha's phrase. She had written to all directors to inform them the Miss Braben and her assistant had disappeared and that as a temporary measure, until replacements could be found, she was assuming day-to-day management. Whittier had arrived the following day, shocked, he said, by Miss Braben's desertion – he had always trusted her implicitly, as did the other directors – and her betrayal saddened him. He was keen to review the books in case she had embezzled. Agatha let him see the accounts. Miss Braben had indeed taken money, he discovered – sixty-one pounds. seventeen shillings and eightpence halfpenny. That was undoubtedly why she had absconded and it would be painful for him to appraise other board members of it. "He kept probing about how much we knew," Agatha had written, "but he was fulsomely appreciative of what I was doing." He had not offered to take any girls on carriage rides. Had he done so he would have learned of the new policy, that a chaperone would always join such parties, Mabel or Agatha herself. On leaving he had professed himself reassured, happy that a difficult situation was being handled so well.

He could not have played it better. Whittier and Mellish and whichever other directors were involved would behave scrupulously in the coming period. There would be no confrontation but they would ensure that a nominee of their own would replace Miss Braben. Calm, patience, and outward courtesy to Agatha would serve them well.

Florence read the letter several times. It worried her that there was no indication as to whether Whittier knew of Sankey's vitriol attack. Mabel had looked embarrassed and had referred to an unspecified intimate matter when he had been solicitous on seeing her wince with pain. He had seemed to believe her, and if he did not know of the assault then there was a good chance that Miss Braben had not contacted him before she fled. If she had not, then he would be unaware that so much was now known about the abuses at Rosewood. But, if he did know, then the chance of other violence could not be discounted. A burglary, apparently disturbed while in progress, could provide cover for murder. It was good that Jack and

212

the two armed men with him were maintaining a watch day and night.

And another detail first chilled Florence, then enraged her. Mabel's examination of the records showed that two of the three girls who had been consigned to a mental asylum had accompanied Mellish on carriage drives. The third had joined Whittier when he had visited, not once, but almost weekly.

Now, more than ever, retribution must be merciless.

*

Susan was shorter than Florence and her clothing would not have fitted, even if there had been some excuse for borrowing it. Instead Florence put on her own plainest dress and found her way to a second-hand clothes shop near Portsmouth dockyard. Washed though the threadbare garments there might have been, she still felt repugnance about touching them. It would be worse still to wear them. She settled for a faded dress that had once been navy blue, for a frayed brown jacket to go over it and for a worn-out cotton blouse to go beneath. A shapeless straw hat carried the remnants of a bunch of wax fruit and she would provide a veil for it herself. Cracked leather boots, worn down at the heels, and an old leather bag would complete her transformation. Pitiful as these items were, she saw another customer, a wan young woman with a baby, eying them enviously. She brought her purchases home in a brown-paper parcel and tried them on in her bedroom. Stooped, and rounding her shoulders, she regarded herself in the mirror. It was troubling to see how easily clothes alone transmuted her, no longer the lady she had come to be, but into a drudge no different to millions of others.

She was to meet Raymond in early evening outside the station at Clapham Junction and she travelled there third-class, a normal, respectable, travelling suit packed in a Gladstone bag with overnight necessities. She had five minutes to wait before the cab – an old growler, with a tired horse – drew up alongside. No word from the cabby, but Raymond's face glimpsed briefly and then the door thrown open from within. There was another passenger, in shabby workman's clothes, forty, forty-five perhaps, with a lined face set in a sneer.

"Mr. Broome," Raymond said. "You'll be accompanying him. He's experienced in this sort of work. Just sit with him when you get there. You'll call him Jem and he'll call you Annie. He's your fancy-man and he's to have a short temper with you if he finds you irritating."

A nod from Mr. Broome but no word. For him the masquerade had already started.

"Where are we going?" Florence asked.

"Bermondsey. A public house, the *Duke of Kent*. It's long way."

"Will anybody else be there besides Mr. Broome?"

"One should be inside already, and two more across the street. Don't look for them."

Light failed, the cobbled streets gas-lit now, the cab moving at a crawl, thronged pavements, singing to an out-of-tune piano coming from a public house, women congregated on front steps, men lounging at corners, the cabby flicking his whip back with curses to deter children swinging on the rear of the vehicle. And the growing smell and sense of poverty.

There was little further conversation, just enough to assure Florence that a room had been arranged for her at a lodging house near Waterloo. Clean and safe, Raymond told her, and two of his people would be on watch outside all night. The cab would bring her there later and another would be there to bring her back to the station in the morning. As he lapsed into silence she wondered exactly how many such people he had, what they really were, what he owed them and they him, how he came by them. He seemed to have as many such people here as he had had in the United States. But here, in contrast to there, there was a greater air of confidence about him, a hint even of invulnerability. A man who rode in the Prince of Wales' carriage in Hyde Park, who undertook commissions for what he termed highly-placed persons, might well feel that.

The cab lurched to a halt.

"Good luck, Mrs. Dawlish." He swung the door open.

"Move your arse, Annie," Mr. Broome's tone one of foul-tempered impatience. "We can't wait all night. Get movin' if you don't want a thick ear." He went first and did not help her down.

They were in an unlit alleyway and Florence fought down momentary panic as the cab moved away.

"How far to…"

"Shut yer bleedin' face, Annie. Just do as ye're told."

It's a play, a charade, she told herself, and yet she felt degraded. *As the part demands.*

"Yes, Jem." She made her voice a whine. "I'll hold my peace, Jem, I won't trouble you."

They passed out of the alley into a poorly lit street beyond, the decaying houses to either side dark but for a few candles seen through open windows, the same miserable gatherings on doorsteps and corners as seen previously. Two more streets, busier, one with stalls selling meat and vegetables that might have been the refuse of some larger market. It was Saturday evening and the week's wages were being spent, might be all gone by the morrow. And then at last the *Duke of Kent*, a palace of gilt and light on a corner, incongruous amid the squalor to either side, light streaming from its windows on the intersecting streets, noise and the smell of beer rolling from its open door. Several children stood or crouched by it, waiting to guide some drunken father home.

"I'm sick of that face of yours," Mr. Broome said. "Stop a clock, it would, Annie. So drop that veil of yers a bit."

She pulled it down just below her eyes and followed him inside.

It was so close packed that it took long minutes to press forward to the bar. Florence felt somebody grope at her as she passed and she slapped the hand away. "Particular tonight, dearie? Savin' it for yer old man, are ye?" The mocking voice from behind was rewarded with laughter. The heat and stench were all but overpowering, the noise demanding shouting to communicate. Nobody seemed bothered by it.

"Sit over there, Annie." Mr. Broome motioned to the women on benches along the wall to the right. His voice dropped. "At the end, the very end."

She understood why when the stout woman drinking from a pint glass shifted cheerfully to make room for her. From here, despite the crowd, she could see along the bar and on to where it turned a right angle.

"You ain't been 'ere before, 'ave you, love?" the woman said.

"I'm visiting me sister. Down from Northampton, just for a couple of days." Florence was forcing herself back into the regional accent she had made such effort to leave behind.

"Nice, that," the woman said. "Family's everything, ain't it?

Florence glanced at the clock above the shelves of bottles behind the bar. Almost ten o'clock. Any time soon.

Mr. Broome pushed his way back to her, a tankard of beer in one hand, a glass of gin in the other. "Put that inside yer, Annie". He

215

pushed the glass at her and he winked at the woman next to her. "Mother's ruin, ain't it? But all the better for that." The woman smiled.

"Ye're such a one, Jem, you really are." Florence made herself laugh. "You ain't safe to be let out on yer own! Not with so many tempting ladies about." The stout woman laughed.

"Enough o' yer lip, Annie. Just drink an' be thankful." He stood before her, drinking deeply and then wiping the back of his hand across his mouth. Florence made as if to sip the gin.

Suddenly she felt his knee against hers, the slightest nudge, saw his head jerk imperceptibly. She looked along the bar, then, at the far side of the corner, and practically facing her, she saw a scrawny youth in a shiny dark suit and with a billycock hat nervously tapping the counter with a coin and demanding service with no great confidence. The servers, intent on other customers, were ignoring him. His pinched features gleamed with sweat and he was obviously forcing himself not to look around. Even at this distance the light glinting on the pin of his necktie told that it was of cheap glass. Florence could look directly towards him but Mr. Broome was part-facing her and watching the youth's reflection in the bar's mirror.

Five minutes passed, the boy resisting jostling by others on either side and resolutely maintaining his place at the bar, feigning interest in the beer he now had bought, eyes drifting repeatedly to the clock. Two minutes more and he was wiping his brow with a handkerchief, his hands trembling as he did. Florence felt fear that his nerve would fail, that he would scurry away before contact was made. He was an office-boy, Raymond had told her, one whose occasional services at a place like that at Cleveland Street earned him more than his regular work. The five pounds he had been promised for playing his role tonight might have seemed an easy windfall when he agreed to it but now, by his discomfort, he was obviously sweating for every penny of it.

Now somebody was pushing resolutely through the crush behind the youth, a thickset figure discernible only by the rounded top of his hat. He reached the bar at the boy's right side and called to be served. Thickset, in a check suit, a broken nose.

And Florence recognised him.

She felt Mr. Broome's knee touch hers again and he nodded almost imperceptibly. He had not moved his head but was watching the mirror, his tankard held to his face.

It makes sense. I would not have suspected it in a million years, but it makes sense.

The newcomer had said something to the boy. Heads nodding, identity confirmed, blood draining from the youth's face as the full enormity of what he was doing was now upon him. The older man had brought his mouth close to the lad's ear – the noise was such that it was impossible to speak normally – and he was speaking. The boy was trying to smile and was nodding. He had been rehearsed in his part. Yes, he was prepared to provide the information, but he'd need a down payment. The other man was shaking his head, the implication obvious. Cash on receipt. If anybody overheard them it would have sounded like some paltry sale of goods. The boy seemed to be pleading now – he was doing better than might have been expected – but the man in the check suit was shaking his head slowly. He slammed his glass down and turned to leave. The boy grabbed him by the arm to detain him, was speaking, was nodding furiously. Yes, he'd do it. He'd take payment later. The older man nodded, said something. The boy fished in his pocket and passed over a folded paper. An address where he could be reached – a false one, some unknowing householder's in Putney taken at random from the street directory. The man shook the boy's hand, drained his glass and pressed away through the drinkers behind.

"Take yer time, Annie," Mr. Broome said. "You've time enough to finish yer gin and' I don't know if I won't take another pint myself."

The boy, still at the bar, seemed at the point of collapse and the server he called to brought him what seemed like brandy. He threw it back, called for another. He had been instructed to wait at least ten minutes more before leaving. The man in the check suit has disappeared. An unremarkable customer would already be following him and Raymond's two men across the street would be seeing them emerge. They would follow, one on the pavement twenty yards behind, the other two on the opposite side of the street, changing places at irregular intervals. It was the system his associates always used, Raymond had said, and it never failed.

Mr. Broome was savouring his second pint. Despite her thumping heart Florence was listening, seemingly fascinated, to the stout lady's account of her daughter's most recent confinement, her seventh. "Nearly killed her, it did, but that don't worry that man of hers. Oh no! There'll be more, mark my words, until he's done for her, the bleeder."

"Time to go, Annie." Mr. Broome pulled her to her feet. "Say goodbye to yer friend."

They left, and took a different route on foot to the one they had come, finding the cab at last in another alleyway. Raymond, as intended, was not in it.

"I'll see you safe to your lodgings, ma'am," Mr. Broome was handing her courteously inside. "I trust that business wasn't too much of an ordeal." His accent was now cultured, his tone solicitous. The bullying labourer had disappeared. Dress this man in evening clothes and he might dine without evoking surprise at the table of the Prince of Wales. As perhaps he did.

But Florence said nothing about the identity of the man in the check suit. It was a lead and Raymond's people would find out more – for there must be more, much more.

And in the meantime she herself had to get one question answered.

23

A different Florence emerged from the lodging house the following morning, once more a lady and with the shabby clothing of the night before packed in her bag. She had hardly slept. Excitement – rather than fear or anger – had kept her awake, an impatience to confirm the truth of that which she now suspected. It was not far to Waterloo Station and she walked there through empty Sunday streets. She left her bag at the left-luggage counter there and took a cab over the bridge and westwards.

This time she entered the Russian embassy by its front door. The footman who opened spoke English with a pronounced accent. Prince Livitski was not here and anyway saw visitors only by appointment. Florence pushed passed and sat down in a hall chair. She presented her card. "Show him this."

The man jerked a bell-pull and presently the butler appeared, though he introduced himself as major-domo. He regretted that Count Livitski was not here. It was Sunday and...

"Tell me where to find him. I'm not leaving and the Count wouldn't like me being thrown out."

"His Excellency's private address cannot be disclosed. If you wish to make an appointment…"

"No!" The most powerful of all words.

At last he conceded. He brought her to a small office off the hall. There was a wooden cubicle in the corner, the interior visible through the glass in the door and with a box that looked like a large studio-camera, but with a circular bell on top, mounted on its far wall. He showed her to a chair, then entered the cubicle and closed the door. He stood close against the apparatus, holding something attached to it by a cord to his ear and winding a small crank furiously with his other hand. After what seemed like several attempts he began to shout at the box but no sound passed through what must be two layers of glass. Florence realised that it must be a telephone. She had read of such things and Nicholas had tried to explain their operation, but she knew there could be only a handful in London. The man was obviously waiting now – somebody he had been speaking to must be doing something – and he was drumming his fingers in impatience. Then he was shouting again in dumb-show, turning to look to Florence – describing her, she thought – and then nodding vigorously, his lips moving to make what she guessed was *Da, Da,* Yes, Yes.

Apologies when the major-domo emerged. It had taken too long to get a connection but he had at last reached His Excellency. He was on his way, would be here in twenty minutes. And if Madame would like to wait in more comfortable surroundings, and like refreshment…

It was a small parlour, luxuriously furnished, with a portrait of the late Czar – barbarously murdered the previous year – above the mantelpiece and one of his portly successor on the opposite wall. Comfortable it might be but there was still an impression of a room intended for official use, for confidential encounters between people of importance.

And below…

Down in the cellars Peter Sankey was still being held, bruised, terrified and cowed at last, perhaps on a hard floor with a single blanket, uncertain if he would ever leave it alive. It was Sunday morning, and otherwise she would have been in St. Jude's in Southsea at this time, and hesitating over the plea for forgiveness in the Lord's Prayer, *as we forgive those who trespass against us.* She repeated the prayer mentally now and once again she halted when she came to

219

the words. *I can't say it. God forgive me, but I can't. I can't forgive for Dorcas, for Emily Gleason and her brother, for the others. They were not delivered from evil. I have no forgiveness for Sankey.* The awareness that had weighed down and depressed her in recent days was strongest now. What she had seen in the public-house last night had hinted at even deeper rottenness than Braden's or Sankey's.

"Florence Hanim." Livitski was immaculate, as always, when he entered. He showed no pleasure in seeing her. "I take it that this isn't a social call? That you must have something to tell me. Otherwise you would be at home on this day and at this hour."

"Walter Staveley."

Shock registered in his eyes.

"Of the *St. James Fortnightly*. It was Walter Staveley, wasn't it?"

"I don't understand you, Florence Hanim." Livitski had collected himself well.

"It was he who provided you with the information about Oswald, wasn't it?"

"I know of Mr. Staveley of course. His journal is well respected." Calm, reasonable, now, a diplomat's voice.

Nicholas had once told her of an old definition. *A man sent abroad to lie for his country.*

"Other than reading that journal on occasion I know nothing of the man, Florence Hanim. I've never met Mr. Staveley."

"But you didn't need to, did you, Count? You — or maybe somebody working for you – would have dealt with his creature. His Mr. Benton." *The man I saw negotiating with that terrified youth in the Duke of Kent last evening.* "Money would have changed hands, wouldn't it?"

"I've told you that I've never met him, Florence Hanim."

"No. but some agent managed the trade on your behalf."

He shrugged. "You and I live in the real world. We know that some things, however distasteful, have got to be done."

"And you had somebody approach Oswald on your behalf. To threaten him with exposure and to promise silence if he provided information to which his position made him privy."

Livitski made no denial.

"You hadn't reckoned on his loyalty, had you? And on his courage? You never expected so much of Oswald." *Nor did I myself.* "And when he refused to cooperate you put the matter back in Staveley's hands. For his Mr. Benton to speak to Chester Brewster. You guessed what Brewster would do – perhaps you had Benton suggest it – and you knew that Oswald's reputation would be ruined, that his friends would desert him and leave him a scapegoat. You knew that he would have to flee the country and that out of bitterness he might be glad to tell you all you needed. And you hoped that following me would help you find him."

"Some good came of that, Florence. I was thankful that I was there when you were attacked. Thankful that I could have been of service to you. And in that other business also. Rosewood House."

"Did you know anything of Rosewood before?" Her mind recoiled from the possibility. She still wanted to think well of him.

He shook his head. "Nothing." Then he smiled. "Some of the names are of interest however, advantageous to me in fact. You've received Sankey's confession. I trust that you'll find it useful?"

"Useful. But very sad, very terrible." She told him that Agatha and Mabel were at Rosewood now.

"And Sankey? What would you like me to do with him?"

She thought. *Retribution. Punishment. Satisfaction.* But sometime there had to be an end to it, if her fury was not to be a cancer that would consume her. *As we forgive those … No, I can't forgive, but I can remit.*

"Keep him for a month," she said. "Then give him five pounds and put him on the street."

She stood to go.

"We won't be meeting again, Count Livitski."

"No. We won't be meeting again, Florence Hanim." He took her hand and kissed it.

And there was something like regret in his voice.

*

Raymond complimented her on her performance the previous evening – Mr. Broome had already reported. Under the courtliness however she sensed that he was not pleased that she had come directly to the Clapham villa from the embassy. She told him of the discussion there, of Livitski's confirmation of her suspicions.

"Did he specifically name Staveley?" Raymond had heard her out before speaking.

"Not as such." It sounded so weak. "He didn't confirm it directly, but I sensed – no, I was sure – that he wanted me to know that it was Staveley who had provided the information on Oswald. I can understand that he couldn't be direct but…" It sounded weaker still.

"And he didn't mention Benton's name either?"

"No." Her elation of the early morning was gone and she was starting to feel foolish. "But there's no doubt that the man I saw last night was Benton."

"He was followed home," Raymond said. "He lives alone in rooms in Deptford. In Albury Street, a respectable address. He showed no suspicion of being trailed from the *Duke of Kent*. And we've checked already – it's like you say, his name is Benton and he does work for the *St. James Fortnightly*."

"What did that boy he met say about him?"

"That he was prepared to pay for information about gentlemen clients. More if the lad could induce friends to do the same. And a lot more still if – and you must excuse me, Mrs. Dawlish for saying this – if he, or one of them, would be prepared to be surprised *in flagrante* with a client."

"He would have been the ideal contact then." *It seems so obvious.* "Staveley wouldn't have been stupid enough to deal directly with Count Livitski."

"We don't jump to conclusions in this line of work, Mrs. Dawlish" Raymond's patient tone might have been well meant but it she found it condescending, patronising, and she resented it. "We need confirmation, cross-referencing with other sources. Staveley might indeed know of Lord Oswald's activities but for any of a dozen reasons he might have had no intention acting on it. Benton might have had access to that information – might have sourced much of it – but he might have been a free agent, acting on his own behalf, and without reference to Staveley, when he contacted Livitski."

"Yes, but…"

"Staveley's a powerful man, Mrs. Dawlish, widely admired. If he is involved, then he will have covered his tracks very carefully. So caution is needed, caution and patience as we investigate. Because what you're interested in is finding that young man Andrew Shepton, is it not?"

She nodded, but felt almost sick. The image of the boy's fretting mother contrasted so powerfully with the arrogant bully she had seen tempting the wretched youth laid out as bait last night. "Andrew might be in that house in – where did you say? Yes, in Deptford."

"He may well be, though I doubt it – Benton seems like the sort who wouldn't take a chance like that. But wherever Shepton is we'll find him, Mrs. Dawlish, trust me in this."

And that is what I will not do now. It is as Nicholas said. That this man could be trusted only up to a point. Nicholas had been uncertain what that point might be. But this is that point now.

"How long do you think this might take, Mr. Raymond?"

"Who knows, Mrs. Dawlish? As I said, we have to move with infinite caution. Staveley must have no inkling of our enquiries. There's no doubt that he already knows a lot that's discreditable about many influential people – what he prints is probably only a fraction of it. And the interests of those people need to be taken into account as well."

"Like those people who wanted you to help Oswald escape?"

"I think you understand the situation, Mrs. Dawlish."

She stood up. "I need to be getting back to Southsea."

"And our agreement, Mrs. Dawlish? I held to my side last evening. You witnessed the meeting and indeed you recognised Mr. Benton. I've no doubt that you'll be delivering the information you mentioned as soon as possible."

"I'm delivering it now." She took the package from her bag, Sankey's confession. Her heart sank as she handed it to him. *I've given away too much, too easily. But it's a debt of honour. It must be paid.*

The thought nagged her even more painfully as the train sped her homewards.

The Raymond I knew in the United States and in Cuba – that man I helped rescue Nicholas, the man whose wife I pretended to be in Santiago, the man who never lost his nerve even when a Spanish gunboat was trying to blow our vessel apart – would not have hesitated to have that house in Deptford broken into. So expertly that Benton would not know it had happened. But he's holding back. Because Andrew Shepton – and I myself – are incidental figures now. If that boy is a big enough embarrassment for certain people, then I'll never know what Raymond finds out.

And there was worse.

If it's to suit Raymond – and the people he refers to, and who are more important for him that I could ever be – those named in the confession extracted so painfully from Sankey will be placed on guard and will be strengthening their defences.

She winced at the memory of the vitriol. There could be worse to come. Not just for herself, but for Agatha and Mabel also.

Florence got back home to Southsea in late afternoon. She sat in the garden and had Susan bring her tea, and she remained there long after dusk, a shawl clasped about her against the evening chill. The villa seemed an ever greater haven of tranquillity now, one she realised she had never appreciated sufficiently before, one where she and Nicholas had been happy. And yet she feared that she could never enjoy that tranquillity again – might not even deserve it– were she to stand back now, when even Raymond, the most powerful ally she had counted on, might have reasons for not assisting her further. The foulness of what she had become aware of, which she felt besmirched by, weighed even more upon her than before. It was all the more terrible for awareness that whatever retribution might be exacted it could do no good for the former victims. Dorcas lay in that pathetic Portsmouth grave and Jemmy Gleason's abused body had been cast like refuse into an ebbing tide. Jemmy's sister Emily, and the other girls whose names would so soon be forgotten – Rose and Lucy and Mary and Rachel – had been traded on from Antwerp and were now untraceable. The mind quailed from imagining where or what they now might be, from accepting that some might already be diseased or dead.

A resolution was presenting itself, one she shrunk from, yet one that kept returning with the strength of unarguable logic. She had never felt more alone for she knew that even if Nicholas had been here, and not on the other side of the globe, she would not have confided to him the intensity of her cold fury nor the action she was now contemplating.

She at last went inside and leafed through the pile of letters and newspapers that had accumulated in her absence. Among them was the latest edition of the *St. James Fortnightly* – she had ordered it from the newsagent – and she leafed quickly through. The campaign against slum landlords was now subordinate to Staveley's crusade on behalf on the phosphorous-poisoned match girls. Accusations in previous editions had not stung Lord Allingham, the Lucifer King, into a response. Florence turned away from an engraving that showed a girl's cheek laid open, the exposed teeth grinning like a skull's. She read the article, and the notice at the end of it, several times. Then she went upstairs.

The room between Susan's and the cook's on the top floor had been kept locked since she had been there last and she had kept the single key for herself. She pulled out the tallboy's bottom drawer, felt beneath the underwear stacked there and touched metal. The small revolver and the box of shells were as she had left them. She held the weapon a long time in her hand – it seemed so light for something so deadly – and doubts still raged within her.

I don't know if the powder inside these brass cases deteriorates over time and becomes ineffective. But if I go ahead, if I can bring myself to it, then there must be no uncertainty.

She broke the seal on the cardboard box and selected a single round at random from the two dozen inside. She placed it in the cylinder and advanced it so that cocking the weapon would draw it under the hammer. The steps she had learned five years before were coming back to her and she took the pistol with her when she went back down to the parlour. She waited there, attempting to read a novel, until she was sure that Susan and Cook had gone to bed.

It was after midnight when she went out into the garden at the rear. Weak moonlight cast deep shadows along one wall and the neighbouring houses were dark. She had heard gunfire before, had heard it too often, and she guessed that the noise this time would not be loud enough, and would be too improbable in this respectable area, to arouse alarm. She stood into the shadows, cocked the pistol, felt the cylinder click into place. She straightened her arm and aimed into the soft earth of the flower bed before her.

The report was sharper than she expected, but also less loud, and the weapon's kick was negligible. She stayed in the shadow for a few minutes more but the noise did not seem to have attracted any curiosity from the houses around. As she went back into the villa she realised that her hand was no longer shaking, as it had been before.

For now she was set on what she must do.

24

Florence wanted to be making this journey to London for the last time – the last for months at least. It might indeed be for the last time ever if what she planned would turn out badly. She longed for this nightmare to be over, to be back in her old routine of letters to

Nicholas, of her piano practice, of walks along the Esplanade, of the mundane concerns of the Sailor's Rest. The familiar station-names slipped past and, try as she might, it was impossible to read a magazine.

She lodged again at the Charing Cross Hotel – she could not bear to think of the other where Sankey had thrown the vitriol – and in the afternoon she walked up the Strand for the few hundred yards to the pillar-framed entrance to Exeter Hall, the capital's huge venue for public meetings. Large letters on the notice boards outside confirmed that the evening's event had not been cancelled. She had feared that for some unlikely reason it might have been. She suspected that if it had been cancelled she would never again manage to screw her resolve up to the pitch to which she had brought it now.

"Seats only in the gallery, ma'am, and few enough of them," the porter who took a shilling for a ticket told her. "It's going to be a big one tonight, packed out it'll be. It always is when Mr. Staveley is talking."

A hansom brought her to Pimlico, an area south of Westminster where she had never had reason to come before. She had herself set down at a distance from the address she had found in the *Kelly's Handbook* and which she had memorised. She had read a laudatory article in the *St. James Fortnightly* about what had happened in the area, how philanthropic trusts had built blocks of flats in recent years to replace what had been one of the foulest slums in London. Maunsel Street, the one she sought, was on the district's edge, its terraced houses prosperous but unostentatious. She walked slowly down the street, past the number she needed – the house was no different than any other – and did not stop, lest she attract attention. She continued on foot back to the hotel and lay down in her room, yet she could not sleep, nor had she any appetite to eat. She resisted checking her preparations again, for she had already done so a dozen times. At last, at a quarter after seven, it was time to leave, a leather bag larger than her normal reticule held firm against her.

The crowds on the pavements thickened as she moved down the Strand, all heading for the same destination. Solid middle-class and middle-aged couples in sober dress – chapel-goers rather than church-goers, she guessed – mingled with earnest-looking younger people. There were fewer workmen or workwomen than she had expected but they had all arrayed themselves in their modest Sunday best. Closer to the entrance the throng slowed to a shuffle. Brief cheering erupted when some admired figure was set down by cab or carriage and a path was cleared for them to enter. Florence edged forward with the crush, presented her ticket, and was directed up the stairs to the balcony. The meeting would be in the smaller of the building's two auditoria, but still large enough to accommodate over a thousand. The seats on the balcony's front rows were already occupied, but even from the fourth she had a good view of the stage. She exchanged courtesies with the couples on either side – solemn board-school teachers from Fulham to her left, and on her right a Unitarian minister and his wife who had travelled down specially from Rugby for the occasion. Florence was grateful that the hum of expectant voices made conversation difficult.

Eight o'clock. A figure walked out on to the empty stage – it was no surprise that it was the consumptive-looking man with round steel-rimmed spectacles, the *Fortnightly* journalist whom she had last seen outside the Kegworth mansion. He raised his arms and the hum died.

Applause followed his announcement of each name. One by one they came out, a Radical member of parliament whose mention evoked cheering even before he appeared, an Anglican bishop, the novelist Mrs. Anna Matthews, a Roman Catholic bishop. Prolonged applause greeted the unexpected arrival of the explorer Jonathan Langdon, just back from the wilds of Borneo. Florence felt the excitement swelling around her with each new introduction – Miss Amelia Bartlett-Rogers, the advocate of women's suffrage, a venerable white-haired rabbi, a Methodist minister known for his work in an East End mission. One by one they seated themselves on the row of chairs at the back of the stage, the Anglican and Catholic bishops exchanging guarded compliments, Mrs. Matthews effusively greeting Mr. Langdon, the Methodist and the rabbi nodding and smiling weakly in confused, uncomfortable proximity. Worthy and well-intentioned as they were, Florence guessed from the air of supressed expectation that they were not whom the crowd had come to hear.

Two empty chairs remained at the centre of the row. The young man swept his arm towards them.

"Lord Allingham," he said. "Lord Allingham of Thanet, Mr. Stanley Allingham, that was, the gentlemen whom many refer to as the Lucifer King – I make no comment on the appropriateness of the title – Lord Allingham has declined an invitation to be here tonight."

The audience erupted into the nearest such a respectable gathering could ever come to unbridled rage, many on their feet and shouting "Shame", not least the teachers next to Florence.

The young man let the polite uproar run for a half minute or more, nodding his head and pursing his lips in mute agreement, before he gestured for calm. There was disappointing news. Mr. Staveley had asked him to relay his apologies. The crowd groaned and Florence felt her heart thump – to have come this far…

Another call for silence. No need to be alarmed. Mr. Staveley had apologised in advance for an inevitably late arrival. Something relevant to this meeting was involved and needed his attention first. Applause rippled, then grew. "We'll wait all night for him if we must," the clergyman's wife told Florence. "Such an inspiring speaker! And such a passion for truth!"

The Anglican bishop spoke first, his tone and delivery those of a practised preacher but the content platitudinous, a speech that could have been equally applicable to slum housing, infant mortality, coal-mine safety or improved sanitation. Florence wondered how many times he had delivered it before with only a word changed here and there. The Radical MP proved a disappointment – he had a reputation as a firebrand speaker but the list of statistics he reeled off about wages, working conditions and disease among the match girls was received in silence by an increasingly restive audience. The mood changed when Mrs. Matthews worked herself up into a frenzy of incoherent indignation, not just on the match issue but on the plight of women – our sisters – generally. Mr. Langdon proved no less popular, especially his anecdotes about the head-hunters he had encountered in Borneo demonstrating their moral superiority to the men – if they could even be classed as such, the Englishmen, he was ashamed to say – who built fortunes on the misery of others. He was embarking on another story of the unspoiled tropical Eden when a rising murmur in the hall caused him to pause.

Florence looked down and saw that the audience below was rising to its feet, turning to the entrance unseen below the balcony and beginning to applaud. "It is he!" the clergyman's wife beside her was shouting as she stood up, and so were dozens of others, those in the front rows craning dangerously over the balcony edge. At last she saw two figures emerge into sight and move slowly up the auditorium's central aisle towards the stage. One was clearly Walter Staveley but a shabbily-dressed woman was leaning on his arm. Her head was covered by a thick black veil. Both bishops on the stage were rising from their seats, the others there also, and the consumptive young man was sprinting down the steps on one side to meet Staveley, Mrs. Matthews close on his heels.

The applause grew as Staveley stood back to allow Mrs. Matthews to lead the veiled woman up on to the stage. Both women paused at the top and Staveley followed. The explorer grasped his hand and shook it – there was something bold and manly about the action – and he drew Staveley to the centre to face the cheering audience. The ladies in it were more vocal than the men, the sense of shared righteous satisfaction almost palpable. Staveley gestured for calm, but weakly, as if it was an empty formality that he did not expect to be observed.

He's enjoying this as much as they are. Cold anger was seething in Florence now.

At last he raised his arms – seriously now. The hubbub died. He pointed to the two empty chairs.

"I understand that a certain noble lord has declined an invitation to be with us this evening." His voice was strong and it carried well. The crowd roared. He waited ten seconds until the noise had reached a crescendo and then gestured for calm. Twenty seconds before there was silence.

He's a master, and he's manipulating this crowd, and they love him for it.

Now he gestured to the two women, one veiled, standing to his right, then addressed the audience. "Might I have your permission, your approval, that I might ask Mrs. Matthews to conduct Miss Ussher…" His arm swept over towards the veiled woman, "… Miss Gertrude Ussher, previously an employee of the noble lord, to occupy the chair her erstwhile employer has declined this evening?"

A cry of "Yes!" from a thousand throats. Women around Florence were holding handkerchiefs to their eyes and men, embarrassed, brushing tears away. Miss Ussher was seated with elaborate ceremony as Staveley moved unhurriedly along the row of other speakers, shaking hands, obviously thanking them for their presence, apologising for his lateness. Florence wondered if she was the only one here who recognised this charade for what it was, a ritual orchestrated to the nearest second for maximum effect. The applause was muted now, the audience turning to each other to share admiration, indignation, conscious virtue. And there was something worse, an impression that the stages of this procedure were well known, that something yet to come had perhaps been seen before, half-dreadful, half-fascinating. It was the feeling that crowds must have shared around the guillotine or the gallows, one both guilty and shameful, and now all the more repulsive for the respectability and ostentatious righteousness that cloaked it.

Staveley spoke without notes, the Yorkshire accent just strong enough to proclaim him as a plain, blunt man, and the enraptured hall listened. Had any other man talked like this then Florence might have wept like so many around her. He began with pay, no worse than in many industries – but that was no recommendation, for Lord Allingham's female employees worked fourteen hours a day for a wage of less than five shillings a week. And that was if they had not been fined – anything from thruppence to a shilling – for talking while working, for dropping matches, for leaving without permission for a few minutes for certain delicate purposes. Yes! And women in other businesses were no better paid, particularly those working at home – he had recently encountered the case of a girl of little more than thirteen who was supporting a younger brother and sister in a garret by sewing ribbons on hats at nine-pence per gross. That garret, he might add, was in a house occupied by fifty-seven other people and owned by a certain Duke, an ornament of the Upper House.

He paused and his bespectacled acolyte brought him a glass of water. He had been moving back and forth across the platform, more effective, Florence saw, then speaking from behind a lectern. Sounds of sobbing, low murmurs of indignation.

But there was worse in the match factories, Staveley resumed, far worse. Phosphorous, white phosphorous, was a poison, as deadly as arsenic but slower, even more terrible, in its action. Slow, merciless and measured in its pace, it destroyed beauty and robbed health. Two European counties – not Britain! No! To our Shame, not Britain! – had banned its use in making matches, Denmark seven years ago and Sweden four years later. And why was it not banned here in this great Christian country of ours? He stood silent for a moment, arms akimbo, as of waiting for the audience's answer, then gave it himself. Because, those in authority had told him, those who profited from its use, had explained to him that doing so would constitute restraint of free trade. Free trade! Freedom to exploit our fellow man and our fellow woman, freedom to inflict injury unspeakable in the cause of profit!

Florence could feel the excitement throbbing around her, the anger and the urge to shout and gesture that Staveley's own mesmeric performance was somehow holding in check. She sensed indignation building in herself against the abuses he denounced, for all that she knew what this man really was, for there was truth in what he was saying, and she saw that the eminent figures seated behind him were no less moved. And yet she was repelled – decency, justifiable outrage, compassion, well-meant even if naïve, were being exploited with a brazenness so bold that none here recognised it.

And this white phosphorous, this substance so dangerous that it had to be stored under water if it was not to combust spontaneously, this substance that had to be mixed with other chemicals before the match head could be coated, this foul substance was not essential to create the humble item so valuable in domestic use. The Danes and Swedes had proved that, had built profitable business venture on less harmful compounds. But not here! Not in this England!

Then silence. He stood before them like a man exhausted, despairing, beaten down by iniquity, and the hall, silent but for the sounds of sobbing, seemed to share his sense of impotence in the face of such immense evil. And Florence guessed what was now coming, what she suspected that half the audience had seen at some earlier meeting, as Staveley looked up, face set in defiance.

"Let us leave here tonight resolved not to rest until we secure justice!"

Behind him Mrs. Matthews was helping the veiled woman to her feet and conducting her towards the stage-front.

"Resolved to secure justice for the exploited! For the forgotten! For those whose lives and beauty count for nothing when balanced against the interest of free trade!"

The veiled woman was to his left now and even at this distance Florence could see that she was trembling violently.

"For Miss Gertrude Ussher! Nineteen years old!"

He reached over, and drew the veil away from her face. From what was left of it.

Florence endured the sight for a moment only, ashamed by her own cowardice to confront it, gasping like all around her at this incarnation of living death. And then her fury deepened, for behind that mask of horror was a woman with a name, with feelings, who was perhaps still loved by a mother who still remembered her as a baby at her breast, by a father who had held her on his knee, by brothers and sisters who had played and gambolled with her, and whom she herself loved no less for all that she must hide her desecrated visage from them. She stood here now as Staveley's freak, an exhibit whom he demanded loudly that Lord Allingham would yet meet in person, even if he had declined to do so this evening, one whom...

But Florence was not listening now. She had come here tonight for one last opportunity to reassure herself that she was not mistaken. And she was not.

Staveley was a monster.

And she would destroy him.

*

Nobody thought it strange that she left the meeting, handkerchief held to her eyes, all too obviously distressed by what she had seen. In the lobby she saw two other women, one quite distraught, being led away by their husbands. She dropped her veil, brushed past and walked to Trafalgar Square before she hailed a cab to take her to Pimlico. It set her down at a distance from Maunsel Street and she walked there unhurriedly. This was the most difficult part of her plan, she knew, for a woman walking alone on the street in late evening – it was now after ten – was liable to arouse suspicion. It was not accosting by strange men that worried her, but that some well-meaning policeman might consider it his duty to conduct a well-dressed lady in safety to her own front door.

She had no idea how long Staveley might remain at Exeter Hall after the meeting, whether admirers might detain him, whether he might go on to some other gathering, whether he would return to his home here alone or with company. When she walked down the lamp-lit street this evening she saw from the opposite pavement that no light burned in the house, that whatever help Staveley needed to tend his bachelor establishment must come in from outside on a daily basis. She turned at the street's end, walked down another, and another, all deserted but for residents and their wives returning home on foot or by cab, but she returned every few minutes to glance down Maunsel Street even if she did not enter it. Her mouth was dry, her hands trembling, and it was an agony to pass respectable couples lest she be offered assistance.

Florence must have walked down the same streets a dozen times, though in different order, when she heard Big Ben chime eleven o'clock a mile away. A man, respectably dressed, had come up to her and, without ceremony, had offered money – two sovereigns, an hour only, his house was near and his family away and he never consorted with anything but clean women. He had backed away and stammered apologies when he recognised the fierceness of her repulse, but the encounter had shaken her. The next man to do so might be less easily intimidated. The walk continued – she must be conspicuous at this hour on these all but deserted residential streets – and yet there were limits on how much she could vary her route if she were to remain sufficiently close to Maunsel Street. Eleven-thirty passed – she was weary of it now – and she promised herself to give up and return to the hotel at midnight if nothing had happened.

Five minutes remained. She was at the end of Maunsel Street again and this time a hansom was entering it at a fast clip. The streetlamp at the corner exposed the passenger space beneath the hood for seconds only but in the soft yellowish light the broken nose of the thickset man within made Mr. Benton unmistakable, another figure by his side but no doubt who it could be. The cab stopped at Staveley's house and Florence saw him dismount and let himself in. Benton remained in the cab and departed with it. He had escorted his employer home and now his work was done.

The street was otherwise deserted and Florence walked quickly to Staveley's door. Her knees were weak, hands trembling more than ever as she held her bag in her left hand and felt inside it with her right to close on the pistol's but. Her finger slipped into the trigger guard but she did not release the safety catch.

A faint glow illuminated the fanlight above the hall door. She reached for the electric bell's button on the left, pressed it, and heard it shrill within. The pistol was out of the bag now and she was holding it before her.

The wait seemed like hours. She was about to ring again when she heard the noise of bolts being pulled back. The door swung back and Staveley was looking at her in amazement. He must have thought that Benton had returned for some reason and for an instant he did not recognise her, but when he did he looked baffled.

"You're that friend of the American journalist," he said, "You're... you're Mrs. Dawlish, aren't you? I don't know why..."

Then his gaze dropped and he saw the pistol.

"Stand back, Mr. Staveley," Florence said. "I'm coming in. And be quiet or I'll blow your brains out."

25

Florence's hand was steady now and she felt calm as Staveley cowered in front of her, his eyes locked on the muzzle pointed towards his stomach.

"Is there anybody else in the house, Mr. Staveley?"

"For God's sake put that thing away and..."

"I asked if there was anybody else in the house."

"No." His shoulders slumped, his voice quavering.

"Where do you keep your papers, Mr. Staveley?"

"In my study but..."

"Take me there."

He went up the stairs ahead of her, passing from the glow in the hallway into the shadows of the landing above. Only the pilot-light was burning there.

"Turn up the gas-lamp."

His hands were shaking so violently that it took two attempts.

"Now lead me on. And remember that I'm aiming at your spine."

She stood in the study doorway as she ordered him to light the gas there also and to pull the window's heavy curtains closed. The light showed a large room, probably a bedroom originally, and one wall carried shelves laden with box files. Two large metal safes, taller than Florence herself, stood against the opposite wall. Between them a large desk, a single chair behind, two in front, a smaller table to the right carrying a typewriter. The room was at the back of the house, protected from street noise.

"Sit down, Mr. Staveley – yes, there, in your own chair."

Florence sat opposite him, the desk between, her pistol steady.

"Where's Andrew Shepton?"

Terror as well as surprise in his eyes. "I don't know who you mean. Why are you..."

"I'm asking you politely, Mr. Staveley." His terrified gaze followed her thumb pushing the safety catch forward. "I shot a man once before, Mr. Staveley. I killed him. He deserved it but he was probably no worse than you. I'll have no hesitation in doing it again. So where's Andrew Shepton?"

He stammered another denial, then thought better of it. "Not far from here. He's safe. You don't need to worry about him."

"Write down the address."

He did so and pushed the paper across, the straggling script betraying his trembling hand. A street in Chiswick, not far off.

"We'll be going there soon to collect him, Mr. Staveley. But there's something more you'll have to tell me first."

A mute nod. A beaten dog, but beaten dogs could still bite.

"You sold Oswald's name to Count Livitski, didn't you?"

"Yes." Almost inaudible.

"Andrew Shepton had gone to you with the story of the boy from the *Brahmaputra* being killed. He told you that Oswald had been present. And when Livitski got to know of it he tried to blackmail him." She remembered Oswald's words. *Not money. Information. Secrets, things vital for this country.* "And when Oswald wouldn't yield, Livitski passed the matter back to you. To inform his fiancée's brother."

"Oswald had a choice. He was given a chance and he didn't take it." Staveley was trying to sound like a reasonable man who had been pressed beyond his limits of patience.

"You made an example of Oswald, just like you made an example of Ludovic Gilpin, that poor lieutenant who shot himself. You made examples of them to terrify every other wretch you've been sucking dry."

"It was in a good cause." He said it as if he believed it. "You know what the money goes to support. My campaigns, my crusades. The good that the *Fortnightly* does. It's not for myself. I live modestly – you can see that for yourself. And those whom I... whom I deal with, there's no other way to hold them accountable, to make them pay for what they do."

"Hold your tongue, Mr. Staveley." Florence felt revulsion now. Money didn't interest this man but power did, the power of the gloating cat over the captive mouse. "The Shepton boy wasn't the first to come to you with such a story, was he? He must have heard that you were in the market for the like. How did you come to know of such happenings in the first place?"

He coloured, looked away, would not meet her gaze. His head dropped. Shame, anger, desperation. In any other circumstances Florence would feel pity.

Almost too late she saw his hand reaching towards the typewriter, realised that he was going to throw it at her, that he was stupid enough to think she wouldn't dare shoot.

She shifted her aim ever so slightly. The report was more ear-splittingly loud in this enclosed space than it has been in the garden and it masked the sound of shattering as the slug smashed into the glass-fronted cabinet behind the desk. Smoke, the slightest whiff of rotten eggs and then dead silence. Staveley was cowering in his chair, lips moving wordlessly, eyes lock in horror.

"I told you that I'd have no hesitation in killing you," Florence's voice was icy. *Nor will I. No more than I would crush some foul insect.* "The curtains are too thick for the noise to carry far and nobody knows that I've come here, or any reason why I should. So tell me now how you got wind of these abuses."

He did not meet her gaze. "It was a place where other men went too. Men with... with feelings like my own. People like you don't understand. And I stopped going there when I recognised who some of them were."

"It was Cleveland Street, wasn't it?" It was a guess, but he nodded.

"Men who believe themselves above the law and are usually right. Some decent fellows among them but others..." Staveley's words were rushing out, as if he had prepared this justification long before, had perhaps needed it to convince himself. "... men who own slum properties, who treat their workers like slaves, whose factories and mines are death-traps, who over-insure unseaworthy ships and send them on voyages they have no hope of surviving. Men who..."

"Rosewood House," Florence said. She had no intention of listening to his explanations, felt it beneath her even to acknowledge his arguments.

He tried to look as if the words meant nothing to him, but his eyes betrayed him.

"You've known about Rosewood for a long time, haven't you, Mr. Staveley? You were frightened that day when we proposed taking those children there. You didn't want Mrs. Bushwick or any other journalist asking questions there, did you?"

His gaze was locked again on the pistol. "You can't blame me. It's those men who..."

"Those men whom Sankey fed your creature Benton information about? Those men you've been blackmailing? Which of them were they? Mellish? Whittier?"

"Not those." His voice a whisper. "Some of the others. They could all afford to pay."

"You were keeping other names in reserve to maintain your income in the future, weren't you? And all the time the orphanage was being used like a brothel." She saw terror, but no remorse. "It's not just Rosewood and the *Brahmaputra* that you know about, is it? There are probably other places like them, aren't there? With other rich and influential men involved?"

"You don't understand what you're getting into, Mrs. Dawlish. These are powerful people, you've no idea how high this goes. You already know enough to get yourself killed and…"

He froze, Florence too.

For there were muffled noises on the stairs outside, cautious footsteps.

Staveley began to laugh, relief and hysteria mixed. "The police! That shot of yours was heard! The police are here, Mrs. Dawlish. You've broken in with intent to murder, a deranged woman with an imaginary grievance against a respected editor. They'll find a gun in your hand and…"

The brass doorknob turning slowly. Florence edged around to half-face it though she still held the revolver pointed at Staveley. And still the knob turned, an aeon to rotate a full half circle and in it agony.

Disgrace, Prison. Ridicule. Shame. Nicholas brought down with me, an object in the Navy of scorn and pity. The officer who had married a servant and who got what he deserved

The door swung open.

Raymond's face displayed as much amazement as Florence's own must. Staveley had half-risen from his chair and he now slumped back with a moan.

"A pleasant surprise, Mrs. Dawlish. And I do believe we're here for the same purpose." Raymond, dressed as if for a city banquet, had regained his composure. "And I think you can put that weapon away now. I've no doubt that Mr. Staveley will be fully cooperative without it." Another man was standing behind him and carrying a large leather bag, such as a doctor might use. "I apologise for not shaking hands, Mr. Staveley. The call isn't a social one and there's no need for you to know my name."

Florence engaged the safety catch and slipped the revolver back in her bag. As she did Staveley rose to his feet.

"Whoever you are, I want you to leave my house."

"Or what, Mr. Staveley? Or you'll call the police?" Raymond smiled as he shook his head. "When I leave here, I'll be taking your papers with me. There are three more men in the hall below – and by the way the lock on your front door is too inferior to have kept even a child out – and there are two coaches waiting nearby." He looked around the room. "There's a lot of documentation here so the sooner we start the better."

Staveley tried to laugh, as if he was master of the situation.

"You'll need to carry those two safes with you then," he said. "The keys aren't in this house."

"Mr. Dobson?" Raymond turned to the man with the bag. He was short and slight and in a cheap dark suit. He might have been a clerk in some minor business.

"Excuse me, ma'am." Mr. Dobson edged past Florence and stood before the safes, looking in turn at the decorative brass bosses on the doors, each adorned with the maker's name. He shook his head and spoke in a tone of regret. "Inferior pieces, Mr. Staveley. It's a case of penny-wise and pound-foolish with the Murdoch and Wharton brand, especially with so-called fireproof models like these. Good enough for a drapery emporium or the like but in the sort of business I believe you're in you'd be well advised to pay a bit more and invest in a Chubb."

"Mr. Dobson is an admired peterman," Raymond said. "He needs some time for his preparations and it's safer that he works alone. So, Mr. Staveley, if you'd care to conduct Mrs. Dawlish and myself somewhere else – ideally at the back of the house– we can continue our conversation there."

They seated themselves in a small library. One of Raymond's other men had materialised – he had the look of a retired prize-fighter – and he pulled the curtains before standing by the door.

"Perhaps you'd tell me how far you got to, Mrs. Dawlish," Raymond said. "And no, Mr. Staveley, I suggest that you keep silent until you're required to speak." And for all that there was no pistol on view now, and that Raymond's voice was soft and courteous,

Florence realised that Staveley was even more frightened now than he had been before.

She summarised briefly. Raymond seemed unsurprised and she suspected that he knew all this, and more, already.

"Neatly done, Mrs. Dawlish," he said when she finished. "Dangerous, mind you – you should have spoken to me first, but very neatly done."

"One point remains," Florence turned to Staveley. He seemed shrunken. "The forged letters in the Rosewood files. Do you know whose idea that was?"

He shook his head. "It would have been Whittier or Mellish, probably both. They needed evidence in the Rosewood files to show that the girls had been sent somewhere trustworthy."

"To fool any innocent board member who asked questions?" Florence seethed as she thought of Agatha and of her mother before her. Both genuinely and naïvely good women, they would have been satisfied, would not have delved further, would have sworn to the probity of the home's management. *As I would have done myself after my first visit.*

"It worked," Staveley sounded almost admiring. "It worked for years. It was the price of admission. A man who wanted access had to provide such cover. Family members, friends, names so trustworthy that they'd be taken at face value."

"Like Lady de Courcey? Doctor Longworth? Miss Lydia Scott?"

"Those, yes. Others like them too."

It had been a double betrayal. Of the girls themselves, but also of the decent people whose names had been exploited by persons they admired, trusted, loved.

"I guess we'll find the details in the safes," Raymond sounded satisfied. "Mr. Dobson will be finished soon. He's fast as well as competent. We should be gone in half an hour, Mr. Staveley. I'm sure you'll have a lot to think about thereafter."

"I came about Andrew Shepton," Florence said.

He's why I'm here. He's the only one who can be saved now.

"Why were you holding him so long, Mr. Staveley?" Raymond said. "You must have milked him already of all he knows."

Staveley all but squirmed. He seemed even more frightened now.

"You wanted him as a live witness, didn't you, Mr. Staveley? To produce when the time was right. When you'd threaten somebody worth all the rest of your victims together. So who is it?"

A shake of Staveley's drooping head – reluctance rather than defiance.

"It's somebody a lot more important than that German visitor, isn't it? Somebody who had ... who had perhaps entertained himself with Andrew Shepton on another occasion? We won't burden Mrs. Dawlish with the knowledge so I trust you'll write the name here." Raymond produced a pocket notebook, tore out a leaf and passed it to Staveley with a silver pencil.

Staveley's hand was unsteady as he wrote. He passed the sheet back and Raymond regarded it.

"What I'd expected," he said.

He stood up and walked to the fireplace, empty on this warm summer evening. He laid the paper on the grate, produced matches from his pocket and lit it. He used the poker to break the charred fragments into powder.

A muffled boom from elsewhere in the house and the slightest tremor. And then the same ten seconds later.

"That'll be Mr. Dobson," Raymond said. "I knew he wouldn't be long."

Staveley walked ahead of them back into his study. The smoke had largely cleared but there was an acrid smell that Florence did not recognise. The doors of both safes had been swung open.

Mr. Dobson was putting his tools and a small bottle of clear liquid back in his bag. He looked up as they entered. "Like I said, Mr. R.," he said, "inferior products, these safes, they really are. Once I'd got a few drops into the locks – hardly enough to blind your eye – that was that. And is there anything more I can do for you tonight, sir? No? Then I'll be on my way. And yes, sir – the usual fee. In the next week if possible. Always a pleasure doing business with you, Mr. R." He left.

The safe-interiors had shelves inside and on them card folders, none less than a half-inch thick, containing documents. Markers on the shelves identified them alphabetically, A to M in the first safe, O to, intriguingly, Z in the second as well as a cash box on the bottom.

Raymond stood before the open doors for a full minute, his delight palpable. Then he said to his man who had been waiting behind "Bring the sacks up here. Take everything. I don't want a single paper left behind."

"What are you going to do with all this?" Staveley's voice was almost inaudible. These files must represent his life's work, his treasure, the foundation of his power. He looked as if he was about to faint.

"Certain people will be taking an interest in it but if you have any sense, Mr. Staveley, you might have made yourself scarce by the time they come to act. I'd recommend South America myself, but a good first step would be Ostend. There's an excellent daily packet service and you could be there twenty-four hours from now. A change of name might also be in order."

Two men appeared with the sacks and began to fill them carefully with files.

"Is that your ready money?" Raymond gestured to the cash box.

"Yes."

"How much? About five hundred? That's good. I'll take a hundred from you for Andrew Shepton – it should be enough to get him to the colonies – and you're welcome to the remainder."

"Thank you." Almost a whimper.

Sankey's destruction had been nothing to this and yet I cannot pity him. Florence's detestation was stronger now than her fury.

Staveley opened the cash box and handed over five twenty-pound notes. He must have sensed Florence's loathing for he said, "It was in a good cause, Mrs. Dawlish. You must know that. Nobody stood up for those slum-dwellers before, or for the match-girls, or for..."

Florence turned on her heel and walked out on to the landing. She wanted never to see this man again and felt befouled by his presence even more than she had been with Sankey. Men were lugging laden sacks down the stairs. Raymond followed her.

"Andrew Shepton," she said.

"He can be collected tonight. Leave it to me. I'll have him held in a safe location until arrangements are made for him. The sooner he's out of the country the better. He won't be left alone until he's on shipboard."

"I want his mother to see him, even if it is for the last time. She should know that he's alive and well. She should have a good memory of him."

Raymond nodded. "That'll be arranged."

"Who will be seeing those papers?" Unease was growing within her. There must be enough in them to bring disgrace, if not formal justice, to dozens who deserved it. But for Raymond they could be stock in trade, items to be bartered, currency in some larger game.

He must have sensed her doubt. "You may be meeting someone who'll be glad to see them. He'll have some questions for you himself. It will be soon."

"And that man?" She gestured to the room they had just left, reluctant to use Staveley's name.

Raymond shrugged. "We'll be leaving him here and he can make his own decision. Probably the usual one in such circumstances. He's a coward no less than a hypocrite. He won't find it easy."

Even now she felt no pity.

"You must get back to your hotel, Mrs. Dawlish. There's a hansom waiting in the alley behind with my other vehicles. The driver's reliable. One of my men will escort you. And you'll hear from me tomorrow."

Her escort, a soft-spoken and well-dressed young man, introduced himself as Fuller but was silent thereafter. She felt exhausted, drained of all feeling and emotion, as the cab rattled over the cobbles. Remotely, as if from another universe, she recognised the looming bulk of the Abbey to the left and of the Palace of Westminster to the right Lights were burning there, some parliamentary debate in late-night session. There might be some wealthy, complacent, widely-respected men in the chamber whose names appeared in the files Raymond had taken charge of.

And then a sudden impulse, a desire to cleanse herself. "Tell the driver to turn on to Westminster Bridge," she said.

Fuller looked alarmed. "I think it's better that you go straight to the hotel, ma'am."

She could see what he feared, the dark, filthy swirls eddying beneath the arches.

"It's not what you think, Mr. Fuller. Take me to the bridge."

He called out to the driver. The cab arced to the right just past the buildings. The bridge's roadway was almost empty, a few other vehicles only and several derelicts slumped in uncomfortable sleep on the pavements to either side.

"Stop at the centre."

Fuller stepped down first, then helped her alight. She noticed that he kept close enough to grab her as she moved towards the downstream balustrade. The tide was at its lowest ebb, glistening slopes of dark filth exposed on either side of the foul black artery winding through the richest, most powerful, city on earth.

Florence reached into her bag and took out the revolver, reached out and dropped it. She fancied that she heard a slight splash.

"Now take me to the hotel," she said.

26

The house was in Berkeley Square.

"It's not Sir Richard's," Raymond had said as his matched bays drew his clarence up Regent Street two days later. "It belongs to a friend who's away, and he uses it for meetings."

Florence had met Admiral Sir Richard Topcliffe only once before, on a rainy November evening almost three years before when he had come to Albert Grove. They had exchanged polite conversation until Nicholas had arrived home, and thereafter the two men had been closeted together. She never knew what had been discussed – Nicholas did not speak of it but a half-year leave of absence in South America followed. He never told her what had happened there, but the nightmares that sometimes woke him seemed to relate to it.

The civilian suit did little to hide the fact that the thickset and grizzled man who opened the door was almost certainly an old seaman. Sir Richard was waiting in the library, he told them. As they were conducted there, Florence had an impression of the house being otherwise unoccupied, despite its rich furnishings and spotless cleanliness.

Topcliffe, immaculately groomed, did not wear uniform. As he rose to meet them she recognised, as before, that the still-handsome bearded face and the courtly manner did not quite disguise the coldness in his eyes. He had been a presence in her life ever since that other meeting, she suspected, even though Nicholas had never confirmed it directly. It was this man who had sent Nicholas to the United States. She had gone with him and she remembered the telegrams that had followed, almost certainly from Topcliffe. She had never seen them, and suspected that they were coded – for Nicholas always locked himself away on receiving them. And those messages had in turn sent Nicholas and her – and Raymond – to Cuba. And Oswald, then attached to the Washington embassy, had been involved too, however reluctantly.

A friend – your husband knows him – would also like to help him, Raymond had said, and *I'm somewhat beholden to that gentleman.* Topcliffe must be that gentleman.

He congratulated her on the success of the Sailors' Rest. He had heard much about it and her commitment to it was beyond praise. He made no allusion to Cuba, even though he must certainly know that her scarred left arm was for her a constant reminder to what had happened there. The pleasantries were soon over.

"You played a courageous and principled role, Mrs. Dawlish," Topcliffe said. "A person whom I cannot name is most grateful for your help in aiding a certain unfortunate gentleman to leave the country. Deeply grateful." He handed her a small leather covered box that had lain on the table beside him. "A small token of thanks, Mrs. Dawlish."

She flipped it open, saw the sparkle of diamonds on the earrings, felt a brief rush of lust for them, then handed the box back. *Quickly, before I change my mind.*

"It was done for friendship," she said. "Please return these with thanks." *I could never wear them. Brahmaputra. Willie Burton. Jemmy Gleason. Andrew Shepton. A German prince. And a name that had not surprised Raymond.*

"I suspected that you would say that, Mrs. Dawlish." Topcliffe accepted the box back.

I could have sold them and I could have used the money to help Mrs. Shepton. They could have supported the Sailors' Rest for a year. And still I could not accept them, could not even bring myself to touch them.

"What exactly is your position, Sir Richard?" Florence said. "I don't feel comfortable to discuss these matters unless I know."

The question did not offend him. "I hold Her Majesty's commission, Mrs. Dawlish, a serving officer, just like your husband. Like him, I represent that Lady's interests, though in ways not always connected with naval matters. In ways not usually subject to public scrutiny but relevant to the fortunes of the realm. And Mr. Raymond provides invaluable assistance from time to time."

"Are Rosewood House and the *Brahmaputra* relevant to those fortunes of the realm?" Florence could not supress her bitterness.

"Most assuredly, Mrs. Dawlish. I've been perusing the documents that Mr. Raymond has collected. I can assure you that they will be used with discretion."

"I don't want discretion," Florence said. "I want justice. I want retribution."

She saw a brief smile flash between the two men, one of tolerant, patronising exasperation.

"I understand your anger," Topcliffe's voice was gentle, soothing, as a parent might explain the death of a beloved pet to a child. "I understand it fully, and I honour you for it. But you must understand, Mrs. Dawlish – and I think you know it already – that most of these people are beyond the reach of the law. I deplore it and I'm no less outraged than yourself. I'm saddened to see the name of the son of a fine man who's been a valued friend since we were midshipmen together. I'm shocked by the involvement of men who are directors of a company I have had some dealings with. I feel for the family of the gentleman whom you assisted. I rejoice that you and your friends are bringing order and decency to Rosewood House. But I cannot lie to you. The vast majority of those involved can never be charged, much less brought to trial."

"And so, no justice?" She remembered the smell of formaldehyde in a corrugated iron shed and the pathetic body that she had saved from a pauper's grave.

"There's justice much rougher than any court can dispense, Mrs. Dawlish. There'll be a word to each of the persons mentioned, a word from one source or another, enough to let them know that their actions and their guilt are known. There will be resignations. There will be withdrawals from public life. There will be sudden departures and residence abroad. There will be contributions to worthy charities. And all the while there will be the threat of exposure, not just exposure in the press, but far more powerfully by word of mouth in society. The knowledge that exposure might come at any time, and that disgrace for them and ostracism for their families would follow, will haunt the guilty until the end of their days. And in the meantime, should any signal service be needed of them for the good of the country, then they cannot but agree to it unconditionally."

"It sounds like another form of blackmail, Sir Richard." Florence was unsure whether his words repelled her or reassured her.

"You're getting retribution, Mrs. Dawlish. You're getting justice. I can assure you that what will follow will be harsher than any stone-breaking in a prison quarry, any months of sewing mail-bags, any endless days on the treadmill. Some will be unable to endure it, I'm afraid, and they'll make an end of themselves."

"Yet the one person who wanted me to have a gift – the same person, I suspect, whose name was written on a piece of paper that Mr. Raymond went to great lengths to destroy – will be beyond all this."

"*Raison d'état,* Mrs. Dawlish." Topcliffe's tone regretful but resigned. "Reasons of state. Some concerns are stronger even than justice. You or I might not like it but it's the reality of the world we live in."

There could be no answer. Florence stood up, ready to leave.

"Before you go, Mrs. Dawlish, there's some news I should have given you earlier," Topcliffe said. "It's about your husband."

Her knees weakened, her heart pounded. *Not Nicholas! Oh God, not Nicholas!*

He had detected her alarm and his tone was gentle. "It's nothing to be worried about. It's just a slight delay before he can bring *Leonidas* back from the Far East. He'll most likely have written to you from Hong Kong about it but the letter cannot have reached England yet. But I have had telegraphic contact – he's well by the way – and he's been entrusted with a diplomatic mission that will cause only a month's or so delay."

"A diplomatic mission!" A sudden image of gorgeous oriental courts, silk robes, mandarins with long moustaches and longer finger-nails, porcelain and Willow-pattern gardens. "Where to, Sir Richard?"

"To Korea," he said. "Just a matter of getting some signatures to treaty codicils. A routine affair but interesting nonetheless."

She knew the country's name, little more. She would have to consult the *Britannica* about it. But, interesting as it might be, Nicholas would gladly have traded this experience of minor diplomacy for the opportunity of action at Alexandria.

Topcliffe saw Florence and Raymond personally to the hall door. He paused there.

"It's better if you say nothing of this affair to your husband when he returns. Speak to him about the reorganisation at Rosewood House by all means. But nothing more. And one final point, Mrs. Dawlish…"

"Yes?"

"You had some dealings with Count Livitski of the Russian Embassy. There's been some discussion with the ambassador, a suggestion that some of the count's activities were not consistent with his role as a diplomat. It was agreed that it was better that he leave Britain immediately. He's a very dangerous man, Mrs. Dawlish."

"Yes," Florence said. "I know that."

*

Florence returned home that evening. There was a deep joy in being there and only now did she realise that when she had last left she had unconsciously accepted that she might never see it again. She wondered – and did not know the answer – if she would indeed have wounded, or even killed, that man in London had Raymond not arrived. She riffled through the mail that had arrived in her absence and no letter had arrived yet from Hong Kong. She gave Cook and Susan a half-crown each and sent them away for the evening, then sat with her piano with the French windows open and the soft evening breeze ruffling the curtains. She did not play well – she knew that she never would now because of her injured arm – but it was rewarding nonetheless. She slept well, as if her mind had decided independently to shut out, however briefly, all memory of what had happened in recent days.

Her feeling of oppression, of awareness of evil, was gone when she awoke but it returned when Susan brought her a telegram at the breakfast table. From Raymond.

The boy would arrive under escort at 10:55 and must leave at latest by the 17:15.

Mrs. Shepton would see her son for less than six hours.

Probably for the last time ever.

*

The youth who came down the station platform with Raymond's Mr. Fuller bore no resemblance to Florence's mental picture of Andrew Shepton. She had imagined an underfed, skinny boy with a pinched face and a shifty expression, somewhat of a double of the youth who had played decoy in the *Duke of Kent*. Instead she saw a well-built young man of close on six feet with broad shoulders, an athletic walk and a handsome face. Whatever else the *Brahmaputra* had done for him, exercise on the masts and yards had given him a physique and bearing of which his mother could justifiably be proud. And, knowing what Florence did, that made it all the worse. He was well, if flashily, dressed.

She did not introduce herself, just told him briefly that he was being taken to see his mother.

"That's fine," he said. There was a trace of a smirk but no word of thanks.

Florence recognised the tough-looking man who had come with Fuller, and was now standing behind Shepton, as one of those who had helped take the documents from the safes.

Fuller nodded towards him. "Mr. Jenkins will be with me when I bring Andrew to his mother's. You have the address?" He had obviously sensed that Florence did not wish to be present at the meeting.

"And what happens afterwards?" Florence had drawn Fuller apart and was speaking in a near whisper.

"Straight to Southampton. The ship sails in the early hours. He won't be left alone until it has cast off. He'll do well enough in South Africa."

"Does he know where he's going?" She knew that he had told his mother before that he was going to America.

"He'll only find out when he's on board. We'll see to it that he won't have a chance to leave the ship."

"Let me speak to him."

There was a dumb insolence about him as he heard her out, an obvious contempt for what she said, a smug satisfaction that he had got all he wanted and wished now only to be gone. Florence saw that he would have been happier to leave without seeing his family and she was glad that she had insisted that he should. For all his manly bearing he would not look her in the eye. He almost laughed at her when she asked if he had a story ready to explain to his mother why she had not heard from him for so long. Of course he had. He had been taken on as an apprentice clerk by a wine merchant and his duties had taken him to Scotland, as they were now taking him to America. Florence saw that he could lie easily. *As easily as I've come to do also.* She was glad that the time for it was over.

"You'll write to your mother, won't you? She thinks so well of you, is so proud of you. She will be so worried about you, your father too when he gets home."

And he would write, he assured her. Two or three times, she expected, until the letters would cease and he would disappear into whatever new and dishonourable life he would make for himself. For he knew now that he could exploit others, maybe more effectively than others had exploited him, and he had the arrogant confidence of the truly amoral that would enable him to thrive where others would fail. It would be better that his parents think him dead than that they should know the jackal he would become.

The burden of knowledge lay heavier than ever on her as she walked away. She knew that in the coming days, maybe even tomorrow, Mrs. Shepton would find her at the Sailor's Rest, would be full of joy that her boy had come to see her, that he was doing so well, that his employers were sending him abroad on an important business errand. No mother ever had a better son, or a more handsome either, and incidents of his babyhood had proved his innate talents. Florence would be delighted but not surprised – she had always thought there had just been some misunderstanding. Boys were like that, she would say, she had two brothers herself and knew how they could be. She would make no reference to her own promise to find him which had dominated her life in recent weeks and she hoped that Mrs. Shepton would forget it in her elation.

It was to the Sailors' Rest that she headed now. The prospect of immersing herself in the small administrative tasks and correspondence that would have accumulated in her absence was attractive. Discussion of roof repairs, haggling over a quote submitted by a plasterer, bargaining with a grocer over a bulk discount, seemed clean, worthy even, by comparison with her recent concerns. On the way she bought a *Morning Post* to read as she took tea in her small office before starting work.

She expected that the first article would have to do with Egypt – Alexandria, she knew, had been pacified in recent days but there was still unrest outside it and speculation that further British intervention would be necessary. Instead she found the headline *"Tragic Death of Respected Editor"* and knew even before reading further who it must be.

He must have been dead for several hours when his cleaning lady had found him. An inquest was pending but initial indications were that the pilot of his study's gas lamp must have been extinguished and when he had turned on full flow to get light he must have been overcome by the influx of toxic gas. Had the heavy curtains not been closed, then natural ventilation might have saved him.

The obituary was respectful, if restrained. The *Morning Post* stated that it had not always been in sympathy with the gentleman's views but they had been held with passionate conviction and he had campaigned for them with an energy that earned well-merited respect from his critics no less than from his adherents. His passing would be widely mourned. There was some speculation in another article as to who would now take over the *Fortnightly's* editorship. Another told that leadership of the campaign for the match-girls had been assumed on a temporary basis by Miss Amelia Bartlett-Rogers. The best tribute to her predecessor would be to maintain his campaign with undiminished vigour.

Florence laid the newspaper down.

And felt only emptiness.

*

Nicholas's Hong Kong letter arrived a week later, just after Florence had returned from a two-day visit to Rosewood House. A new supervisor had been installed already, a middle-aged spinster who had been a matron at a major London Hospital. Agatha had approved the selection but it appeared that Mabel had driven the process of finding and appointing her. Mabel herself was about to return to the United States. She had recovered fully, she said, and though her scars were hidden Florence still noticed the occasional wince of pain. Agatha would remain at Rosewood for another week, as would Jack, who still maintained his nightly patrols of the grounds. Mellish and Whittier had already resigned from the Rosewood board. Agatha's father had emerged from seclusion and was approaching acquaintances eminent in ecclesiastical and business circles to act as replacements. A friend of his who had retired from parliament to write a biography of Plutarch and edit a new edition of his works had agreed to replace Oswald on the board of the *Brahmaputra*. The task immediately confronting him would be to help select a replacement for Captain Wilton, who had resigned his post without explanation and was believed to be emigrating to Brazil.

Something had been achieved, Florence thought, something to protect the girls now at Rosewood and the boys on the *Brahmaputra*, but there had been no help for those who had preceded them. There was justice of a sort for Willie Burton and Jemmy Gleason and Dorcas Hayward but Emily and Rose and Rachel and Mary and Lucy, girls whose names she would never forget even if she had never known their faces, were beyond help in some nightmare world that began for them at Antwerp. And there were others, dozens perhaps, quiet, withdrawn servants who would never speak of carriage rides at Rosewood but would be haunted forever by memory of them.

She turned with relief to Nicholas's letter, as full of solid detail as it always was, satisfaction with the *Leonidas's* dry-docking, the excellence of the Hong Kong dockyard facilities, his pleasure in meeting a senior officer whom he had admired when he was a boy, the extraordinary growth of the colony's trade since he had last visited it, as evidenced by some statistics he knew she would find of interest. He trusted that she would like the silk shawl he had bought for her, and another for his sister Susan, whose latest confinement must be by now imminent. His return to Britain was being delayed by an unexpected order to visit Korea for reasons of diplomacy but he expected to be back no more than three weeks later than previously expected. And he sent his love. It was like all the other letters she had from him, factual, dense, lacking on this occasion even the most awkward humour, and yet somehow conveying the commitment to each other that had not failed them even when they had faced death together.

I miss him, badly, as he misses me, and yet I may never tell him of what has just passed. Just as he has never told me of what happened in South America.

*

For a week or more she raced through the *Morning Post's* pages, as soon as it was delivered, for mention of some other name to follow Staveley and Captain Wilton in that procession of shame that Topcliffe had predicted. She knew what she wanted to find – Rear Admiral Dale (Retd.), the ship-owner Sir Charles Pugh, the politician Lord James Wigworth and the vile Reverend Martin Thursley whom she guessed had warned Dolly Braben that she was being investigated. And other names, men whose moral degradation had been described in that appalling confession by Peter Sankey. She hungered for their punishment with a passion that was both cold and relentless, yet she knew that its satisfaction would be as empty as when she had learned of Staveley's death. But it was one further death that taught her that she must quell this hunger before it consumed her, that she should no longer trawl for news of retribution lest it embitter her forever.

The story was carried in the *Morning Post* and, at greater length, in the *Portsmouth Argus*. Lieutenant Frederick de Courcey, a promising young officer who had been serving on the royal yacht *Victoria and Albert,* had disappeared when the vessel was crossing the Solent during stormy weather. It was believed that the unfortunate young man must have stumbled and fallen overboard and his body had not been found. Neither Her Majesty nor any member of her family was on board at the time but royal condolences had been conveyed to his grieving parents, the Port Admiral at Portsmouth and his wife Lady Adelaide. Admired by his brother officers and loved by the lower-deck, the exemplary young officer's merits would undoubtedly have earned him senior rank had he not been cut off in his prime.

Florence sent a letter of condolence, probably one of hundreds, and she received a black edged card in acknowledgement. She had held off from approaching Lady Adelaide to outline what had transpired at Rosewood – an explanation was due since her signature had been used – but she quailed at the thought of where inevitable questioning might lead. It was a relief to know that in the period of mourning there would be no invitations to tea parties, no well-meaning attempts to atone for earlier snubs. But there was no avoiding the meeting when she did receive an invitation a month later.

They met in the same parlour as before. This time Lady Adelaide was already waiting for her. She looked twenty years older than when Florence had last seen her, her face haggard and her eyes dead. They sat. Florence could only find conventional words of sympathy, empty, trite, inadequate, but no worse than any others when set against the immensity of grief. Then, polite enquiries about Mrs. Dawlish's husband and his ship, a brave attempt at normal conversation. And, at last, Rosewood.

"That home you spoke to me of before, Mrs. Dawlish. I understand that so much good work is done there."

Florence confirmed it. There had been some problems, some misunderstandings, but they were now resolved. Her friend Lady Agatha, Lord Kegworth's daughter, had the matters in hand.

"My husband and I have been wondering how best to commemorate our son. You probably know that his body wasn't..." Lady Adelaide dabbed her eyes. "That there is no grave, although there will be a memorial tablet in church. But we thought there could be something more, something he would have liked and that we believe you might be willing to administer. A trust to be set up in his memory that would contribute to the annual costs of Rosewood House."

"I could think of nothing more appropriate."

"He was a good son," Lady Adelaide's voice was breaking. "No mother could have a better."

"No," Florence said. "No mother could have a better."

The End

Historical Note

The activities at the Cleveland Street brothel were finally exposed in 1889. Telegraph messenger boys who worked there were prosecuted and given light sentences. No clients faced court proceedings, though over twenty suspects – many of them aristocratic or otherwise prominent – left Britain hurriedly. The government was accused of covering up the scandal to protect clients' names. Allegations of involvement of a person at the pinnacle of society have never been proved, though an American newspaper – which could not be sued for libel – named him at the time. Public outrage at the case stoked the prejudice that homosexual behaviour was an aristocratic vice that preyed on working-class youths. As such it paved the way for the merciless destruction of Oscar Wilde six years later. Homosexual acts between male consenting adults remained a criminal offence in England until 1967, and for longer elsewhere in Britain – a situation often referred to as "the blackmailers' charter".

Adam Worth (1844 – 1902), alias Henry Judson Raymond, did exist in real-life and featured as a character in *Britannia's Shark*. He was to continue his successful criminal career – and double life as a respected socialite in Britain – until 1892, when he was convicted in Belgium for an uncharacteristically bungled robbery of a major cash transfer. He served four years and on release promptly stole £4000 worth of diamonds in London to finance his new operations. He returned thereafter to the United States and negotiated a deal with the Pinkerton Detective Agency. This involved return of the Gainsborough portrait of The Duchess of Devonshire, which Worth had stolen in 1876, against a payment to him of $25000. He returned to London and died there. He was buried, under the name of Raymond, in Highgate Cemetery, not far from Karl Marx. In his own lifetime he was referred to by senior Scotland Yard officers as "The Napoleon of Crime" and is believed to have been the inspiration for Sir Arthur Conan Doyle's Professor Moriarty, whom Sherlock Holmes described by the same title.

The campaign in Britain against use of white phosphorous in matches was espoused from the mid-1880s by many leading social reformers and it prompted a boycott of one of the major companies involved. The Salvation Army took up the cause and set up its own match factory – using safer materials – in 1891 in opposition to established manufacturers. It was not however until 1908 that the British Parliament passed the White Phosphorus Matches Prohibition Act. Had this been done a quarter-century previously – following the lead of Sweden and Denmark – countless lives would not have been so hideously blighted.

A personal message from Antoine Vanner

I hope you've enjoyed *Britannia's Amazon* and also the other books in the series, *Britannia's Wolf, Britannia's Reach, Britannia's Shark* and *Britannia's Spartan* (which runs in parallel in time with *Amazon*). *Britannia's Mission* and *Britannia's Gamble* follow sequentially.

You probably know how important good reviews are to the success of a book on Amazon or Kindle. I'd be very grateful if you could post a review on www.amazon.com or www.amazon.co.uk.

Your support does really matter and I read all reviews since readers' feedback encourages me to keep researching and writing about the lives of Nicholas and Florence Dawlish.

If you'd like to leave a review then all you have to do is go to the "Britannia's Amazon" page on Amazon. Scroll down from the top and under the heading of "Customer Reviews" you'll see a big button that says "Write a customer review" – click that and you're ready to go. You don't need to write much – a sentence or two is enough, essentially what you'd tell a friend or family member about the book.

Thanks again for your support and don't forget that you can learn more about Nicholas Dawlish and his world on my website dawlishchronicles.com and blog dawlishchronicles.blogspot.co.uk in which I write short articles based on research which is not necessarily used in the novels.

I hope you'll enjoy the bonus short-story that follows – ***Britannia's Eye*** – which casts more light on some aspects of Nicholas's childhood that have been alluded to in other books.

Yours Faithfully: ***Antoine Vanner***

Britannia's Eye

April – October 1857

There was blood on his handkerchief when he coughed, spots only, nothing comparable to the blood that would flow so copiously at midday.

Ralph Page had lodged in a cheap pension near the Gare Saint-Charles, Marseille's principal railway station, one night only, arriving late the evening before and now leaving early for Toulon. It had taken a whole day to get here from Pau, with short breaks between connecting trains at Toulouse, Narbonne, Montpelier and Arles. There was nothing remarkable about an obviously consumptive middle-aged man in well-tailored but worn clothing to arouse suspicion when he posted a letter at each stop. They would arrive at a nondescript address in a London suburb within two days and be on a desk in Whitehall three hours later.

The summer sun was merciless as the train – a local one – crawled across the parched Provencal landscape. The carriage windows were open – Page was travelling second-class, as befitted his shabby-genteel appearance – but it still felt stuffy and he coughed intermittently, forcing other passengers to keep their distance. He had tried to tell himself that his chest was no worse than it had been a year before, but now he had come to accept what was inevitable. Forty-three seemed very young for this. He had nine months left, a year at the most, the doctors had told him, and the prospect saddened rather than frightened him.

But Armand Brisson had even less time, a small internal voice reminded him, not nine months, not one, not even a week, but just under three hours. The ghastly machine would have been assembled before dawn and the crowd would even now be gathering before it. Was there already a priest with the wretched man now, were any words of solace capable of easing his terror? Page himself had seen death enough – the fighting on the Levantine coast sixteen years before had been particularly brutal and, paymaster or not, he had joined in the storming of Sidon and Acre – but that killing had been in the heat of battle, and had nothing of the cold, systematic nature of what would happen at noon.

He did not need to be on this train, he told himself, he could have been in London, even in Shrewsbury, by now. He had dealt fairly with this man and owed him nothing more, had never even seen him. Brisson has been paid, well paid, through three levels of intermediaries. Even when he was arrested the dockyard draughtsman must have known that his offence would not have earned death but he had panicked, had stabbed and killed one of the gendarmes sent for him, and then tried unsuccessfully to cut his own throat. Now it was to be cut for him.

And all the while the small voice reminded Page that it was he who had brought on this terrible morning. He was unsure what had committed him so whole-heartedly to this squalid game. Was it love of country, or the desire to blot out awareness of his own shortened time by throwing himself into an activity he excelled in? Bad health had forced him to leave the Navy but his aptitude for information gathering and analysis had allowed a semi-invalid living at a French spa to be more useful than he had ever been in the service.

He left his valise at the station in Toulon – it was lightly packed but even then the effort of carrying it from the platform jaded him – and he checked again the departure time for the afternoon express to Paris. A quarter past two. Long enough. He would not want to tarry here.

The Place de la Liberté was close to the station, a few hundred yards, but that was enough to tire him. It was just after eleven o'clock and a crowd was already clustered in the north-eastern corner of the enormous square, trees and high buildings to the side offering shade. He moved among them, edging his way to the front. Most were poor, some even ragged, and there was a strong smell of unwashed bodies and garlic and cheap wine. There were as many women as men – and some of the women carried babies, or had older children clinging to their skirts. Crude jokes were evoking shrill, forced laughter. A few stolid bourgeois, well-dressed, some with equally stolid-looking wives, were scattered through the press. A vendor was selling, for a few sous, badly printed sheets that purported to be Brisson's last confession. Page bought a copy. It was obvious that Brisson had never seen it and it consisted of high-flown statements of contrition, of admonition to learn by his failures. It mentioned the policeman's death, but nothing more, and the details were so vague that it was likely that, but for Brisson's name, the same text had been used on a dozen previous occasions of this sort.

Page reached the front, an invisible line patrolled by bicorne-hatted gendarmes with drawn sabres. They were encountering no difficulty in controlling the crowd. There was a sense that the event was mildly interesting and entertaining, but not one to evoke sympathy or partisanship.

Only now did Page look up and see the rectangular frame set up on the low scaffold, the triangular blade already raised. A dignified-looking man in an immaculate frock coat and a top hat was gravely, unhurriedly, instructing two blouse-clad labourers to make minor adjustments. There was a horror about the calm meticulousness, the systematic preparations, the carefully positioned basket, the open coffin to one side of the hinged plank now standing vertical. Page had never seen this spectacle before, had despised the bravado with which some English residents at Pau boasted of having seen several such. But he had brought a man to this. That small, nagging internal voice that grew louder as he felt his own time ticking ever more quickly away had told him he must be here. Despised as Brisson might be, he should have one in this crowd to mourn for him, to feel for him, even if he would never know.

Several officials, one with a tricolour sash, arrived in a coach and mounted the scaffold. They shook hands solemnly with the grave man with the top hat. The crowd was falling silent, dead silent, as a closed van escorted by mounted police emerged from a side street. And then the dreadful procession.

The condemned man was smaller, older too, than Page had visualised. His head had been shaved and the collar had been ripped from his grubby shirt. His eyes were locked on the ground ahead, avoiding as long as possible the sight of the guillotine. He had probably been dosed with brandy, for he was staggering slightly and was being steadied, not unkindly, by a guard on his left. On his right a priest, pallid and trembling, was reading from a book – gabbling rather – and he seemed almost as terrified as Brisson himself.

His body is still healthy, his lungs sound, Page thought, just as mine are failing slowly. But in five minutes he will be dead and I will still be living. Nine months, at the most a year. Why had Brisson done it? Would he have said that it was for the dying mother or the sick wife or the crippled child who were so often cited and who might, or might not, exist? It was never to buy revelry and women beyond their reach, never to settle gambling debts, never to have money to squander in a quantity so far above their pay that it must arouse suspicion. The fifteen-hundred francs that had bought a drawing and a dozen documents had also bought a life.

Page forced himself to watch until the end, turning away only from the last foul manoeuvrings with the basket and coffin. The sight would have disgusted him at any time, but now there was something worse, loathing for himself, revulsion for the temptation that he had offered and that Brisson had accepted, acceptance that there could be no undoing.

And recognition that he would do it all again if the opportunity arose.

Even though his own final darkness was nearer by the day.

The crowd was breaking up in silence, sobered, perhaps ashamed. Page was coughing again into a handkerchief that was increasingly sodden with red.

It would only be a few hundred yards back to the station but it would seem like a thousand miles.

*

He had never liked his solicitor brother-in-law, his dislike growing into a grudge after his sister Jessica had died in childbirth, her baby with her, seven years before. He had come back to Shrewsbury only four times since then, visits needed for discussions with his agent about the half-dozen farms he owned near the town. He had never expected that a childless cousin's early death would bring them to him. The life of a local squire did not attract him – and did so even less when he grew ill – and the rents brought in from the tenants were meagre. Common sense told him that he should sell them but he shrunk from breaking his last link to an area his sister had loved.

Yet now, in Shresbury, Andrew Dawlish's concern for him was touching. He had insisted on Page lodging with him, had disguised whatever reluctance he might have to taking a consumptive into his house, had assured him that the three children would be desolate if their uncle were not to stay. Page realised now that, for all the roughness of his manners, for all his liking for alcohol and his addiction to smoking-room stories, for all his leering way with housemaids, the Shrewsbury solicitor was moved by a pity for him that he would never openly express. He had never referred to the illness, though its progress was so outwardly unmistakable, had arranged with clumsy kindness for a doctor friend to dine with them so that a social as well as a medical bond was established. He had taken on himself all arrangements for the meetings with the agent, for the visits to the farms, with a solicitude that ensured that no one day's work or journey would be too much for an ailing man. Only now did Page recognise how much this man had been scarred by his wife's death. He was ashamed that he himself had not given the comfort of shared grief, that he had recoiled from a brotherhood that would have ignored superficial coarseness, the randomness of fate.

The children liked him, were eager for his company. James, the eldest, and his eleven-year-old brother Nicholas, were importunate for stories of the Navy. Susan – thirteen, vivacious and painfully like her mother at that age – was keen for details of life in France, of the elegance and grace of the women there. Page told her of his housekeeper, of her daughter Clothilde – she was almost of the same age – and of life in Pau. The sleepy spa town in the foothills of the Pyrenees, that was renowned for its pure air, and that attracted its colony of British invalids by its low costs, seemed to the girl vastly sophisticated compared with her own English market town. Page thought briefly about bringing her also back with him – but no, with her growing woman's intuition she would perceive more about Madame Madeleine Sapin than her younger brother Nicholas ever would, more than Page would ever want her to know.

Andrew Dawlish must have guessed that there was a reason for this visit other than a routine review of farm accounts with the agent but he made no allusion to it. It was left to Page himself to raise it a week after his arrival. They were sitting together after dinner, Dawlish drinking too much port and Page restraining. He noticed that his brother-in-law had not lit up one of his usual evening cigars – he must have noticed that he himself had stopped smoking. Talk of the farms, of wool and cereal prices, satisfaction at the agent's honesty. And then silence, and about it an air of hesitation, yet of mutual recognition that truth could no longer be denied.

"I'm dying, Andrew."

Page had never put in words before. He was surprised how calmly he found himself saying it.

Protestations, unconvincing protestations, that there was no question of it. Too-quick assurances that he had never looked better in his life, that he'd see the whole family out. But a catch in the voice and an unwillingness to look him in the eye.

"I'd like you to be my executor, Andrew. I'll let you have the will tomorrow." It had been drawn up by another solicitor three years before when he had at last accepted that residence in Pau could only delay, never cure. The provisions he had made then still stood.

"It won't be for a long time yet," Andrew Dawlish tried to laugh. "Maybe it'll be James rather than me who'll have to execute it." His elder son was already apprenticed to the business, was showing aptitude for it. His future was assured.

"Nicholas will get the farms," Page said. "Susan will have a little money also. She's a fine girl and she won't want for suitors, she'll be well looked after in time, but I'd like her to have something. But Nicholas will have to make his own way. As well as the farms he'll have some money from me too." He did not mention that the remainder would go to Madeleine. Not a fortune, but enough to buy her a generous annuity. She owned her house, would not need much to maintain respectability. And a hundred pounds in francs for Clothilde, for a *dot*, a dowry.

"It's generous, damned generous." Dawlish failed to sound surprised. It was hard to imagine any other settlement. There were no other close relations.

"I'd like somebody to remember me, Andrew."

"But they will, Ralph, they will." The assurance recognised the inevitability of the outcome.

"Not just a kind word when my name is mentioned. Somebody who'll have loved me like a father." As he had hoped Clothilde would do, but despite her outward charm there was a chill air of calculation about her. She would not long mourn him.

"Like Nicholas?" Dawlish said it gently.

"Yes. Like Nicholas."

"You want to take him to France?"

"It will be good for him. He can learn the language." Page despised the tone of pleading he found entering his voice. He wanted this badly. "My housekeeper's daughter is about the same age. They'll play together and he'll learn French from her. It'll stand him in good stead later. Knowing another language is never a burden to carry."

"How long would he stay, Ralph?" The concern was obvious, though not specified.

"A few months. Only until it gets too bad with me. He won't see the worst of it." He had heard that the boy had woken with nightmares for months after his mother died. At four, old enough to remember her. He still fell into silences when she was mentioned. He should not be brought close to another death.

"Did you talk to him about it, Ralph?"

"I thought it better to talk to you first."

A silence. A question hung unspoken in it. Page answered it.

"I may have a year. I wouldn't keep him for longer than six-months. He'll be gone before he sees me bed-ridden."

And to his surprise Page saw tears glistening in his brother-in-law's eyes.

It might have been the excess of port that made him maudlin.

*

The boy had been easy in his company while he was in Shrewsbury. Page tired too easily to ride and a hired trap brought him to view his farms. Nicholas often followed on his pony, a competent and determined rider, a less spectacular one than his elder brother James, who flew over high fences with such casual elegance. Nicholas had not been told that the properties were intended for him but his questions about their running were spontaneous and intelligent. He seemed to find it easier to talk with his uncle than with his father, to whom he showed respect rather than warmth. It might be that he resented, perhaps unwillingly, unconsciously, the loss of his mother, just as Page did that of his sister. Quieter than his elder brother, Nicholas still had much of the innocence of early childhood about him and seemed dependent – over-dependent perhaps – on the robust affection of Mrs. Gore, the old widow who had been nurse of all three children and was now housekeeper.

That the boy was coming with him made the parting at the Shrewsbury station less difficult. Page knew, and his brother-in-law knew, that he would never come here again. Regret for chances missed, for a friendship that should have been, hung heavy but unspoken between them, memory too of a grief that should have been shared, realisation that past coldness counted for nothing in the face of what must now be. Nicholas's presence gave them the opportunity to talk instead about trivial practicalities – train-changes at rail junctions, the night's hotel-booking at Weymouth, the prospects for a smooth Channel crossing to Saint Malo the following day. Mrs. Gore provided another welcome diversion, bursting into tears as a distant whistle announced the train's imminent arrival.

"Oh Mr. Page! Do look after him well!" She was hugging Nicholas to her. "The poor little lamb never spent so much as a night from home! And now you're bringing him among the heathens who murdered their king and queen!"

Susan, moved by her nurse's words, also flung herself on her brother and wept. James was trying to maintain a manly reserve but was close to tears himself. Nicholas himself was trying to choke back emotion. They had never been parted before.

And so there was no opportunity for a formal farewell between the two men. They were both glad of it, that there was nothing more than hands pressed, a "Thank you, Andrew," and a "God bless you, Ralph", both heartfelt.

The stationmaster blew his whistle and waved his flag and the train lurched forward.

Towards a life's end.

*

Nicholas had never seen the sea before and the crossing entranced him, all the more so since it proved unseasonably rough and he could be proud of not being seasick. His trepidation about leaving home was forgotten in the excitement of new discoveries and the mood continued on the three-days of easy rail-stages to Pau. Yet even so Page arrived exhausted at each evening's hotel, one sodden handkerchief guiltily hidden, another half-soaked, the boy trying, with courteous sensitivity, to make no mention of it or of the coughing he must surely have heard in the night from his adjoining room. He had picked up the rudiments of French in his Shrewsbury grammar school and was now eager to learn, and Page to teach, new words and phrases.

Madeleine – Madame Sapin – was genuinely delighted by him, and he by her. She lavished on him care and affection like Mrs. Gore's, taking infinite but kindly pains to teach him expressions and idioms, to correct his pronunciation, to guide him around the sights, such as they were, of Pau. He accepted her for what she seemed, a housekeeper. Worsening symptoms had necessitated separate rooms and Page had not shared a bed with her for almost two years. He kept a distance from her – one that hurt them both – lest the slightest touch communicate his disease.

Clothilde, a year older than Nicholas, seemed wary of him at first, but that soon passed. They played easily together and it was from her that he picked up the language fastest. A routine was quickly established, he escorting her gravely each morning to her convent school and continuing on to the small academy for sons of British invalids run by the clergy of the town's small Anglican church.

English boys came back several times to the house with Nicholas, one of them already showing the early signs of the malady that was killing his father. Page welcomed their games, their enquiries about his naval life that Nicholas must have boasted of, their relish in his stories – he had been little older than them when he had been on board *Albion* at Navarino. It was risk and action and danger that fascinated them, and yet it was his quieter, colder, secret accomplishments that he must never speak of that had been more deadly. An invalided naval paymaster with a gift for codes and ciphers, for clandestine manipulation and exploitation of weaknesses, had proved more valuable to Britain than a squadron of warships.

The days seemed to be passing ever more quickly now. Each small pleasure was tinged with sadness – summer's blossom, scented shade, the hum of bees, slow walks with Nicholas and Clothilde and long conversations with them when he was forced to sit and rest. Madeleine never spoke of the illness directly but he was moved by her endless solicitude for his comfort, by the favourite dishes she prepared herself, by the tears he saw welling in her eyes when he found her looking at him when he woke from a doze in garden shade. He had always read a lot, but now his appetite for knowledge was insatiable – history, travel, scientific works – hungering to know all he could before… before that unknown but nearing month and day and hour.

And still he worked. The communications still arrived, indirectly, from the only three contacts whom he had ever met in person – and in each case once only. They were the filters, the highest layer of several, that shielded him from the squalid web of greed and weakness and treachery that he depended upon. Their caution and their discretion could be relied upon, for each knew that his fall would be theirs, that the weaknesses that had brought them into his orbit could not bear exposure. Innocuously worded, assurances came that some clerk or draughtsman or dockyard supervisor needed money, that some army or naval officer with an extravagant wife or demanding mistress or mounting gambling debts was on the edge of despair, that some deputy or petty minister had a taste for young boys and even younger girls. All could be open to an approach, not immediately perhaps, but at a moment when one single item of information might be beyond price, when the fate of nations might be in the balance. The new French Empire had been Britain's ally in the Crimea but their interests were diverging now. France still smarted from her humiliation four decades before, was as eager as her present monarch to restore the glory his uncle had lost. Britain was already investing heavily in forts to protect Plymouth and Portsmouth and England's southern coast. The day might come when…

When I am no longer here. When none of this will matter to me anymore.

Yet he worked, as efficiently as he ever had, perhaps even more so. He was resolved to do so to the end. It was not patriotism alone that drove him – though that was part of it – but awareness that this was the only thing he had ever excelled in, that it somehow gave meaning to his life.

And other than a few men in Whitehall, to whom his passing would be nothing more than a temporary inconvenience, nobody would ever know of it.

Not even Nicholas.

*

Page's hope that the boy would come to love him was fulfilled, each day together a pleasure, diminished only by awareness that it must end in a few months. Their conversations were long and satisfying, made even more pleasing by the innocent naivety of some comment reminding that he was still a child, that awareness of the evil of the world had not yet dawned upon him. He was hungry for stories of his mother's childhood, of Page's life at sea, of foreign parts and of dangers survived. He had found Southey's *Life of Nelson* in the small library and had drawn diagrams of the main actions, discussing them as gravely as if he himself was one of the Band of Brothers, and his uncle the great admiral himself. Yet even now something of the brutal realities of society were coming to weigh upon him.

"Why does Madame Sapin not go to church?" he asked one evening. He had got over his initial suspicion of Catholics, reassured that the horrors illustrated so graphically in the copy of *Foxe's Martyrs* Mrs. Gore had regaled him with on so many Sundays were now gone for ever. It was hard to imagine Madeleine ever wanting to burn anybody.

"She's such a good person that she doesn't need to," Page said.

"But we go to the English church. And Clothilde made her communion at the convent. It was a great occasion, she said. She had to have a beautiful white dress for it. And she goes there to mass each Sunday."

"That's because the nuns demand it. But they can't force Madame Sapin to do the same if she doesn't want to."

"I'm glad of that, Uncle" The sight of nuns still intimidated him. Mrs. Gore had not laboured in vain.

And yet it was not the nuns who had driven Madeleine away. When Page had come here first, as her lodger, she still went dutifully to mass each Sunday with her large prayer-book in an embossed leather cover. It was only months later, when they had come to love one another, that she had suddenly begun to stay away. She had never spoken of it to him but he seethed when he thought of what secrets might have been wrung from her under cover of the confessional, what threat of damnation had been held over her by a prurient curé. Quiet, modest, kind as she was, she had the courage to choose love over the risk of Hell's fire. She could bear it for now, while he was still with her, but he worried how she could cope with the ostracism when he was gone.

Then, one by one, the English boys stopped coming, nor did Nicholas in turn seem to spend so much time at their houses. Page assumed that his growing fluency in French was perhaps inclining him to friendships with the brothers of Clothilde's friends. Many English residents in Pau, many here for upwards of a decade, could still speak no word of the language and were vocal in their contempt for the local inhabitants. It was inevitable that their sons should share their attitudes and their ignorance. Page was glad that the boy was no part of this, that Madeleine's and Clothilde's obvious affection for him, and his for them, made him as much at home in Pau as in Shrewsbury. It was comforting to see, but not without sadness. There was more blood each day on the handkerchiefs. Nicholas would have to leave in another month, six weeks at most.

*

"Ralph, Ralph!"

He had fallen asleep in his study – he often did so in the afternoons. Madeleine was shaking him gently. She looked alarmed.

"It's Nicholas." She pronounced the name in the French way. "There's something wrong. Clothilde told me that he rushed to his room when he came back from school. He locked himself in and wouldn't open the door to her, or to me when I went up. But I could hear him sobbing."

He went up. The sobbing had stopped. He knocked on the door, got no reply, then said, "Whatever it is, Nick, you can tell me." He tried to laugh. "There's no problem the Royal Navy can't solve. Like shipmates, Nick, like shipmates."

Another five minutes of forced humour. His heart melted at the thought of the misery of the child within. And at last no answer, but the click of a key in the lock and the door swinging open.

He caught a glimpse of the black eye and the blood on the chin and the torn clothes as Nicholas hugged himself to him, face hidden, sobs choked back. Page held him for a moment, then pushed him away reluctantly but gently. Fear of infection had forced him for weeks now to keep the boy at arm's length. He guided him to the bed, sat down beside him on it. He waited for two minutes before speaking.

"You were fighting, Nick?"

A miserable nod.

"Nothing too bad about that. We've all done it, me, your father, probably even the Reverend Augustus Lyall. I'd say he was a demon in his youth."

The idea of the grave and white-haired minister of Pau's English church ever putting up his fists brightened Nicholas slightly.

"I hope you gave the other chap as good as you got yourself, Nick."

A nod, with a hint of what might be pride.

"Just the one?"

"Three." He named them. "And a lot more I thought were my friends just by stood laughing and didn't help me." It was obvious that this hurt him more than his bruises.

"Do the masters know about it?"

A shake of the head.

But they will, Page thought. From what he'd seen of the fathers of the three boys it was possible that they were already complaining to the headmaster. And rightly or wrongly he himself would stand by Nicholas. One against three deserved support.

"How did it start, Nick?"

He turned away, shook his head. Page could sense anger, deep anger, as well as hurt.

"Were they bullying you?" There had been no hint of it previously.

Another shake of the head. Better to wait.

"I hit Fothergill," Nicholas said at last. "His nose started to bleed."

"And then his friends joined in?"

"I thought they were my friends too. Pritchard and Villiers."

"So they knocked you down, sat on your chest, gave you a damn good beating and a few kicks for good measure?"

Nicholas looked at him in alarm, as if Page had already heard of it and knew the details. But it was the standard course of such encounters and in his own early days afloat there had been many. Followed more than once by undignified bending over the gunroom chest, a half-dozen painful cuts with a rope's end and a forced reconciliation signified by a reluctant handshake. Like most officers he was to tell of it with some pride in later years and to assert that it had done him a world of good.

"Why did you hit Fothergill?" It seemed out of character.

Silence. Head turned away.

"Had he said something?"

A nod. The anger was even more palpable now.

"He said something about Clothilde. He wouldn't take it back."

"What did he say?"

"He said she was a bastard."

Page felt a stab of cold anger within himself. "Do you know what that means, Nicholas?"

"He said that she never had a father."

"Her father was an admirable man. An army officer. He died bravely for his country in Algeria."

Yet Page himself often wondered if Captain Claude Sapin had ever existed. Madeleine had been evasive and he had never pressed her. There was no framed miniature in a place of honour.

"And he said that Madame Sapin was …"

"No need to tell me, Nick." He reached out, laid his hand on his shoulder. "You'll meet lots of Fothergills as you go through life. They won't matter. But people like Madame Sapin will. You know what she is, a kind, good woman, the best I've ever known. And she loves you and I know that you love her."

She had come to Pau eleven years before, a widow with a baby. Captain Sapin had died poor, she said, but her family in Lille – Pau must be further from it than any other town in France – had helped her buy the lodging house. A spa town patronised by English invalids was an ideal place for one. But she must have been an embarrassment to her family, for she never returned to Lille, nor did relatives ever visit her, nor post arrive.

And none of it made any difference. She was the only love of his life and he should have married her. It was fear of what would follow if he was ever unmasked, arrested, tried, that had held him back. Her life would be unbearable and the stigma for Clothilde worse still. Better to let others speculate that snobbery had deterred a retired British officer from marrying a French lodging-house keeper

"You know I love her, Uncle. Just like Mrs. Gore. And Clothilde's my sister, just like Susan."

"I think that's worth taking a beating for, Nick. Especially if you gave as good as you got."

He nodded fiercely, the tears gone, pride and defiance manifest.

When this boy is a man he will be one to reckon with. He'll be loyal and brave and honourable, a good friend but a very bad enemy. He may forgive, but he'll never forget. And I'll never see it.

Page stood up, gestured to the boy to do the same. He took his hand and shook it.

"I'd have been disappointed in you if you'd done anything else, Nicholas."

And he himself would settle matters with the Reverend Augustus Lyall, and with the fathers of Fothergill and Pritchard and Villiers, if they came complaining.

They didn't matter. But Nicholas did.

*

The deterioration was worse by the day now. Three months at the longest, maybe less, he had been told. He still felt no great fear, but regret nagged him, however much he thrust it from his mind. Many of his contemporaries would live another forty years, would realise ambitions, would see children marry and those in turn have children, would see inventions and changes that would have fascinated him. Madeleine's patient sorrow hurt him badly. She had wept when he had told her frankly how long was left and had spoken of practical arrangements that must come, but neither he nor she mentioned the subject again. They continued to be content in each other's company and grateful for it, words unspoken because there was no need to say them, the brief touch of hands all they could allow themselves of intimacy, petty concerns of housekeeping discussed as if they would endure for ever. Clothilde must know too, for there was a solemnity about her, less laughter, excessive courtesy, over-solicitousness about his minor comforts.

It was time to send Nicholas home. He wanted him to remember the time here with pleasure, the walks together, even if they had been shorter than he would have wished, the naval battles fought on paper, the stories of storm and danger and the delight of mastering skills. He wanted Nicholas to remember a man whom fear had never conquered – even though he had known fear – and whose life had been governed by duty, loyalty and honour. For yes, even in the duty he was now handing over to another there had been honour, for all that the instruments he had employed were squalid and contemptible. It was better that Nicholas return to England in two weeks, under the care of a clergyman who had come to visit an ailing relative, than that he should witness the last and most distressing stage of all.

And so at last the inevitable talk, not in the garden or study, where it might have sounded too formal, but on the slow morning walk – slower each day – to the Parc Beaumont.

"Do you want to enter the Navy, Nicholas?"

He had hesitated about asking the question lest by doing so he influence the boy unduly, lest Nicholas feel an obligation to what he must know was a dying man. But in recent weeks there had been no disguising Nicholas's interest in the Navy and his unwillingness to spend his life in a British market town. His experience of travel, short as it was, and of a different language, had clearly inspired him to think of a career in the wider world.

The boy did not answer directly. They reached the park, sat on a familiar bench in the shade.

"It's not an easy life, Nicholas, and you wouldn't be rich. There are other things you could do and you'd have money to support you while you study. Not just the law. Medicine perhaps or…"

"I want to join the Navy." Fierce and unfeigned determination in his voice.

"Then I'll write to your father." Andrew would not be surprised – he had raised the possibility himself. "And if he agrees, I'll write to some old naval friends. They'll make the necessary arrangements."

Then a long silence. No outward emotion, but a sense that the boy had recognised the full import of the decision.

"I won't let you down, Uncle," he said at last. "I won't fail you."

"I'll never doubt that." Tears were starting in his own eyes.

"Are you going to die, Uncle?" The tremor in Nicholas's voice told that he must have been screwing up his courage for days to ask this directly.

"Soon, Nicholas. Very soon." He paused, let the boy collect himself. "There's nothing to be afraid of. It comes to everybody in the end."

Nicholas was weeping quietly now and was ashamed of it.

"You can do one thing for me, Nicholas. I want you to care for Madame Sapin and for Clothilde too. Not to be with them all the time, but not to forget them. And to be as a son and as a brother to them whenever they need help. You'll do that for me?"

"I promise, Uncle."

And then they stood up and walked back to the house together.

In silence. And never closer.

*

He had strength enough to make one last journey if the stages were not too long. He would have liked to bring Nicholas on board a British ship, where friends of his own would have been welcoming, but there was no opportunity for that now. But Toulon was relatively close, the great French naval port set in a great three-quarters circle bay backed by mountains. There would be warships there, glimpsed from afar, but he would be able to explain them to the boy, to

271

enumerate the masts and yards, to comment on the intricacies of anchoring and of departure. It was the sort of excursion that he would have liked to make again and again with Nicholas as he grew, advancing over the years to adult equality. But now it could be for only once ever.

It was the same route he had taken a scant few months before, but they had to stay a night at Narbonne – exhaustion saw to that. Nicholas, like Page himself, made no mention of the illness, ignored the coughing and the scarlet patches on the white handkerchiefs, talked with interest of what they were to see. At Nimes they were guests of a retired British major who was devoting his ample means to investigation of the extensive Roman remains there. He was an old friend, Page said. The boy did not need to know that he had never met the man before, that he knew him only by correspondence – much of it encrypted – and that there were certain confidences – last confidences – that could only be shared orally. For all that it took only a short train journey to reach it, Page was so exhausted on arrival that he had to lie down and Mr. Monkton – no mention of military rank, but a genuine scholar – was glad to bring Nicholas to see the Roman amphitheatre and the surviving town gates and temple. Delighted by the sites and by his host's explanations, the boy slept well that night, unaware of the low murmur of male voices from the floor below, interspersed with the sound of coughing, that continued into the early hours.

And so the next day to Toulon, another long gruelling day in a hot compartment – they were travelling first-class, a small indulgence – and they had it to themselves. The wait for transfer at Marseilles seemed endless as Page remained slumped on a bench while Nicholas fetched him coffee. The station was crowded – hurrying businessmen; ladies in their light summer finery returning from holiday, their servants fussing over luggage; bourgeois women smug in their gentility; healthy children who might live to the middle of the next century; workers in shabby blouses; bewildered peasants still dusty from the fields and here for some lawsuit; new conscripts, half-elated, half-apprehensive, still in their civilian garb, being herded into wagons. The scene would never have struck him as unusual previously, but now there was a poignancy about it that moved him. *They will still be alive a few months – weeks – from now, and I will not. All of them unaware of the richness they have of life, all valuing it too little until it is too late. And yet though my body rots my brain is as sharp as it ever was, my affections as intense.*

He felt sadness weigh down more heavily upon him than ever before, not for himself alone, but for Madeleine and for Nicholas and for Clothilde. The love he knew they bore him was both a burden and a comfort. He felt tears start to his eyes but he brushed them quickly away as he saw Nicholas returning with the coffee. They sat in companionable silence until it was time for their train.

Page was on the point of collapse when they arrived at Toulon and without the boy's support he would not have had the strength to reach a cab outside the station. A paroxysm of coughing overtook him as he told the driver to avoid the Place de la Liberté – the memory of the brandy-befuddled man being led, eyes downcast, to his bloody end was more dreadful now than ever. Rooms had been booked at a hotel on the eastern fringes of the bay and he lay down immediately, never touched the tray of food brought later to his room, was too exhausted to talk long with Nicholas.

He slept for less than half the night. It was not the coughing that kept him from sleep – it was so much part of him now that he hardly noticed it – but the same sadness and regret that had overtaken him on the railway platform at Marseilles. Death itself did not frighten him, though he dreaded how the last unknowable moments might be. His religious belief had always been lukewarm, his observance weaker still, but at this extremity he felt confident of mercy awaiting him beyond that final curtain. He prayed only for courage during the passage – as he had so often done in his life. A man should never ask for more.

The sight of Nicholas's face at breakfast cheered him. He had been up at sunrise, had walked along the eastern shore, delighted by the movements on the water, by the fishing boats returning with their night's catch, by a warship weighing anchor and nudging slowly into the open sea beyond. Page made no mention of his difficult night and resolved that this would be a good day, one they would remember with gratitude, whether it would be for a month only or for decades.

They walked very slowly to just short of the great circular fort at the tip of the peninsula bounding the bay's eastern side. A bench beneath a tree close to the water's edge offered rest and shade. From here, looking westwards, they could see where the young Napoleon had made his name, an unknown artillery officer who had established his batteries to make the harbour and dockyards untenable for a British occupying force some sixty years before. Excited by the prospect of this trip, Nicholas had read voraciously about the siege, and was now identifying the eminences where the French guns had been sited. It had ended badly for Britain – the Royal Navy forced into ignominious retreat, resources abandoned to the enemy – and even worse for the French Royalists who had been left behind to face merciless revolutionary vengeance. A career had been launched here that had brought misery to millions from Lisbon to Moscow, from Amsterdam to Aswan. It was better to die unfulfilled, Page comforted himself, than to have such as that on his conscience as his time slipped away.

But there is still one person I must answer for. Armand Brisson. His blood on my hands.

A small naval squadron was leaving port, a brave sight, six ships-of-the line, wooden two-deckers with gun-ports chequering their sides. They were vessels little different from those Admiral Hood had withdrawn from here in 1793, from those which the British blockade had caged in port here for much of the long years that followed. But with one difference. Their yards might be crossed, their sails ready to be unfurled in open water, but black smoke was spilling from the single thin funnels just ahead of each main-mast, and frothy wakes betrayed unseen screws churning beneath the counters. Page recognised the vessel in the van as – most appropriately – the 90-gun *Napoleon*. Her sister *Algésiras* was directly astern. They had been designed from scratch for steam propulsion, had not had boilers and engines and screws crammed into them as an afterthought. He knew their dimensions, their framing and construction, their sailing characteristics, their coal consumption, their magazine capacities, better than their own captains did – for he had paid for the information. Seven years old, the *Napoleon* had earned admiration during the Crimean conflict as perhaps the finest warship afloat.

"They're magnificent, Uncle" Nicholas was excited by the sight. "But ours must be better, mustn't they?"

"It doesn't matter," Page said. "Their day is done. You'll know different ships."

For already he knew. At the close-by Arsenal du Mourillon a ship was being laid down that would make these stately wooden vessels as irrelevant as oared galleys. Encased in iron plate, *La Gloire* would briefly be invulnerable to the gunfire of any warship afloat. And for all the secrecy that the French had tried to surround the project, *La Gloire's* details were already known in Britain. The weakness of a draughtsman called Armand Brisson had seen to that, and he had paid for it with his life. A ship, more powerful still, even more strongly protected and more heavily armed, was already under design for the Royal Navy – the name, *Warrior*, had already been chosen – and together these two vessels would initiate what must be a new race for naval mastery.

And I won't see it. But Nicholas will.

The boy caught something of his pensiveness and did not pursue the matter. Then long quietness, shared awareness that a day like this would never come again, that the final parting would come four days hence after they had returned to Pau.

When Nicholas broke the silence he used the same words as he had spoken once before.

"I won't let you down, Uncle," he said. "I won't fail you."

And Page answered as before. "I'll never doubt that." Emotion made him turn his face away. "I'll never doubt that, Nicholas."

Then they walked back, very slowly, and again in silence, to the hotel.

The End

Printed in Great Britain
by Amazon